For Nanny Polo and Nanny Dear
A creative bent and steady hand was all that was needed

Read this, ideally wearing
a monocle and smoking something
from Havannah, not necessarily a
cigar.....

Yours ever,

H.C.fox

Chapter 1

On the day that Doris Thudd was ejected into this world, twixt the legs of her poor mother, the Greek god Aphrodite clearly had other things on her mind. That most radiant goddess of beauty and *l'amour* had been doing a solid morning's work on the 20th March 1910. She had already blessed many thousand new born babies with rosy cheeks, beautiful eyes, soft hair and cheeky smiles. It was just another day on a cloudy precipice at Mount Olympus. Unfortunately, it would seem that when it came to giving Doris her equitable dose of good looks, the door bell on Aphrodite's bit of rock must have rang. Perhaps there she met a mountain to mountain salesman with samples of chemicals to get difficult ambrosia stains out of her shag. Annoyed and distracted, when she returned to her work she'd missed over a hundred new-borns, one of which was Doris.

Alas, after a difficult childhood, acne strewn puberty and a career in the family business as a Blacksmith, she had been left with a ruddy, pock marked face, straggly brown hair and a figure best viewed from the front of a tablespoon. An only child and underwhelming as a school pupil, she had reluctantly but faithfully agreed to learn the family trade, adding scold marks and hard skin to her beauty regime. Stuck in the small village of Lank-on-the-Wash, her lot in life was fashioning wrought iron gates, posts and horseshoes for meagre pay, little thanks and small chance of meeting anyone who would want to be straddled by her broad and slightly varicose thighs.

And so it was, that on the 20th March 1940, Doris's thirtieth birthday, she arrived at her smith's yard, alone, tired by life's unfair dollop of seclusion. She unhappily stoked the furnace, smudging coal on her overalls and face. Glumly, and with a glassy expression she set to work on a fire guard that hopefully a passerby might purchase; and yet with a stroke of Lady Luck's fair hand, who should stride into the yard that day but a handsome Frenchman.

As Doris honed a shaft of iron with her hammer, she failed to notice the sound of approaching horse hooves. They clopped to a clattering halt, but still her attention was squarely focussed on the ringing *clang* of metal against metal. Finally she became aware of the crunch of boots landing on the gravel nearby and then two black and shiny leather uppers appeared under her gaze. Startled, she looked up and there found a devilishly handsome body and face beaming back at her. Unaccustomed as she was to small talk, Doris dropped her head again in embarrassment and carried on bludgeoning her hammer into the metal so heavily that if she had buffeted the molecules a whisker harder, she would have inadvertently discovered nuclear fusion.

A hand slipped under her oily chin and gently averted her attention back to it's owner. Her eyes leisurely travelled over the immaculate black leather riding boots and sauntered up the stranger's muscular legs to his generously packed jodhpurs. Above the waistline there was a white shirt, open at the top, allowing a hint of dark chest hair mixed with a dash of toned frame. As the grand inspection of the homme du jour concluded, her eyes met his, taking in that chiselled face, wispy black moustache, slender lips with a curl of mischief about them and those delicious green eyes.

Before she could yell, "Butter my tuppence," Doris managed to put her hand in front of her mouth. Alas her loins trembled like an uninhabited flat that had not been lived in for years due to the underground trains that passed nearby making it an unfit dwelling. This was a fitting metaphor for the state of Doris's love life, as it had been five long years since the last time a tenant had slipped into her residence, which regrettably was also the first time. Somewhere in the Norfolk countryside there was a church verger who had succumbed after the annual village fete. Plied with too much scrumpy, he was on the precipice of passing out when she set upon him. There may have been a lollypop splint involved; regardless it was still very harrowing for him all these years later. Meanwhile Doris, whilst briefly sated, felt like she was only at the entrance door of the dinner party that should have been her love life, looking in upon the happy people eating canapés and then running off hand in hand to give each other a good seeing to. Meanwhile, Doris could only stand at the window and sniff the entrees.

"Bonjour Madame, perhaps you could help me. My horse seems to need some attention in the way of new shoes and as I passed through the nearby village, your services were recommended."

Doris paused, not seeming to understand the question. At last she slapped herself in the face and re-entered the orbit of her small reality with a, "Kay." She took the reins from the stranger's gloved hands and led the horse into the open front of the workshop, tying the leathery straps to a rail attached to the crumbling interior wall. She dragged an old wooden stool and a bucket of horse shoes over, plonked her backside down and got on with the task at hand. As she worked she occasionally dared to glance up at the stranger who stood aloof, leaning on the wall opposite, seemingly grinning at nothing in particular. Was it Doris? Surely not.

Half an hour later, sweating and grubbier than ever, Doris's four hoofed masterpiece was complete. The stranger minced his way over towards the horse and inspected her handiwork.

"Ah, very good Madame, you are an artisan for sure."
Doris allowed herself a look at his swarthy figure and fell head over heels in blossoming love, eventually issuing a, "S'alright."

But before she could discuss the goodish sum that such craft would deserve, the stranger patted down his side and exclaimed, "Ah mon dieu, I must have mislaid my wallet at the hotel where I'm staying. Madame, je suis desole."
Doris harrumphed, feeling duped by his charm and reached down for a crowbar that seemed to be lurking with villainy against the nearby wall. Alarmed, the stranger put his hands out and exclaimed, "Madame, now I am a man of my word! If it is not too much bother, will you escort me to my lodgings where I will pay you double?"
Doris thought about the jobs she had on, a couple of brasses and that was it; they could wait, she wanted her money. Birthday cakes don't buy themselves, especially if no one else is prepared to buy one.

As Doris arrested her service for the day and shut up shop, the stranger lazed against the flank of his horse and sparked up a Gauloises, grinning occasionally at the blacksmith. She locked a sturdy chain into position across the front doors of the workshop and gathered her belongings for the quick walk back to Lank-on-the-Wash. Just as they were about to set off, the stranger raised his hands in apology again and turned to his newfound tour guide of the wilder and more hairy parts of Nelson's county.

"Madame, I have another idea which perhaps I could suggest? Yes, I could pay you double, but then what do you have but not a lot more, no?"

Doris seemed to be following his logic and nodded for him to go on.

"Well now, I am only staying in the area for a fraction of time but regrettably I have no one to escort me to the dining table this evening at the local hostelry. The pleasure would be all mine if you would accompany me, for an evening of polite conversation and du vin?"

Doris stopped dead, literally dead. She'd had a heart attack from the sheer sensation of his words caressing her brain. That someone as actually beautiful as him would ask her to dinner was shock enough for a coronary and whatever du vin was, she was sure it was bound to be an erotic experience, potentially involving a van. Fortunately at that precise moment, the static energy generated from her nylon overalls electrocuted her in the chest and a tragedy was averted.

"Lorks! A slip of a Frenchie accommodating me with dinner. What a birthday treat for little old me ," she replied, sounding her most feminine but still spoken with the gruff tone of a closet trannie. Her claim to be 'Little,' was also up for serious mooting.

"We will meet then in the Nags Head on the high street, perhaps at seven?" said the stranger. Doris nodded furiously whilst he bent down to kiss her rough steelworker's hands, placing his soft lips upon her dry knuckles and coming up coughing from the tang of sulphur and phosphorous.

Having thumped himself in the chest a few times, he mounted his steed, gave a devil-may-care wave of his hand and turned the horse back towards the village. Doris reciprocated and then realising that she had learnt nothing about this charming Frenchman, bellowed, "But I don't even knows your name!?!"

The horse eased to a halt. The stranger glanced over his shoulder and replied, "Men have been known to call me a charlatan and a cad, women just call me, Philippe De Castagnet!"

He tossed his head back and got the steed to rear up, showing off like a child pulling wheelies on a bike. This had the unexpected effect of causing him to lose balance and Philippe fell to the dirt track below with an altogether sharp thud. Doris winced. Mildly cut and embarrassed, Philippe got to his feet, brushed the powdery dust of the path off his shirt and cursed at a big hole that was now ripped into his jodhpurs. He climbed back on his horse and geed it to a canter, disappearing along the small lane. Doris pondered their future happiness together and set off for home, realising that a good five hours of makeup were required.

That night, loins were stirring like a primitive Kenwood Chef as both parties approached the Nags Head Hotel in the remote village of Lank on the Wash. Fully refurbished recently, the landlord, Ken Slagbatter had ensured that despite the pub's small size, if gave off warmth and comfort with is rosy hearths and velveteen cushioned chairs. The suites upstairs were functional and allowed five travellers to rest their weary heads at any given time.

As an unknown precursor to what we now know as a Gastropub, Ken also maintained a kitchen which served an excellent brown meat and potatoes, just as long as that was what you wanted, as it was also the beginning and the end of the menu. When an unfortunate customer was to ask what type of meat it was, Ken would wearily look up from the ale glass he was polishing and say, "Brown". The colour was never in question, the provenance to which animal it belonged to was. Regardless, it was the fairest of the local dives and where our two star-crossed lovers were to entangle, twixt slabs of beef and spuds.

After exchanging difficult introductions due to Doris's complete memory loss of Philippe's name, calling him Plimpy instead, they settled in for an evening of small talk, booze, brown meat and flirting. Doris had surpassed all previous efforts of femininity and even managed to borrow a dress for the evening. Floral and ill-fitting, it heaved at the seams like a top sail in a force nine hurricane threatening to expel its cellulitic contents at any moment. Furthermore it did nothing to ease Philippe's concern that he might be about to bed a man but with his goal within reach, he pressed on.

Emptying the contents of his sizeable wallet on cognac and whisky, he finally convinced his quarry to retire with him for the evening and they tottered up the stairs, giggling all the way. Philippe's room was comfortable with a small double bed forced into the corner, adjacent to a window looking out onto the all too plain Lank-on-the-Wash high street. They perched on the edge of the bed, planning their next moves as nervous lovers do, the slats underneath creaked and gave off a nervous energy at their potential impending end.

They were under the covers quickly, Philippe making love like a gigolo, Doris making love like a roadside accident involving a generous amount of concrete mix. However, using his finest moves including one called, "Mr Petanque goes to market and buys an unusually large horse," he soon had her mewing like a blue whale calling to its young. Unexpectedly she rolled on top of Philippe and rode him to the big finish. Doris fell off him and lay there, happy and depleted, he had certainly made an impression. However, for the recently flattened Philippe and his two freshly cracked ribs it felt more like an imprint.

After wearily moving himself onto his elbows and in some pain, Philippe reached down off the bed and retrieved a packet of Gauloises from his jacket on the floor. He sparked up two of the cigarettes and passed one to Doris. There they lay, silently puffing out the petit-mort that had risen in both of them. Ten minutes passed and now a deuced more relaxed, Philippe engaged in a little post-coital pillow talk.

"I notice, Madame that you are very good with your hands. Perhaps you could have been an artist of the paint instead of the steel." He drew on his cigarette, focussing on the wall opposite the bed.

Doris turned and cuddled into him, placing her rough hand on his hairy chest and causing his eyes to bulge as a cracked rib underneath complained. "Well, tis a kindness for you to say, but no. Blacksmithing has always been in our family's blood. My father was a smithy and when he was syphilitic, it only seemed right and proper that I stepped into the breach, though I longed for the bright lights of Norwich!" She looked animatedly at Philippe, who ruffled her hair whilst searching for the word most opposite to worldly in his mind.

"So the lineage of your craft is perhaps, a hundred, two hundred years old?" Philippe pressed.

"Oh, longer than that my love, my ancestors were mentioned in the Doomsday Book. We were making horseshoes before horses were invented."

Philippe mulled over this last point, eventually finding it implausible.

Doris frowned, coal smut, the backs of horses' legs and the occasional turd down the collar were her lot in life and she knew it. Days began with curling steel U's and ended the same; they sat on racks, pointed downwards like unhappy cartoon faces, extolling misery with every coming dawn.

"Ca c'est formidable, mon cherie," mused Philippe. "I do love ancient history. Do you perhaps have any artefacts that you could show me? I'd be more than happy to stay awhile to examine them and you, more closely." He turned and gazed into her eyes, trapping Doris under his illusion. Doris fell for it immediately.

"Oh really? Oh that would be terrific!" she gurgled. As she spoke, Doris tossed over in her mind, wild rambling thoughts of long walks together in summer meadows, fumblings in hayfields and sex, lots more lurid heaving sex. Perhaps she could teach him the craft, lure him away from majestic, romantic France and into the agricultural and flat world of Norfolk. They would raise children, wildly strong but beautiful. Her mind danced across such images like a hippo practising ballet.

"I'd love for you to stay a while and I'd happily put you up in my dwellings." She took a drag on her cigarette. "There was one object, something of an heirloom........"

Philippe perked up, eager to find out the truth. "Go on," he urged with considerable tension in his voice.

"Well, aint much really, but my old man kept a beautiful statue, about twelve inches high and it was cast in lead. It depicted that queen from olden times that was from around these here parts, Queen Boudeewassname and there was a second piece, her chariot. The detail, the intricacy, it must have been cast by a true master, it's a stunning piece of smith artistry."

Philippe begrudgingly decided he could stomach one more night of unbridled trampling and ventured a suggestion.

"Perhaps, Madame after we rest you may show it to us, er me? I'd be very keen to appreciate such a piece." He stroked her broad thigh.

"Alas, someone took it from us," Doris frowned. "My awful mother god bless her soul, had an affair with the local land owner behind my father's back. In a particularly low moment for the Thudd name, she tried to blackmail the land owner who then threatened to evict our family from our lodgings. As recompense, the bastard took all we owned, including the statue and then gave it to his son, like some ridiculous toy. I couldn't begin to tell you it's whereabouts now."

Philippe stiffened and for the first moment of their brief entente, looked positively disinterested.

"How unfortunate for you. It is a shame, I would have liked to have seen it." He turned away from her, literally giving Doris the lukewarm shoulder. "Now perhaps I should return to France before the Germans invade. It seems ever more likely that the Nazi threat will focus their attention on my homeland." He lay down to sleep, facing the wall and coldly ignored his emotionally wounded bed partner.

Doris frantically tried to recover the situation, touching his arm. "Oh, but I'd still love to spend time with yer!"

"Perhaps," Philippe replied hollowly, still staring at nothing but the whitewashed plasterwork of the room. He changed direction with his questioning. "A name, do you have a name for the villain who so unscrupulously took away the sanctity of your mother and father's marriage?"

After a brief pause to compose herself, Doris squealed, "It was them toffs up the hill at Udderly Park, the Bryant-Lukelys!" Doris looked visibly rattled and a tear slowly crept from the corner of her left eye. She was immediately comforted by the warm, gentle, manicured hand of her bed partner around her waist.

"Calm yourself, my petit pomme," cooed Philippe. "Only bad things happen to those who steal. For now we sleep." Doris had other things on her mind though and rolled back on top of Philippe cracking another rib.

A few hours passed and the room and its contents had fallen into total darkness and silence. An occasional lazy and half-hearted snore came from one of its occupants. But also in the blackness, a man's eyes blinked and using the merest suggestion of light from the outside moon trickling in through the window, he grew accustomed to his surroundings once again. He waited patiently whilst his prey slept on.

A further half an hour ticked by, but then outside the room a squeak from a floorboard gave up a further presence edging along the corridor. Philippe knew perfectly well who it was. He began to fire his muscles into life, gently, silently moving the bed sheets aside. He'd been pinned to the wall by Doris's substantial bottom and had to perform quite an impressive straddling manoeuvre to step over her, off the bed and onto the floorboards of the hotel bedroom. He straightened, letting out a small wincing sound. Three cracked ribs; still it was worth their price and besides, seduction was always the best method of espionage. Torture and murder were far too easy and doubly messy in the long run, though Philippe was well versed in all three. He surveyed the floor for his long-johns and discovered that they'd been thrown off in the moment of high passion landing handily a good ten yards away on the windowsill illuminated by the moonlight. He tottered across the room and slid them back on.

The door handle was clearly being turned from outside in the corridor, as on the opposite side, the handle in the room began a slow, careful descent. When it could turn no more, the door moved partially open but without the sound of the catch touching anything. Given relief by the moonlight, a silhouette of a head and it's right shoulder peered round the short opening that the door had allowed. Philippe's mouth curled into a cruel smile. He gathered up his shirt, trousers, socks and boots into his arms and padded out of the room.

His new companion said nothing as they descended the darkened staircase for the ground floor of the inn and the front door which had been expertly lock-picked by Philippe's accomplice. Once outside in the cool March air, they took a moment to check their surroundings, the dark main street of the village showing no signs of life. Casually, both men slipped down a narrow alley to the left of the pub and Philippe quickly dressed. Peering back out of the darkness, Philippe whispered, "Herr Von Schuler, the coast is clear, we can leave."

A large, rough looking hand seemed to descend out of the night and purposefully squeezed at Philippe's shoulder, pulling him back in.

"Are we able to obtain the artefact?" whispered a coarse, deep germanic voice. "The Fuhrer will be most displeased if we cannot complete our mission."

The meaty paw on Philippe's shoulder contracted on his collar bone and caused him more than an unpleasant amount of pain.

"No Monsieur," Philippe gasped, "But, I have a name.........."

Doris Thudd lay asleep on her back, gently snoring. At nine in the morning or thereabouts, a particularly loud crash of pans from below in the kitchen shook her from her happy dreams. This was three hours later than her usual start for work and she momentarily panicked. Her eyes focused on the ceiling, what if she'd missed that large order, that war commission for ten thousand horseshoes? In fact why was she even in this bed? Then the previous evening's unlikely but wonderful events played out in her head, the talking, the fancying, the thrusting. She smiled, closed her eyes and reached across to the other side of the double bed, feeling for the lithe Frenchman who should have been laying there. Sadly her arm encountered nothing but the cold cotton surface of the bed sheets. It was fine, Doris was half expecting it. Should Philippe and Doris have ruined a perfect night by promises of more evenings together, a relationship, marriage? *No,* thought Doris, *Philippe wanted it to be special, and now he's heading back to France to tell stories of the devilishly handsome blacksmith he had a fling with in England.* Doris lay there contented; even if her own perception of reality was a dream, she would happily take it. They were but ships that passed in the night, he a small dingy, she a Royal Navy destroyer. Unbeknownst to Doris though, she had also given away the whereabouts of a secret long forgotten. A secret so important and provocative that two men were now in search of a legend which if proved true, would bring Doris, Lank on the Wash, Norfolk and the rest of Britain to their knees.

Chapter 2

Benedict Bryant-Lukely was an excellent shadow-boxer, at least the World Championship belt holder for mildly flabby dandies with nothing better to do with their time, and this morning was no different. There he stood in the large entrance hall of his fashionable Kensington apartment, opposite the gilded three foot tall mirror, dressed in his Harris tweed waistcoat and suit pants, all six foot and broad. He smoothed down his receding bed-hair with a dab of spit. Benedict, wrinkled his eyes, gave that substantial grin of his, pleased with his chosen look for the day and began the customary twenty seconds of jabs and hooks which said to him, *You're alright you! You're a bit of a bob n weaver, a bit crafty.* It was a ritual he'd performed ever since the age of seven when his father had taken him to see an amateur boxing match. He'd loved the circular, vicious ballet played out by the pugilists that day and had danced a fisty dance every morning since. He felt it made him look *tasty* in the words of the cockney brethren that shared the crowd that evening. In truth, if Benedict looked *tasty*, it was in the very edible sense of the word, being rather like a trifle, soft and fruity. It would even be fair to say that in matters of the heart and of bravery, Benedict was a coward. Regardless, he had bested thousands of imaginary opponents over his years. Today there was one minor change in the boxing card though. Benedict's housekeeper, Mrs McDoughty, after years of being aware of dust building up behind a small cabinet kept in the hallway had moved it to clean the varnished floorboards. Having done this, she'd put the cabinet back into what she thought was it's original position. It was in fact, an inch further away from the wall opposite the mirror. This subtly altered Benedict's perception of his space and on a particularly deft right jab he connected with the glass which then rudely shattered into as many pieces as possible all over the hallway rug and floorboards below. He looked at his hand; a rather simple looking cut striped the knuckles of all his right digits as blood began to colour the wound. "Oh bugger," said Benedict, as he tottered backwards and bounced off the perception-altering cabinet. "Mrs McDoughty!" he called, as the rising blood started to spill from the wound and down his wrist. Despite hating the sight of claret and feeling queasy, it was decision time: either ruin a perfectly decent white shirt which was fashionably cut and tailored in the most dapper way, or forever tarnish a beautiful Persian rug, passed down by his great grandfather, with a dark maroon bloodstain.

Mrs McDoughty looked down at the Persian rug and pulled a dour, salty, pinched scowl. Blood was a pain to shift and this classless rich oaf had just sacrificed a wonderful artefact like a tissue. Mrs McDoughty was a dumpy Scottish woman from Glasgow who was a devout catholic and held the general belief that the majority of life was mortal sin. Servitude under the stairs was possibly the best career imaginable for her, as it allowed Mrs McDoughty to feel altruistic in her housekeeping of a master and yet at the same time continually besmirch his name regarding his appalling moral standards. She particularly enjoyed her time with Benedict Bryant-Lukely as he really didn't seem to have any purpose in life making an ideal target for scold at every available opportunity. Her hair tied up in a smug bun, with no makeup, she would much rather be scrubbing the rug clean whilst murdering some classic hymn with her reedy pipes, than mollycoddling this bungling fool who'd just punched out a similarly priceless item. She spitefully pressed a fresh hanky, drenched in witch-hazel against the cut, causing Benedict to whine and glare at her.

"I require a woman's touch Mrs McDoughty, not that of a navvy applying tarmac to a road, thank you!" He raised his hand, examining the gash, glad the cut wasn't deep and that the blood seemed to have clotted. Benedict took out another hanky from his trouser pocket and wrapped it round his mangled paw. Mrs McDoughty tutted once more at the rug, rolled it up, nonchalantly shoved it under one arm and clumped off to the kitchen, muttering about clumsy idiots with two right fists.

With his sports injury sustained, Benedict was left at sixes and sevens. He sighed and ambled into the sage coloured sitting room, finding his usual spot in the comfiest worn brown leather armchair. Benedict slumped down, bored and slightly despondent. If his morning was a pot of beer, it had been gloriously half full and loaded with promise, but the violent mirror mugging was the sip that tipped it into half empty territory.

It was April, and in the course of the first four months of the year Benedict's achievements listed as waking up, dressing, eating and drinking. What to do? He drummed his fingers on his lap. There was the phoney war of course and Norway was currently taking quite a beating. Some of his elders had already suggested that he'd make a smashing officer, so he should venture forth and help out in foreign climes. Plenty to do here as well, dig for victory and all that. None of it was for Benedict though, especially the fighting part; the thought of being shot at didn't seem much like fun. He'd rather leave that to the tough, bully beef tommy, wait for it all to end and then reap the benefits of black market opportunities to spread the wealth around. He gave a deep disinterested sigh. Regardless, the problem was, Benedict didn't know what to do at all.

Benedict's family had a rich heritage of being barristers and his father, Lord Spurgeon Bryant-Lukely had been a fine silk until ill health brought retirement. Benedict's older sibling, Chalfont had been mooting champion at Oxford, had residence in Lincoln's Inn and was likely to be a QC in no time at all. Benedict had had the same opportunities; he'd been schooled at Foulsham Private School for Boys and got into Oxford on a good word from the old man as his academic abilities were nothing to write home about. He'd chosen English as his subject, but reviews from his lecturers were mixed: "Critical analysis of Wordsworth about as rich and compelling as a grocery shop receipt," was the highest accolade he'd received. He'd roared and rousted with the best of them in the Bullingdon Club and was thoroughly involved in the dinner episode where Worcester College woke up to find the entire outside of their halls had been painted banana yellow. Benedict was a laughing stock and after two years of playing the fool, womanising and convincing his father that things were going well, the game was up.

He was outed at the family Christmas cheese and wine bash on the estate near Lank-on-the-Wash. His brother, ever keen to score significant points with his father had started to make enquiries of Benedict's progress. Chalfont was still chummy with a number of lecturers and soon realised that Benedict had been struck off the student records for failure after his first year. He exclaimed this point about Benedict in spectacular style at the highlight of his father's utterly dull speech in front of the fireplace to well wishers at the shindig. When Spurgeon began to say what progress Benedict had made at Oxford, Chalfont, pompous and double chinned, had piped in with how marvellous it was that the family could afford the two hundred pots of banana yellow paint that went into defacing a college and his father shouldn't be surprised to learn that the only education Benedict was getting was how to manage a bad dose of the clap. And so Spurgeon curtailed his son's allowance somewhat (though a husband and wife, their seventeen children, two horses, a cat, a dog, the husband and wife's croquet partners and their spouses could still live handsomely and afford to finance their own republic through it). This did limit Benedict's champers and hampers lifestyle and thus he faded as a burgeoning starlet of society circles. Whilst his peers went off to become barristers, surgeons, doctors and politicians, Benedict had no academic start in life to fall back on.

In the bloom of his twenties, Benedict decided to become an antiques dealer and through a sizeable capital investment begrudgingly handed down from Spurgeon, had set himself up as an importer of Asian antiquity. However, one of Benedict's less positive traits was hoarding and slowly but surely, the contents of his freshly rented warehouse in Wapping made it's way to his abode in Kensington. He still kept the bars of London buoyant with cash and had become a dab hand at the Charleston, but now at thirty two that was all he'd amounted to. By now, friends and girlfriends who'd been flappers and boozers had settled down, married and were working on the next generation of London socialites. Benedict was alone, and rudderless in a sea of possibility.

Benedict heard the latch on the front door rattle and the noise of Kensington briefly flooded in from the outside. He peered round the side of his chair like a shy child. Entering the flat was Caruthers, Benedict's butler, carrying some groceries he'd picked up for Mrs McDoughty. Caruthers resembled a highly polished cat. There was a graceful, aloof air to the man. Similar in age to Benedict, he was sleek, from his bryll creamed hair all the way down to his effortless walk. He'd only recently gained employment in the Lukely household as the replacement for Albert, an old, wiry but kind valet with what looked like candyfloss hair around his ears who had been in the service of the Lukelys since Benedict was a nipper and had come to London with him. A decade of cleaning up the mess from Benedict's parties and Albert had become ill, not long after, departing for the great servants' quarters in the sky. Deeply saddened by losing his old friend, Benedict had reluctantly advertised soon after, following a misunderstanding between him and an iron where Benedict had felt that by removing the ironing board from the equation and just ironing the clothes on himself, he'd create a massive timesaver. After a visit to the local burns unit, he'd eagerly waited a week for the initial flurry of responses and it quickly became apparent from his application that Caruthers was the man up to the job. The valet's references were impeccable and had come from the best estates and on this basis alone, Benedict appointed Caruthers without so much as an interview. This had proven to be a mistake, as whilst his new man was able to dispense with his duties in the easiest of fashions, Benedict had not been able to get a handle on Caruthers at all. There was an arrogance to the butler and he possessed a tongue as quick and as devil-may-care as a rat setting off mouse traps using a dead mouse it had killed earlier that morning. Benedict knew himself to be a bungler, but his butler's ripostes were often brazen and it was not his place to point out Benedict's shortcomings. Benedict was unsure whether it was his status, whether Caruthers was just shy, or whether he'd made a grave error in employing the man. But Benedict suffered fools gladly and everyday would try and strike up an unwanted friendship with him. Today, he leapt from the chair to greet

Caruthers in the hallway, who was staring with no emotion at the mirror frame, sans mirror.

"I say, Caruthers. Guess what happened to the mirror?" Before Caruthers could answer, Benedict added, "I might have gotten into something of a scuffle with it. Didn't think much of the pleb on the other side so I er, buffeted him a good'un." Benedict gave a knowing smirk, desperately searching his butler's reaction for approval.

Caruthers didn't laugh, he just stared at Benedict's excited face. Nothing.

My God, this man is bereft of humour! thought Benedict. "How unfortunate then, that the pleb is a reflection of you sir...."

Caruthers let the comment hang in the air for too long. He walked away, down the stairs to the servants' quarters in the basement. Benedict made a noise like a balloon with it's air being let out and certainly felt deflated.

"There are others out there, in far worse circumstance who would willingly do your job for less money you know!" he bellowed, waiting for a response that never came.

His shoulders sagged, he'd been wounded by the comment for he felt it was an accurate depiction of himself. He was a shadow boxing moron with absolutely no agenda. The apartment was feeling incredibly claustrophobic this morning and Benedict felt he needed the hubbub of London to feed any opportunity into his mind. Peering out of the window, it seemed like a warm April day, so deciding not to take a coat but wearing his suit jacket, he grabbed his wallet off the coffee table and departed.

Chapter 3

Despite the European politics of the day, London was still relatively cheerful on Saturday 20th April 1940. Yes, Hitler had invaded Poland and the Netherlands and he was trying his worst in Norway, but Britain was still largely in a period of phoney war. So the country whistled chirpy songs about keeping sunny sides up and dug for victory. The sun shone down in Kensington and as he toodled along, Benedict realised he needn't have even bothered with a jacket, taking it off and folding it over his left arm. His wallet was also generating heat as it rubbed through his tight trouser pocket on his right thigh. *Note to self, must cut down on the pork pies,* he thought as he strolled. He took five minutes to amble through his local park, stopping to admire the flower borders and to chat to some formidably beautiful women sitting on a bench. When the conversation inevitably ran out of steam, they made their excuses and walked away. Benedict was never going to meet anyone and settle down at this rate, and besides, what did he have to offer, other than the old plush? But then sometimes, that was all that mattered.

Benedict had passed a corner newsagent earlier on and deciding a bracing read of the news might help, retraced his steps back a few hundred yards to pick up a copy of The Times. He steered his way round some small idiot in a cheap navy blue suit and bowler hat who was spinning like a top on the pavement, wielding a large trunk, looking lost. Having reached the kiosk Benedict took out his wallet and counted out the small change for a copy of his paper of choice. The newsagent took the cash with the obligatory "Cheers Guv," and Benedict folded the copy of the Times under his arm.

Tristan Wynd was already having a hell of a time in London having gotten completely lost in it's size and majesty and literally lost in that he hadn't got a clue where he was. As a farmer from Camarthenshire, he'd never ventured further than Cardiff and having run his arable farm for ten years had not taken a holiday until lately. The last few seasons on the acreage had been good and with some reliable farm-hands year in, year out, Tristan had saved up to take a holiday in the capital. He'd listened carefully to old Tom Jones when down the Two Valleys Union Pub. Tom was a retired Locomotive Engineer who'd claimed to have passed through London's many taverns thousands of times, but who in reality had only ever made it as far as Tring.

"Wear a smart suit and a bowler hat at all times," Tom had said confidently, basing his extensive knowledge on the pictures he'd seen in the business sections of the broadsheets left in the carriages by commuters. "You should be able to ask the King if you can take residence in Buckingham Palace for a few days. You are, after all, a subject of Wales and of Britain," he'd added in his thick welsh brogue.

Tristan had indeed taken this advice, marching right up to the Palace gates and asking with all intent and honesty whether he could stay the night. Unaccustomed as the statuesque guards were to demonstrating any eye contact or emotion, the particular soldier he'd questioned was compelled to relinquish his duties by creasing on the floor with laughter, having to wave Tristan away being doubled over and giggling hysterically. Tristan thought there must be a common rule that everyone except outsiders knew which made his request ridiculous. Like perhaps this day, a Saturday, was held in reserve by His Majesty for dusting and polishing. So without the King's hospitality, where to go from here? He knew the Chelsea Flower Show was in London as he'd seen it mentioned in his Farmer's Digest and that had always seemed magnificent and pretty so in a slight hole, he decided that was where he would turn his attentions to next. Soon he was in Kensington, spinning around on the pavement, causing an obstruction with his heavy suitcase.

For Benedict, wedging the newspaper under his armpit had been plain sailing, but actually removing the wallet from his trouser pocket, with a freshly cut and bandaged hand and a jacket on top of it had been a painful experience. Now, sliding it back in to what was becoming an obstinate and rather tight entrance was going to prove tricky. Slipping the tip of the brown leather cash holder in, was a quick victory, but with a paper under the other arm which to all intents and purposes he didn't want to drop, Benedict was making a meal of getting any further push to make the wallet go into the limited space. He danced about the pavement, undulating his legs to wiggle the damned thing in but all to no avail.

It was at this point, Benedict was shoulder barged at speed and slammed into the grimy pavement below him. Benedict was violently blown to the floor as nearby pedestrians gasped in shock, but this was no accident. The adept mugger knocked down his prey and in one agile motion scooped up the brown leather wallet which Benedict had been carrying. He was away like a gazelle as Benedict rolled over and yelled, "I say, stop that man!" But the other few people on the street were in as much of a daze as Benedict and proved no trouble to this particular villain as he scampered further on. The only view Benedict got of the perpetrator was when at about sixty metres away the mugger looked over his shoulder to see if his victim was following. All Benedict saw was a tanned face, bright eyes, but the rest was obscured by the shoulder and a woolly hat. Satisfied that Benedict wasn't hot on his heels, the mugger returned to looking ahead and ran on.

This is impossible, thought Tristan, still milling about in a circular fashion and occasionally wiping sweat from his brow. Most of the hotels and bed and breakfasts in the Kensington area had, he felt, extortionate pricing schemes. He'd tried seven and frankly was getting the pip with the West of London. People bustled by and were generally ignoring him, if not even a bit rude, not what he'd been told at all. But Tristan was a pragmatist, so he set down his suitcase and put his hands on his hips. *What would I do, if this was the farmers' market and I was trying to buy an inexpensive ram?* Fate intervened at once and sadly Tristan never got the answer to his own question. Right in front of him, a fleeing man tripped over the bulk of his suitcase and cart-wheeled over, skinning the stranger's palms as he reached out and thudded into the pavement. Tristan immediately went to issue his sincerest apologies, but the grubby stranger was up on his feet and away again before he could get the words out.

Tristan spotted that the poor chap had dropped his wallet so he picked it up off the pavement. However, just as he was about to call out, a voice yelled from behind, breathless but with conviction, "I believe you'll find that's mine!"

Tristan span round to see who was addressing him. It appeared to be a tweed suited, balding gentleman, with a strong forehead, slightly piggy eyes and who had just developed a rather alarming wheeze. Unsure of the claim, Tristan decided to ascertain this for himself as just a moment ago it clearly was in someone else's possession, so he unbuttoned the wallet and therein found a number of members' club cards. Tristan put his hand out to halt the oncoming man and said, "But first, I'd like to know your name please sir."

"Benedict.......Byrant.....Lukely," rasped Benedict as he pulled up short of the man currently in possession of his wallet. He placed his hands on his knees and drew in great gulps of air.

"....And your date of birth?" quizzed Tristan. He'd found it on a card for the *Bubbles Bottoms and Sunshine Club*. Tristan, who had been brought up on the most wholesome of values came to the conclusion that he was dealing with a well to-do pervert.

"11th February 1908, that man was a thief, now give me back my wallet," replied Benedict with more than a dash of impatience and impoliteness in his voice.

Tristan looked once more at the small documents he'd assembled and replied, "Fair enough," handing it over. Benedict snatched at it, angry at his own impotence in the entire mugging affair. He begrudgingly issued a half hearted thanks before beginning his merry waggle of the one handed wallet pusher dance again.

"I say, could you?" said Benedict, desperate for the embarrassment to end.

"It would be my pleasure," replied Tristan in a chummy way, always willing to help.

After a further five minutes where the wallet was in the pocket, then out, then in again and having had to apologise to a policeman who had approached them about disturbing the peace with unruly hollering and dancing, finally, Benedict had a chance to appraise the man who had foiled the mugging.

He was small, well, small in Benedict's six foot four eyes, but probably around five foot seven inches. But he was also sturdy, not stocky and he clearly worked hard for a living. The chappie was toned and his skin had some colour. His face had a gentle, unassuming almost passive look, though it had been marked by the sun. Hazel eyes and brown hair, neat and tidy with a side parting. Benedict was not fond of the way he'd dressed; the navy suit he was wearing looked awful and his trousers were at half-mast, Benedict wondered if someone with a naval background had recently passed away in this stranger's family. And for some reason unknown to him, he was wearing a bowler hat on such a roasting day. But Benedict conceded that both of them looked equally hot and sweaty.

"I owe you a debt of gratitude sir and perhaps by the looks of it, a crisp beverage. Now er, what do I call you?"

Tristan had only just clicked that he'd inadvertently foiled a mugging, "Oh er, Tristan sir, Tristan Wynd at your humble service. And think nothing of it, just doing my civic duty." He shrugged his shoulders and bowed slightly to make the situation even more awkward.

"Let me help you with that, it's the least I can do," ventured Benedict, reaching down for Tristan's case. He heaved on it with his one good paw and nearly put his back out, dropping the trunk in the process.

"It's no bother," said Tristan taking the case strap in hand and lifting it with ease.

After a short walk they arrived at one of Benedict's favourite haunts, The Crumb Sieve Tea Rooms and there they settled into some comfy chairs with a pot of Earl Grey and a terrine of sandwiches and cakes. Tristan was especially hungry as he'd previously found the pricing of such goods in the local area as much value as the hotels. He helped himself to the ornate sandwiches on pristine white bread without the crusts and washed it down with the unusually perfumed tea and a heavy scone with clotted cream. As he chuckled to himself, he spat crumbs everywhere, then laughed some more. "Honestly, I've never had such luxury."

Being of a more amiable composition, the two chaps began to talk. Over more tea, Benedict learnt a lot about his new acquaintance. Tristan explained that his family had been extremely lucky when he was a boy. His father had been a farm hand for many years and subsequently life had been tough for the Wynds, earning little more than enough to live on. However, a neighbouring farmer had been experimenting with the concept of filling his sheep with helium, in his eyes removing the usual hassle of driving the flock to market by tethering them to a string and treating them like balloons. Unfortunately, on his maiden flight, the concept had proven too successful and on leaving the barn he had set off with buoyant, high pitched bleating ewes into the blue yonder and was never seen again. The farmer was declared mad by the local vicar who took umbrage at that sort of experimentation on God's creatures, especially in terms of where the stopper valve had been inserted. As there had been no next of kin to inherit the lands the farmer left behind, they were raffled off as part of that year's parish summer fete. In such a brilliant twist of marketing, the vicar scored a direct hit with the idea and there had never, ever been such a busy coming together of fairy cakes, second hand trousers and tat like it due to the draw of the grand prize. The Wynds, down on their luck purchased only one ticket but that one ticket proved to be the winning entry and the land was theirs.

The Wynds had been extremely successful and had introduced new breeds renowned for the quality of their wool. Tristan had been eager to follow in his father's footsteps and had taken over the running of the farm aged twenty five. It was all he'd ever wanted to do, so he'd missed out on further education, seeing little point in it given that farming was, he felt, his destiny. He was very much hands on and had built that small but muscular frame from working out in the fields all day. Tristan loved the physical conquest of a struggling ewe or being able to mallet a fence post, deep into God's own soil. Benedict found himself liking that quality about the man opposite. He was an earthy, optimistic character. It was a part which Benedict did not have, cynically removed by the matter of fact black or white nature of London.

When Tristan asked Benedict what he did for a living, there was an awkward pause. "Oh well, I, I just am by definition, I'm, er, me." Benedict flapped his arms by his sides like a penguin as if this would help to explain things. Tristan looked like he wanted to say something encouraging, but Benedict interjected first. "That is, I mean to say, I've been things - a stock broker, an antiques dealer and well, I'm rich and frankly, quite happy. I mean, do I need to be defined by a job title? No, so why can't I be a lover, a rogerer, a party goer?"

Tristan thought he'd be helpful, "Have you thought about joining the army, a man like you would easily merit a commission?"

"And be shot at? No thank you. I know that people say we should all pull in for the big win, but I'd rather wait to see how the land lies first before I play my hand." Benedict dusted his hands off as if washing himself of the issue.

The afternoon was trudging on towards evening and Tristan still had nowhere to stay. He slowly raised himself out of his chair, "Well, thank you kind sir for your hospitality....."

"Oh, you're going?" Benedict was immediately deflated. He'd enjoyed having some different company from the other unemployable rich goons he usually biffed about with, not that there were many left. "Where are you staying? I'll walk you there."

"Well if I'm perfectly honest, I'm not entirely sure. You see, I was going to Buck..."

"Well, why not bunk up with me if you'd like to; it's the least I can do after bravely besting that mugger."

"I wouldn't want to trouble you."

"Oh, no, no trouble at all! I'll have Caruthers make up the spare bedroom. No sir, tonight you will billet with me and we shall enjoy a night of merriment and jollity, for I have two tickets to a variety showcase!" Benedict had been intending to use them to woo Penelope Lovely-Mills, but in his laziness hadn't gotten round to it.

A wide, foolish grin spread across Tristan's face, "Well sir, it would be an honour and a pleasure, consider me your house guest. You see you come to London and everyone is as friendly as at home, I knew it!"

Benedict thought Tristan's optimism was ill founded but still, he reached forward to carry his new friends case and immediately stopped before putting his back out. "I think you'd better take that".

"Right you are!" replied an excited Tristan.

Chapter 4

The tickets that Benedict had scalped were exceedingly well placed. That night, the Palladium was a feast of music hall and variety brilliance. Opening the show was Mavis Doyley and her fifty handbags, an act which involved a middle-aged housewife with a blue rinse juggling a selection of luggage. Following that was a footlights sketch called Occu-pie, an explanation of the German retaking of the Rhineland, Anschlus and invasion of Poland through the use of custard pies to the face. Then on came the well known spoons player Alfie Clemm with his new introspective ladle show and finally the headline for the evening was the Creosote Gang with their medley of Glen Miller hits played on the jew's harp. It was a cavalcade of low budget, knees-up entertainment.

Their sides firmly sown back into place after splitting them, Tristan and Benedict were drawn to the boozy nightspots of London. They found their way to the bars of Covent Garden and visited a brothel dressed up as a pub called the Old Love. This oak panelled yeomanry, heavy with the thick fug of tobacco smoke, offered extra gentlemens' relish upstairs so was always popular with the troops on leave and tonight was no exception. Benedict and Tristan fought their way to the beer soaked and cigarette stained bar and squeezed into enough space to be able to bellow at the ample barmaid for two pints of ale.

More than two pints of ale later, Tristan stood fast at the bar, soaking up the atmosphere. Benedict on the other hand, feeling his morals and inhibitions eloping together, had a different agenda. Tristan caught sight of him being led up the stairs to one of the pub's private rooms above, by a sharp looking lady in an outfit which would have made Caligula feel like having a quiet night in with a good book.

Earlier on, Benedict had staggered out of the gents after a successful trip and had goosed this lady, dark eye shadow and greasy hair all piled on top on top of her head. She'd spun round and levelled a stiletto blade at his adam's apple, explaining that "touching such apparatus, costs, sunshine." Benedict liked someone who drove a hard bargain and happily accepted the terms of her brusque deal. So here was Tristan watching the only person he knew in London going up some stairs to an unknown room where invariably he would meet a sticky end, one way or the other.

In the time it takes to fulfil the requirements contained in the job description of being a harlot twice, Tristan had been swept up by some merry squaddies in town on base leave. They'd spotted him looking gingerly for company at the bar and he'd immediately become a sort of regimental mascot with lots of ruffling of the hair and filthy songs of which he couldn't quite hear the important parts above the hubbub of the room. Thus:

"Norah worked at the knocker shop, where she shined the shiniest of knockers,
She'd show anyone a knocker or two, from squaddies, bosuns and dockers,
Norah was the easiest of girls and therefore without any luck,
If she liked you, she'd shove her knockers in yer face and give you a damned good...."

Tristan had missed the ending again and again and eventually managed to shout into the ear of the private nearest to him, "Excuse me, would you mind repeating that last song? I didn't quite hear the punch line."
In full rousing chorus, the ditty started up again. This time, Tristan heard the ending. It didn't feel it right to judge and so he raised his eyebrows and replied, "Oh."

It had reached past closing time and there was no lock-in on this particular night. Very slowly the pub began to drain of the din of revelry as the squaddies filed out, heading for their billets, but there was still no sign of Benedict. Tristan approached the bar and waving at the scrawny rat-faced landlord asked if he could retrieve his friend from the private rooms above. The publican grunted and gave permission with a toss of his head towards the stairs.

Having climbed the wooden hill, Tristan tried the first door he came to and was swiftly presented with a naked bottom betwixt the legs of a woman. A resounding "Oy!" by the owner of the hairy peach and the door was slammed shut in his face. It had been an eye opener of an evening for Tristan, who in fairness was saving himself for that special lady. He had greater success with the next door along, as there, strewn across the mattress of a truly filthy looking room was Benedict, snoring heavily, with his trousers round his ankles but his long johns still on. The hard looking prostitute sat next to him on the bed, also still clothed, legs crossed, bent over, coolly smoking a fag.

"This one yours then?" motioned the scarlet woman.

"I believe so," answered Tristan in a shrinking tone. He didn't know what to say. "Has it er, has it been a successful evening?"

"Of sorts," replied the prostitute, her voice ragged by years of thirty Rothmans a day and various effluvia. "Your friend passed out before he could fulfil his duties, meaning I've had to do very little, sort of a night off really." She stretched and yawned, "Well, I say night off, he'd have been the third tonight."

Tristan resisted the urge to pull a disgusted face. Suddenly though, the nameless lady was up on her feet, deftly reaching to her boot and then the stiletto blade was once more in her hand, tip pointing at Tristan.

"But I still want paying though," she growled.

"Oh, I see, verbal contract was it?" replied Tristan with nervous enthusiasm, trying to resolve the situation as calmly as possible and ensuring that both he and his companion left with all their body parts intact. He reached for his wallet, to which the prostitute snatched it away from him to take what she required. She handed it back to Tristan with a knowing wink. He checked to see what she had taken, expecting to see nothing but the inner lining staring back at him. In fact she had only taken the most modest of sums.

"Very reasonably priced," he unintentionally said out loud, forgetting the company he kept.

"Beg pardon?" replied the prostitute.

Ignoring the question, Tristan nervously walked over to Benedict and propping him up under his friend's armpit carried him out of the pub, trousers still dusting the floor, to find a taxi home.

The journey back had been eventful. Benedict had woken from his happy baby-like slumber to find that the cabbie had evidently decided to drive to Kensington via the Giants Causeway in Ireland. It seemed to take forever and included the world record attempt for the most hilly cobbles ever driven over. Benedict's face explored new shades of green never before seen by the human eye. It was a pity only Tristan was there to witness it and he was feeling pretty rum too.

Soon the vomit express pulled up outside the garbled address that Benedict had given twenty minutes ago. Tristan took in a deep breath of fresh air as he stepped out onto the road and jogged round to the other side to open the door for his booze-disabled friend.

Benedict fell out of the vehicle like laundry tumbling from an overfilled airing cupboard. He briefly crawled on all fours to the curb and a trickle of saliva abseiled from his mouth onto the dirt below. Desperately just wanting to feel better in a nice soft bed, Tristan shepherded Benedict with two hands, like a farmer giving direction to geese. Benedict started to climb the stairs to his town house, but stopped halfway to sit on the shallow set of steps and survey the street, very happy with his squinty eyed self. Tristan asked for the key. Benedict managed to find his wallet in his jacket pocket, but the key was missing.

"Buggr, mst've left it in th'hose. Jiz knock an wek Miss McDuffty up."

Tristan had only met Mrs McDoughty once when he'd first arrived and even in that brief encounter knew she was not a woman to be trifled with. Still, a feather pillow was worth her verbal slings and arrows. He approached the black, glossy painted door, ready to knock and then paused. The door was already ajar.

"Benedict, is London really that safe that you can leave your front door open at night. I mean I'd heard rumours about it's friendliness...."

"No, s'full of cheeky cockneys who'll winkle all y'loose change out of you if they get th'chance, terrible, terrible place, hic!"

"Then, for why is your front door open?" said Tristan over his shoulder, still staring at the door.

This comment sobered Benedict up a jot and he swung himself round and up onto his feet. He slowly reached the door and inspected the lock with grim, drunken intensity. Knowing that his friend would be no use in confronting a burglar, Tristan placed a flattened hand onto Benedict's stomach, forcing him back onto the blackened railings to the side of the door. "Stay here for a moment please, I'll just go and check to see if everything is as it should be."

The door gave an unforgiving creak as it began to move open under Tristan's gentle push. Nothing but darkness and a short foot of light by the door was his reward. Tentatively he edged into the hallway, only the gloom framing the furniture therein. He called out with his reedy pipes, "I say, Mrs McDoughty, are you there?" No one responded to him. He edged further forward, finding a long umbrella in a wooden rack and picked it up to use as a rudimentary weapon. Benedict burbled from behind, "Wasss goinon?"

Tristan ignored him, raising his makeshift bludgeon, ready to strike at an unseen assailant. He'd now reached the lounge door. It too was ajar and so he knocked it softly with his foot, moving it further open by an inch. It was it this point Tristan heard the muffled sobs of a woman. He called out, again soft mumbles were all he heard in return, "mmmph phuf, mmmph!" His fear was now tangible and his hangover gone. Tristan gave the lounge door a heavy kick. It swung fully open, meeting a bookshelf on the other side with a resounding bang. He looked in, umbrella at the ready to clobber any villain or at least protect them from a rain shower. It was now he noticed that the room was in total disarray. Even though still only gloomily lit, the difference in tidiness compared to the hallway was staggering, something was wrong. Another noise and now he was drawn to the centre of the room. He allowed his eyes to focus and gasped in shock. There, hog tied and gagged in the middle of the floor was a silent Caruthers and a particularly distressed Mrs McDoughty.

Chapter 5

An eerie chill ran through Tristan's body; the bastards had used every draft excluder in the house to tie up Benedict's servants. Assessing the scene quickly, Tristan had left the hog-tied captives in the lounge, much to the squeaky muffled chagrin of Mrs McDoughty. He'd immediately telephoned the operator and within ten minutes, the police had been despatched. In the mean time, Tristan had helped Benedict into the hallway, where he promptly collapsed on the rug, totally without comprehension of the gravity of the situation. Instead he started kissing the ancient fibres and saying how he'd never bleed on it again and how his days as a shadow boxer were behind him, that he would become the finest shadow boxing columnist if the Times would have him. Tristan, had then moved to pull down the gags of Caruthers, who reacted to freedom without emotion and gave nothing away other than a thankful smile. Mrs McDoughty on the other hand began to babble Glaswegian at him.

"Whodyerthinkyarbladdyscamprinofflythatyaweebastad!" Tristan understood perfectly well what she said and uttered a "sorry," as he worked on the knots behind her. Caruthers had stood up on his own steam but Tristan needed to help the visibly shaken woman up onto the chaise, where she fell like a like period maiden with consumption. She lay on her side and yelped, "Och, I thought it were the end of dees. Will ya be a luv and fetch me a strong tea!?"

"Oh, right you are," replied Tristan, scuttling off to the kitchen whilst Mrs McDoughty wept wet tears onto the red velvet of the chaise. Caruthers had settled into an armchair and had positioned himself, crossed legged and looking like being in need of a good cigar.

As Tristan busied himself with tea making duties, Benedict had also found his way down to the kitchen and was crawling on his belly toward the deep freeze. Now wasn't the time to admonish his new friend for being a lousy host during a crisis but he was crawling along the floor weeping.

"Good Lord! When did I fall onto a giant grammar phone, Tristan would you be a dear and remove the stylus, I can't stop revolving."

Ignoring Benedict, Tristan made up a brew, a pot of coffee and set off back upstairs with a tray including cups and saucers. He poured a cuppa for the quivering housekeeper and handed it to her. Her hands all of a dither sent the brown liquid splashing over the side and on to the wooden floor. "Perhaps not just right now eh?" said Tristan as he took the saucer back off the housekeeper.

The moment gave Tristan the chance to look around. The sitting room had properly been worked over. Upholstery had been cut through and left in a ragged state. Books had been flung off their shelves, trinkets and ornate pieces of pottery smashed. The floor was a sea of household flotsam, the hallway was the same.

The doorbell rang and Tristan oiled off to answer, where two policemen greeted him. In their defence, the police had come quickly. However, they were as effective at gathering clues as a blind man trying to assemble a two thousand piece jigsaw puzzle of a plate of baked beans. "Evening sir, I'm Constable Randolph and this is my colleague, Constable Lemon. I believe you've had something of a theft," said the older officer in front of a much younger companion. The man who spoke was in his early fifties, about five feet tall with a greying moustache framing his lips and a policeman's helmet, shadowing the rest of his shaggy dog-like face. He resembled a sad looking Highland Terrier. His colleague, Lemon, had already taken his helmet off to show a tall, lanky man, with a boyish face, pink but not ruddy cheeks and circular spectacles perched on the bridge of his nose. It looked like a father – son, constabulary convention between two unconventional parents. Tristan ushered both in and after a preliminary wander around the house to ensure the perpetrators weren't still there, they set about taking statements from each witness. Caruthers set the scene well; he'd been dusting in the lounge when he'd heard a noise in the hallway and walked over to the front door. There he was overpowered by four men in balaclavas wielding household objects used as rudimentary clubs. They'd found Mrs McDoughty in the kitchen and carried her into the lounge against her will, whereupon both of them were tied up. The assailants then looted the house for what they could. Giving a quick glance round the room, Caruthers could see that a large amount of silverwear, candlesticks and picture frames had gone but only a thorough clean up would disclose what else had been pilfered.

When Lemon had tried to interview Mrs McDoughty, he realised the gift of shorthand was missing from his professional repertoire, as her quick Glaswegian tones had gone back into overdrive with her recollection of events. "Soyasee,itwasnaeformetosaystopyecannaetakethatasawa sherethenooonthefloordeeinnothinwuthagaginmamooth." He tried, he really tried, but he looked back at his notepad and realised that he had a collection of dancing worms meaning absolutely nothing. Only one word, at the end of the balletic dance of his pen had any semblance of legibility, "Mooth." At that point he just pretended to take notes. It seemed only right to feign interest.

Constable Randolph interviewed Tristan, who retold the story of his entrance into the house after a nights drinking and how he had found the burglary.

"And, you say it's not your house, sir?"

"No, it's Mr Benedict Bryant-Lukely's, I believe there's a hyphen involved."

"Thank you. And where is he to talk to?"

"Oh, he may well be in the deep freeze, Officer......He's not all there after a heavy night on the sauce."

"......right, and how long have you known your friend?"

Tristan became animated as he was pleased to be asked, "Oh literally hours. You see I foiled Mr Lukely being mugged on the street only today. As a mark of gratitude, he's very kindly invited me here as his guest. Apparently, Buckingham Palace is currently occupied." He winked at the policeman knowingly, causing Randolph to recoil a little.

Randolph studied his note pad, "Hmmm, I do find it a little strange that in the course of a day, there had been not one but two instances, involving you, and that having been let into not only his abode but also into his trust, suddenly Mr Lukely is burgled. Is there anything else you want to tell me Mr Wynd?" In his mind Randolph had just solved the greatest whodunit of all time.

Tristan caught the gist of what Constable Randolph was implying and crisply replied, "Certainly not Officer, is there something you'd like to ask me?" He squared his puffed out chest at Randolph, who backed down a little.

Randolph tucked the pencil he'd been writing with above his left ear, dislodging a cigarette he'd placed there for a quiet moment. Later on, in the dark, he'd try and smoke that pencil and suffer much frustration before finally realising his error. The policeman folded his arms.

"Well it's our job to be suspicious sir. There is a risk of confidence tricksters weedling their way into the homes of the rich and may I say slightly naive people......or it could just be your common garden burglary."

"And that's your assessment?"

"Yup. I mean obviously you'd have had to be in cahoots with the gang and the only way we could prove that would be to catch them and get a confession, which therefore involves finding them and the loot first and let's be honest that's probably more than my job's worth. So maybe we are getting ahead of ourselves a little, but understand me Mr Wynd, when I say, everyone is a suspect."

" Are you a suspect, Officer?"

Lemon looked over and answered for his colleague,

".....Probably."

"Well, I can tell you now Officer, when you do catch the thieves, and I sincerely hope you do catch them, you will find I won't be implicated in any way. Now if you don't mind I have a stranger's lounge to clear up," replied Tristan, visibly hurt by the Policeman's comments.

"Lemon, I think we're finished here, let's be on our way and allow these people to get to bed," said Constable Randolph, the effort of his words draining the room of any further energy. Lemon nodded. The two of them reattached their helmets, tightened chinstraps and set off into the London night, questioning whether a pie and mash shop might be open at this hour.

There appeared a dishevelled figure at the lounge door. Benedict it seemed, had managed to get his head to stop revolving and used the Icelandic chill of the deep freeze to great effect. He looked very much like his suit, crumpled. He massaged his sore temples.

"Bloody hell Mrs McDoughty, the Women's Institute parties are getting a little rough and negligent aren't they? I won't stand for it you know," he croaked.

Mrs McDoughty went a shade close to crimson, got up from the chaise and crossed the room to stand nose to chest with the weary Benedict. He was then awoken and sobered further by the swift stroke of her hand meeting his cheek. He felt the girth of her wedding ring slap his chops like a meat tenderiser. She stormed off with an insulted and slightly high pitched "Hmmmph." Benedict looked at Caruthers and Tristan for answers.

"Was that warranted Tristan?"

Tristan solemnly nodded. He wiped some debris off one of the chairs and sat Benedict down to explain the last two hours.

By four in the morning, the ground floor of the house had been largely cleansed of the after affects of an aggressive ransacking. Caruthers had been particularly efficient with the use of a dustpan and brush and after scant thanks, was released by Benedict for what was left of the night to retire to his quarters. A brief inspection and Benedict had deduced that the burglars had stolen a substantial amount of silver cutlery, some silver picture frames, a collection of antique gold coins and a priceless Wedgewood plate. He stood in the middle of the room, hands on hips.

"Damn it all, Tristan, this is the last bloody thing I need at the moment, it's as welcome as a German at a meeting of the anti-sausage league. I mean how the bloody hell did they get in? There's no smashed window and the door doesn't seem to have been forced! How did nobody hear the shindy from outside?"

"The two coppers you had here, said that it looked like it wasn't forced at all," replied Tristan, concerned with his own innocence.

"Well, I mean it can't have been you as you've been with me all day and night," said Benedict. Tristan breathed a sigh of relief as he'd been feeling like public enemy number one after Randolph's haughty assumptions.

"....and it couldn't have been Mrs McDoughty. Her customer service skills are an inch short of being non-existent and she knows it's only me who will employ her. And Caruthers, well, his references seem to stack up." Benedict wracked his brain. In their excitement, as they left for an evening's theatre and boozing, had they left the door open? He slipped his hand into his trouser pocket and pulled out his wallet. He opened the flap where he kept his small change and more notably, his house key.

"Alas, I've been hoodwinked!"

"I'm sorry?"

"When I was mugged.........it was all for the house key. That's how the cheeky pinheads must have gotten in. It must have been a setup from the moment I left the house!" Benedict slumped into an arm chair, winded by the revelation.

Standing in the aftermath and unsure how best to console him, Tristan ventured, "Tea?"

"No, I, I just think I need to finish up here and turn in if that's all right with you?" Benedict asked.

"Oh by all means, by all means. Yes, I think we've had quite an eventful night."

Tristan was keen to earn his keep and spotting a pile of books that had been collected up but not restacked, eagerly gathered them and placed the various tomes on the bookshelf near the hearth. He stood back, pleased with his work. That was until they leapt from the shelf and littered the floor once again. He looked over at Benedict, "Sorry."

"No, not your fault," replied a confused and seemingly distant Benedict. He walked over to where Tristan was and scanned the floor for something. "It's not here."

"Er, I'm not familiar with your house seeing as I've only known you half a day. You've lost me."

"The bookend has gone as well. To fill you in, I used to own a lead model, a carriage, played with it as a boy. Bloody heavy thing it was, used to make peoples knees bleed if I chose to drive it into them. Hence it was the smallest thing I owned which could support the weight of those books. Looks like they've had away with it."

"Valuable I suppose?"

Benedict laughed. "No, that's the daftest thing. The perpetrators of this crime clearly had no idea what they were doing. It's just a worthless, heavy lump of lead. It'll slow them down if anything. If they have any sense they'll have jettisoned it into the Thames by now, the fools."

Having had one last look around the ground floor of the flat, Benedict called it a day, night and early morning. He led Tristan up the stairs and bid him goodnight at the guest bedroom door. He then turned back to his own dwelling, flicking on the light switch, only to see that his room had been tossed as well. He'd completely forgotten about his room and was quite discommoded. Presently, the mattress was vertical on the wall with all his sheets strewn everywhere. Drawers hung, exposed, looking vulnerable as their contents seemed to want to escape from the trauma. Clothes from his cupboard were thrown to the floor, like spurned playthings for the selfish counterpart hangers above. There was no place to start, and certainly no end to this mess, especially at this time of the morning. Benedict lowered his mattress into it's more natural state of being horizontal on the bed frame, stripped off, found two pillows and a sheet and launched himself onto the bed like a superhero instantly deprived of the power of flight. Daylight was beginning to wave at him through the bedroom window, but Benedict would not see it for eight hours.

Chapter 6

It had reached that time in the morning where the only thing that could be heard was one's thoughts. No one was up yet, not in Whitehall. Two hours earlier, the streets had been filled with revellers making their way home, pearly kings rolling out barrels and 'proppa villuns' tracking their evening's prey with long cloaked intensity. Villains were also in Kensington that night and now, as the night considered day's offering of bringing light again, nothing moved but the breeze, and three overly large shadows swiftly covering ground to an old school hall in the East End. The occasional scuffle of their shoes could be heard as they ran over dimly lit pavements, but nobody cared as householders drifted ever more nodward.

The school hall had been disused for a couple of years. In a previous incarnation it had been the Urchin Street Primary and had taught the three Rs to the local scruffs. Sadly, educational reform had brought a much larger school to the area, which had forced three of these little parochial halls to close. It had briefly been resurgent in a second life as an events hall for jumble sales and the like but sadly, the war had made times thrifty and people became reluctant to part with their second hand goods, rather making do and mending. Once more the red brick walls and corrugated iron roofed little building fell silent. Tonight though, it was inhabited. Somewhere, in the clamouring darkness of the hall, sat a man on a wooden chair, bent over a desk, reading a letter by the flame of his lighter. His silhouette could have been mistaken for an adolescent, kept back for the longest detention on record. This was no teacher's reprimand and task he was reading though, as the brass lighter's flame gave occasional dances of light onto the page and showed there the swastika of the Third Reich and German handwriting. He studied the letter intensely, then after digesting it's meaning set fire to the paper, allowing the amber and crimson edge to grow and consume, until his fingers began to burn. He dropped the flaming morsel and watched it bloom in heat and then die back to ash. He waited another five minutes in the darkness, alone only with his thoughts.

A noise outside, a rustle. The silhouette's hearing picked up, only his heartbeat racing and the wind previously, but suddenly more. His hand moved to his belt where he drew the cold steel of his luger out, ready to fire first. He'd always found that the best offence was not defence but to get in first and not give the other party a go. Steps outside now; he knew who it could be, but could not be sure until properly identified. There came a soft knocking on the wide oak door frame. The noise cannoned round the hall.

The silhouette whispered, "Yes."

A reedy voice whispered back, "I would like a gateaux."

After a pause, the silhouette questioned, "I am serving gateaux, which would you like Sachertorte or Vacherin?"

"Sachertorte, s'il vous plait."

A moment's contemplation and the silhouette strode across the room, his boot footfalls giggling the floorboards. Sachertorte had clearly been the gateaux of access. He slid the bolt backwards and lifted the latch to the door, easing it open so as not to anger it's sore and rusty hinges. Two other male silhouettes joined the original, the largest and thickest with the bulge of a substantial hessian sack thrown over his shoulder. When he moved, the bag gave off the metallic rattle of a cutlery drawer. The man who had opened the door, latched it closed again and then strode gracefully across the wooden floor boards to the desk where he originally sat. He reached under the school table, bringing out an old oil lantern. Sitting it on the wooden surface he took out his lighter from his pocket and lit the wick in the lantern's glass housing. Slowly, the flame took hold and grew strong to throw out it's dim glow across the room. The host to this little midnight party was revealed to be Philippe De Castagnet. He gave a wry smile as he stared at his two accomplices and eagerly shook hands with each.

"Chevalier, Poubelle," he said as he congratulated both.

The gang were neither well disciplined or had come from the background of rigorous precision or excellence that the military might imprint on them. Philippe had chosen them on the grounds that his pool of potential candidates for this mission reached the heady heights of.....two, in fact the two he had in front of him. There was Chevalier, a sinewy five foot six, a militant from the day he was born and in prison more than he was a free man over his fifty two years of life. He hated the British purely for their cuisine and Philippe's ideology appealed to him greatly in that he might get to bash some people who had no concept of the use of garlic. He had some brains and generally was the voice of the two accomplices. Poubelle was clearly the muscles, and if not the muscles then just the heavy bludgeoning force that was happy to be paid and cause ruin. He was a strapping six foot eight and rotund in a planetary fashion. Things would literally bounce off him without much cause for pain. For his size and sheer bulk, he was incredibly subservient, but this was due to his remaining brain cells having something of a disagreement with each other and had since refused to cooperate. So he was led rather than ever being a leader, but he seemed happy that way. He just went along with the status quo and as long as there were things to dismantle, he was a happy chappy.

Poubelle, moved to the side of the hall where three of the old school desks had formed a row to create a flat working surface. Clumsily but purposefully, he upended the sack onto the desks' surfaces. Metal rattled and clanged angrily as if annoyed by it's sudden exit from the bag onto the desks below. Poubelle, pleased, turned towards his master and promptly received a slap to the face. He recoiled, hurt and looking like tears were just round the corner

"Idiot!" De Castagnet growled. "No one is supposed to know we're here. The neighbours will think we're opening a late night cafe with that cacophony."

"I'm sorry Philippe," replied Poubelle in a deep voice, wringing his hands in apology and trying not to cry.

"It matters not, a minor oversight on your part" replied De Castagnet, his eyes only fixed on the spoils now strewn in front of him. Philippe searched for his prize, forks, serving spoons, no. Not on the surface. He looked under the final desk of the three and exclaimed "Ha, bon!" He squatted down, retrieving whatever had fallen below and standing up, turned to reveal what he was holding. The object was an ornate carriage cast in lead. It was heavy; he could feel the warm pressure of blood building up inside his finger tips. He sat it on the desk and walked back over to his original waiting place. He reached into a tool bag down by the side of his chair and withdrew a chisel and a thick faced lump hammer. Back with the carriage, Philippe gave a quick smiling glance at his companions, placed the tip of the chisel vertically into the leaden base of the model and then landed one swift and vicious blow to the top of the long metal pole. After an explosive bang, the room fell silent again. Philippe put the chisel and hammer down and admired his handiwork. The ornate cast model had been split in two and it was clear that underneath the carriage there was a small cavity. This was what Philippe had bet his life on. He slipped two fingers into the crevice and hooking them round, his nimble digits happened upon what he'd only believed to exist from old wives tales, long forgotten and only whispered about in certain circles. He knew how old and fragile the object of his attention would be, but Philippe had neither the time or the patience of an archaeologist and went about extracting the item with his fingers as best he could. He turned to show his fellows what this whole adventure had been about, a tiny roll of parchment.

Ever so carefully, Philippe unrolled the paper. It was so fragile, evaporating to powder at the edges with every single movement. An unfortunate jerk of the arm and the whole roll could tear. But by slowly teasing it open, the parchment flexed until it lay flat in the palm of his hand, no bigger than a grocery receipt. Philippe looked up and gave a knowing eyebrow raise to his colleagues, who were staring blankly at him. On the parchment lay the answer to so many questions, but which would raise new ones, a riddle. Philippe read aloud:

The High Cross to show her journey homewards
The sapphire for the lands which she vowed to defend.
Philippe looked up from the scrap of parchment in his hand, a smile on his face. The same happy, mildly inane grin was now emanating from his associates. Nothing but smiling though, no celebration or words of congratulations and slowly, the grins began to crack as lactic acid attacked their facial muscles. Finally, one of the burglars had the courage to ask. It was Chevalier that piped up. "Um, pardon Philippe, erm, what exactly, does that mean?" Philippe boxed clever with the question, "Yes, well I'd expect that of you, I'm sure it has little meaning to one so un-learned."

"Forgive me," replied Chevalier, "But to know what our end goal is, may yet inspire us further, perhaps you could inform us?"

"You'd like that wouldn't you?" said Philippe still dancing with the answer of what he now had in his possession. "Well..........yes."

"How can I put this? The truth is.........I'm not entirely sure." Both Chevalier and Poubelle groaned with deflation. Philippe almost crumpled up the antique document as he desperately wanted to ball his fists, but he took a deep breath, counted to ten and then an epiphany popped into his head. He turned to his men.

"No, this is not all of it, there is more, another statue, did you bring the other statue?" He started frantically searching down by the sides of the desks where all the stolen loot had been spilled, nothing. His men were looking confused and shrugging their shoulders. Chevalier piped up "There was only ever the carriage, boss."

"No, no, no! There must be a second piece! I was told it was the carriage AND a statue of Queen Boudicca. Oh please tell me they are still together. Did you rigorously search the house?"

Chevalier flushed with colour that Philippe could not see in the dim light, "We messed the house up a little bit, took the statue and then..........I stopped to quickly sketch some amusing caricatures of the house keeper we'd just tied up."

Philippe slapped his forehead in despair. "Oh sacre bleu. Well if you want something done, you may as well do it yourself. Fair enough gentleman, we will have to sortie the house once again and this time I will be in attendance so I want no mistakes, no waylaying of our mission!"

The pair gave him a unanimous nod, which gave Philippe the impetus to begin one of his ridiculous pep talks which to him were empowering, but to everyone else just made him seem largely pretentious.

"And then once more gentlemen, the Napoleon's Original Brotherhood shall rise again!" said Philippe, thrusting the parchment into the air, waving it like it a revolutionary ticket.

"Philippe, what do you mean again? I thought this was the initial 'push' so to speak," asked an inquisitive Chevalier. Philippe coughed with embarrassment and said, "Oh, pardon, yes this is the first attempt of which you mention."

"And, though it may be disagreeable to comment, but the acronym for our society is NOB." added Chevalier.

"Nob?"

"Nob."

Philippe paused, looking for a smart reply and falling short of the mark. He settled with, "Yes, well it was better than our previous ghastly efforts: 'The West Avignon Terrorist Society,' and, 'French Armed New Nationalist Youth Heralding An International Revolution!'"

"And I thought we were doing this because the Germans are paying us to?" asked a nervous looking Chevalier, really pushing his luck.

"Well, yes, that as well, enough! So many questions tonight! Now, contact our man on the inside, we need another date and time to thoroughly inspect Mr Lukely's property. He clearly doesn't know what he holds, help me tidy up, we must return to our lodgings before the dawn light."

The gang bundled the items into the sack again but then lobbed the bag into an old broom cupboard. The spoils were immaterial to them, they'd got what they'd came for, or half of it at least. Philippe smoked a Gauloises with impatience whilst the two henchmen finished up and slowly they all filed out. The front door closed, the latch dropped and the sound of trudging feet gently softened. All that could be heard was a stifled conversation.

"......How did the caricatures turn out?"

"Bon."

"May I see?"

There arose a snigger from disappearing voices.

Chapter 7

In Benedict's flat, the next week passed relatively quickly and the presence of Tristan really helped biff the time along. The front door locks were changed as a precaution to the now missing key, Benedict's primary concern being that it was in the hands of tea leaves who had so expertly dealt with Caruthers and Mrs McDoughty.

On Benedict's pleading to stay as gratitude for the mugging, Tristan had been accommodated for the entire length of his holiday. Once order had been restored to the house, Benedict had felt a sense of purpose in his life in being able to show Tristan around the fine monuments of the capital. As the week passed, he started to feel a twinge of sadness in potentially losing someone who did not judge him for the over-wealthy, purposeless fool that he was. He wished he could keep his new friend around for longer and briefly considered whether the servants' quarters could be turned into some form of comfy dungeon. Regardless, time stopped for no man and as Tristan had enjoyed the theatre so much on his first night in town, Benedict had planned a proper send off, by purchasing two tickets to see The Amazing Arthur Snoad and the Fifty Whistling Tea Pots, which the Evening Standard had rated as "Tour de force! A riotous hour of music hall tunes whistled through the steam of Britain's favourite beverage container!"

Tristan had nearly fainted in excitement when Benedict showed him the tickets he'd procured and as they were going out for a beano, Benedict had decided to give Mrs McDoughty and Caruthers the evening off as well. Mrs McDoughty, had given praise indeed by saying, "Ah, whilst yer a wee prat most of the time. You're a real gentleman the noo." She was spending the night at her local church group, where she could hold court on the recent tale of an evil, overpowering land owner, acting in a particularly un-samaritan way when the poor damsel in distress had been hogtied in the middle of a burglary. Caruthers on the other hand had just assured Benedict that he would make himself unavailable for service that evening. The valet never gave much away and the bonds between master and servant were as fragile as the day they met.

Benedict once again had the pleasure of looking at himself in the mirror. But this one was a simple wooden framed affair. Tristan had wanted to thank Benedict for his kind hospitality and had dragged Benedict into a local craftsman's shop he'd spotted during the last half hour of their final excursion into London. Benedict had naturally moved towards the gilt-edged frames, but after five minutes searching, Tristan had let out a highly audible gasp of pleasure at finding the oaken one now resting in Benedict's flat. The wood was slab-like and at least eight inches across from the edge of the frame to the beginning of the mirrored glass and had a gentle rise and fall to the dark, grainy surface. It was completely Tristan, simplistic, purposeful, plain and not to Benedict's taste. However, a gift was a gift and Benedict was gracious. It also secretly reminded him of his new chum, but he wouldn't admit to as much. So there he now stood in a new, freshly pressed dinner suit, white dress shirt and dickie. He slipped his hands into the spacious trouser pockets and admired his dapper self. There came a clumping noise down the stairs and there appeared Tristan, wearing a brown pinstripe suit, his spare for the holiday. He walked into Benedict's reflection and started struggling with his tie, much to Benedict's annoyance.

"How do I look?" he asked Benedict.

"Perfectly adequate."

This was lost on Tristan, who smoothed down his jacket and added, "Good, shall we be off then?"

Benedict checked his pocket watch. "Actually, yes we'd better be making tracks if we want to make dinner before the performance."

Benedict had another surprise up his sleeve all along, and dinner at the Dorchester was it. Amongst the proprietary setting, never had such savouries been devoured with lip-smacking aplomb. Disgusted gazes were shot down long noses of the other dinner guests regarding the overly vocal noises coming from a happy Tristan. Then when the dessert trolley was brought forth, Tristan nearly passed out at such intricately decorated sweets. After an hour and a half, coffee and mints, both men sat, bloated. Tristan, sagging in his chair, let out a long, "Phhhhhhhhhhhhhhh," from his lips, stifled a belch and said to nobody in particular, "Well I'll tell you something for free, it's going to be bloody hard going back to the mutton down the Baritone Valley Club, no mistake." He rubbed his belly which made a nearby diner frown and tut with disapproval. Benedict gave a wry smile and added, "They are rather a good host, the food is quite palatable here. I remember once, prior to Mrs McDoughty starting, I had nothing in the house but bread and a block of lard. There comes a time in a man's life where if he is stranded in the arctic, he might have to resort to eating the porcine substance, but whilst I don't like to show off my wealth, one bite of that filthy luncheon was enough to make me dine here for an entire fortnight!"

"So I suppose that explains the slight belly then I guess," replied Tristan giving his diagnosis.

"Erm, yes I suppose you are right. The food is quite rich, after all. Anyway, I'll see if I can get a waiter's attention to pay the bill. I say waiter?"

The two men stepped into a taxi outside the Dorchester and quickly they were moving again through the streets of the capital. Both sat in a pleasurable silence and with amiable mood, Tristan enjoyed the sights of a bustling London evening, whilst Benedict thought about the theatre. The thespian life really appealed to him with it's colour, it's pageantry. Benedict had a vivid imagination which the theatre easily quenched and he often dreamt of what it would be like to stand at the front of the stage, chest thrust forth, hands tense with emotion, spouting words as a Hamlet, or a Montague or a Puck. His Benvolio at the Foulsham Private School for Boys production of Romeo and Juliet had drawn the appropriate but muted applause of upper class parents not wishing to draw attention to themselves. However, he knew that if he ever told his father or brother, Chalfont about his desires, it would be met with silence, then humour, then a thorough beating with a wooden tennis racquet for being a colossal whoopsie. And as for music-hall? Whilst the family might enjoy the occasional trip to see what in their eyes amounted to poor people displaying their ability to play washboards, it was just ammunition for his pompus double-chin of a brother. No point in dreaming that then eh? At least he had tonight to enjoy, another rip-roaringly fun spectacle. Benedict patted his jacket pocket to feel the slim rise in surface against the fine material that two tickets would make. But the pocket lining was in seclusion. He patted harder, as if the slapping of material would reveal them. All he felt was the muscle-less chest that lay underneath. Tristan noticed his friends face turn purple and the hand to chest gave rise to him thinking that Benedict was suffering from chronic indigestion or worse, a coronary.

"Oh that's torn it!"

"Heart attack?"

"What?"

"Are you having a heart attack?"

"What? No you bloody idiot, I've forgotten the tickets! Oh what a hole, I'm such an fool!" shouted Benedict.

"Well, no bother, we'll just get some more when we're there," said Tristan, trying to be helpful.

"The Amazing Arthur Snoad? Are you completely off your lemon?! The box office would have sold out in half an hour. Nope, we've missed it! We've bloody well missed it because of me. Oh that's just the pip!"

Tristan didn't think much of Benedict's fatalist approach or language and tried to reason with him. "Well look here, it's only forty five minutes to the show's start and by my calculation, your place is about half an hour ride either way right? I warrant we might miss the first fifteen minutes, ah but his tea pots will just be getting warmed up."

Benedict stared Tristan down, but then grinned and said "Wynd, I like the cut of your jib. I say driver, back to Kensington please!"

They made good time. Whilst the phoney war was just that, the amount of military vehicles, barrage balloons and anti aircraft emplacements had made people nervous and the traffic in London on an evening was considerably less. In fact with the cabbie's knowledge, if Benedict could get in and out of his house quickly, they would probably only miss the first five minutes. The situation could be salvaged after all.

The driver pulled over to where Benedict asked him to stop. As quick as he could, Benedict had opened the door and was stepping out of the car, risking having his heel run over. He spun round and yelled, "Be right back, don't go anywhere," over the engine noise to which Tristan shrugged, like he would know where he was going.

Benedict bounded up the four steps to the front door, two at a time. He slid the key into the lock effortlessly and the door clicked open, so far it was all going to plan. The house was peaceful and quiet. Good, if the tickets weren't where he thought they were, he could think and wouldn't have Mrs McDoughty harrying for all sorts of randomness. He was sure he'd left them on the mantle-piece in the lounge. As he moved into the living room, his eyes settled upon where he thought he'd put them last. *Damnation, they're not there!* His eyes naturally panned left to something else, something that didn't belong in the usual picture of his home. It was at this precise moment that the true nature of Benedict's predicament was revealed. Standing about five feet to the left of the fireplace, was a burglar, about five foot six, all swathed in black, wearing a balaclava.

It was like the hunter, meeting eyes with the careful deer in a forest. That moment of absolute still tranquillity before the world would explode back into it's vulgar and violent evolutionary form. However, the man was a decoy. The true assailants were behind him. He felt a large shadow creep over him, looming, threatening. This character must have been behind the door. Another was sitting on a chair, just past his field of vision to his left. It was this character that the very real threat came from. Whilst he couldn't see the man, there was suddenly a cold point pressed on the back of his head and the mechanical chat of a weapon being loaded. Very carefully and slowly, Benedict reached for the sky.

"Good evening Monsieur," said a gentle French voice behind him, Benedict assumed it was the owner of the gun. "I wondered if you would permit us a moment of your valuable time. Ah, we understood you would be attending the theatre this evening, Arthur Snoad I hear. What impeccable taste for tea-pot based nonsense you have. However, we will not keep you longer than necessary, allowing you to still attend this rendezvous if you are willing to assist us."

The Frenchman's words burned in Benedict's mind, how did they know he was going to be out? Was this a set-up job, what on earth was the previous burglary then?

"I, I can assure you that if you were looking for anything of value, you pilfered it last time, if it was you."

"Oh, you are quite correct Monsieur. However, my comrades suffered from what I can only call, bungling incompetence and failed to retrieve a little je ne c'est quoi from your property. Perhaps Monsieur, you would facilitate the process of finding it?"

The Frenchman seemed well spoken and quite reasonable despite the fact that he had the cold barrel of a gun pointed at the side of Benedict's lemon. Unfortunately this gave rise to Benedict's cockiness and a wave of xenophobic bile.

"Now look here my onion munching Frenchie cove, I know Frogland can't be the nicest place to live at the moment, what with the sausage-eating hun breathing down your neck. But the fact remains that you're in my country, stealing from the very people who will no doubt come to the aid of you surrender monkeys yet again. Now I'm going to count to trois and if you're still there when I reach trois, well, I shall be very cross."

The Frenchman giggled and then bonked Benedict on the top of the head with the butt of the gun. "Very funny Monsieur and may I say how brave of you. You are right to deduce, that I am per'aps a man you could have the words with. But I must tell you Monsieur, the problem a trois does not come from me. Regardez, the man facing you."

Benedict didn't need telling where to look; he hadn't actually managed to pull his eyes away from the chaotic, snarling mouth in a balaclava in front of him since he'd surprised this little party with his entrance.

"That fellow, he hates the English just on the basis of your cuisine. A foolish chef from Bath once tried to feed him a Yorkshire pudding. They later found that same chef, dead in the shape of a giant croissant, made entirely of pudding batter. He would happily tear you limb from limb and it wouldn't even be personally against you Monsieur. He just hates your country. Now, if you will, regardez the substantial shadow cast over you."

Benedict looked down and noticed that a very tall, bottle shaped darkness was cast over him, giving off a gentle swaying motion.

"The owner of that shadow, I would not call him a villain like myself monsieur, no. He is a confused, simple and playful fellow who just happens to weigh the same as a rhinoceros with a taste for eating anything, up to an including limestone. It just so happens that he has the wingspan of a small plane and muscles of a pneumatic pump. He is also incredibly loyal and once again, I couldn't vouch for all your limbs after five minutes 'dolly time' with him Monsieur. Alternatively, there is just me, a lithe and handsome kind of fellow who makes small talk with my captives. I'm holding a gun and could just finish you off by squeezing one bullet out of the chamber. But the choice is yours no?" He asked the question with the friendliness of a parent asking a child if they wanted to go to the seaside or fairground.

"You make a valid, if not long winded argument," replied Benedict. He sighed and then said, "How may I be of assistance to you this evening?"

"Ah, how very kind of you Monsieur, bravo." Benedict felt the tip of the gun come away from his skull and a mock clap was given behind him. "Now, what we would like to procure from you this evening, is a second piece to a two part puzzle. On our first little sojourn to your abode, we happened upon a statue, a statue of...."

The French assailant didn't get a chance to finish his request, as a fourth masked man climbed out of a cupboard to Benedict's left. He hadn't noticed this one as his view had been obscured by the open cupboard door. This man had something large in his hand and started waving it with urgency. He'd clearly found what they'd been looking for just as Benedict had entered the room. It was a figurine, one that Benedict had not clapped eyes on since moving into his town house. A lead weight he'd played with as a child but that had been brought with him to London and quickly filed away into a cupboard, forever lost from thought, until now. It was a statue of Queen Boudicca.

"Ah, bon. So you see Monsieur, we do not need your assistance any more, neither should we detain you from seeing a mundane theatrical production involving ceramics and hot water. And best of all, no harm has to come to anyone."

The angry short assailant in front of Benedict growled something at his French companion. There was an awkward pause, a build up of lactic acid was beginning to make Benedict's arms ache, so much so that he had to monkey grip both hands together just to keep them supported and up in the air.

The Frenchman laughed, "Ah, je suis desole, it looks like I must be the villain of the piece after all Monsieur. You see, my colleague has made the incredibly valid point that if we were to leave you, you would make an excellent and keen witness. Therefore we have no choice and I will be killing you after all. As an added disappointment I intend to do it the 'Cowardly Frenchie' way and shoot you in the back of the head for what you said about my great country. So no open coffin at the funeral of Monsieur Bryant-Lukely I'm afraid. Oh well, Bon soir!"

Benedict closed his eyes, confused and scared. *How did they know my name?* He winced and felt his lunch drop before the shot was fired.

Tristan needed a wee, in fact really needed the toilet in epic proportions. He needed to use some facilities so badly that he was sure his choices were to either spend a penny or suffer terminal kidney failure. He'd actually desired a number one when they left the Dorchester, but Tristan was always lazy about his bladder, feeling that there were more pressing things to do. Now he was suffering the consequences. Ten minutes had passed since Benedict had entered the house and Tristan had counted every second of that time. Now he had reached critical bladder mass and was ready for an explosion in the back of the taxi. He wasn't sure how well the taxi driver would take to being showered in hot urine. So after waiting a final minute, he threw open the taxi door, yelled, "Don't go anywhere," at the cabbie and legged it across the road to Benedict's flat. If Benedict found the tickets and got back to the taxi before Tristan and he had to wait, my goodness there would be hell to pay, he thought. With that concern in mind he flew through the open door and began to attack his trouser fly with vigour in a bid to be ahead of himself once he'd reached the toilet. Unfortunately, by having his hands stuck to his crotch region and unable to counter balance his travelling velocity, Tristan lost footing and began to corkscrew wildly, bouncing off one wall and pin-balling into the living room. There he collided heavily with a man's back.

Benedict still had his eyes closed and his hands up in a monkey grip when the loud shot rang out. Being so close to his ears, all Benedict could hear now was a very solid "eeeeeeeeeeeeeeeeeeeeeeee!" and the feint muffles of struggle around him. He was violently catapulted forward, but had time to think *must have been the impact of the bullet through my head*. Eyes still closed he landed on something warm, woollen and squirming with fisticuffs. *This is not at all what I thought death would feel like*, he registered and then took a peak. Expecting to see himself on the floor from an ascendant position, like an angel looking down on the recently departed, instead he caught a swift right hook to the eye. The light came to him and so did his hearing and Benedict quickly realised he was on top of the French Yorkshire pudding murderer. Around him mayhem broke loose. There was the distinct sound of some beefy animal roaring in pain and he distinctly heard Tristan say, "Oh no you don't!" Meanwhile the madman that had made such a comfortable landing for Benedict, had now managed to clamber on top of him and was raining fierce jabs down all over Benedict's person. Suffering this onslaught of fists, Benedict raised his arms out to protect himself and looked across the floor to something, anything that would serve as protection or a weapon. As the savage pummelling began to bruise and cut, Benedict worked his fingers like a deft spider across the wooden floor to the cornerstones of the fireplace and there, found an ornamental brass poker. Grasping, he swiftly brought it up and with blind luck accurately met the nose of his assailant in a devastating, schnozz breaking whack. The recipient of the blow recoiled off him, hands to nose dripping claret, screaming in pain. Benedict looked back in time to see that Tristan wasn't faring much better than him as the large giant of a man who was now bleeding from a wound to the leg caught him squarely with a meaty forearm and sent Tristan flying into the far wall, knocking the breath out of him. Tristan crumpled to the floor as a familiar villainous French voice obscured from view by the giant fatso shouted "Allez!"

The raiding party was quickly exiting and the large wounded thug and his hidden boss had already disappeared out of the lounge and presumably the flat. The angry man, glared at Benedict through his hands which were cupping his newly rearranged conk, then vaulted Benedict also fleeing. The burglar with the statue in his hand now tried to do the same, displaying a graceful hurdle of Benedict. Benedict was having none of it though, reached up and managed to grab a handful of trouser leg as the villain passed over. He brought his quarry down with a thump. The masked thief looked back at Benedict grasping at his trousers and growled through his teeth as they struggled.

"Oh no, not you as well, you don't get to leave with my property in your hands!" Benedict yelled as he wrapped his long fingers round the burglar's leg who was now kicking wildly at his arrester's hands. Inevitably he made contact with a painful snap, bending Benedict's index finger on his left hand to breaking point. Over-reaching his pain threshold, Benedict howled in pain and cuddled his bent digits as the burglar clambered to his feet, grasped the statue and began his escape. However, Tristan had caught his breath and chased the assailant out of the lounge. He struggled to keep up with the speed of the man though and the burglar was out the front door with the statue a good few seconds before Tristan reached the open door frame. He looked out onto the street ahead and saw the black silhouette of the assailant step out from the pavement into the road, casting a quick glance back towards the house, ignoring the startled face of the taxi driver who had just seen three other masked men scamper past with urgency. Unfortunately for the burglar, he had missed the true impending danger, which was not Tristan but a tipsy army corporal driving an empty troop transport coming the other way. Both met in a sickening crunch just as the burglar had stepped past the taxi. The several tonnage of the lorry caused such momentum that the silhouette that Tristan was watching was catapulted a good fifteen feet before bouncing in a disorganised and snapped dance prior to flopping onto the tarmac. The startled driver slammed on the brakes, stopping short of the body by a matter of inches. Despite the darkness, Tristan could see in the glare of the lorry's headlamps that the silhouette would not be running any further, ever.

The young corporal, who up until that point had been having a relatively uneventful night, shot out of the driver's door and was with the lump in the road in seconds. Wishing that the freshly deposited dollop of human was still alive, he could see the bad hole he was in and promptly burst into tears. Meanwhile Tristan had shouted back for Benedict to come quickly. Both men scampered down the steps, covering the short distance to the accident. The driver was inconsolable, babbling, "S'not my fault. Just wasn't there and then he was. It was like a magic trick gone wrong."

"Sadly I believe the next Houdini has not been mown down tonight lad. Come on, it's alright." Tristan put his arm round the young lad and tried to comfort him. "He's probably not dead. It's wonderful what hospitals can do nowadays." Tristan looked back and saw the true extent of the random collection of limbs and knew instantly that he was not helping the situation. He took the corporal to the side of the truck, just out of sight of the body. The cabbie was also now out of his cab. He yelled across, "What the bloody hell just happened?"

Tristan looked over and yelled back, "There's been a terrible accident. Would you be able to go into the house please and phone the police? The telephone is in the hallway. You can't miss it." The cabbie nodded and ran into Benedict's flat.

Benedict was in something of a glassy daze, this was the horrendous and no mistake. Why was all this happening, what or who was this man and why was the statue the be-all and end-all? At no point had his father given him the items in question and said, "Now then lad, that's a priceless antique I've given you there. Don't play with them like you would your lead soldiers." No, in fact, the very opposite; he'd given Benedict Boudicca and her chariot to play with as Benedict had decapitated all his soldiers to quell a potential coup (he'd stood on one of them by accident and it had hurt him to the core). So why Queen Boudicca and her carriage were so important were beyond his estimation. He looked over at the fatality beneath his feet. Dead or alive he was determined to hear some answers, though he hadn't quite figured out how to work around the dead part of the equation.

Benedict bent down and gripped the top of the deceased man's balaclava, intent on reanimating the corpse enough so it could speak and he could issue a bloody good telling off. He whipped away the woollen covering to reveal the face of the assailant. It slid over the dead man's head only to show the bloody face of......Caruthers the Butler?!

"Bugger me with an extremely wide, voluminous encyclopaedia," said Benedict quietly, his eyes glued to his former valet. Automatically Benedict biffed the dead servant on the nose. That had been coming a long time, albeit a little late in the day and was ever so slightly frowned upon by the growing crowd of onlookers.

By now other neighbours and passers-by had stopped to see what the commotion was about. Tristan had also looked over and propping the non-commissioned man up against the side of the lorry, strode over to Benedict, grabbed his arm and pulled him assertively away before he could deliver a second blow to the recently departed villain. He softly said, "Come on now, let's not make a scene."

A scene it was though and as they stood there they could make out the pathetic non-threatening tringing noise of a British police car's bell becoming louder as it worked it's way through the maze of London's streets. That car, joined by a second had pulled up outside the crowd and five bobbys had stepped out, pulling down their jacket tails and assessing the scene. They were efficient, establishing a cordon to redirect traffic around the street and performing duties to deter those not involved to move away and go back indoors. Two familiar faces approached Tristan and Benedict, who were still standing over the body. Tristan looked up, "Oh heaven help us, it's Randolph and Lemon. Jack the Ripper will sleep safe in his bed again tonight."
"Evening gents," said a happy looking Constable Randolph. He peered over the body, "Oh dear oh dear. Someone been trying to give a lorry a cuddle eh, corr dear. What a mess." His put his hands on his hips, "What happened then?"
Tristan blinked at the laziness of the man in such a bleak situation, "Well Constable, Benedict and I had returned early from a night at the theatre..."
"Oh yeah, out convincing this gentleman to part with more of his money were you sir?" Randolph nudged a stunned Tristan in the ribs.

Tristan thought it pointless to argue and just continued. "We arrived back and there was a burglary in full swing which my friend got caught up in. I desperately needed the toilet and I stumbled into the living room and stopped Benedict being shot. The bullet ricocheted round off the coving and hit one of the burglars, a large chap, on the leg. There were four of them in the room and we struggled with them until all but this chap had made their escape." Tristan gestured to the body. "He broke free and got a good start away from the house and by the time I'd reached the front door, he'd just stepped out into the road. Seconds later the poor chap in the lorry slammed into him."

They looked over at the young corporal who was sitting on a nearby bench, wrapped in a blanket with a policeman giving him a hug. "Honestly Officer, it wasn't his fault, the burglar blindly ran into the road and at that point he'd had his chips."

Lemon was frantically scribbling away on a pad, worried once more by his barely legible pen marks. In the past week, the police station had been in awe of one report that Lemon had submitted where according to his notes, during an attempted murder the accused, 'had demonstrated expert knowledge in the martial art of morris dancing and had proceeded to threaten the victim with a sharpened toddler.' He'd already lost the thread of this scene and was wondering how he'd squeeze the words, 'equator, steam engine and inflatable mischief' into his next report.

Randolph cast a good glance at the body, "Lemon, go get a blanket from the car, there's a good lad. I think we need to give our rather dead friend here a bit more privacy." Lemon scuttled off. Randolph tapped his top lip with his index finger. "Anything else we need to know gents?"

"They were French," added Benedict, having clarity for the first time since the event happened.

"French you say? Well that is interesting............interesting," added Randolph, not sounding interested in the slightest. He nudged Tristan in the ribs, "Well, at least that means you're off the hook doesn't it lad, hey?"

Tristan flicked him a sarcastic smile in acknowledgement of the comment.

"Indeed," said Benedict trying to get the officer to behave more seriously. "What you might find interesting though, is that the man at our feet was formerly my valet."

"Crikey, now there's a twist. And I suppose that's how they got in, I take it?"

"Sounds like a relevant theory," replied Benedict, now understanding why he mistrusted his butler so much.

"Well, we'll rifle through his pockets at the morgue and see if any identification turns up. Mind if we have a butchers at his quarters sir?"

"By all means, cellar floor, second on the left," replied Benedict. Randolph whistled at a nearby officer and sent him in to the house to make an investigation of Caruthers' room.

Remembering slightly more of his job description Randolph said, "Ooh, did they er take anything?"

"The statue!" blurted out Benedict, forgetting entirely why they were here in the first place. His eyes trailed away from the body and saw the leaden Boudicca a mere few feet away in the dark. Randolph followed his gaze and walked across to the item. He bent down and picked it up, holding it like he'd won an award. He walked back to the two men and flipped the statue over in his hands.

"Worth much is it?"

"No," said Benedict. "There's the rub, Officer. Of all the luxury goods in my house, they chose this which has little if no real or sentimental value. I've got stuff in the deep freeze which is worth more than this."

"And it's in no way attached to a larger, more collectable set?"

"Not that I know of, they made off with the carriage in the first burglary, but even together they're more of a blacksmith's folly than a real piece of artistry or antiquity."

"Don't get boastful sir, it's not becoming of you," added Randolph, showing his roots more than a peroxide blonde in need of a colour and set.

"Odd," said Randolph adding nothing more. He looked down at the ground for any further clues. The young corporal was being questioned by another colleague, an ambulance had just pulled up and Lemon was trying to figure out how the phrase "chimpanzee festival" had ended up on his pad without having written it.

"Right, well thank you very much gentlemen. We'll take it from here. We'll step up the amount of bobbies in the area to prevent a repeat performance but I don't think you need to worry."

"You don't think they'll return a third time then?"

"Nah, I think to return at all was exceptional. Nope, change your locks but with the larger police presence I don't think you'll be seeing them again. Well, my officer inside will be out in a jiffy, I'll bid you both goodnight." And he turned and left the two men shrugging about what to do next. Just as Tristan had mentioned a nice cup of tea, Randolph turned and shouted, "Oy! Excuse me," at them. Neighbourly curtains twitched.

"What now?" asked an exasperated Benedict.

"Nearly forgot to give you this," Randolph said, running up to their position and bumping Benedict's chest with the statue.

"Er, thank you," replied Benedict, taking the large lead weight. He and Tristan walked with effort back to the house.

With a policeman there checking for prints and any evidence of Caruthers, Benedict and Tristan stood in the lounge awkwardly, the wait for him to leave causing jaunty angles in their postures and uncomfortable silences to ring out. They stood, with nothing to say for a good fifteen minutes. Eventually Benedict broke rank and walked to the door, shouting up the stairs, "I say Officer, I could get you a brandy if you fancy one?"

"No thank you sir, not while I'm on duty," came the call back down from the hidden voice above. Benedict moved back to standing with his hands resting of the back of an armchair. Tristan had moved to the bay window and was peeking out of the dark blackout curtain on to the scene below. The carnage from earlier was beginning to disappear now. The ambulance with Caruthers in was long gone to the morgue, as was the young corporal who had been escorted off to the Kensington police station with a policeman for further statements and to calm him down. The truck was being moved off the road by another bobby and the rest were leaving, returning the street to relative normality. Tristan turned back from the curtain and looked at Benedict, not sure of what to say. "Warm for the time of year, eh?"

Benedict took time to think of his reply. "Well, it is April I suppose."

"Oh yes, that might account for it," replied Tristan, scratching a spot on his arm through his jacket. "Feeing okay after the little rumble earlier on?" he asked adding a mock boxing motion.

"The fullest of health thanks," replied Benedict nonchalantly. Secretly he was scared witless by the whole event. He needed to redecorate the lounge, but it could have easily been done for him in a nice pink colour called, 'Brain at Dusk'. Secondly, the scrawny, mad, English-hating Frenchie he had wrestled had completely bested him. If his wandering hand hadn't had the chance encounter with a fireplace iron this could have all ended with himself and Tristan being the ones discovered not long for this world, rather than his traitorous valet, Caruthers. Benedict decided to return the courtesy. "And you?"

"Oh, I've ad worse scrums at the annual pub rugby match," replied Tristan trying to sound impressive. The awkward silence fell back over the room. Fortunately it was broken to everyone's relief by the policeman coming back down the stairs with a black bag full of evidence. He paused by the doorframe looking into the living room. "I've had a good look round gents and I've found some fruitful identification documents which could help establish the true identity of your butler. Well, I'll bid you goodnight." And with that he has out the door and into the one remaining police car. Immediately both men relaxed.

"Did you feel tense? I felt tense and I don't know why I felt tense," said Tristan, babbling. "It felt like I was on trial."

"I think that's how everyone must feel, strangely guilty of crimes which you haven't committed. And despite no guilt, you feel like you're about to be collared for giving the King's wife a jolly good slap on the rump with a cricket bat."

"Feels more like a snow shovel's worth of guilty rump slapping to me."

"Indeed, Brandy?"

"I think I'll join you in a large one please."

Benedict poured two large cognacs from the crystal decanter on the drinks cabinet and then passed one to

Tristan. Both men sank into the leather armchairs nearest to each other and brooded on the events.

"Well if I can say one thing about London from my travels, it's that it's not paved with gold as some from my village would say," said Tristan with some bitterness.

"No sir, it's paved with pavement stones and nothing else. If you're lucky you might find a shilling, but that's your lot I'm afraid. And if you've time to spare, you can witness an armed robbery and have the opportunity to foil it."

Tristan chuckled. Both of them looked particularly dishevelled, their dinner attire dusty and slightly ripped.

"So after all that commotion, is the little leaden lumpy lady alright?"

"Erm pardon?"

"The statue man, was it worth the thrill of the chase? Is it in good nick?" Tristan clarified.

Benedict hadn't really thought about it. He reached over the arm of his chair and grasped the statue which lay on the floor. Drawing it closer to him he could see that the violent skirting action off the road surface outside had removed Boudicca's nose and a hand. As he gripped it, turning the statue this way and that, he felt the main section of her body suddenly break apart, almost like she had waited for this moment to shift off to the afterlife. The soft lead had obviously been weakened in the incident and with a short but resolute chink had just snapped. Benedict looked at Tristan and said, "Well if you need any guttering replacing on your farmhouse, I've got the metal in ready supply." He drew his hands apart showing the fractured torso in two pieces.

"Ah, not salvageable then," added Tristan.

However, Benedict looked down and was incredibly surprised by what he saw. The torso was hollow and something old and yellowing had clearly inhabited it's insides since it's smithing.

Both of them saw it; Tristan stood up and looked at Benedict, who was now trying to work out how to remove whatever it was without damaging the yellowing tidbit. He put the statue down and ran upstairs. Tristan could hear the sound of urgent footsteps on the floorboards and then within a minute Benedict was back downstairs with some very small tweezers. Benedict saw the look on Tristan's face and added, "Not mine, er they were in an ornate makeup box which my mother gave me for when I have company of the female variety."

By Benedict's rather defined brow raise, Tristan didn't buy it.

Regardless, Benedict picked up the broken statue and began to get a little leverage on the old object's strange cavity filler. Slowly, gently, Benedict pinched with the tweezers and raised the item up and out of the hole. It was a small piece of parchment, folded over so the crease was at the top, where Benedict was currently trying to pull it from. It's age betrayed it's quality though and with every miniscule tug the crease began to deteriorate. Tristan was not helping by adding the occasional "Ooooh, easy there," which Benedict would head off with a menacing glance. As it came out, it was clear that the blockage was very much at the top as the paper began to move more easily, until at last Benedict held the folded parchment in the prongs of the tweezers. It was not without damage though and as Benedict unfolded it, years of being bent double in the cast meant that the scrap came away in two parts in Benedict fingers. "That's torn it," quipped Tristan.

"If you have something better to do, I suggest do it, especially if it involves throwing yourself off something high," replied Benedict slowly, eyes constantly on the parchment.

Tristan apologised whilst Benedict turned the paper over and there discovered, as luck would have it, that the tear had occurred between two lines of a poem. It was an old inky scrawl. He put the pieces together and read it out to his audience of one:

All false is this above provided
By heinous words of ill-founded power
Come the crown which once Boudicca wore
British rule is installed and Rome shall cower.
Four rubies that were taken from foolish Claudius
Coronet of Wales for beginning and end

"I'm presuming there's more but it seems to have been torn away," added Benedict peering at the inky smudges which decorated the perforated edge of the parchment.

"Well, would you believe it?" Said Tristan, gasping in wonder. He had no idea what it meant. "Is this some kind of artisan's trinket they put in all statues, Like the penny in a Christmas pudding?"

Benedict cast his mind back to his brief sojourn into the antiques trade and considered all the objet d'art he'd ham-fistedly broken by accident and the absolute lack of bits of paper with odd riddles scribbled on them. "No, not at all," was his conclusion. He read it through again.

"So what it's essentially saying is, whoever holds Boudicca's crown restores British rule?" said Tristan, piecing the rhyme together.

"Certainly sounds that way."

"And, er, is that something that exists?"

"Well from my days at Foulsham, it was never something that cropped up in history class. All we were really taught there was that the Romans didn't like bends in the road, everyone hates the French and occasionally the Spanish, and the Greeks when not thinking out loud had unusual tendencies involving boys. That's a pretty fair summation of what I learnt. And Britain has had lord only know knows how many different monarchies which were rife with Johnny Foreigner so it's probably nothing." There seemed some finality in Benedict's words. He didn't mean it though. "Bloody exciting stuff though eh?"

"Oh yes, in the most furtive sense," continued Benedict. "I mean, who knows the history of this document and why it was tucked away for so long. It may have been a relic from Boudicca's age itself. Fascinating, absolutely fascinating."

They had reached the point where their extremely limited knowledge of ancient Britain had found it's cul-de-sac and exhausting fatigue had crossed paths, leading to an inevitable break in conversation and the thought of what to do next. The truth was, Tristan was due to go home.

"So then, that will give you something jolly interesting to pursue when I'm off tomorrow, back to sunny Wales. Gosh, I'm sure you'll have lots of peace and quiet once I'm gone. You'll probably be glad of something to do, having that riddle to tackle."

Benedict was modest in his response, "Oh I'll probably just drop it off with the British Museum and let them do their worst. Got a friend there, Tommo, very enthusiastic ale drinker."

"Oh, er right," said Tristan, surprisingly hurt that his new friend didn't want to continue the adventure or more importantly invite Tristan to tag along. "Well I suppose it's back up the hill to Sandy Bedfordshire for me?" he asked rhetorically. "Is there anything I can do before I turn in?"

"Thank you, you've done plenty already. No no, I'll square up round here as much as I can and then head up myself. What time is your train back?"

"Eleven thirty," replied Tristan.

"Ah, well that gives us plenty of time for me to rustle up a fried breakfast in Mrs McDoughty's absence. I'm not without some culinary skill." Benedict had forgotten about Mrs McDoughty. "Oh Christ, how am I going to tell Mrs McD what's happened? She's not been fully settled since the last break-in. Oh there's the bloomer, I might lose a butler and a housekeeper if I'm not careful. I'll have to work out a way to break it to her gently. She's back in the afternoon so I should have plenty of time to juice the old lemon and come up with something."

"Best of luck with that one," replied Tristan. He stretched his arms out and jested, "Well, it's time for me to take my own rickety suit of armour off and clank up the wooden hill, Good Sir Lukely, I bid you adieu!" He swept his hands down in a bow for good measure and then skipped up the stairs but when out of sight his shoulders sank. Back to farming for poor old Tristan. Back to five in the morning starts, hard cold nights, sheep that were predictable in their unpredictability and a small town, small people, small attitudes. Secretly, he'd loved the bustle and energy of London and especially found the danger element of the past events exhilarating and just the ticket. It was a good old dose of high drama and he felt more alive than he had in years. The prospect of returning to the valleys was not appealing.

Benedict sat for a while on his own downstairs, enjoying the peace that had at last returned to the flat. It gave him a chance to pick over the events of this most unusual evening. He still had the tattered old riddle to hand and kept on going through it in his mind almost as if to see if it would magically lengthen and make some sense. He'd turned the page over, flipped it upside down, held it to the light, put it into the shade, screwed his eyes up at least fifty times for each category of action but perception and meaning did not radically alter. But then, he knew this was hardly surprising. This wasn't work for an antiques dealer, no codger in a fusty smelling room full of old clocks and random tea strainers could answer this question. Benedict knew this needed an archaeologist or a historian; there would be no solving of the puzzle tonight, if at all. The painful truth was that if anyone would want to study it, they would probably want it for their own ends or their museum's collection. This was going to be tricky. Who could he rely on who would have the expertise to know precisely what this was all about and who would also be willing enough to give up the game without getting all political about information sharing? Tommo at the British Museum was an absolute swot, but would likely drop the artefact in his pint, no. Then there was Shady Pete, he'd have the initiative but not the knowledge, which kind of defeated the object. Plus Shady Pete wasn't just a clever name, he cast dubious shadows further than a forest of giant redwoods.

Then it clicked, a plan so brilliant that Benedict thought that it made Isaac Newton look like a bit of a thicky. Without further ado, Benedict headed off to bed at the early hour of the day, highly unlikely to get any sleep what with his mind now filling in the gaps of what he proposed to happen.

Chapter 8

Tristan was in. Of course Tristan was in. As soon as Benedict told him what he intended to do he was in. In fact it was positively rude of Tristan to ever assume he was even included. But as soon as the plan was divulged, Tristan without thought clapped his hands together and said, "Lovely stuff, when shall we leave?"

Benedict smiled and playfully said, "Thought there was a flock of sheep that needed tending to."

"Well, actually they're more than capable of looking after themselves, unless of course, you don't want any company. I have taken up a good week of your time already?"

"Oh I wouldn't have it any other way old boy," replied Benedict.

So far, Tristan had only travelled around London with Benedict either on foot, on the underground, or in a cab, so it was a fair assumption that Benedict had no other means of transportation. Tristan was wrong. As they left the Kensington apartment that morning, Benedict mentioned that he was taking Tristan to see his phantom. Tristan wondered how this fitted in with the newly concocted plan and had visions of talking to an eccentric spirit, living in a graveyard, who would radically defy any belief system which Tristan may have had. Instead, after five minutes casual stroll they had reached a gravelled cul de sac where a long row of locked garages were built. Benedict walked three doors in and approached the fourth, number eight. The lock-up had a set of hinged wooden doors painted in a loud green gloss and was in reasonably good condition. He felt in his top pocket for the key, which he then pulled out and slid into the central lock on the right hand door. Through a lack of any regular use, the lock initially did not want to give but eventually, after a grating sound came from the cumbersome mechanism, Benedict successful twisted the key and asked Tristan to grab hold of the left hand door. Both pulled their respective doors away, the wooden bottoms coarsely running over the uneven gravel until the garage was open. Old, damp air spilled out and filled their nostrils. Inside was a large sloping lump, as big as the room itself, though a little lower than the ceiling. Covering the odd shaped object was a substantial dust sheet. Benedict whisked it off like a magician plying his trade with the old tablecloth trick and the lump underneath was revealed in full glory.

"Oh, that really is something quite beautiful," said a misty eyed Tristan.

"Present to myself on my thirtieth birthday. She really is a gem isn't she?"

Both men were staring in admiration at a beautiful, well polished and immaculate black Rolls Royce Phantom II. The light that entered the small space played across it's chrome features and danced over the round saucer like headlamps.

"Ever driven one of these?" enquired Benedict proudly.

"Can't say that I have, though I expect it's similar to a tractor."

"Yes, well with that ansnwer you won't be driving it today either. In fact it will probably take me a moment to get all my own driving faculties in place. Been a while you know, but I'm sure for an adventurer like me we'll be sailing in a jiffy!"

Tristan stood outside whilst Benedict entered the large workspace and clambered through the driver's side and into the seat. He slammed the door shut and for a moment, Tristan was watching what amounted to a silent movie about a gentleman who had briefly forgotten how to drive. The faint wafting of a "Bugger," or a "Well that's clearly not working," came through the windscreen until at last the brilliant tiger of an engine came to life. It's motorised roar as Benedict gave a little too much throttle paralysed Tristan, but the feeling in his legs returned as the vehicle lurched forward out of the small garage. In three clear jerky movements the Phantom stopped next to Tristan and then the engine coughed out in a comical stall. Benedict enthusiastically pushed the passenger door open to a non-plussed Tristan.

"Soon get used to it, hop in and we'll go for a spin in the surrounding countryside." Understandably, Tristan saw what looked like an elegant but obvious death trap driven by a man clearly tutored by the Grim Reaper school of motoring. Tentatively, he slid into the passenger seat and closed the door behind him.

Seven angry pedestrians and a man knocked off his bike later and Benedict and Tristan were shipshape, motoring along quite happily into the Essex sticks towards Chipping Ongar. The Phantom had survived the collision with the pensioner and his pushbike remarkably well, but then a car nearing three tonnes in weight was always going to come off best against the spindly and now bent frame of an old bike. Benedict had tried to claim that the bicycle would corner better bent into a right angle and in fact the pensioner should claim ownership of the trademark to the "Rightcycle," but the old man was having none of it. Once the old cove had been silenced by being compensated for his trouble, leaving London had been remarkably easy and they rolled along unannounced towards Benedict's brilliant idea.

Benedict had imparted his epiphany to Tristan first thing that morning. The concept was simple, who did Benedict know who had the substantial historical knowledge to be able to explain the background behind the riddle, yet who would be old and infirm enough so as not to get any clever ideas of pursuing it themselves? Only one name sprang to mind. Professor Trilby Effingham-Wright.

Effingham-Wright, or Trilby to everyone who knew him, had been Benedict's old History Master at Foulsham. Benedict had realised that when he had dismissed Tristan's comment about whether what they had been taught at school could unearth the reason why this piece of paper came into his possession, actually Tristan was in the right area. Although Benedict and his counterparts had only been taught the essential major events within the context of time and many of the boys hardly listened, Trilby was an expert disguised as a teacher. How did Benedict know this? Firstly, it came across in the passion in which Effingham-Wright taught. This small woollen haired man enthused about British history. Be it the Tudors or the Boer war, he would stand in front of the blackboard, his arms flailing with expression, the look of disdain as only the most physically challenged brainy oiks listened. Secondly, as any boy who had suffered a Trilby detention in his study could verify, his room was a veritable museum of coins, helmets and other pieces of antiquity that would make some local museums blush with jealousy. And finally, and the icing on the cake, Trilby was once a very well respected historian who had a rather hefty fall from grace.

Trilby had been a leading historian, a star member of the Society of Antiquaries of London whose opinion was sought on rare pieces of parchment and art the world over. He'd keen a key point of contact on Roman antiquity for a number of archaeological digs across Britain and was often seen near the neat ditch of an excavation in a muddy field, washing a fragment of pot or examining an eroded skull. He'd be there, work boots, brown trousers, thick navy blue jumper barking out instructions in his raspy voice. Effingham-Wright was the jewel in the British historological crown, except there was but one flaw in his nearly flawless professionalism; Trilby was a colossal gambler and larcenist.

His addiction to the thrill of the pinch came to a head when he was invited to assist with a dig in Singapore which he'd fought tooth and nail to be a part of. Oriental history was not his specialism but being so revered by the historical community he was given permission to join the expedition, much to the protestations of some rival historians. As it turned out they needn't have been worried about him stealing their limelight, for as soon as the ship docked in that colonial part of the orient, he was not seen for the first two days. After forty eight hours, a small group of archaeologists did the right thing and knocked at his apartment to make sure his health was up to it. This was the early turn of the century and local medicine was more likely going to turn you green and have you claiming that you'd invented Ireland. Trilby was in his mid thirties at this point so it was unlikely and unlucky that he might have been struck down by a virus. But it certainly looked that way when he answered the door, only in a pair of khaki shorts, sweating profusely, beads of the stuff rolling off his pale, hairless, pigeon chest. He blocked their view of the small room, but the hum of stale sweat and booze eeked out of the room all the same. They asked of his health as he wasn't looking as chipper as normal. He tried his hardest to assure them he was not deficient in vitals. Gently they explained to the red and sweating half naked historian that whilst the orient must contain many a tourist trap to visit, they had hoped to see him at the dig, due to his wealth of experience. They had after all, already dug up a number of skeletons and artefacts. A blushing Effinham-

Wright replied that when he was feeling up to it he would grace them with his presence. Suddenly, the archaeologists heard some uncomfortable whispers emanating from the room. The eminent British Archaeologist Sinclair-Ceefaive, a creative man who was quickly surpassed by all his colleagues in the field, started towards the door.

Trilby let out a defeated sigh of "No.....please stop."

Too late, Sinclair-Ceefaive pushed the door open and there, revealed in literally all it's glory, was a remarkably detailed model of Hadrian's wall and a set of forged title deeds. Apparently Trilby had been demonstrating the wall as a marvellous defence against the English and the Scottish to a group of misguided oriental businessmen, missing out the part where depending on how you were disposed to either country would probably also be quite important to consider unless you wanted to spend the remainder of one's days on the wall itself. How Trilby had managed to construct such a wonderful demonstration was anyone's guess. What was clear was that the wall was the star attraction in a very high stakes game of poker and that Trilby had a serious problem. Regardless, before anyone could say, "Where did you find the modelling paint?" Effingham-Wright had been kicked off the dig and was on a ship headed back to Blighty where he was promptly arrested, not before stealing Sinclair-Ceefaive's wristwatch and monocle out of habit.

It was only his reputation, connections and his problems being treated as 'tendencies' that saved Trilby from prison. As a double whammy of bad luck, word of Trilby's unusual exploits reached society circles faster than he could travel. Soon all stakeholders who had come into contact with the man realised that they'd lost paintings, figurines, shoes, lacy unmentionables and hairpieces to the habitual thief. Effingham-Wright became a figure of scorn and revulsion. The Society of Antiquaries literally threw him out, two of the senior members escorting him by the armpits into the street and then threw him to the floor, to ensure he knew he'd been thrown to the floor. The Natural History, V&A and British Museum wouldn't touch him with a bargepole, presumably because they assumed he would attempt to pilfer it and gamble it away to a foolish gondolier. Struck with shame and unable to find work, Trilby hid in the darkest corners of London, matched rumour with form and engaged on a torrid rampage of dice, shove ha'penny and 'how many fingers am I holding up?' until his funds were spent. Eventually, the small sallow frame of Trilby realised he had exhausted his credit and welcome with the sharks he consorted with and was out on his ear. Alone, with nothing but a dirty hanky and half a deck of cards for comfort, Effingham-Wright found a park bench and began a modest but far cleaner life as a tramp. However, he was saved from anonymity by an opportunistic headmaster: Jessup Wimple.

Jessup was a Foulsham man born and bred. He'd been schooled there and from an early age had enjoyed the sound of his own instructive and patronising tones. At Durham University, he found his degree in education just the ticket and through bootlicking and working his contacts, quickly established a job back at his old school as an English teacher. Here he flourished, becoming a favourite of the boys and fellow masters and it was only the work of a moment, where, at the age of twenty eight that Wimple became the headmaster. He was enthusiastic for learning, introduced better methods of teaching and found talent wherever it hid and it was in this way he found Effingham-Wright. At tea with the local vicar and other gentry from the area, the lurid story of Trilby had been mentioned; the clergyman naturally shrieking in abhorrence to the events as they were told. A light-bulb went off in Wimple's head though as undoubtedly Effingham-Wright had historical knowledge in abundance, what a coup for the school if he was brought back from the brink. Wimple broached the idea thus: He suggested to the various parishioners that it was their civic and Christian duty to help a person previously held in such high esteem who had perhaps fallen on stony ground of late. He got their attention and continued to explain that he would like the opportunity to rehabilitate the man, utilise Trilby's considerable knowledge for his boys and would keep a stern eye on Effingham-Wright to ensure he did not fall back into bad habits or try and involve staff or children in a game of jacks for cash or pinch plimsolls and stationary. Not seeing Wimple's own selfish intentions but only seeing the act of good faith and charity, the parishioners agreed. So on a particularly brisk October morning, having been tipped off by friends, Wimple caught a train into London, and carrying a large briefcase made his way on foot to Saint James's Park where there on a bench, he found a bundle of rags asleep. Whilst the owner of the rags snoozed, huddled against the cold, Wimple placed the case on the bench by the foot of the tramp and worked the latches on the lid. Inside was a pristine but heavyweight copy of Plutarch's "Moralia". He took it out of the case, took a step away from the bench, held the tome up horizontally and let go of it. Down it came, banging the air around the ground with an almighty clap.

Suddenly woken and irritated, the unmistakable white cloud of hair that made up Effingham-Wrights's head emerged from the rags, along with the smell of grease and unwashed skin. Wimple, who was particularly anal about his cleanliness, gagged at the cheddary smell. Trilby's

normally reaction would have been to bark at the intrusive stranger to be about his own business but just as he was about to, he caught sight of the veritable classic laying on the pathway beside the bench. Surely it was far too much of a coincidence that this stranger had caused such a commotion with such an interesting tome, one that had been debated and quibbled over for years and years by fellow historians? No, clearly this was a message.
Enfeebled, the aging tramp looked up, squinted and said, "You have my fullest attention for a midday without a bottle of something to take the edge off, now what do you want?"
 "Quite simply, I want you to teach at my school, buck up your ideas and in return, I'll pay you a school master's wage and see that you are halfway respected again. I'll leave you with these. Good day."
Wimple reached back into his briefcase, pulled out a written job offer, threw it onto Effingham-Wright's blankets and walked off towards Park Lane. Effingham-Wright sat up, shaken by the suddenness of events. He looked at the wonderful text on the floor and then at the job offer. There really wasn't anything else to consider.

Trilby Effingham-Wright became the History Master at Foulsham School and the gamble paid off for Wimple. Wimple got a highly knowledgeable historian who just about tolerated the insolence of his pupils, Trilby got some form of a life back and toned down the larceny and gambling though he dabbled from time to time, but only a bag of sweets here, a hand of gin there. He was candid and frank about his previous life and hence it was that the boys came to know about his previous indiscretions, using himself as an example of what short happiness a pony on a horse each way could bring, but in which the long term consequences were often problematic. He wasn't a conventionally bad man and he believed in trying to pass on his knowledge to the best of his ability, but old habits die hard and the school often shielded Trilby from the verbal slings of parents whose children had had their tuck boxes pilfered.

As they sped through the Essex country lanes, past green fields of young wheat and adolescent lambs beginning that slow decline from woolly gambling energy bundle to thick, stocky plates of Sunday roast, Benedict imparted Effingham-Wright's background to Tristan. Tristan had a faint look of disgust on his face. Where he came from you might play whist in the pub for matches or pennies, but he thought it terribly poor form to gamble with Hadrian's Wall, no matter how old and crumbly it was. Benedict replied, "Well, it may not be your cup of tea, but what can you do? As he used to say, 'All of life's a gamble boys.......' Besides, we can't judge him now, he's about to become our technical expert, so chin up old chap and try and ignore him if he half inches your socks."

Shortly after the silences in the car became awkward, they had reached Chipping Ongar, and took a left turn onto a narrow track through a small wood. The chalky road gave a satisfying rumble under the wheels of the Phantom and after fifty metres of curving right, the car was in the middle of a small turning circle, in front of a chocolate box cottage, surrounded by the woodland. It was so sickly sweet that Tristan felt a sudden urge to book an appointment with the village dentist. The front of the cottage displayed large sash windows and a wild cottage garden surrounding the front door.

It felt good to get out of the car. While Tristan had never been in a vehicle that was so fleet of foot, the ride still left a lot to be desired and he felt sure his buttock shaped tractor seat would have given a more comfortable experience. Benedict stepped out and tapped his jacket pocket, just reassurance that the mystery document hadn't flown away as they sped along. He could feel the soft slip of parchment underneath. Both men trudged their way to the front door over the grimy white chalk. Benedict pressed the doorbell and the trill of an electric ringer was heard the other side. There was a momentary pause, then the sound of footsteps on a wooden floor. A reedy voice piped out, "Be there if a mo, just buzzing about trying to find the old slippers."

The front door was confidently wrenched open by a small old man. Benedict instinctively knew it was Effingham-Wright; that shock of cloudy white hair on his head, the well oiled skin, a faint whiff of aftershave. He was wearing a white shirt and beige silk neckerchief, navy blue trousers and leather sandals. Sickeningly he was in the fullest of health for a man in his seventies.

"Yes, well hello, what can I do for you today gentlemen?"

"Professor Effingham-Wright, perhaps you don't remember me?" enquired Benedict. "You taught me at Foulsham?"

Trilby looked confused but not irritated, "I'm sorry, I find it hard to place people nowadays, dotage and all that."

"The name is Benedict Bryant-Lukely."

Trilby took out some oval reading glasses from the top pocket of his shirt, popped them on his nose and reached out a hand to run over Benedict's jaw. Benedict thought this was not entirely necessary but Effingham-Wright was his man and so he would suffer the odd fondling.

"Ah, so it is, Lukely my dear boy. What has it been, five, ten years?"

"Approximately fifteen I believe," replied Benedict.

"Good lord, is it really that long? Well, how time flies." He nodded in the direction of Tristan, "And this is an old pupil as well, are you?" he asked.

Benedict answered on Tristan's behalf, "Well no, Professor Effingham-Wright, I'd like to introduce you to a friend of mine, Tristan Wynd. Tristan is a farmer by trade."

"Oh, how lovely for you, all fresh air and manure I suppose."

Tristan was still not sure what to make of this small old man, but he'd just seen him steal the parchment from Benedict's top pocket when Trilby felt Benedict's face, so he just smiled back.

"Well, let's not stand on ceremony all day, come in, come in." He waved them through to the hallway and they were ushered into a comfy living room. If the outside had the charm of a picture book cottage, then the inside did not disappoint either, all low ceilings, uneven floors and ancient wooden beams. Benedict could not guess how old the house was, but by the thick cut stone walls, guessed probably seventeenth century. Trilby had added his own flair, with tapestries and paintings, Benedict recognised a small Titian and a Bernini; clearly they had been half-inched at some point from someone else's collection and the culprit never found.

"Sit, sit," insisted Effingham-Wright as he rubbed his hands, "I've just put a pot of coffee on. Do either of you play bridge? What am I talking about of course you do. I'll be back in a jiffy."

The two gentlemen sank into a soft futon, spattered with cushions. Tristan yanked one out from behind, that was tilting him into Benedict and flung it into one of two equally squishy armchairs opposite. On a coffee table between them were a stack of old books and a copy of the parish church news. Tristan looked down past the arm of the futon and noticed a well read copy of the day's newspaper on the floor, specifically turned to the horse racing section. He shook his head solemnly. Benedict heard the sound of footsteps outside and through the net curtain saw Trilby throw a blanket over the Phantom and then try to freewheel it into his shed. Fortunately, as it was so heavy, it stood firm and the old man threw in the towel after two attempts with a resounding. "Bugger it". Benedict shook his head and laughed. Same old Trilby.

"You do realise he's already taken the parchment?" asked a concerned Tristan. Benedict nodded his head, this was all part of the plan.

Shortly after, Effingham-Wright appeared carrying a tray laden with coffee and cups and saucers. He set it on the coffee table and poured each of them a cup, then sank into one of the chairs with his bespectacled eyes fixed on Benedict. He took a sip of the hot arabica juice and then posed the question which had entered his mind on answering the doorbell.

"So, it isn't everyday that former schoolboys visit me. In fact, if I was feeling particularly bitter about it, you are the first. I must enquire then, is your presence for a game of any stakes poker, a vendetta for a poor mark I once gave you, or a guilty conscience for a prank once served? Or are you just giving care to the elderly?" Benedict played the game. "We happened to be in the area and I thought we'd pop by."

"Oh do give me the courtesy I deserve, I'm not an octogenarian yet" chided Trilby. "Come now, I'm far closer to my death than I am the day I was born and consider my time fleeting; so whilst I hope you enjoy the coffee, I must press you for why you are here."

"Well, if you really wish to cut to the heart of the matter, my motives are purely selfish. I wish to use your brain."

"You can't have it, I'm still using it, at least until the end of the day I hope, maybe even tomorrow," he jested. "Ah, so come to pick up some tips from the old master have you? I heard a rumour on the rounds of tea with the Vicar that you were dabbling in antiques yourself."

"Dabbling is the exact extent of my actions. I found the items perhaps a little too collectable."

Trilby looked around at the walls of the lounge, inspecting his army of paintings and trinkets, "Yes well a problem shared is a problem halved. I digress, so still in the trade and wanting an objective opinion I take it?"

Benedict pursed his lips, took a moment and replied, "Not exactly. Something may have come into my possession which is slightly unusual. But I don't have it with me now."

"Well who does?"

"You do..."

Trilby looked away guiltily. "You make rash accusations based on old form sir."

"You took the item from my breast pocket when I reached the door, a small roll of parchment. But I'm not here to admonish an old codger for being a petty crook. Please, read it."

Trilby gently unfolded the paper, adjusted the glasses on the bridge of his nose and read the strange verse underneath. He looked up at Benedict, who could sense Trilby's next question.

"It was hiding in an old statue of the aforementioned Queen Boudicca. In an impossible sequence of events I was burgled twice. The first time they took the carriage and the second time came back for the Queen. However, we happened on them and before you could say "inflamed situation" all hell had broken lose and the one who took the statue lay dead in the middle of my street having been hit by a lorry."

"Most surprising," added a captivated Trilby.

"Any initial reactions?"

"Well, the riddle clearly depicts a situation whereby whoever holds the Queen's crown, restores rule to Britain, that's the clear and obvious interpretation of what it says." Tristan, who had kept quiet up to this point felt a strange relief come over him. "Our point exactly, as easy as that then eh?"

Trilby found Tristan's answer rather blithering, "Yes, interesting but it doesn't mean for a minute that the crown exists or that there is any truth in the matter young fellow-me-lad."

"Oh," said Tristan, eyes drawing back to his knees in ignorance. Effingham-Wright saw this and wanted to bring the scorned chappie back into the conversation.

"All I'm saying is, you are right, that is what it says, but the riddle is moribund Mr Wynd. Let me explain...." Trilby settled back into his armchair. "What do you know of Queen Boudicca?"

Benedict gave a sizeable "Um," and took a moment to stare at the ceiling. At last he had his best answer, "Rule Britannia and all that?"

"Not even close to a good answer. Britannia is nothing more than an image, thought to be the very late Duchess of Richmond," Tribly giggled. "Let me see, where to start. I think I can strike the appropriate chord." He cleared his throat, ready to teach. "The Roman empire had extended to our shores and invaded around the first century AD. However, some Celtic tribes had allied with the Romans to form an enduring peace. One of those tribes was the Iceni, based in modern day Norfolk. Prasutagus was their leader, Boudicca his wife. In his will he left his kingdom jointly to the Roman empire and his daughters. However, on his passing, the Romans took the land for themselves, flogged Boudicca and raped her daughters. Understandably more than a little browned off, Boudicca formed an alliance with other tribes willing to fight the empire. The Roman governor of the time, Gaius Suetonius Paulinus, had focussed his attentions on Wales so Boudicca and her allies sacked the town of Colchester and the temple of Claudius, a great insult to the Romans. To give you an idea of the anger of the Celtic nationalists, they also slaughtered the entire Hispana Roman Legion sent to relieve the settlement. Suetonius, surprised by the ferocity of the assault, returned to Londinium. Any guesses what that is called now?"

Benedict raised his hand and said excitedly, "London!" Trilby hadn't seriously been expecting an answer, but paused and then said, "Er, correct," much to Benedict's satisfaction, shooting a smug look at Tristan, who was secretly hoping there wasn't a test at the end. Trilby continued, "On surveying his defences, he realised the size of the operation was untenable and withdrew from engaging with Boudicca. Nobody had expected such a revolt as this and therefore the way was clear for Boudicca to sack both St Albans and Londinium. The Britons massacred thousands of civilians, thought to be traitors to this island. Suetonius's only possible response was the scaliest of vanguard actions, massing his troops in the midlands. There then began the battle of Watling Street, the largest encounter between the Romans and the warring Britons. Historians argue about the exact location of the battle but from the varying accounts the general location is thought to be somewhere along the road from London to Shropshire, hence Watling Street. Regardless, through tactical endeavour, Suetonius's legions won the day. As to Boudicca, accounts are not clear. Some say she died in combat or committed suicide. Others tell of her succumbing to illness. What is not known is where she was buried or perhaps more importantly in your case what she was buried with. If she really was a Queen, we can theorise that she had some sort of crown. But there are no foundations as to what it looked like." He waved the piece of parchment in the air. "As to this leading to some kind of leadership of the country? Folly my dear fellows, folly. Perhaps a revolutionary blacksmith's fancy. The oldest relevant piece of literature regarding the throne of this country and the responsibilities of the crown are fully laid out in the Magna Carta. Nothing else supersedes it."

"If only we had more to the riddle," replied Tristan, "There's clearly a tear at the bottom of it, you can see the ink from the high points of words at the tear line."

"Well, what you have clearly missed, my dear boy, sorry, old habits, old chap. What you've missed is that if the burglars had the chariot, then there is the likelihood that a second and perhaps final piece of the riddle was contained therein. Hence they came back for the first part. If we had both pieces this would be much easy to sally forth and investigate. Ah, but it would be a fool's errand anyway. As I've just explained nothing trumps the Magna Carta. Therefore, in conclusion, I would say bad luck to you for your two burglaries, but it's time to scratch the fixture as searching for recompense from an artefact which we cannot even establish if it exists, is sadly, not forthcoming. Now, is there anything else I can do for you today gentlemen? Perhaps I can offer a spot of lunch before your return to wherever you've come from today? I have a lady friend coming over just before noon. She's old crumpet and a poor dominoes partner but is well met in the culinary department."

Benedict had had the wind taken out of his sails, he blinked and said, "Just as an aside, as we're having such a lovely spot of weather, if we were to continue looking where would we start?"

Trilby raised an eyebrow. "Not easily dissuaded are you? Well, you will note that the riddle mentions 'foolish Claudius'. If you really have the ginger to investigate, why not start in Colchester? That's where a prolific 'Claudius,' lived. The army barracks there have a history stretching back to that period of time as well. Why not visit and pester the curator of the local museum. You never know what stone you might turn over but I feel confident all the cobbles in the local vicinity will have been rotated several hundred times already."

Benedict paused, deciding whether to continue. The alternative was to return back to London, no plans, feeling wary by the phony war and loneliness. At least he had this straw to cling to. "May I have my parchment back please?"

"Certainly, but if I may, I'd like to take a copy of the text." Trilby saw Benedict's look change to suspicion. "Just so that I may continue to assist you of course. I still keep my fingers in a lot of pies."

"I bet you do," muttered Tristan.

"I may be updated with a piece of archaeological enquiry which I can telegram you about. One never does know quite what will be unearthed next."

Trilby was out of his chair with an agility which gave away his excitement. Despite Trilby's negative assurances and best attempts to pooh-pooh Benedict's find, Benedict was beginning to doubt his choice of expert. There was something about the old rotter that Benedict didn't trust.

With Trilby temporarily gone, Tristan asked the question. "So that's that then I suppose?" Benedict turned to him. Tristan too had a deflated look on his face. "You know, unless you want to.....I mean I've nothing better to do today?"

"My thoughts exactly. No, there's more life to this yet. I'm not going to let some historian discard us with words so easily and ruin our tea party. If there's one thing my father taught me, it's that perseverance leads to results."

"Oh, and is that why your father's not very happy with you then?" Tristan asked innocently.

"Just be quiet," replied Benedict. "Now, where is that Professor with my riddle?"

"Here I am," replied Trilby coming back through the lounge door. He was wearing a beaming smile and was carrying a further silver tray. On it was the parchment and a full looking brown paper bag. He set the tray down, giving the parchment back to Benedict and passed the brown paper bag to Tristan.

"Had a ham hock on the go, roasted it a couple of days past. I've made up some ham and cheese sandwiches for your journey".

Tristan, warmed by this generosity took the bag with thanks but then noticed when he looked down past the brown bag that somehow, Trilby had stolen his left shoe. He glared at the culprit.

Trilby winked, "Old habits, dear boy, old habits. Just larks to see if my skills were still there." He pulled Tristan's shoe out from under his chair and handed it back.

 "Well, thank you for your assistance, regardless. Let's hope nothing more comes of this conflict between Germany and the French eh?" said Benedict

"Quite," replied Trilby, "The last thing we need is another terrible war, I remember the previous shindig only too well. Wars not only kill men, but they repeat history we already know and add nothing new to text books. They also have a nasty habit of further burying relics of the past."

They all moved to the front door, dutifully shook hands, took general direction on how to get to Colchester and soon the Phantom was moving again. Benedict concentrated on the direction and on the conundrum Trilby had posed in that there really was nothing to go on. His train of thought was interrupted by rustling and munching next to him. He looked over.

"These sandwiches really are delicious", answered a cakey voiced Tristan, insufficient in bringing any further wisdom to proceedings.

Chapter 9

The afternoon had grown long when the Phantom rolled
into the middle of Colchester. Both men were tired and had
sufficiently burned the fires of all possible conversation into
embers. The invention of the car radio was a blessing that
was more than a few years away and after several
conversations including what they wanted to be when they
were children (Benedict, a doctor, Tristan, a giant), what
qualities they found most attractive in women (Tristan, their
compassion, Benedict, pendulous bosoms) and theories on
how Hitler had managed to anchluss Austria, reclaim the
Rhine and Saarland and invade Poland without so much as
stern look from any other country (Benedict thought it was
capitulation from an under-armed deterrent, Tristan thought
Hitler was jammy) they were talked out. Beyond talking
about the varying type of sheep and cows they passed,
mainly inspired by Tristan, they had run out of things to say
and were slightly bored by each other's company. So it
was quite the relief when the outskirts of the old Roman
town came into view. Soon they had made their way
through the suburbs to the ancient heart of England's first
capital. Of course, neither of them had any idea what they
were looking for. Tristan remained easy and tranquil which
caused Benedict more frustration as he was no help at all.
Eventually, after twenty minutes of doing circuits around
the centre, Benedict growled, "Oh bugger this," and swung
the car violently to the side of the road in front of a very
startled old lady taking home her groceries.

Having retrieved an onion from underneath the Phantom,
Tristan enquired, "Hello there, please could you direct us to
anywhere where there might be a bit of ancient Roman
antiquity?"

The old lady shrugged, took the onion which had committed suicide when the car had pulled up and hurried on her way.

"Blast," exclaimed Benedict from the driver's seat.

"I think I was too specific," said Tristan. Having got back into the car, he dropped his window down and shouted to the other side of the road where a pimply schoolboy, all in his school greys with satchel, was meandering home.

"Scuse me young lad," asked Tristan, "There any museums round 'ere?"

The young boy paused for a second, ascertained that the two men probably weren't the villainous Hun as promised in various pieces of propaganda and searched his noggin of the area between his house, his school and the high street, which was the geographical extent of his wisdom. Fortunately one museum fell within his tiny jurisdiction.

"Oh yes, there's Colchester Museum, it's Colchester's oldest museum actually and tells the wonderful history of our wonderful city," he said proudly.

"Well done laddy and where might that museum be?" asked Tristan, this seemed to be going well.

"Oi! Think I give up information for any old Tom, Dick or Harry? Clear off!" Clearly the schoolchild was not as cherubic as first thought. Tristan was horrified.

"Excuse me young man, do you speak to all your elders like that?"

"All the time, especially if they're a nonce off the street who likes stopping young boys."

"I was merely enquiring.." Tristan didn't get the chance to finish his sentence.

"A shilling," the boy shouted.

"What?!"

"A shilling or I stroll on Squire," the boy insisted.

Tristan's face was agape, framed by the rolled down window. He was at once puzzled and bemused.

"Well really, bloody youth of today, no respect," said Benedict. He slid a hand into his trouser pocket where he found some loose change and flipped the shilling out onto the quiet road. The young scamp was upon it immediately and then examined the currency like a jeweller would inspect a crystal for imperfections. Satisfied he turned to Tristan and said, "Four streets down the way you are pointing, turn left and climb the hill, look for the big castle shaped thing and you'll be there. See ya mister." The boy skipped off down the road making decisions regarding which sweet stocks to invest heavily in.

The Museum of Antiquities, Essex, was different to what they expected. In fact, as they drew up outside it, they realised it was a castle; Colchester Castle to be precise. Despite having been open since 1873, neither Benedict or Tristan had had the inclination to visit. So it's red bricked turreted square façade came as quite a surprise as they arrived. Furthermore, as it was late afternoon and not during any holiday, the sparse tourists were gone, the school trips departed and the place was entirely theirs. Both men stepped out of the car and enjoyed the feeling of immense freedom in their stiff legs. After much bending and procrastination, they headed across the gravel to the gothic archway which formed the entrance to the museum. Benedict grabbed Tristan by surprise and stopped him from entering.

"What's our back story?"

"What what?"

"We need an excuse! Look we can't just go marching in there waving a scrap of parchment, looking like a bunch of glory hunters!? People will suspect something ripe is afoot."

"Yes, but isn't that technically what we are?"

Benedict thought long and hard about that statement. His only defence would be to say something xenophobic about beating rotten Frenchies to it.

"Well yes, but at least we'll be beating the rotten Frenchies to it." Benedict wished he was quicker witted.

Tristan had an idea, "Why don't we pretend to have a profession, perhaps something associated to the crafts contained in the museum?"

"I'm an assorted collection of ears, what did you have in mind?"

"Ooh, I know how about we say that we are specialist Polishers." Tristan seemed pleased with the idea, "Yes, let's say that we specialise in the restoration and polishing of antique wood, metal and precious stones and all we are doing is enquiring whether they may have use of our services and we can go on from there."

Benedict was less impressed, "Well it's less juicy than a month old apple core left down the side of a chair, but I can't think of anything better so it will have to do. Now, should we give each other false names?"

"Going a bit far isn't it?"

"Not if the police get a whiff of what we're doing?"

"Right, well you can be Mr Gerald Updike and I will be Mr Rhodry Jones."

"Why?"

"Why not, you asked for names," replied Tristan quite heatedly.

This ridiculous conversation was ended when the large oak door they stood in front of swung open and a tall balding bespectacled gentleman popped his head round.

"What's all the racket gents? If you don't mind, the museum and it's grounds are supposed to be a place of historical value, peace, quiet and contemplation."

"Do beg our pardon," schmoozed Tristan, "We were just quibbling over our previous piece of custom. Allow me to introduce ourselves. I'm Rhodry Jones and this is my assistant, Mr Gerald Updike."

Benedict looked miffed at being the assistant, but stuck out his hand and said "How d'you do."

As the hand was offered, the bald head moved from round the door and was soon joined by a long thin body dressed in a black warden's uniform. His substantial hands engulfed Benedict's and worked his arm like a water pump. He talked in a farty high pitched voice. "Geraint St John if you please sirs, I'm the Museum Warden. Are you er looking to visit or is there something else I can do for you today gents?"

Tristan replied, "We were in the area and wished to enquire whether you have any speciality polishers who service the relics in your fine facility. Both myself and Updike can work wonders on antiques with nothing but a dab of Brasso and a cloth. We can turn dull, dusty exhibits into award winners. Would it be possible to speak to your chief antiquarian about facilitating our abilities?"

St John contemplated their request and nodded replying, "Well, it's like the Mary Celeste today if I'm honest. Doesn't really get busy for another couple of months, when the schools break up for the holidays. No harm in it I supposed. Follow me gents." He pushed the door wide until Benedict took hold of it and St John walked inside. Benedict let Tristan pass, and hissed, "Assistant!? Bloody cheek, I'll give you Assistant!" He cuffed his Welsh accomplice round the back of his head.

The museum had the mixed smells of earthiness, damp stonework and old timber, the pong of ancient history which pervades every museum and church. They wound their way down the close walled stony passageways of the castle, into a large wooden panelled chamber where glass cabinets displayed roman coins, pottery and the odd extinct mammal. After a good five minutes of walking, Benedict guessed they were towards the opposite end of the museum. They walked through a further collection of suits of armour and then passed through a side door into a large high roofed space, almost like a warehouse. Inside was a higgledy piggledy collection of tea crates with dust covers strewn over them and random artefacts standing on pallets, presumably for display or transport to other museums across the Country. They walked towards the back of the room where off to the side were two small wooden huts that had been built into the wall of the castle as temporary offices. One of them had it's door open and grammar phone music crept out, opera of some-sort. Benedict had never had the time for it himself, the language barrier always leaving him cold. On this particular record, a woman with a beautiful voice sung in a heartfelt way which relaxed the soul and suited the peaceful atmosphere. Tristan thought it was the loveliest thing he'd ever heard.

"Miss Warner!" shouted St John, about ten metres from the door. "There are a couple of salesmen here to see you."

The grammar phone needle scratched off the record and an eerie silence befell the open space. Benedict was guessing from his previous experience as an antiques dealer and dislike for opera that Professor Warner would be a dreadful, pompous, frigid, know-it-all who would simply waft their best attempts at gaining information by pretending to be polishers away with the deftest of swishes from her aging hands. So it was a great surprise when the first thing to venture from the door was the soft clack of a stiletto heel, followed the lithe and sexy shoe itself. Then a long, lustrous stockinged leg followed by another, both of which could be best described as going all the way up. Next was a swishing blue and white polka dot dress, fitted perfectly to the hourglass shape of the body inside. A pert bosom on top, fair skin, red lipstick, doe like eyes and dark brown locks that fell softly around a feminine neckline. She was the kind of woman where if a man's loins didn't stir from just her walk, they should make their way to the cemetery immediately as they could only be recently deceased.

She stopped in front of the two men, her soft red lips spreading into a wild smile, showing her pearly whites underneath those kissers. St John left them to it.

"You're a woman!" said Benedict, almost a knee jerk reaction to his assumption of a wrinkly old dear's leg coming through that door first.

"Gosh, you're clever, have you ever considered becoming a human biology lecturer at Oxford?" She laughed as she shook his hand. Her skin was like silk in his palm.

"And an American!" added Benedict stupidly.

"Oh, you're two for two today Mister." She slipped her hands onto her hips, "Lillian Warner, Professor of Ancient History for the University of Illinois. I've taken a secondment over here whilst they look for a new curator. And you are?" She offered her hand to Tristan.

Tristan's voice found the highest octave it could and nervously squeaked, not with the caper they were now part of with their back story, just with shyness in front of such a perfect woman. It would not have surprised Tristan if he had found that there was no gramophone music previously and that it was just her voice instead.

"Tris....Rhodry Jones at your service Ma'am". He found himself bowing slightly as he took her hand. "And this is my Assistant Geraint, I mean Gerald! Upkite – dike!"

"I beg your pardon?"

"Updike, sorry." Benedict urgently needed to take over the situation. He was as emphatically aroused as Tristan but had more experience with womankind and though would almost certainly come off as a bungling idiot, could at least make conversation.

"We are here today to offer you a most valuable service Ms Warner. We are polishers and restorers of the highest quality and we would like to offer our services to your establishment, should you have any French polishing, dust removal or most importantly any gemstones which we can bring a certain je ne sais quoi to."

Lillian pursed her luscious lips together, "Okay, so what relics have you worked with recently?"

Tristan, blushing but feeling as if he was on a cloud around this pretty young woman said, "Well we've recently add our hands on them Elgin Marbles and Michelangelo's David was a doddle. I've even seen the King's crown jewels." Tristan found this incredibly funny and burst out laughing

"Michelangelo? You've been to Italy recently then?"

Benedict knew this was a trap. A trip to Florence was highly unlikely in the current climate. He suspected that Italy would have it's borders closed as part of their pact with Germany. He stepped in front of his blundering colleague.

"Excuse my friend, he's drunk."

"You're his assistant?"

Benedict grimaced, "Yes, that's true. God knows we're trying to help by getting him to see a Doctor." Tristan was bent over behind him, red faced, still laughing to himself out of sheer desperation. Benedict wrung his hands together and continued "Respectfully, we haven't polished the Elgin Marbles or been to Italy at all. We are just highly skilled polishers trying to make our way in the world and wished to enquire whether we can be of service to you."

"Well, the veneers on most of the glass cabinets could do with a fresh glaze, but we tend to manage a lot of the dirty work ourselves," replied Lillian. Benedict couldn't even imagine dust falling upon Miss Warner, let alone her chipping a nail whilst scratching away residue off a fragment of an iron-age spear head.

"I see," Benedict pondered, scratching his chin. "I think we were hoping for something more challenging, perhaps some precious stones."

"Sorry gentlemen, I don't have any."

Benedict looked disheartened but persevered, "Oh, I think we both presumed that with Colchester's ancient history, some fine wares may have been retrieved. We specialise in buffeting diamonds and other gems back to a high sparkle."

"So you're not as green as you are cabbage looking then?" Lillian ribbed Benedict. "Well, sorry to disappoint you guys but we really are just the dusty relics round here. Some of the gemstones would have ended up in the royal collection but certainly none have been excavated on any digs within the last fifty years."

Benedict was crestfallen. He gave it one more chance. "Do you know of anywhere else in Colchester where our specialities might receive a warmer reception?"

Lillian paused for a moment while in thought and then shook her head.

"Sorry, the only other place which would have use of your services would be Colchester Barracks. They've a lot of ceremonial pomp and circumstance when they're on parade and use ornate swords and what-not. I wouldn't go near the place myself, too many troopers deprived of contact with women."

Benedict laughed at her comment, "Well hopefully, we won't come in for as much particular scrutiny. We'll bid you good day."

"Oh please, the pleasure is all mine and make sure you come back to visit the museum, you shouldn't leave with at least seeing some of it."

Lillian showed them to a transit door at the back of the warehousing area and explained how to make their way back round to the front. Just as they were about to walk away, Tristan, who had been trailing behind Benedict like a naughty chimp turned to Lillian and said, "Who was that woman singing on the record before we arrived?"

"Maria Callas, she's a relative unknown. It's beautiful isn't it?"

"Oh yes, quite, quite beautiful," mumbled Tristan.

Benedict grabbed his monkey-like chum by the arm and pulled him away, "Come on."

As Tristan was forcibly led round the corner, the brief encounter with the most wonderful lithe set of pins attached to a woman, had set a fire under his heart, his need to utter some declaration of love unbridled within him.

"She was nice, wasn't she?" he enquired.

Benedict gave a low patronising "Yeeees," in response. Truthfully he had also found her more than adequate and the flame that was currently kindled in Tristan's heart was also matched by an equally raging blaze in Benedict's. He tried to kid himself it was indigestion or trapped wind. But an airing of the bestial breeze couldn't make him feel any better. Lillian was sharp as a thistle and had spirit. She had immediately disarmed him with her wit and cut him down to size with eloquence. And he liked it.

Chapter 10

Whilst to be in the sheer presence of Miss Lillian Warner had caused the day to brighten and a tightness to form in both of their britches, the news that there wasn't an awful lot of sparkly objects which might pertain to any Nationalists versus Romans type mystery left the boys dissapointed. Knowing that only the thinnest of hope existed, they had traipsed silently back to the car, climbed in and then driven aimlessly through the streets of Colchester again. Deep in thought, reality struck only when Benedict was so lost to his own imagination that he curbed the beautiful steel cap of his front left wheel in a negligent scrape. He stopped the car immediately in the quiet street. There was no one about; everyone had finished for the day as the late afternoon became evening.

Tristan turned to Benedict, "Shall we go home and just write the whole thing off?"

Benedict dwelled on the words, conceding defeat and replied, "Righty ho, but shall we at least get some dinner in us first? It's been a ridiculous day and I could murder an ale."

The Phantom rolled up outside the Rifle Butt, a Tudor pub in the town centre, fully replete with a whitewash exterior, black painted beams and more importantly a chalkboard offering, "Grub voted as the best in this local area 1940!" As they had not found another pub offering food in the local area, both felt that the competition must have been thin at best, but it would serve. Benedict noticed that a chemist next to the pub was still open.

"Listen, I've got a thumping headache, I'm just going to nip in there and procure something for the pain. Order me an ale will you. I'll be a second." Tristan nodded and the two men clambered out the car.

The pub was large and comfortable. It was a warm, well lit space and was able to feed at least thirty customers. It obviously did a roaring trade and clearly was living up to it's award winning reputation as it was nearly full of chattering couples, families and men supping ales, tucking into pies, steaks and sausage and mash. The odour would tantalise even the most dour of nostrils and Tristan had a hard time not to look like the Victoria Falls of drooling. Benedict found Tristan at the bar coveting two pints of a dark beer. He passed one to Benedict who took a long thirsty draw from the light foam top.

"Should you be having that if you've just been taking something for your head?" asked Tristan.

"Oh, the chemist thought it was something else, gave me liver salts," replied a particularly evasive Benedict, eyes darting away from the truth that Tristan was searching for.

"Makes no sense at all, but I'm not particularly knowledgeable on science," replied Tristan.

They found a bench and both ordered the steak and ale pie with chips. Benedict ate hungrily, having passed on Trilby's sandwiches from earlier. He finished well before Tristan who was savouring each mouthful. However, whilst Tristan was enjoying his meal he had become concerned by Benedict's general demeanour. It was clear that this feast had given Benedict his second wind, as he was now staring out into nowhere in particular, concocting a further plan. Finally, Tristan put down his knife and fork, finished his pint of ale and sat back in his chair.

"Is it er, is it home time now?" Nothing but silence followed. "Benedict, are we going home now?"

"It just seems, like, such a waste," Benedict began. "If we were to leave here now and not try the barracks."

Tristan thought this was coming. Even he knew that as Lillian mentioned it back at the museum, the dumb thought would somehow seep into Benedict's consciousness. That was where the devil on his shoulder would poke him with his trident and say, "Go on, have a jolly good crack at breaking in." There was no stopping it. Tristan so far had enjoyed the spirit of adventure and more to the point, the legality of it. So at this point Tristan thought he'd better ask the question.

"And how exactly do you intend to enter said army barracks, seeing as I'm a mere Farmer and you are conspicuous by your absence as a rank or conscript." Benedict picked up his knife and pointed away to two gentlemen in army fatigues in the corner who were enjoying plaice and chips. "They look like a couple of regular army chaps, probably from the base. Let's ask them if we can tag along to the barracks when they return. If they tell us to stick it, no harm done, we'll jump in the Phantom and toodle off back to London and you can catch your train in the morning."

Tristan was surprised at the simplicity of the plan and felt relieved by it's eagerly anticipated failure. Even he knew that most military facilities were for authorised personnel only, the chances that they would be allowed on site were between slim and none. This was over before it even started. By this time tomorrow he'd be on a train from Paddington back to the valleys.

Benedict craned in to whisper. "Look, I don't want to discuss our business in front of all these people. Let's continue with our veil of secrecy. I'm off for a jimmy in the gents, allow me five minutes and then you can ask the two squaddies to come with you to the toilets." Benedict rose from his seat and nipped down the corridor down by the side of the bar to the gentlemen's facilities to relieve himself. Tristan relaxed, taking in the sights and sounds of the pub, then curled a pea round his plate so it left an arty trail of gravy over the china. He looked at his watch, five minutes had passed quickly. Tristan stood up and walked to the snug behind him where the two squaddies were supping pints and making crude jokes.

"Excuse me gentlemen," Tristan began, "Can I ask you to accompany me to the facilities please."

"Not a noofter are you?" asked the one directly facing him, a swarthy looking chap, with a animal quality to him and the signs of a previous career in amateur boxing from the shape of his nose.

"Oh I hadn't thought about it like that!" exclaimed Tristan, "No no, my friend has a confidential request to do with army matters that he'd like to make and due to it's secret nature, cannot divulge this information in the middle of a family pub. We are not, as you say, noofters."

Mr Swarthy looked at his companion, an oily looking man with a spotty neck. Spotty neck reckoned with a cockney accent, "Can't hurt, can it? Might be able to strike up a bargain with them. Not as if the King's shilling is going to set us up for life Alfie."

Swarthy looked displeased to be parting from his beer, but nevertheless, scrunched his lips together and said, "....alright."

Tristan, who had no idea what was about to go down, gave a far too happy, "Excellent," and turned towards the lavatories with the two squaddies following. He pushed the gloss blue painted door open and was immediately hit with the delicate scent of piss and cleaning products. The urinals were directly in front of him and to his right was the side of one of two cubicles, opposite which were the first of the sinks. Tristan presumed Benedict was waiting in this gap, so he rounded the left hander with the two squaddies. Benedict was not there. This was awkward; he called out once, a high strain in his voice as the soldiers looked unhappy.

"He said he'd be in here," said a panicky Tristan.

Mr Swarthy sighed and then started to make a pounding motion with one ham-like fist into the palm of his other. Both men walked menacingly towards Tristan who began to cower.

"We don't like tricks do we Alfie?" said Mr Spotty.

"Oh I like tricks Ted," replied the swarthy gent, not removing his glare from Tristan's slowly wilting disposition. "I'm about to teach our little friend here, the instant panda trick."

Tristan tried to make light of the situation and whimpered, "Alfie and Ted then, well at least I'll know the names of my assailants. I suppose that makes it a little more personable."

The glaring continued until spotty Ted turned to swarthy Alfie and looking confused said, "Ted, I really didn't understand the panda thing? I didn't follow you..."

"I'm gonna give him two black eyes aren't I?!", Alfie replied. To everyone's delight but Tristan, this cleared things up immeasurably.

Tristan had now walked backwards into the wall behind him. There was nowhere left to go. Cubicles to the left of him, sinks to the right and his way out of this sanitary alley of ablution blocked by the two men he'd intentionally invited in there. Where was Benedict? The only direction available now was to lower his altitude and his back slipped down the wall until he was crouched on the floor looking up at his two potential muggers.

"You really don't have to do this you know. Anyone could walk in at any moment."

Swarthy Alfie drew his fist back, grimaced a smile and said, "We'll take our chances th..."

Before he could finish, a hand gripping a handkerchief slipped over Alfie's mouth. In shock, Alfie took a deep breath and felt a wave of nauseating sleep drown him. He hit the floor with a thud, unconscious and no longer the master of panda eyed ceremonies. Ted spun round, not totally sure what or who had just dropped the better equipped of the two of them at fighting. Benedict stood there, self assured, with a handkerchief in hand as a weapon. He raised an inviting eyebrow at Ted who accepted his invitation by swinging a southpaw left hook at Benedict's jaw line. Benedict hardly flinched as he took a brief step back to allow the punch to whistle past him. As Ted overreached, Benedict stepped back in and slipped his pocketsize white cotton weapon over Ted's face. Like his army pal who was already lying on the floor, Ted was quickly down as well.

Benedict gave the pile of bodies a smile and said, "And a nighty night to you too." He looked over at the still crouching Tristan who was covering his head with his arms, like a primitive ape man.

Tristan looked confused and terrified. From under the cover of his limbs he gasped, "Ohhhh Benedict, what have you done?!"

Benedict smiled again knowingly and then pulled out a small green bottle from his inside jacket pocket. "The most tender of white lies earlier. I didn't have a headache at all. I just popped into the chemist to buy this." He referred to the bottle, "Quite astounded they gave it to me considering I didn't have any medical identification on me."

Despite Benedict showing the bottle, Tristan still looked confused.

"Chloroform old boy," said Benedict as he shook the bottle. "I soon realised that if we were going to get into Colchester Barracks, we couldn't just ask at the gate. Don't be ridiculous. So I took my chances and lo and behold, two squaddies were in the pub, how lucky. Right, I'll squeeze into Knuckles McGinty's clothes and you can wear the Captain Spotty's effects."

Tristan didn't comprehend at all; the whole situation was totally out of hand. "Where were you? I thought I was going to be beaten within an inch of my life!"

Benedict giggled again, feeling exhilarated by recent events. "So sorry Tris old pal, you were never in any danger. I was hiding in the first cubicle. As soon as they'd walked past to give you six of the best, I sprang out and sent them off to Sandy, Bedfordshire."

"So, so what now?" exclaimed Tristan. "I'm supposed to be all happy for you saving me and slip into something more comfortable or appropriate for impersonating military personnel!!!!! Have you gone completely out of your mind?!"

"Well I thought you might be a little more thankful considering I just saved you from the thrashing of a lifetime," Benedict replied pompously.

"A beating?! You have just assaulted two men of His Majesty's forces and now you're asking me to dress up as one of them? My God man, if we're caught we could be tried and hanged as spies!"

"And your point is........" asked Benedict, with no appropriate defence for potentially committing treason.

Tristan surveyed the situation. The two squaddies would be out for a good six hours at least. He'd seen the impact of chloroform on his Uncle, who was put under when his favourite ram had taken a dislike to him and made it his business to break off one of it's horns in his Uncle's backside. He wasn't immediately cognisant when he came to either. Applied to these two not so bright sorts, that would buy them some more time. Stripped of their dignity, the men might be found in the gents, wearing nothing but their long johns. That in itself would look rather funny and cause the local constabulary to ask some questions.

Lonely nights in them barracks I reckon, thought Tristan. Still more time added to the clock.

"Alright, in for a penny in for a pound." He slid across from his crouching position to spotty Ted and started to unbuckle his trousers.

As he fought to get Alfie's shirt on, Benedict mumbled, "Splendid," from underneath.

Soon both men were wearing ill fitting uniforms. While Benedict was about the same width as Alfie, Benedict was a fair few inches taller, thus his trouser bottoms proudly stood at half mast, as did the jacket which finished just below his belly button, showing the shirt underneath. Tristan's feet were a size larger than the black polished boots he was wearing now. Notwithstanding the stiffness of the leather, his toes were squashed in at the end and the footwear was already crippling him.

"Oh these boots are enough to ruin anyone's posture, we won't be long will we?"

"Couple of minutes tops, we'll hit them hard amidships and be home for tea and crumpets before they realise. If these chappies were out to dinner it's bound to mean they were on leave or given a pass. We'll just nip in, say that I forgot my monocle or some other ballyhoo, have a quick oil around the place and then scamper back out again, no harm done."

Benedict walked to the toilet entrance and peered out. He momentarily disappeared into the hallway but returned within a hare's breath.

"Excellent, there's a back entrance to the pub adjacent to the loos. Help me drag the two men out there, and we'll squeak out to the front and jump in the Phantom."

Thankfully no one entered the loo in the next ten minute span of time, otherwise they would have seen two poorly tailored squaddies dragging firstly a greasy looking chap in his vest and johns out into the yard before being placed behind a bush. They then would have witnessed a similar scene but with a more difficult logistics exercise from a far bulkier chap also down to his pants and a pile of civilian clothes stuck on his stomach, like an unusual ironing board.

When both the denuded squaddies had been placed into a position which could be seen as, "Giving each other a bit of a cuddle in the bushes," Tristan and Benedict picked up their own civil effects and made for the side alley which bordered a row of terrace houses. As the dusk of the day crept over into evening, the only people in the street were a couple of grimy looking kids played hopscotch on the floor of the alley in the distance. They would never be accurate witnesses, so Tristan and Benedict strode out of the pub's back yard, into the alley and back around to the front where the Phantom waited.

Chapter 11

The Phantom ambled past Colchester Barracks just once as reconnaissance, but that was enough to realise that the site was vast, sprawling in fact and one couldn't just nip over the wall to take a look. It was well protected with high walls and enough barbed wire to ruin the hem of a nicely tailored suit of plate armour. The only way in was past one of two guard stations which were posted at either end of the huge enclosure.

Once the brief reconnaissance was complete, Benedict pulled the Phantom into a side street of terraced red brick houses. Night was approaching and the street lamps had just begun their flicker into activity, with a gentle glow in the building darkness. Under the dull light was a quiet road with some residents earning just enough to own a car. A couple of black Morris motors were parked on either side. The Phantom looked out of place and risked being pinched but it would have to do. Besides, in and out and pop the kettle on was still the motto, although the sheer sprawl of space which the barracks took up meant that they were either going to have to incalculably lucky or it would be like finding a needle in a hay stack. Two or three lines of enquiry was as much as they were going to be able to pursue. Nevertheless, it had already been half an hour since Tweedle-dee and Tweedle-dum had been knocked out and there was a good ten minute walk for Benedict and Tristan to the nearest guard station ahead. Just as they were stepping out into the hushed darkening street, Tristan said, "What shall we do with our civvy clothes?" nodding to the pile in his foot-well.
Benedict thought for a moment, neither of them had rucksacks and even if they did, they might be searched. "Just leave them here."

"What if someone pinches the car?" asked Tristan nervously, hoping for any twinge of conscience which might stop Benedict from getting them both sent to the gallows.

"I think that's a chance we're going to have to take, now buck up, we've not got long to do this."

Benedict and Tristan hurried along the dark streets until they found the perimeter wall of the barracks, tall, dark and imposing above them. The guard post came quickly into view. A young soldier with a rifle slung across his chest, puffed on a cigarette. He saw the two poorly dressed soldiers ambling along. In the darkness, he could not make out if it was an officer so he spat out his woodbine and drove it into the ground with his boot. As the two misshapen soldiers hustled into view, the guardsman bristled slightly at having lost his ciggie for no reason, and barked "Halt, who goes there?" rifle and affixed bayonet pointed at Benedict and Tristan.

For his sins Benedict had not quite figured out how to hoodwink a guard in his grand plan, but his hand instinctively went to his trouser pocket and there thankfully he found Alfred Robeson's papers. Not sure what he was showing, he whisked them from the pocket, up to the soldiers face. The documents were rather tatty and worn from having sat in Alfie's pockets for a while and the constant in and out of having to show them as identity. Tristan, clocked what Benedict was doing and followed, feeling Ted Jones's papers there. He nervously took them out as Benedict had, a worried sweat beginning to collect on his brow. The soldier squinted with suspicion at Tristan's state.

"Ere pal, your mate alright?" he asked Benedict.

Benedict looked at colleague and realised that his friend was melting with shame. "Oh he's fine, just a dodgy sausage at lunchtime. You know how it is – using up all the meat, even if it might have come from parts of the pig best not mentioned."

On cue Tristan retched at the pavement.

The soldier looked at the pair of them. They looked non-army, tatty, outgrown. He deadpanned, "Good job there is a war on fellas. My quartermaster would have you shot if he saw your uniforms."

Benedict gave a reassuring, "Mmmmmmmm". The guard snatched at his papers and took them to the street lamp that illuminated the small sentry gate.

"Bloody hell fire!" he exclaimed.

Oh shit, the game's up! thought Tristan, taking a couple of steps back in preparation to leg it and in all probability get mown down by a volley of gun fire.

The soldier re-slung his rifle onto his shoulder and hurried back to the two fake squaddies. "Why didn't you say it was you?!, Crikey, you're very late." He looked at his wristwatch, "You're on in half an hour."

Benedict craned forward, "Beg pardon?"

"You're on in half an hour," the guardsman repeated.

"On?" Benedict asked carefully. But before he could get a response, the guardsman had lifted the gate and caught sight of another soldier coming up to go out.

"Oy Bill, can you take these two down to the mess room? They're the soppy sods that are performing tonight."

"Right ho," shouted Bill. Benedict looked confusingly at Tristan who mirrored his companion's expression.

"Well, at least we're in," growled Benedict under his breath as they walked through the gate towards the squaddie twenty metres in front of them; where they were going and what they were so clearly supposed to do performance wise was clearly another matter altogether. Tristan certainly wanted to know what he was letting himself in for by the sound of the occasional squeak emanating from his lower half every fourth step.

They were met by a nearly seven foot plug called Bill. The giant soldier strode silently slightly ahead of them leading the way into the unknown, his calm and dopey features looking from side to side and giving a casual wave to a passing colleague or two. Meanwhile, they had walked far into the main complex and past old, well used quarters which housed soldiers and had educated them in the ways of disabling and killing men for centuries. There were more temporary structures too, wooden cabins, designed to hold the quick expansion of man power should the war with Germany escalate into a wider conflict. They ambled through the main parade ground, past football pitches, cumbersome assault courses and firing ranges in the fields around the complex until at last they walked silently toward an open side door of the largest of the red bricked buildings, burning with the light from inside and a pissed off looking sergeant, pacing outside. He saw the trio and strode in an obvious and enhanced fashion towards them, all ten metres worth of distance. Bill casually announced his guests. "These are the two you've been looking for Sarge," and he idly strolled off, clearly focussed on other things.

The sergeant major was a caricature of what a sergeant should be, short, hat jammed onto his small head, barely leaving space for his eyes. He had a small moustache, almost reminiscent of Hitler himself and surely the basis for many awkward discussions behind his back at dinner parties. He walked and used his muscles in such a clipped angular fashion that anyone else would think he was severely disabled. Sadly this vicious little man was like a hyperactive jack russell; his neck pulsed with the everyday venom and harassment of his men. Happy is the man whose work is also his leisure. He was so upset by the supposed lateness of these two men for God only knows what that he felt the need to speak in words missing most of their opening letters.

"Ere the ell a you been then lads?! Ou'd leave me embarrassed like this in front of my ommanding fficers!?"

"We're terribly sorry," volunteered Benedict, still not entirely clear what he was apologising for.

"Oh, erribly orry are we?!" the sergeant replied calmly and then exploded with, "Ell, you will be sorry when I've ad mi pound of flesh on the parade rounds 'omorrow lads. Do you know what it feels like to do an infinite amount of ress ups lad? Just cos you're from a different egiment, doesn't mean, you can go PANSYING OFF, when a little army iscipline is equired." The P in pansying covered Tristan in enough spittle to wash in for a month. Unfortunately he did not have soap or a towel to hand.

"Erm."

"It bloody urts! Ow, get yourselves in there and get changed before I report your ittle acksides to your ommanding officer back in Aldershot!"

To assist both men, he gave them a boot up the bottom as they walked into the brightly lit room and then he strode off into the night.

Nothing made any sense. Here they were, exactly where Benedict wanted them to be and yet they were trapped under the confines of some role of which was yet to become apparent. This room which they had entered seemed to be some sort of storage facility, but for items you'd need for running a briefing, a conference, a lecture or a play. There were a couple of lecterns, a series of drapes and clearly the odd painted back-drop or two from plays, not to mention a number of props, including a chicken suit and a number of jolly roger flags. Tristan began to piece together the mystery.

"Right, well clearly, we're not from this garrison, I mean Alfie and Ted aren't."

"Mmm, the sergeant major definitely alluded to us being from Aldershot, so why are we here?"

"All the bits and bobs in here would suggest....are we giving a talk on something?"

"I bloody hope not. Unless it's on oiling round the best eateries in London, the game really is up."

"But I'd have thought that briefings about upcoming military strategy would be given by a ranking officer and not this late at night, and also Sergeant Big Chops would never have been able to scream at an officer."

"Good point, but it doesn't answer the question of why we're in here."

Tristan walked towards a blackened corner of the room which led to a short corridor which was also completely dark. He took the few steps along it and was led to a larger area. Wooden floorboards creaked as he took step after step. In the darkness, he did not see the chair in front of him and as his foot struck he overbalanced. Tristan put a hand out to his right expecting to find a solid wall to steady himself with. Instead he met with the heavy but giving cloth of a stage curtain and fell through the material and onto the stage on the other side. As luck would have it, nobody was about but Tristan understood the enormity of what was afoot. This was a performance room, no doubt. Rows of about a hundred chairs had been laid out in neat order and in the corner was a grand piano, presumably to accompany the act on stage. Tonight, perhaps Tristan and Benedict were to be the star performers? He picked himself up, dashed back behind the curtain and ran the short way to the holding area.

"Benedict, Benedict, I think we're definitely performing tonight. I've seen the stage. Oh crikey, I hope it's hymns. It's the only thing I'm good at!"

Benedict had his back turned to Tristan and was looking in a long tea crate which had sat in the room for as long as they had, but no one had bothered to check it. The crate was now open. He did not turn around. "I'm afraid it's much worse than that."

Tristan looked puzzled and moved towards Benedict and the trunk. Benedict handed Tristan a card over his shoulder, still not daring to make eye contact. Tristan read the new information.

"We're a detachment from the Royal Artillery Concert Party!"

He joined Benedict at the trunk and looked into it. There was a mass of coloured chiffon, sequins and glitter. Tristan read the final sentence on the card.

"The Royal Artillery Concert Party presents, 'Them Dames from Damascus?!' Oh that's soured the cow's milk..."

Benedict reached into the trunk and pulled out the first outfit on top, a purple bustier with a green chiffon flapper skirt and a dark haired wig. This was clearly meant for the bulkier of the two, Alfie. Benedict then took out Tristan's number for the evening, a slinky, sequined black sleeveless evening gown, short blonde curly wig and feathered headband. Also in the trunk were a pair of knickerbockers each, presumably to flash the men with, a lot of makeup and a pair of foam boobies. Thankfully, also at the bottom of the chest was the entire act, written down on a series of cards.

Tristan looked despondent, beside himself with anxiety, "I never thought my lot in life was to be hanged by the neck until I'm dead for being a treasonable cross dresser. That's a fine end," he added with sarcasm. Benedict said nothing whilst he flicked through the cards, further insulting Tristan by his lack of response.

"Did you 'ear me, we're going to be collared as some kind of unusual spies. What are we going to do?"

Benedict seemed somewhat upbeat about it all. "No, no. I think we've got a plum role, have a flick through these, it's all perfectly simple. All the gags and songs are written out and the song words are to popular tunes everyone knows. All Alfie and Ted had to do was arrive, powder up and then perform. I say, this is a cushy number!"

"Eh what?" said a baffled Tristan. He snatched the cards from Benedict's hands and browsed through them. Annoyingly, Benedict was right, the cards were an idiot's guide to the performance and even had when to flash their undergarments on them.

"It's easy. We don't even have to be of Shakespeare quality. Whilst we could back out, it would mean that I, I mean we, leave unfulfilled and we'd raise suspicion. We'd run the risk of bumping into three people who have seen us, the guardsman, that squaddie called Bill and God forbid the sergeant."

Tristan could see Benedict's point. "Well I suppose we've no other option, but the time is now seven, the show starts at seven forty five according to this top card. We'd better get dressed and learn these lines."

Forty five minutes later and both men were decked out in their cross dressing finery. Benedict looked how a big man with ample brown chest hair would look in a bustier and skirt, awkward and out of place. Tristan had fared better as his lithe but toned frame was more feminine and the cocktail dress fitted well, the game only being given away by his quite hairy legs and wind weathered face. But with a goodish amount of dark eye liner and some lipstick he at least would pass for a drag act. As they were supposed to be from hotter climes, Damascus to be precise, both had smothered themselves in a pot of thick brown face paint, the end result looking like both had had an accident with a prototype chocolate fountain which had exploded.

"How do I look?" Tristan asked Benedict?

"You look like a cross dresser. And I?"

"You look like an idiot."

"Excellent, well we're both fittingly attired for forthcoming events then." Benedict replied with chirpy sarcasm. "Know you lines?"

"Barely," replied the morose and oddly sultry looking Tristan.

"Good show old man, lets break a leg then."

"I bloody hope not."

"Figure of speech old boy, thesp speak for good luck." Benedict nonchalantly gave Tristan a hard slap on the bare back to motivate him towards the hidden corridor and the steady murmur of male voices that had started to build from the dark corner.

Both men stood in the darkness of the curtained stage, smoothing down their garments which kept riding up as they walked and warmed up with lunges more akin to a game of rugby. Inside the storage areas where they had changed, the crowd had been background noise, but out here, the throb of jovial voices, laughing and cavorting was overbearing. This only served to amplify the terror in both men. What if they were no good, forgot their lines, frozen like statues with stage fright? And what if they were found out? Benedict had only now begun to compute now that actually, what they had done is assault two soldiers of His Majesty's army, impersonated soldiers of His Majesty's army and then entered Ministry of Defence property under false pretences with intent to cause theft. This was squeaky cheek time. He looked over at the second player in this double act. Tristan was visibly sweaty, no better than when they'd come in and it was causing his makeup to run so that he now resembled a much worse for wear flapper after a particularly hard night on the gin and Charleston.

A head peeped through the curtain, causing Tristan to jump. The bespectacled face piped, "Alright lads, I'm Warrant Officer Warboyes."
Oh goody, a military ooliceman! thought Benedict. Warboyes continued, "I've got the set list through the post, so I'll just give you a quick ta daa on the old joanna and we'll be on our way? Yes? Brilliant" and Warboyes vanished before either of them could register an objection. The crowd begun to hush under a multitude of whispers until at last only a gentleman coughing to clear phlegm could be heard. All went silent.

The tuneful "tad da!" of the piano rang out all too quickly and the stage curtain moved to the side in a yank that lasted the slimmest of seconds. Suddenly, Benedict and Tristan were fresh out of darkness to cower in. Instead two spotlights now exposed them opposite approximately ninety army officers and non commissioned personnel all guffawing at the ridiculous figures now standing there to put on a show. Both men froze so badly it was like watching a staring competition, who would blink first? Within the first few seconds of awkwardness a voice broke the uncomfortable silence.
"Oy darlin, what's your bra size?" There was a giggle or two amongst the ranks.
Benedict, from the deepest recesses of his tiny pot of courage, found the nerve to speak and confidently rounded on the heckler, a cheeky jack-the-lad twenty something, all

hair oil and polish. He let a moment go past and said deadpan, "Forty, same as your IQ."

This brought an "Oooooh!" from the crowd.

Tristan now found his voice and crossed the stage to the young man. "What's your position laddie?"

The slightly embarrassed and red cheeked soldier said, "Rifleman".

"Big gun eh? Compensating for something?" Tristan pushed his tongue into his cheek as the audience roared with laughter.

"Ooh, get her," added Benedict thumbing in Tristan's direction.

They'd won the audience over quickly, so without further ado and nerves steadied, Benedict moved centre-stage and announced, "Gentlemen, I'm Enid and over there is the ravishing Eartha. Together we are them Dames from Damascus!"

A roar went up and quickly the ivories were once more tickled by the bespectacled Officer Warboyes as the first song of the evening began.

After breaking down those initial terrifying barriers, it was plain sailing all the way. Benedict had been one hundred percent right, this was a doddle. The crowd was boozy, wanting to be shown a good time and didn't even mind when the two trannies on stage used their cue cards, if anything it made it funnier as it forced Benedict and Tristan to adlib. Their songs included, "Simon the simple Syrian", "My camel's got the hump with me, luckily I've got two humps", and somehow through belting out a cornucopia of racism and bawdy songs, intermingled with flashes of knickerbocker, the lads sailed through the performance. After a finale of the Damascus Damsels Pyramid Dance, which involved rotating their foam breasts to their front and back with changes of direction, they brought the house down to a standing ovation. They gave a modest bow, as smirks crept across each their faces. Benedict shot Tristan a knowing look that they'd pulled off the big show off as they exited stage left.

Benedict ran into the stage store room and gave a hurrah of happiness as Tristan similarly bounced up and down with excitement, his face a swirling vortex of browns, blacks, blues and skin tones from the sweat. Both were buzzing from the performance. Tristan grabbed Benedict's arms and squealed "That was AMAZING! I've never done anything like that in my life, never even had the courage for it!"

"Well, I'd hope it's not every day you dress like a nancy," Benedict wryly joked.

"Aw, you know what I mean!"

"I do, I absolutely do." Benedict suddenly was on a different plane staring out upon a great imaginary plateau, "Did you see me out there Tris? I was electric; I had the audience cooing and eating from the palm of my hand?!"

He was swiftly kicked off his plane and back to reality by Tristan's next question.

"Like pigeons?"

"Quite. But, I mean," Benedict gestured with his hands, "I could do that, I could actually do that for a job. What do I care for money? I'm richer than twenty of you put together. Sorry, that sounded distasteful. What I meant was that the energy, buzz and applause; that would become my meat and drink."

A calm but clear voice issued from behind them, from where the stage exit to the room was. "Perhaps not until after the war though eh?"

They turned around and there was an officer standing in the doorway, arms clenched behind his back. They had no idea what he'd overheard and Benedict quickly tried to replay the entire post concert conversation in his head to see if the game was up and they'd need to make a sharp exit dressed as ladies. As luck would have it, the young captain hadn't cottoned on. He stepped into the room and extended a firm and brief handshake to both of them.

"Allow me to introduce myself, I'm Captain Underhill. I'm currently the Mess Officer on duty."

He spoke in soft effortless tones, but underlying it was that sense of purpose, diligence and ultimate responsibility that would be drilled into all the candidates from Sandhurst. He gave them a small round of applause, "Bloody good show tonight fellas, bloody good show. You controlled the baying mob well enough that the baying mob would now like to buy you both a few drinks. We're just across the corridor from the performance room; we have a nice little bar established there. Come through imminently if you will." He heel-turned and was gone into the blackness of the stage and din of happy voices and chairs scraping on the varnished floor beyond.

Both men took a long look at each other. One thing commendable about the products they wore was that despite all the energy, nerves and sweat, the brown face paint refused to budge.

"This stuff's going to take hours to shift."

"What do you think? Go as we are? Might be a bit odd."

Benedict wrinkled his mouth, "Oh I don't know, the baying mob want them Damsels from Damascus, let's give them Enid and Eartha in bonhomous form. Besides, they're more realistic than if you and I get scrubbed up and go as our true selves in ill-fitting uniforms."

Tristan sighed, he was getting used to this by now. "Right, in for a penny...again."

"That's the spirit," replied a smiling Benedict.

They walked back through to the stage, down into the seating area which was now strewn with displaced chairs. Benedict pushed the entrance doors outward and they entered into to a long corridor, painted in a cream gloss but which showed the brickwork underneath. With the lights which glared overhead, it had the look of an old Victorian hospital. A few groups of men chatted and leaned against the walls, occasionally giving the performers the eye but mostly ignored them or patted them or squeezed their shoulders as they passed. But it was the noise coming from the opposite room which drew their attention, through two wooden framed glass doors. The glass was opaque but through the light in the room, Benedict and Tristan could see heads moving, hands and glasses of alcohol being raised and it felt like the whole world could hear the rowdy singing beyond. "Roll out the barrel" was already in full swing and a tuneless cacophony of football terrace singing was underway to much laughter. Benedict gave Tristan a look and said "Shall we?"

Tristan raised an eyebrow of concern and stepped forth, like two unlikely female cowboys pushing past the saloon doors. But the piano did not stop playing, the room did not fall silent and tumbleweed did not roll silently across the imaginary town behind them.

They were welcomed by a sound akin to being badly placed in the middle of the field for the first time that the Greeks and the Trojans met in combat and suddenly, hands, faces and sloshed beer were upon them, cheering, ushering and cajoling them forward into the throng. Someone shouted "Barman line em up," and before they could say, "No, I couldn't possibly," they were stood in front of the bar facing a free pint of ale and a free shot of whiskey each.

Cries of "Speeeeeech, Speech!" went up amongst the majority and then the noise died down again to a murmur. Benedict hadn't prepared for this, he had no cue cards to rely on this time around. But he didn't have to think for long. He'd bullied them all night with tart acidic jokes about what Hitler didn't have and what the size of a man's gun meant, this time he'd play to their strengths. Besides, he was taller than Tristan and most of the soldiers in the room and also a far better master of ceremonies from all the champers bashes he'd squandered his small fortune on. Whereas before he was a man in drag, he now raised his glass and became a man in brown camouflage paint, wearing a dress.

"Gentlemen, please, a toast! To your kind and fierce hospitality, to King and country and to giving Gerry a damn good rodgering should he require it!"

An instantaneous hurrah went up and everyone gulped a voluminous amount of ale out of their pint pot. More handshakes and back slaps issued forth. An endless rotation of men came to them to shake their hands and make merry. Several asked if they had agency representation, one asked if they had boyfriends. He was clearly a very much mistaken chap. Soon, a more careworn standard piano was tinkling in the corner and the songs and swaying with pint glasses aloft began. Regardless of Benedict and Tristan's motivation towards the Colchester Barracks, the moment was descending into a very hazy and drunken blur.

It had already been established that Tristan Wynd could hold his own when it came to the old alcofrolics and once more, five or six pints later, he was steady as a rock. Perhaps he had come out of his shell and his guard was down a little more than usual but generally, sober would be a word that would not look amiss in a sentence about his current situation. The same could not be said for Benedict. For a big man, Benedict had absolutely no constitution. Literally the sniff of the barmaid's apron and he would spend an entire hour tacking like a yacht down a street. Six pints and walking was not an option. He was slurred, he'd happily tell an angry Rottweiler he loved it and in his frock on this particular night he became more and more ludicrous. His long black wig was now on askew, brown makeup smeared across his face and the most preposterous ideas were now issuing forth from him.

"Come on lads, let's steal a barrage balloon and set sail for Gerry land. When we'll get there, I'll flash my arse and th'war will be over by Sunday lunchtime, n we can all have wurst n sauerkraut!"

The lads in the room laughed with and at him and then turned back to their conversations until the next pearl of wisdom was delivered. Whilst Tristan was steady and enjoying the moment and the sing-songs happening, Benedict was becoming unsociable, bandy legged and the world had ever so slightly started to rotate to the right. He also hadn't gone to the loo yet and was on the verge of having an accident. He clapped a hand on a random soldier's shoulder.

"Scuse mate, don' spose you know where the gents are do you?"

"Course, just through the entrance, turn right down the corridor and the latrines are the third right."

"Thhhank you, they sound wonderful, let'ssssss holiday there sometime."

Benedict then left the confused looking squaddie and started to bang his big frame through the crowd, faking smiles and pleasure as more congratulations came his way. He started confusing the situation.

"Yes, thank you, me and my wife are honeymooning in Bognor, you shhhould see the palm trees, they're majestic." and "Thankkkyou, I never thought I'd win the Olympic gold medal for choosing beef over chicken, but four years offff meticulous training have paid off. Was worried for a bit by the biggg Romanian, he was alllways the favourite, was mine anyway haha!"

Finally, and thankfully, just before he started to lose his rag and the contents of his bladder, Benedict had cut a large, constantly diagonal path through the throng and out into the corridor. A coolness bathed his sweaty forehead. He hadn't realised how the masses in the bar next door had simply heated the room to intolerable levels. He stood in the relative peace of the corridor for a moment, eyes closed, smelling the tang of fresh gloss paint that was in the air. He then set off left down the corridor instead of right.

Second right, no, third right, or was it fourth left? It didn't really matter, the initial wrong turn had taken him into a completely separate section of the building. He started trying random door handles, rooms which led to quarters and bureaus, all of which were locked. Benedict briefly found himself in a gymnasium. He couldn't find the light switch but the door's opaque glass let light in from the corridor and it cut a dim swathe into the large exercising space. He could see whole climbing apparatus folded in against the walls and medicine balls of varying sizes lined up at the far end. One looked just big enough to sit on. So in a fit of malady and loneliness he thought he'd park up for a minute or two. Why was he here again? No idea. Regardless, in his current state it took six attempts to sit on the ball before his body gyroscope and it's alcoholic influence dumped him off anyway. It was highly uncomfortable in any situation regardless of Benedict's current state. Eventually he turned to the large wooden ball and said, "That's the last time we'll share a bed. Praps we'll meet again, praps not."

The medicine ball stared back at him unashamedly brazen and caused Benedict to wobble backwards before he landed on the gym's entrance door and tottered back out into the corridor.

There were more pressing things on Benedict's mind, namely his bladder. Unfortunately, his brain had now solely focussed all it's time and energy into saying, "Look old chum, it's go for a wee now in a dignified way, or release the metaphorical hounds, and you receive a soaking beyond respectable levels. Those are the only two options, five seconds to decide and go."

Benedict groped his crotch area through the skirt, and gave an, "Oh dear," before happening upon one final door which was unlocked. Not clocking what the room was for, he threw the door open and the next moment had hitched his skirt up and was standing, urinating into what looked like a vase. Steady waves of relief grew within him as he gave a satisfied "aaaaaaaaaah". A great weight had lifted off him, namely, his bladder. He found himself looking to the ceiling and thanking God for the creation of unlocked doors, though in doing so lost concentration and dribbled a little bit down his left leg.

After a good minute of draining urate from himself and shaking off a few drips, Benedict straightened himself out as best he could. He was still absolutely inebriated. Wobbling a little, he steadied himself against the wooden doorframe. His vision was a constant transition between focused, blurry and then occasionally back to focused. His eyes were three seconds behind the rest of him. As he straightened up, even he could see through the mire of his drunken haze that the room was twinkling at him. Objects gleamed as the dull light from the corridor spread into the room. The edge of metals shone and smooth conical objects reflected what little light there was. The powerful and enquiring mind of Benedict drew the immediate conclusion, *mmmmmmmmmm shineeee!*

 His hand that was supporting his weight against the door began snaking around the wall, careful not to lose grip and topple Benedict to the floor and potentially into a vase of wee. Instead it found the light switch. Benedict's index finger strayed into contact first with the raised base of the switch housing and then the little up and down nub which currently prevented electricity from bathing the room in a heady light. Not for long though, as Benedict's finger, almost as eager as he was to see sparkly things, teased the switch head up. A satisfying click and ready-made instant light poured into the room from the single bulb in the centre of the room. It was not an easy or pleasant brightening of surroundings, but a coarse invasive whiteness, only made worse by the many twinkling objects. Benedict groaned and grimaced by the painful invasion of his head by the light and shielded his eyes from the bouncing rays. Slowly his eyes adjusted, no mean feat considering the state he was in. Out of the blue, he realised his location, he gazed in awe at the myriad of unusual objects in this treasure room. Treasure room? Surely not. He didn't have long to raise questions though as his hand which had been grasping the light switch housing had decided to gently begin a trundle down the wall. Benedict lost balance and crashed into the vase. The container tipped and he was reminded of it's contents as they began to spill onto the floor and splashed his thigh. He gagged at the strong urine and chundered a little, spitting onto the floor. He clambered up again annoyed at having come into contact with the foul liquid, not only on his thigh but to stand back up he'd put his hand right into the puddle. He wiped the rank wetness on his frock and looked around.

Large colourful standards leant against the wall, brass framed and at least five foot tall with their material depictions of war below. There were two suits of armour, cold steel resting in a position as if filled by a swarthy baron, a broadsword held at the waist with the tip in front of the eye slit of the helmet. Sashes lay in racks to the side. Five carronades, three next to one wall, two opposite them sat polished and looked ready to discharge their small but perfectly formed deadly contents at each other. This was not a treasure room, this was the barrack's parade room!

Benedict looked round, enjoying the pomp and circumstance of it all. Giggling, he snaked his way over to the suit of armour in the far corner. He flicked the metal twice with a finger which gave a satisfying ting. Benedict's face changed and took on a shameful, naughty tinge to it. His cheeks flushed like a child looking to steal a sweet as he reached forward and started to prise open the fingers of the empty shell of the knight. One by one the hinged armour around the digits uncurled until at last Benedict could see the hilt of the sword. Gingerly he pulled at the haft and overbalanced by the sheer weight of the sword metal as he took it. He lost control and swung the mighty weapon into a row of parade helmets lined up the side. Benedict apologised profusely to nobody in particular as they rattled and bounced off the floor. No one came to see what the cacophony had been about and the child in Benedict's confidence grew. He giggled naughtily and began to pose with the sword, initially knighting one of the fallen helmets, before drunkenly posturing and grandstanding in front of the other suit of armour, like an incredibly masculine Amazon with no dress sense. He felt cocky, but his opponent, a suit of armour, held his gaze firm and it's stare caused an uneasiness in Benedict. So he bowed, nearly falling over in the process and then turned to leave. It was at this moment he saw something and remembered. He had not yet inspected the wall that made up the corridor side in the room and there alone, resting on two red felt covered brackets, was the most beautifully sculpted rapier. It must have been the parade leader's sword, but it was worthy of royalty. The metal filigree around the haft was intricate but not deficient in austerity, enough to decorate and protect the sword-bearer's hand. But emblazoned in this decoration were four extraordinary rubies. Rubies? Benedict swore that this was possibly the reason why they were here, but couldn't be sure. He stared long and intently at this beautiful weapon and the treasure it contained, and then promptly passed out.

Chapter 12

Considering he had slept on a chair, sat backwards on it so he could lay his hands and then his head on the top of the back rest, Tristan had slept happily and soundly. It must be said however, that if one was to do this every day of life for a normal sleep period of about eight hours, without the amount of sedation that Tristan had undergone, a fellow would probably end up with a displaced vertebrae and piles. However, considering the party had ended at one in the morning and it was now five, Tristan had slept well. He was alone, in the bar where they had been welcomed as returning heroes, still dressed as some demure but manly female entertainer and still very much covered in brown camouflage greasepaint.

The sparrows were already chattering in neighbourly anger at each other in the bushes outside. Tristan awoke hung over, but only to the point where there was a gnawing, warm feeling in his stomach and nothing that a decent fry-up wouldn't fix. After rubbing the sleep from his eyes and stretching out, he looked down at his party frock and the chair and remembered where he was. Whilst there was no doubt Tristan could hold his drink, this did not mean that booze did not play tricks on him. For starters, he still forgot why he was there and instead cast his mind back to the previous evening's entertainment. He looked out across the bare room, bar stools and chairs, scattered round the bar and the air stained by the stale fog of cigars and fags. He was filled with the appreciation of quietness and the joy that an actor on a successful opening night who has stayed after everyone else had gone home might have, to savour the moment. Despite looking like a drag queen that had met an unfortunate end in a butterscotch factory and smelling of day old sweat, whiskey vapours and fags, this moment was beautiful, quite quite beautiful.

Things were not so chipper for Benedict however. He had woken up in a start, the morning call going up around the site to get up, stand by your beds up two three! Thankfully he was very much alone. He smelled mildly like he'd pissed himself and more importantly he couldn't move his arms.

Something had totally paralysed him. What's worse was that Benedict had reached this unfortunate end standing up, oh and he was blind. Nothing but cold blackness. What evil wrongdoer had spiked his drink with such a concoction as that which could cause temporary or permanent blindness? Benedict guessed that perhaps one of the lads had been posted somewhere far far away and had returned with a vial of something likely called "Creeping Paralysis." He was frozen in place and Benedict began to panic. This poison was making him feel cocooned in something too, something hard which he could not escape from and what the Devil what was this? His hands were clasped and raised above his head. Had some utter bounder snuck in as he lay helpless and strung him up? Had the devious Frenchie found him again? He struggled and in that moment of sheer panic, realised that he clanked. Benedict stopped, fuzzy headed and feeling sick. He shook his left leg out and immediately heard metal contacting metal in the knee joint. A thought crossed his mind; Benedict lowered his chin and then flicked his head back violently.

As he expected, suddenly he could see and thankfully for him there was a mirror on the opposite wall which spelled out his predicament. Memories of the night before came flooding back. He was still in the parade room and a dim light from the corridor flooded the room through the glass in the door. Apparently after passing out, Benedict had come to again and thought it would be a marvellous idea to wear one of the suits of armour, hence by flicking his head back he had raised the visor at the front. After what must have taken about two hours of drunkenly strapping the various chest plates and arm guards to his person, he had popped on the helmet and picked up a rapier. THE RAPIER, of course! He let out a minor squeal of excitement from within the suit. But then came reality.

The dawn wakeup call in the distance had done nothing for his memory and only now did the enormity of the situation hit him. The previous day, he and Tristan had drugged two visiting squaddies, impersonated them to gain access to Colchester Barracks, dressed up as a drag act as part of a touring concert party and then got heinously drunk with all involved. The original intent had been to find the four rubies mentioned in his little scrap of a riddle. And he'd done it! Through pure luck he had drunkenly stumbled into this little treasure chest of a room and found a sword with these priceless stones embedded into the hilt. It had to be it; it might not have been but considering the likelihood of finding gems in a base full of working class squaddies, Benedict refused to believe there would be a heavy abundance of priceless artefacts. For them to left in this weapon meant this sword had to mean something to the base; it had to be the four rubies. Only now, Benedict had a problem.

It appeared that in his armoured haste, Benedict had swung the rapier up over his head, presumably to bring it down for full effect on some imaginary foe. Only he had raised it with such vigour that the point of the sword had swung directly into a wooden beam above his helmet and had lodged stuck. The protective hand armour had also locked up, so he was unable to free himself from this striking position. Benedict had then passed out again and slept for an hour in the suit before the dawn chorus arrived. Regardless, he was now tired, on the verge of vomiting on himself, weak and his arms, sapped of any residual strength could not shift the point of the sword from the wood. He had no ideas of the whereabouts of his partner in crime and sooner or later two very groggy, half naked squaddies would either be padding their way to the nearest police station or back to the barracks to raise merry hell and get even with their assailants. Furthermore the base was rousing and he could hear boots hitting the tarmac outside. He hoped there wouldn't be a parade today as they would find a greasepaint coated man smelling of widdle dressed in a suit of armour looking like he was about to kill someone. Benedict panicked. He couldn't call for help but desperately needed some. The longer the both of them were in the base the more likely they would find themselves in the clink. He made muffled moans as he jostled himself, eventually jumping up and down as much as he could under the circumstance. The sword seemed virtually glued to the wood. There was only one thing for it. Benedict gripped the haft as hard as he could, difficult considering his hands were already stuck. He pulled down on it and with an effort greater than his true strength, began to raise his heavy armour clad legs off the floor. It was like lifting a steel blanket. He heaved with everyone he had, nearly popping a blood vessel until at last his legs were raised slightly into the air. Benedict now had his full body weight attached to this very militaristic swing. He moved his legs forward and back just to generate a little motion. Just when he thought he might explode in a colourful display of pressurised blood and sick, thuck! The sword came out.

Benedict came down with a mighty crash and delivered the full weight of the suit of armour and himself onto his tailbone. It wasn't pain that hit him but a wave of numbness, a ringing in his head. Benedict knew he should get up, should get the armour off of himself quick smartish, but he couldn't move, didn't want to move. He lay there for five minutes whilst the numbness played all over him and finally he received a dull throb in his lower back. He groaned, rolled over on his front and pushed himself back up onto his feet. This was exhausting, but it wasn't over yet. He staggered, looking for a vessel into which to vomit in as a sickening heat peaked in his temples. Unable to find one, Benedict chose the corner of the room at right angles to the door and spent his load there, gagging and trying to force up more which hadn't decided it would depart yet, that would come later. He stopped, the acrid twang of spew in his mouth, saliva dribbling from his chin. Benedict spat out a few droplets onto the spattered floor. That expulsion of last night's excess made him feel twenty percent better but he could not stop, there was an exit to seek and only luck and the powerfulness of his hanky of chloroform could be relied on. Working only on logic, as the memory of climbing into the suit defied him, he quickly found all the right leather straps and buckles to peel off the various guards and plates. Benedict tried to do this as quietly as possible but the metal still generated a clang or a ting as it touched surfaces but still no one came. The mess halls and sleeping quarters must have been some distance away and Benedict reasoned that loud noises, like guns and metal were probably common to a place like this where soldiers were conditioned for combat. What's more, on getting up from the fall he had put the full force of his weight on the shaft of the sword and he'd broken it off at the jewelled hilt, handy!

At last, Benedict stood there only his long-johns, his choice of outfit for this morning? This season's collection for the trampy-whore about town. Benedict pulled the skirt back on and loosely fitted the brassiere again. He adjusted the wig and was then hit by the stale cigar smoke and hints of dried sick located therein. Benedict popped the important bit of the rapier into a side pocket in the skirt so it bulged at his thigh. He ran to the corner gagging and reaching again but no more vomit came. Benedict got up, panting. He steadied himself and then walked to the door, gingerly pulled on the handle, opening it to a crack and peered out into the corridor. Benedict realised he was in one of the last rooms of this long building as the corridor finished abruptly to the right of the room, a large window flooding the corridor with natural light. No one was to be seen, but neither was there any signage of where he'd been, the direction he'd come from or where Tristan had ended up. Maybe Tris was already in custody, clapped in irons and ready for a military court-marshal. Benedict felt his gall rise again. He swallowed hard, his body unable to regulate his temperature yet, his back already moist with unnecessary perspiration.

Benedict padded out into the corridor to the left and quickly reached a branching hallway. He stopped but there was no time to consider and explore each direction. However, something in him said that this was not the way and having no greater compass then gut feeling he pressed on. Another left corridor, this one he took feeling somehow right. An intersection of corridors, three decisions to make! He assessed each option, preferring to go right and then worked out where his internal steering was coming from. For each option, as he turned his head, there was a feint smell of the previous night's activity. Generally there was nothing, but some corridors contained the smallest hint of whiskey sweats, stale beer and cigars. Hoping it was not him, he'd picked these corridors in the hope of leading him back the bar.

After a few twists and turns the smell grew stronger until at last he stood in front of the saloon doors. He pushed one gently and peered in. Benedict saw the back of a lone, not overtly feminine woman sitting the wrong way round on a chair, legs splayed in the most undignified unladylike way. He whispered, "Tristan," with urgency. The woman's head swivelled and Benedict saw the mucky, oily painted face of his companion smiling at him. Tristan pulled himself up from the chair as Benedict slid into the room quietly. Tristan looked genuinely pleased, which baffled Benedict.

"What a night eh?!"

"Yes, we really need to leave....."

"Yes but, oh, I could get used to this showbiz lark. We were triumphant, a tour de force and then, well, I've never had so much booze bought for me in all my life. The constant goosing was a bit much mind. I feel like I've sat on a pin cushion."

"That's spiffing but we really need to leave."

"And I'll tell you another thing for free," Tristan laughed, "By bloody hell you can sing, I think. It might have been a vague memory caused by the beer." Tristan put his hands on his hips and sighed happily again.

"Tristan, why did we come here?"

Tristan stopped, hands still on hips, smiling at Benedict and a moment later the smile clanged to the floor, "Oh bloody hell....."

"Exactly and if we don't start making an exit now, we'll have two very burly and angry squaddies turning up in their pants and wanting a very, very good explanation." The last words came out as a hiss.

"Crikey". That was all Tristan could say on the matter as both started to jog towards the bar doors. They pushed through and were immediately met by the sergeant major from the night before. Benedict's sweaty chest met the brim of his hat. There was an awkward moment of tension as both Benedict, Tristan and the sergeant tried to comprehend this coming together and formulate what the correct etiquette was. Frankly, it seemed as if the game was up and he was here to cart them off to a temporary cell. Tristan let out a high pitched and very embarrassing short, gust. Naturally, the sergeant major spoke first.

"Ull yerselves tagetha ads!"

Both Benedict and Tristan stood to attention, Tristan bringing his hand up to salute. The sergeant yanked his hand down and grumbled, "Idiot," at him. Most shockingly, the sergeant then tried to smile at both men, but it looked more like a grimace, as if he was passing a particularly difficult stool. He then quietly muttered, "Ust come to congratulate oo both on a ob well done!"

Both Benedict and Tristan looked at each other perplexed. The sergeant continued, "Ell, don't ook surprised, you was well ecommended. Must admit it aint ormally my up of tea! Ut on this occasion, it made us all it our ants with aughter as the mericans ould say!"

Benedict took a modest bow and replied, "If by donning a pair of high heels and cracking off a series of nob gags, we've managed to keep the British end up sir, then by golly you can superglue the wobbly things to the soles of my feet!"

"That's the spirit you ig oofter!" said the sergeant as he drove his hand enthusiastically into Tristan's back, nearly concussing him in the process.

"Do be sure to write that up in your report to Concert Party HQ!" Benedict suggested. He then gave the sergeant a little wave to signal the conversation was over, "We'd best be off, two hour cleanup job this." He drew an invisible circle around his face and gave a smirk.

"Of course", the sergeant gave a cough, "Well , I'll eave you to it, afe ourney," and he walked off down the corridor and rounded a corner further down. Benedict and Tristan turned to each other with a look of sheer terror.

"That was close!" said Tristan.

Benedict nodded and replied, "God only knows why I asked him to write it up in the report. What's it going to say when this all comes out in the laundry? 'Though the two men were imposters, possibly German spies, they did put on a jolly good show and a hop in the step of a miserable, womanless and possibly predatory sergeant major!' Worked though, come on let's leg it before we're discovered. It may already be too late but there's only one way to find out."

Both scuttled into the concert hall opposite. It was dark without the evening's searing lights but they picked their spots well and missed clattering into any of the chairs which were still strewn about. They ran up the middle isle, onto the stage and through the exit into the changing and props area. They were delighted to find that everything was as they had found it the night before. They both agreed, so as not to look totally ridiculous, they should at least change back into the squaddie uniforms, rather than leaving the base as a couple of cross-dressers. Quickly, both struggled out of corsets and knickerbockers and back into the shirts and trousers of regulation army wear. They ditched the frocks and all other accoutrements back in the large chest supplied by the concert party. Whilst Tristan slid his buttoned up shirt over his head, Benedict took out the sword haft and shoved it into a small rucksack that was nearby. Having managed to get his head through the top hole and one arm in a sleeve, Tristan saw the small bag and asked, "What's that for?"

"Oh just, you know, should we need provisions. Thought it might be useful as we've got nothing to carry food for the journey back or if the worst comes to the worst and we go on the run."

"I sincerely hope not," replied Tristan with a disapproving look.

Benedict changed the subject. "Are you ready to go?" Tristan patted himself down, just to make sure, but then remembered that his own normal clothes were still a good ten minute jog away. He nodded and exuding as much confidence as a pair of would-be crims who were about to be caught red-handed could, strode out the back door into the parade yard, chests out and with a bold statuesque walk.

It was still quiet as they moved through the exterior of the large barracks, retracing their steps from the night before. They only passed one or two soldiers walking about; a couple of them pointed remembering the previous evening's entertainment and would give them a complementary "Wahey!" to which Tristan would give a warm smile and nod in return. Others just looked on perplexed or muttered. Neither of them could figure out why if they were not being stopped and arrested, some of the men still took exception to their persons. Tristan asked Benedict and he replied, "Probably religious, they don't agree with chaps making fools of themselves in drag. I can't blame them really."

Under the circumstances it made them feel very uneasy and they were glad when the guard station they had come in to the barracks from appeared in view. They approached the station and a trooper came out. Thankfully he was clearly one of the audience from the night before and immediately broke out into a wide smile.

"Belly laughs last night lads! Good show!" He drew a finger round his own face, "You not, er taking that off though?" Tristan realised that in their haste they had neglected to remove their dark makeup and probably looked like a pair of badly made up Indians. "Of course!" he exclaimed. Benedict had to cover up the blunder and added, "Of course.......er we are. But alas, the concert party failed to pack any make up remover and cotton buds, strong stuff this. Would you happen to know of any shops or chemists around here where a couple of girls can pick up supplies?" The squaddie chuckled in the spirit of things and replied, "Turn left out of here and it's your first right, there's a chemist there."

"Excellent, thank you so much for your help." Benedict elbowed Tristan.

"Ouch, yes thank you!"

The sentry let them through the small gap that marked the end of the base and the beginning of normal civilian life. Fortunately the guard's initial instruction of, "left out of here," was exactly where they needed to go, but as they walked adjacent to the wall, their turning was a good few streets down. They walked with pace, heads down until they passed the first street on the right. A voice shouted from behind them, "Oy mates, take that right, that's the street you want. Oy, no, you've gone too far!"

"Just keep walking," Benedict said, head down as they strode on.

"Hey, I say chaps!" the voice said, ever more in the distance.

At the other entrance point at right angles to the one Benedict and Tristan had just passed through, the sentry there sat on an old wooden stool, feet on the small table in the sentry house, with an old rag, giving the top of his boots a spit polish. He briefly looked up to check the weather and in the distance, coming down the terraced road, were two red faced, sweaty looking men in long johns. They were sprinting towards the barracks. The guard's first thought was, *unusual physical education gear. These two must have really done something wrong for the sergeant to do that to them!* How little did he know.

Not that it mattered, for as they eagerly recounted their mugging in between great gulps of air and the situation now facing the base to the shocked sentry, two black and white minstrels turned a corner into another terraced street. Thankfully they found the Phantom still there, with the piles of their clothes in the back seat. In a heartbeat, Benedict and Tristan had thrown themselves into the car, performed a textbook three point turn and shielded their faces as they passed the barracks wall back on their way out of Colchester, returning to a state of normality. Seconds later the whiny rise and fall of the alarm peel at the barracks rang out for a good mile.

Chapter 13

The chase by nothing but pure guilt and an unknown and unreal predator made minutes pass like hours. The Phantom rolled out of Colchester and into the Essex countryside with effortless grace and yet it felt like a donkey stuck in quicksand. Every minute passed too slowly, every second seemed like one second more until they were caught. The buzz and nervous excitement of what they might do had now been replaced by the realisation of the seriousness of what they had done and the potential consequences if they were caught. Whereas only Tristan had been aware of how muddled and wrong the situation was when mugging those two soldiers and entering the barracks, Benedict now fully shared his concern as those actual events had taken place and there was not a court in the land that wouldn't convict them if caught. So they pressed on, silently, no words passing between them, only imminent capture on both of their minds.

After what felt like a day, but in reality was little more than an hour, it felt like enough distance had been put between Colchester and themselves. Having passed through a nice picture perfect Hertfordshire village, Benedict drew the Phantom over to a gated field entrance and stopped the engine. As nothing but the idle mooing of a field of cows penetrated the car, he rolled his head back and gave a large sigh. Tristan got out of the vehicle and was sick immediately. Benedict caught a whiff off the pungent bile and joined him, bent over, vomiting onto a hedge.

Tristan felt dirty and unkempt. Every day in Wales, he worked up a healthy sweat earning an honest living and would come home, bathe for a good hour and always be as fresh as a spring morning for dinner or the pub, or just for the next shift in the fields. But here, his stinking, sweating, sickening odour smelt like he felt, soiled and dirty. He looked up from his bent over position and noticed a freshwater well pump next to an old hay barn. It dripped clean water enticingly. Tristan wiped the acrid sick from the corner of his mouth and slowly made his way over. He felt physically drained after turning his stomach inside out but found the strength to work the long arm of the steel pump. He ducked under as cool refreshing water began to pour over him. It was a warm day, but the liquid hidden far underground was crisp and cold. Feeling a hundred times better and without regard for any potential passersby, Tristan stripped his army uniform off and gave himself a thorough clean, using the shirt as a flannel to remove some of the grimy face paint. As the mixture was grease based it was impossible to clean without something to turn it into an emulsion. However, by scraping the standard issue shirt across his mug at least some of the paint was reapplied to the cloth. He picked up the rest of his uniform and quickly zipped over to the Phantom's driver side wing mirror. His face looked better, still a little like he'd been working all day on an oily car, but better that than impersonating a man whose face had been pushed into a chocolate cake. He turned to Benedict and issued a stern instruction, "Your turn."

Surprised, Benedict did what he was told and washed whilst Tristan moved to the passenger seats in the back of the Phantom to dress and feel a little bit of home comfort from his own clothes. He pulled his shirt on and was reaching for his trousers, where Benedict's small rucksack lay on top. Tristan tugged the material of his clothes away causing the bag to roll and spill it's contents onto the gravelly road below. The cat or rather the haft was out the bag.

Benedict heard the metallic clink of the sword haft he'd stolen hit the dirt. At that moment he was rather exposed, in his pants rinsing his hair. The only satisfactory explanation he could give within the minute was, "Ah, yes".

Tristan bent down to look at the haft of the broken rapier. He could clearly see the rubies which encrusted the hand guard. He looked up at Benedict, eyes clearly blazing with anger. Benedict took on the appearance of an apologetic coalminer having a wash and could only shrug.

"Got what you came for then!?" asked Tristan with bitter rhetoric. Tristan stood up, pulled his trousers on quickly, tightened his belt and then climbed back into the passenger seat, slamming the door and nearly irreparably damaging the car in the process. Benedict was going to pick a bone with him over it, but on the basis of recent events he was hardly sainted. Benedict could not think of any witty jibe to save the situation and as the car door slammed shut he simply rolled his eyes at what he thought was prima-donna like behaviour. He had forgotten of course that it was his actions in the past two days that had put them in this situation.

Benedict stepped away from the refreshing water pump and moved to where his treasure had fallen out the car. Picking the metal item up, he turned the sword haft over in his hands. Any precious stone thief would have made the effort to lay their hands on such a beautiful amalgamation of smithing and jewel craft. It happily shone in the sunlight as he rotated it's beauty. He'd done some largely questionable things in his time, but this was plumbing new depths. Whilst his past had occasionally fringed on the selfish or immoral, this was assault, impersonating a member of the armed forces, espionage, theft? What's done was done, but this was adding up to a sizeable prison sentence and it also made a mockery of the armed forces security arrangements during a burgeoning war. Prison might be the lenient option, he was likely to get a good kicking and then be hanged at this rate. And he knew he'd dragged a man he'd little known for over a week into this mess as well. But that was Benedict's way, constantly blundering into things like a bull in a china shop, without having thought through the substantial ramifications.

The passenger door was briefly opened and Benedict's clothes were ejected by Tristan onto the grassy verge, done like some angry housewife who'd caught her husband gambling away the family silver. The car door slammed shut again. Benedict sighed and ambled over to his random distribution of clothes. Still feeling heady and hung-over he stumbled into his trousers and dressed himself fully. He had no idea what to say to the man, how to explain it, but he took a deep breath, opened the driver's door and climbed into the driving seat. He swung the door shut and after the initial "thunk" from the two pieces of metal meeting, there was nothing but silence and two men, facing forward with everything and nothing to say to each other. A minute passed and the breeze picked up briefly and buffeted the car. Trees nearby caused quick shadows across the bonnet with their spring green leaves. Tristan could make the silence last as long as he wanted; he was a patient man and could see no value of speaking to Benedict. Benedict was quite the opposite and found Tristan's silence infuriating. It niggled and pinched at him. Wanting to broach the subject and get on with life, Benedict gestured with his hand and said, "Look". Well, that was enough. Tristan had won the silence contest and verbally fired the opening salvo.

"No, you bloody look! Have you quite finished being Raffles the gentleman catburglar yet, or should I expect to arrive back in London holding a couple of Faberge eggs and the treasure of the Sierra Madres?"

Benedict could only answer with fact. So as not to cause embarrassment, he said, "Tristan, the treasure of the Sierra Madres is fictional."

"I bloody know it's fictional! I can read, I've read the book! Good grief man, what were you thinking?!"

"I just, I was, I was in a situation where the opportunity presented itself. I didn't mean to go looking for it in the state I was in. I woke up and I was kind of.....attached to it I suppose."

"Two days ago I was a Hill-farmer, now I'm the Billy the Kid!"

Benedict tried to calm the situation down, "I do think you're over reacting."

"Am I? Theft, assault? Any of those lovely things ring a bell?"

"That's not really a fair assessment." It was a fair assessment.

"Oh, you're delusional man. Look at you, with your, I'm a toff, I'm all posh I can do what I want attitude."

"Now hang on a tick, there's no need to bring class into this."

"Fair enough, but I do object to being dragged around on your crackpot japes. I've only known you for a week and I've committed more crime than most would in a lifetime. Now, if you please, I smell of vomit and stale booze. I want to go home and have a long bath and then catch the first train back to Wales. I want nothing more to do with these shenanigans." Tristan folded his arms and looked away, out of the window

Benedict knew there was no arguing with him, mainly because he was right. So he opened the car door, ditched the army uniforms over the hedge of a nearby field and clambered back in to the Phantom. Edgy silences were meat and drink to them both for the next two hours as they rumbled ever forward, back to West London.

With the Phantom safely tucked under for the night in it's dust cloth in the small garage amongst the other lockups, Benedict and Tristan hardly said a word as they walked home. Tristan couldn't bear to look at the small rucksack that hung at Benedict's side, knowing the deeply illegal contents contained therein.

They were greeted at the door to Benedict's apartment by Mrs McDoughty who had just added the finishing touches to the house after giving it a thorough clean, post burglary. As this was the first time Benedict had seen Mrs McD since the incident, he raised his hand in some sort of apologetic manner. She was unsurprisingly curt in her answer.

"No need to comment, Mr Lukely sir, I received the full story from the neighbours housemaid. That was of course after I'd nearly had a heart attack and rung the police to report the fact that you'd clearly been kidnapped due to all the signs of a struggle. A Constable Lemon informed me of the goings on. Muriel next door further furnished events. So, don't you worry about me. Now I have a brew on downstairs. It was specifically for me, but you're home now, so I'll make up a tray whilst you wash whatever the two of you have been up to off your faces."

Benedict could detect that her rate of speech was increasing, indicating that the female and Scottish equivalent of Mount Etna was ready for an eruption, he faintly answered, "Right, thank you Mrs McD," as he walked through to the lounge.

She walked off towards the stairs, muttering, "Couldn't leave a note yer selfish bassad," under her breath.

Benedict looked at Tristan and rolled his eyes, looking for any sign of agreement or the spirit of team. He was found wanting.

Despite the relaxing power of the Earl Grey blend, Benedict's body had begun to stiffen and set in the big armchair where he sat. Tristan had since climbed into a big copper bath of warm water, prepared with great tutting from Mrs McDoughty. Benedict suspected that he would be fetching his own bath water if Mrs McD had anything to do with it or that in a fit of pique at his request, she'd easily lift the ridiculously heavy bath tub up and hit him with it.

After a flurry of activity from the floorboards above him, Benedict heard the clump shht, clump shht of male footsteps carrying something that was scraping the tip of each stair coming downwards. It was Tristan, washed and shaved, in his favourite navy suit, with his travelling case. He put it down by the door as Benedict moved into the hallway.

"So, you're off then?" he asked.

"I think it's for the best, don't you?" Tristan responded calmly.

"At least let me walk you to the station. There's all sorts of street urchins out there," Benedict suggested, hoping to find some common ground.

"I don't think that will be necessary. You forget, but not two days ago I pinned a man with a gun to the floor. An urchin pales in comparison." Tristan gave a friendly chuckle, but it was clear he was leaving. He walked to the front door but briefly turned back to Benedict.

"I nearly forgot. I won't be at my home address, not that you've got it, thank goodness. I think that until the smoke clears, along with my name, it's best for me to avoid my farm. People will gossip if they see police snooping around, so I'm going to spend some time lying low at my cousin Gwyffan's farm in Powys. He's always got an open door for me and I think it best that I remain there until you do the right thing and take back what's not rightfully yours."

"Oh, I hadn't thought of that as an option," said Benedict genuinely, it had not even crossed his mind to.

"Well, you should do, so I'd very much appreciate it if you'd write me at my cousin's address, just so I know that the all clear has been given."

He handed over a small scrap of white paper, torn from an envelope Tristan had found in the bin in his room. Benedict looked at the neat handwriting, spelling out the address for the farm in Llandrindod.

"Okay, yes, I suppose I can do that for you".

"I hope you make the right decision," Tristan said softly.

"Well, this is me then, thanks for showing me round. It was certainly an unusual stay."

"Quite," Benedict added, extending his hand and meeting Tristan's in a firm but emotionless handshake. With that, Tristan opened the front door and bounced the bottom of his case down the short steps to the pavement and was gone into the late afternoon sunshine of the capital.

Benedict closed the door, paused for a moment, staring at his ghastly unkempt reflection in the mirror, casually dwelling on the events of the past twenty four hours. He then called for Mrs McDoughty.

"I say, Mrs McD. Any chance of running another bath? I could really use a good soak."

Not a peep came back, yet she was clearly in the house. *There goes her Christmas extras* thought Benedict. He had two choices, go to bed now, covered in whiff and grime but rest up and deal with the mucky sheeted consequences tomorrow, or face the physical machinations of pouring several heavy buckets of hot water into the bath himself. Normally, the softer, easier option was the clear winner, but he looked at himself in the mirror again to assess the situation and decided to put his back out for a change, which was exactly what happened next.

Chapter 14

The next two days in the Bryant-Lukely household were spent in bed. This was because, in another labour saving attempt which didn't quite go to plan, Benedict had gotten an almighty back sprain. His brilliant concept was to heat the bath, rather than the water. So, employing his formidable team of one (himself) he had heaved with the strength of Samson to shift the bath towards the lit fireplace in the bathroom, putting his already knackered vertebrae under enormous duress. It was only a matter of seconds before something went and Benedict found himself prostrate on the floor with only the whitewashed ceiling for a view. Calling, "Mrs McD," or "Mrs McDoughty," didn't seem to warrant a response from the middle-aged battleaxe. Yelling, "Oy! Who pays your wages anyway!" was the clarion call.

She stood over him, gloating briefly. "Oh, have we had a bit of an accident there? Let's get you up and in the tub." Mrs McD had put his arm round her shoulder and hoisted him firmly upright, sending a jolt of pain through his back. He stood, swathed in towels whilst she worked, humming to herself as she filled the bath. Mrs McD then calmly said, "I'm not sure how we're going to do this, but the hot water will steady the pain some." Again she propped him up as they moved toward the tub. He started to lean forward, giving grunts of dissatisfaction from the chronic pain in his back as he gripped the side. He tried to cock his leg over the rim of the tub, but that didn't work. Now he found it impossible to straighten up and worried and the thought of a life bent double. Mrs McDoughty took the initiative and pushed him in head first, causing a tidal wave of water to go shooting out the other end of the bath and for Benedict to nearly drown and get his spine bent entirely the wrong way as he slid front first into the hot suds. Ironically, it seemed to completely alleviate the dull ache and for a brief moment Benedict wondered if Mrs McDoughty had ever been a chiropractor in a previous incarnation.

Since the bathing incident, Benedict had been laid up in bed. He had flattened himself into the soft down of the mattress, confused at how he should be feeling. A part of him wanted to continue the manic flailing of the previous week, he'd never felt so alive. Plus the police could come a knocking any moment and that gave him a buzz akin to being terrified and exhilarated at the same time. But on the other hand, laying there waiting for something, anything, gave him a fantastic moment to take stock of things. As only one option was really feasible whilst his vertebrae nursed themselves back to health, he thought deeply about what he'd stolen from Colchester barracks.

He'd moved the rucksack to the side of the bed and several times, when he thought Mrs McDoughty was about her business, would take the rapier haft out, admiring it, considering it, judging it, letting it judge him and his worth. There were two very distinct trains of thought with this, the most alluring of spoils. Taking the moral high ground, Benedict totally understood that he had stolen and in actual fact caused a hell of a lot morebother than that. The gold and ruby encrusted item he now held did not belong to him and he'd committed numerous crimes to get his hands on it. Furthermore he'd dragged along and implicated some poor Welsh sod, who he half liked and felt pity for. If he was pulled kicking and screaming up this high moral vantage point, there were two options open to Benedict. He could hand the sword haft in, but that was problematic and inflammatory. The questions would be numerous and troublesome. How did he come into it's possession, how did he know to hand it back when there'd been no mention of it in the London press, doesn't he look awfully like the tall chap wearing a skirt and camouflage makeup as reported? That was definitely a no then. The other option was of course, to lose it. Once he'd made a full recovery, there was absolutely nothing stopping him telling Mrs McDoughty that he was out for the afternoon, taking the rucksack with him, driving the Phantom to somewhere close to Richmond and lobbing the loot in the Thames. In all likelihood a local fisherman downstream might net it, or some scavenger on low tide might happen upon it, half buried in the silt from the river. Either way, suspicion would quickly switch to them. Suddenly he'd almost have no motive. If the fuzz came a knocking, they could happily search the flat, he didn't have it. And why would they come a rap tap tapping against his door? He was rich, from good stock and in absolutely no need of something glittering to fence for the right value. He also had no connections to Colchester, no links at all and they were wearing camouflage paint and dressed as ladies for a large part of the evening. The only person who could possibly finger them was the museum's security guard and the lovely, delicious Lillian Warner. He thought of her soft red glossed lips again and melted for a moment. Benedict shook the image from his head and continued adjudicating. Other than two people, this was virtually the perfect crime. If he threw it away, he'd have had no motive to go after such an object other than a suggestion made by an old teacher in Essex. He was clean.

Of course, there were always two sides to the coin though and when Benedict inspected the other side, his prior argument also made perfect sense to keep this sparkly object. Firstly, the fact that the haft was so delicately beautiful made Benedict feel like it would be a criminal act in itself to toss it into the Thames, though this might have been Benedict's addictive personality talking. That was always his problem as an antiques dealer, he could never give his stock away. And this addiction now kicked in, defying reason. Why should he give it away? If it was nearly the perfect crime, nobody would ever come troubling him to cough up the loot because nobody except a hill farmer who wanted nothing to do with it knew. And most importantly of all, this item, this sword haft with it's ruby garnish, went a long way to proving that the parchment, still neatly tucked away in his jacket pocket, was not the fanciful scribbling of a day-dreaming blacksmith, but very possibly real. He had in his possession, the unlikely and long hidden first piece of the riddle. How could he give that away now? If anything he was doing his country a service by providing an unusual and anonymous place of safekeeping for this artefact. If he and Tristan could sneak onto a large army barracks without so much as a by-your-leave, he was sure that the renegade bunch of Frenchies could try it also, although security now would be ridiculously tight after the embarrassment the barracks was faced with. He tossed the sword haft around in his hands, like he tossed the decision around in his mind. There was a return to respectfulness and a move away from illegality on the one hand and shiny objects, high adventure and ancient mysteries on the other. This was not a decision to be taken lightly, but a decision had to be made nonetheless. Benedict figured time was his enemy here. If he held onto the loot and did nothing, eventually the story might appear in the papers though it had been hushed up so far. And Mrs McDoughty, moral busy-body hypocrite that she was, might tidy his room one day and take a peek into the rucksack. Then pandemonium would break lose. No, if he was keeping it, it was for the original purpose, to solve the riddle. He'd keep it well hidden and give himself four or five weeks to solve the puzzle. If he couldn't, Benedict thought he might pluck the stones out of their fixings. They'd make a fine pair of earrings or a pendant for a lady friend or wife one day.

Benedict heard the faint trill of the doorbell ringing. He waited a moment to hear the put-out steps and sighs of Mrs McDoughty going to see who it was, whilst mumbling that she was not the valet. But the doorbell was left wanting as nothing but the occasional sound of London echoed round the house.

"I say, Mrs McD, would you mind?!" Benedict yelled.

There was still no reply. Even his housekeeper wasn't that rude. *Bugger, she must be out*, he thought.

The doorbell rang again, two short trills, as if there was impatience in the finger of the doorbell presser. Benedict stared up at the ceiling as he had done for the past two days, resigned himself to the fact that this was the moment he would leave the comfort of his bed, and then groaned and wheezed his way to an upright position. The bell went a third time and Benedict bellowed down the stairs as he threw on a dressing gown, "Yes, alright, I'm an invalid, there's no call for impatience!"

He finally reached the door and nearly fell over weak kneed when he saw who was on the other side, a policeman, Constable Lemon in fact. Guilty, red faced, high pitched conversation from Benedict then ensued. "Oh hello Occifer, I mean Officer, what can I do you for today?"

Lemon, looked Benedict up and down, taking in his garb, finding it strange as it was one in the afternoon.

"Sorry sir, have I caught you at an awkward time?" Lemon politely asked, pushing his round specs up the bridge of his nose.

Benedict looked down at himself and said, "Oh, pardon. No, not at all, bad back you see, been laid up for the past couple of days."

"Oh, apologies sir, I hope I didn't get you up."

"No no," assured Benedict, waving away the comment. "Been up a while, just making a pot of tea, can I interest you in a cup?" That was a stupid idea, bringing in the fuzz whilst the stolen artefact was just upstairs, a wave of nervous heat nearly made Benedict retch.

"I'd better not sir, just doing my beat at the moment, very kind of you to offer though. I was just checking to see if you'd had any further disturbances or seen anything else suspicious following your incident a couple of days ago." Benedict paused, looking at the young policeman, all good intentions and naivety. Benedict pinched his lips together, looking like he'd really considered the question and then said, "No....no, I haven't." He feigned interest, "Any good leads your end?"

"We took a good look at the poor chap that got splattered by the lorry, but there were no identification papers on him." Lemon paused to consider what other intelligence they'd gathered. He startled himself with surprise, "Oooh, we know that he's possibly French," then he looked disappointed, "But I think you told us that."

"Well, it's good to see how my taxes are invested," Benedict sarcastically remarked.

Lemon didn't get the insult and tipped his helmet in acknowledgement, "Kind of you to say, doing our best sir."

Benedict rolled his eyes, "So, to summarise, you have come here to check everything is okay and whether I have any further information other than the statement and scene of crime investigation you completed two nights ago."

Lemon thought it over and then drew a conclusion, "Yes, I think that just about covers it."

"Jolly good, well if I find a baguette in the fireplace disguised as a firearm or anything, I'll let you know. Now if you please I must rest. Good day Officer."

"Cheerio," said the happy but gormless Lemon as the door closed in his face.

As soon as the latch clicked shut, Benedict leant on the back of the door and breathed a heavy sigh of relief. That could have been a lot, lot worse. *Thank heavens for police incompetence even at my own expense*, he thought. Still, that brief meeting with the authorities had clarified his mind. To continue his personal quest and hold onto the loot for the time being he needed to be away from London, away from acting suspiciously around Mrs McDoughty and the police. But where? It was at this point he noticed the scrap of paper with an address on it, in very neat handwriting, resting on the hallway sideboard.

Chapter 15

As plans go this was possibly as citrus fruity as the assistant to Constable Randolph, a bit of a lemon. But in his panicky state, it was the best that Benedict could come up with at short notice. And like all bad ideas, once Benedict was drawn to it, it was like being a moth seeing a very bright light bulb.

Benedict had packed and readied himself for at least a fortnight's worth of escape. This was to be a time where he could ponder and reflect on the riddle and whether any further leads could be generated from it. He'd taken out the small parchment and read again the next line in the mystery.

All false is this above provided
By heinous words of ill-founded power
Come the crown which once Boudicca wore
British rule is installed and Rome shall cower.
Four rubies that were taken from foolish Claudius
Coronet of Wales for beginning and end

Coronet of Wales, it was a puzzler. Had there been any kings of Wales? Not to do the people of Wales a disservice, but he'd neither learnt about them at school or ever heard any passing person mention them. It was all God save the King, Henry VIII and what Elizabeth did next. Britain was British, not Welsh. Benedict thought he'd go away and think on it for a while and if the answer was not forthcoming, he'd bin the haft for some lucky tramp to find and keep the rubies for himself. It was more than a little recompense for being left out of pocket for the burglary. This seemed a sensible enough stratagem. Even the location of his little break away seemed logical, Wales. However, the exact location, considering the item he was taking and moral dissonance he'd already put one particular man through on this quest, could not be considered a tip top idea.

He'd left two hours after Constable Lemon had departed. In haste he'd had no time to explain his actions to his housekeeper so Benedict scribbled a half-hearted note to Mrs McDoughty on a note pad and left it on the sideboard by the front door.

"Dear Mrs McD. Sorry to desert you again at short notice. Feeling awfully down-at-heel over recent events and need some time away from the big smoke. Have been told of a delightful farm over in Powys. Am going to take in the air for a fortnight. Back soon, help yourself to the larder, ~~not that that's stopped you before; have you seen your ever expanding reflection recently? It's like a new universe is forming wearing a pinny.~~ Here's a shiny shilling for your trouble. Love and yours ever, Benedict".

He'd then closed the door to his house, stepped out into the afternoon haze of West London and made for the Phantom in the little lock up.

Benedict had left at entirely the wrong time of day to ensure he'd reach Llandrindod at any reasonable hour, but it didn't bother him. The sense of wanderlust was making his exit from the capital feel relieving and he liked the idea of finding a small, off the beaten track inn or hotel to make his bed for the night. At about nine in the evening, he found a small bed and breakfast outside Cheltenham and checked in for the night.

After the best night's sleep he'd had in a long time in a soft springy bed and a full English breakfast served by the dough armed hotel owner, he was refreshed and ready for his journey through Herefordshire and across the border into Wales. Benedict regularly stopped at the road side as the ride in the Phantom was beginning to wear thing on him and for the additional requirement to stretch out his back which was still not quite right. Making good time, he ploughed through the English countryside until the major roads at last gave way to small country lanes and the signs were in both English and Welsh. The rolling countryside was not bereft of beautiful scenery and regardless of his motives, Benedict was already feeling his cares slip away. The small farmhouse he was heading for was near Llandrindod, mid Powys. He knew the book of maps he'd brought would only get him so far and after finding the market town, he asked directions from a middle aged woman on the high street, worn down by her two eager progeny that were scampering around her feet on the pavement. She saw him coming and looked delighted to have some normal adult conversation even if it was just which road to take.

"Good woman, could you tell me the way to Fourth Hill Farm please."

"Oh, no bother, though you'll need to turn your car around. It's straight up this lane here, about a mile and then you'll see their sign post and mail box up the right at a cross roads. You can't miss it. Oh, the Bradfields, lovely couple. Can't have kids though, I'd give em mine if I thought they'd take them! Staying long?"

Benedict hadn't prepared for this next question, and said, "Er yes, cheerio." He then turned the Phantom around in the street and sped off in the opposite direction.

Disgruntled by the lack of conversation, she grumbled, "Bloody foreigners, don't ask me how my day is going will you! William put down that cat stool, you know perfectly well where it's been!"

Benedict's car wound it's way through the tight cobbled streets of the Welsh town, past pub and post office until he was out the other side and speeding through country again. The woman had been accurate with her directions as the small country road, flanked either side with a field of cows and a field of sheep, gave way to a cross roads. On the right hand direction there was a sign saying Fourth Hill Farm and a post box. Benedict took the Phantom round the corner onto the dirt track. A late spring shower suddenly started to beat heavily on the roof of the car to meet the percussion of the tyres rolling over old mud and pebble alike. The dirt track ran over a brook and then swung left to the large expanse of an old stone farm house with a beautiful front garden in bloom from the great weather they'd been having, old barns loaded with hay and a gaggle of geese making their way across the yard. Benedict swung around next to one of the barns and peered out of the driver's side window. The singular black cloud was soaking probably a couple of square miles, directly where Benedict had travelled. It did rather make him look like a portent of doom he thought. The rain was thick stuff though; the heads on some of the flowers were bent over, struggling with the sudden weight of the rainwater heaving at their petals. He could have waited for five minutes and it would have passed, but his arrival had been noticed as a net curtain in one of the front windows twitched and shortly after, the front door had opened.

A smallish woman in a floral dress and pinafore was standing crossed armed in the farmhouse doorway peering out. There was nothing for it, it would be rude to sit in the car. He opened the car door and scuttled round to the boot. Shielding his head by pulling his tweed jacket over it, he lifted the boot lid as a proper soaking was administered. Benedict yanked the leather handle of the travel bag out of the compartment, slamming the lid shut and then jogged elegantly across the courtyard to the lady at the front door. As he arrived she took his bag, flung it behind her and pulled out a towel that had been tucked into the tie of her pinny. The woman engulfed Benedict's face and wet hair with it, the soft material finding moisture and caressing it off him. He was guided blindly into the hallway and the front door closed behind him. He put his hands up to his towelled face and finished the job, drying his top half to a perfectly acceptable damp feeling. He pulled the towel away, handing it to the unfamiliar stranger behind him.

Benedict breathed in the aroma of the house, a slight dash of mint, mixed with a boiled vegetable smell. He was in a short hallway with a staircase just after a door ajar on his left where he could see a comfortable looking sitting room. Further down the hallway he could see a door on the right which was presumably where the dining room was and then a final doorway at the end opposite the entrance where the vegetal smells were emanating from, the kitchen. Wellingtons on newspaper lined the wall where he stood.

Benedict smoothed down the thin, soft hair that remained on his quickly receding hairline and turned to the short lady standing next to him, beaming up, all rosy cheeked and smile lines. She had a round face with quite a tight curl to her long frizzy and slightly unkempt hair. Her face showed time in the sun and laughter and there was mischievousness about her looks. She smiled widely at him, clasping the wet towel in her hands. He grinned back full of cautious gratitude. She immediately took the opportunity to get the first word in and very helpfully set expectations.

"Now then dear, are you a funny religion, a door to door salesman or a confidence trickster?"

Benedict didn't think a confidence trickster would answer yes, but also thought that by answering no, it wouldn't cloud her judgement, "No."

"Good, because if you are, then a good towelling off is all you're getting before I send you on your way. Now, who are you?"

"Yes," Benedict had to think on his feet as the entrance to the farm had all been too quick. "I'm Benedict Bryant-Lukely," he extended a hand which was pumped vigorously by the woman. He assumed that as a working farmer's wife, her hands would be all hard and calloused, but instead they were baby smooth.

"What lovely hands you have," Benedict complemented. The smile widened to the point where it threatened to slide off her face, "Bull's semen my dear, I swear by it."

Benedict felt a lot less like shaking her hand.

"And I am Mfanwy Bradfield. So then Mr Lukely, what brings you to Fourth Hill farm on such a changeable day? Not brought the weather with you I hope."

Benedict thought back to him being a portent of doom when he arrived and raised an eyebrow.

"I too hope not. No, I was invited here by, I believe, your cousin? Tristan?"

She chuckled, "Oh, he's not my cousin. No he's my husband's, Gwyffan". She looked past Benedict and shrieked "Tristan? Someone here for you dear!"

Benedict noticed that there had been a good humoured murmur and occasional laughter coming from the kitchen. It got louder as he who was summoned approached the door.

"......and he said, it wasn't sausage...it was a", Tristan clapped eyes on Benedict, ".....horses........Hello?"

Benedict went into his act, "Ah Tristan old chum, how are you?" Benedict walked up to Tristan and slapped his back, thereby knocking the poor man into the wall.

Tristan laughed an uncertain and nervous laugh and said, "Well, this is a surprise........"

"Yes! Thank you for inviting me to such a plush old farm house, didn't you tell these lovely people I'd be coming? They look surprised!" Benedict said with false bravado and smiles.

Tristan was rather lost for words, "Er well, I...."

"Don't introduce me then," replied Benedict jokily, bounding forward to shake the hand of gruff looking man who had now appeared behind Tristan.

"You must be Gwyffan, Tristan's told me all about you!"

That was a complete lie and Benedict felt his rear end tighten as he waited for the obligatory, suspicious response. It didn't come, in fact, Gwyffan fell hook line and sinker for the act and reached forward to meet Benedict, "Nothin dirty I ope." He winked, grinned and tugged on a pipe with his lips. Mfanwy had come forward to join them, Tristan still looked like he'd just been mugged and was rather dazed by the whole affair.

"Well there's always a warm bed and mutton for friends of the family. It looks like the shower has passed, have you anything else to carry in? Gwyffan could pop out and get it."

"Slave driver!" Gwyffan joked.

Benedict cast his mind to the boot of the car and could only think of the sword haft in the duffle bag.

"No no", he replied with too much urgency, "Nothing else to come in, just me and this bag I'm afraid."

"Lovely," said Mfanwy who took up the leather handle and began to walk up the stairs to an unseen guestroom.

"Well, I loves a good guest and there's only just one condition on you staying..." Benedict waited for Gwyffan's request with keen anticipation.

"We've just had a lovely lamb lunch. Tristan is the washer upper, you can be the dryer." He amused himself, chuckling as he took another tug on his pipe and then slapped Benedict with a damp tea towel.

Benedict hated washing up, hence why Mrs McDoughty existed in his life.

Despite the vigour and noisy energy that the plate washing created as the house's finest china was cleansed of carrot and gravy, the atmosphere between Tristan and Benedict could be sliced with a knife and served with a refreshing cup of Ceylon tea. As they were alone in the kitchen, Tristan made sure only to focus on the suds and their contents underneath the water, racking up the clean crockery and pots and pans. Benedict looked on with tea towel in hand. They were the epitome of a broken relationship and so he thought he should say something.

"Lovely views of the back garden," he said, voice higher than normal and raspy from a dry throat.

Tristan did not look up. "Why are you here?" he asked as he ran the hot, wet cloth through a steel pan, eyes squarely on the task at hand. He was clearly nonplussed.

Benedict sighed and walked across the expansive kitchen to a pine sideboard where pretty plates were racked on their sides, held by a slender wooden banister in front of them. He slid the plate he'd been drying into position.

"Well, I thought long and hard about what you said to me when you left and if anything it gave me some clarity on the situation?"

"And what decision did you come to?" asked Tristan, not looking over his shoulder.

"Well I decided to get out of London, come up here, didn't I?!" replied Benedict with a hint of obtuseness about him.

Tristan span round, dripping cloth in hand. "Hardly a decision then was it? No clarity there, you still got it?"

Benedict paused and said, "It's in a safe place for now, I need some time to get my head straight, but I'll probably end up ditching it."

Tristan tutted and turned away, "Safe place? Knowing you, it's probably in the boot of your car."

Benedict flushed red behind him.

After the climax of pot washing duties and the eventually placement of said pans in their correct home by the ever busy Mfanwy, everyone settled into comfy armchairs in the bright and colourful living room. A large bay window which looked out on to the driveway and a field of sheep to the right, provided substantial light and the open space which stretched to the back of the house was inviting and happy. Colourful throws covered the careworn armchairs and paintings of green fields and autumnal shades graced the walls. A sizeable wireless rested in the bay of the window. All kicked their heels back and supped from pea green cups and saucers.

The ever smoking Gwyffan reached down the side of the sofa cushion where his buttocks were resting and rather than bringing up lint and a penny or two, pulled out another cob pipe. He reached down the other side and there found his leather packet of pipe tobacco. He deftly fingered the pouch open and started to eagerly filling the bowl. As he worked, he spoke to Benedict.

"So then Mr Lukely, how do you know old Tris?"

It was time to lie again. Benedict considered that there was a risk that Tristan could totally expose him for a liar, but if there was one thing he knew from their brief friendship, it was that Tristan hated overexposure. He would just have to sit there and simmer.

"Oh this old cove and I, we've known each other for a while now," he said. Out the corner of his eye he saw Tristan begin to squirm a little in his chair like a worm on a hook. "It turns out we're both keen Philatelists."

"I luvs a bit of philately!" Gwyffan expressed.

"No dear, you luvs flatulence," Mfanwy corrected.

"Oh yes, that's right." Gwyffan produced a little squeaker to emphasis his point and giggled.

Briefly looking disgusted, Benedict continued, "If I may continue, we're both part of the National Association of Philatelists, or NAP for short."

"Sends me to sleep, I'll give you that", said Gwyffan, Mfanwy threw a cushion at him.

"We attended the same annual general meeting back in November last year, in Bristol, got chatting and had a lot in common."

Gwyffan lit up his pipe, "Didn't know you were a stamp collector Tris?"

"Oh yes, stamps, dead keen me," he deadpanned. "Can't get enough of em, might be addicted to the glue on the back." He glared at Benedict who couldn't hold his gaze. Benedict continued talking at his hosts.

"Yes, Tristan recently had a lovely stay with me in Kensington."

"Very eventful it was."

Benedict gave an overly fake laugh and said, "Indeed, and Tristan mentioned that he was coming to see you and that the air in London paled in comparison to the tonic-like winds of Mid Wales."

"Can get a breeze up here, no doubt," added Mfanwy.

"Well quite," replied Benedict, "And having felt in quite a malaise, I thought I'd try the free tonic."

He could have left it there and by golly Tristan hoped he would, but he didn't. "And as the absolute encore, Tristan was telling me of some of the wonderful mythology of the place. Dragons? Daffodils? Leeks? Sheep? Wonderful stuff."

Benedict's vehement stereotyping of the Welsh people as a race thankfully fell on deaf ears as his hosts just looked on a little perplexed.

"But the story that really took my breath away was that there used to be a Welsh King! Couldn't believe it, I thought that the monarchy of the British Isles had all started at 1066 with William the Conqueror but no, apparently Wales was doing it's own thing a lot earlier!"

Tristan slid into his chair further, apparently trying to merge with the seat cover out of sheer embarrassment.

"Couldn't believe it! What was the chap's name again? Lewis? Lewin?"

Mfanwy had the answer, "Llewellyn you mean?"

Benedict poured on a further generous helping of mock surprise, "Yes, that's the fellow, stupid old me with my Lewins! What a fascinating story!"

"Oh really, what have you heard? I don't know his story either," said Gwyffan with genuine interest.

Benedict had overstepped the mark now, he could have stopped at hearing of Llewellyn, kept it clean. But no, he had to overegg the pudding with a story.

"Well, that obviously….he was not a man………a man to be…….trifled with…….killed a few….dragons and…………apparently………….he used to be friends with Queen Boudicca?…….."

"Blimey, you seem to know a lot about this stuff Benedict?" said Gwyffan, following his statement up with a perfect smoke ring.

"Apparently so," replied an unhappy looking Tristan, speaking for his houseguest.

"They reckons he's buried round here don't they Gwyffan?" said Mfanwy.

"Oh yeah, forgot about that. Over by old Cwmhir Abbey, last resting place of the great king so they say."

If Benedict's ears could have pricked up any more he'd have looked like an overexcited collie discovering the recipe for Winalot.

"Oh really?" he looked at Tristan with an evil glint in his eyes, "How….very…..interesting." Benedict licked his lips and returned his attention to Gwyffan. "Is this last resting place close by?"

"Crikey yes, it's about a fifteen minute walk, just off the village. Not a lot to see though, just a disused monastery, all faded, crumbly stonework and the like."

"But still, I'm sure we.." he looked over at Tristan, "can fit in a little amble down some lanes to take it in."

"I think I'm coming down with something," replied Tristan, trying to escape the inevitable.

"Excellent, then it's settled. If the weather improves, you can take me there tomorrow and the fresh air will do you good," chimed Benedict.

"Too right," added Mfanwy, "You've been moping round this house for the past two days Tristan. About time you got out and stretched your legs."

Tristan could do nothing but give a deeply resigned sigh.

The evening passed in a haze of port, cheese and biscuits. After the journey, Benedict could have done with something more substantial, but he understood they'd had a full leg of lamb for lunch and he didn't want to intrude. Mfanwy and Gwyffan were also more than capable hosts, keeping his glass topped up and the Glamorgan Blue coming while ensuring the conversation was at the very least amusing. Furthermore, the news that King Lewellyn was close at hand was enough to take his mind off his cheese-lined stomach. Suddenly and coincidentally, coming up here had been the peachiest thing that could have happened and given direction to the broad plateau of options that had previous stretched endlessly in front of him. He would keep the sword haft, at least until he had ruled out any connection or evidence of Llewellyn from the riddle. Crown of Llewellyn; surely it was safe to assume that it had been found by now? How did one mislay a jewel encrusted circular hat of gold? Assuming of course it was made of gold, it could have been made out of stereotypical leeks and daffs he thought. But the mere mention of his name was hope indeed. The heady port was sending Benedict to sleep and after too much conversation it was time for an early bed. Benedict made his excuses and made his way upstairs.

Chapter 16

Morning came and Benedict awoke with an energy and vigour he hadn't felt since he was nine when he had successfully found his Christmas presents two days early thereby informing him of the toy artillery set he was getting and what uses he could put it to in annoying his brother Chalfont. As he swung his legs over the side of his comfy billet, the smell of sausages and bacon, crisping in a pan not too far away filled his lungs. The sun was shining through the thin curtains of this box room, illuminating the mauve floral wall paper. The birds were singing and everything felt right with the world.

Having wash and dressed and wearing a white shirt, brown sweater and olive chords, Benedict literally danced down the stairs towards the kitchen and the full English that was waiting there to increase his cholesterol issues. He shimmied to the table, ignoring Tristan's bland staring, instead embracing Mfanwy to her surprise and then giving Gwyffan a squeeze of the shoulder before explaining it had been the best night's sleep in a long time and that he felt like a new man.

"That's the Welsh air for you," explained Gwyffan, tending to the pink side of a banger.

After the erroneously named hearty breakfast and a couple of mugs of strong tea, Mfanwy performed admirably at the task that Benedict had been trying to figure out how to do whilst mopping up egg and grease with a piece of buttered bread.

"Looks like you've got a lovely day for your walk your two."

Thank you thought Benedict. He looked, wide eyed at Tristan, who dismissed his longing puppy dog-like looks.

"I'm not really feeling up to it if I'm honest," Tristan replied.

Mfanwy, ever the terrier with a bone on all issues, barked back, "Oh come on you miserable so and so, go out and get some sun. The summer's come early and you're as white as a pond lily! If I'm perfectly honest, you're under my feet and the rugs could do with a beating. Now get out there, treat your friend with some hospitality and show him what we've got to offer, go on!" And she shepherded Tristan out to get his shoes. Benedict gave a friendly smile as thanks.

Shown to the door and with the recommendation of the Wily Stag as a good place for a spot of lunch, both men headed out, waved off at the front door by Mfanwy. They walked with the awkwardness and shyness of two nervous schoolboys on the first day of term. If it had been starchy and difficult in the house, it was unbearable now. However, once out of earshot and down the driveway, it was clear that Tristan had had enough and was first to fire a verbal salvo.

"This is a ridiculous hunt you know?"

"I beg pardon?"

Tristan stopped and turned to Benedict, "This, this search. I know what you've heard. There you were making up a story about how we knew each other, which was about as factual as Grimm's fairytales by the way and would see you lynched by about three quarters of the local population. You've spouted your little lies about some random stamp club and then thrown in Llewellyn from the riddle, just for good measure. Having received an unusual and surprising response that Llewellyn may have actually existed, your reasons for coming up here have now changed from decision making about the riddle to continue to finding the bloody thing. Well I can tell you now sonny, you're in for a day of disappointment!" He turned back and began walking again.

Benedict continued also, unperturbed by the attitude just shown to him, he'd rather been expecting it.

They trudged along the farm track for a further few minutes. Then Benedict asked the question that had been burning in him since Tristan's little outburst. "So you knew about Llewellyn then?"

They stopped and faced each other again. Tristan seemed more humane this time, the rollicking before seemingly having released a lot of pent up frustration.

"I did, it's one of those myths that you hear about as a child. And I knew that if I told you about it and that my relatives lived round the flaming corner of the alleged burial place of King Llewellyn, you would continue to pursue this pointless and at times illegal whim. I'd rather not have anything more to do with it."

They set off walking again. After a pause, Benedict talked as they strolled up another lane outside the village where Cwmhir Abbey was signposted.

"Look, I threw Llewellyn in as I was stuck for knowledge of anything Welsh. Llewellyn sounds Welsh. I suppose I rather hit the jackpot."

"I suppose that's one way of looking at it."

"Look, I understand if you want out. We've done some daft things together already which for most would be the final spasm. But regardless of kings and crowns and old riddles, you're a chum, a pal, a friend. I had more fun in London with a complete stranger in a week than I had with all my jumped up society friends since I've known them. You've made me full of joie de vivre Tristan Wynd. If nothing else, come up to the abbey with me, let's see what there is to see and then I'll treat you to a pub luncheon and we can spend the rest of our short time relaxing. Do you play bridge or cribbage?

"Not in so many words, no."

"I'll teach you."

"As long as I don't have to distract an entire brigade of soldiers again, I'll think about it."

He gave Benedict a nod and the fragile bond of friendship was repaired.

Sadly, Tristan's outburst was not far from the truth. It seemed that this really was folly in an area that frankly looked like a folly and the weather soured with Benedict's mood. They passed through a wooded copse and there on the other side found the ancient ruins of Cwmhir Abbey. Whilst the dark stonework still held together despite the elements, to form walls and the occasional arch of a former window, the ruins were patchy and the interior non-existent, grass and weeds occupying what was formally an important religious space. Cwmhir was erected in the eleventh century and had been a much contested site prior to it's dissolution. Now, stone walls and a peaceful soft whistling of the wind was all the abbey could offer. The wonderful clear blue sky that Benedict had awoken to was slowly being replaced by thick grey cloud and once overhead, a soft, miserable drizzle began to make it's way down. Neither Benedict or Tristan had anticipated the change in weather and so both were slowly getting drenched by the unsuspecting mist falling from the heavens. Tristan knew it was time to go, but also knew to humour Benedict, letting him probe every remaining wall and lump if they had to, to prove there was nothing in the riddle that connected the mysterious Llewellyn to this place. Besides, it was hardly a renowned tourist spot and they were alone in their investigations.

After a good hour of peering, poking and picking, Benedict was well and truly beaten. He felt his shoulders fall and realised he was sopping wet. He looked at Tristan, who peered back at him from rain covered eyebrows and offered an apology.

"Sorry, for dragging you out in this."

"Oh it's no bother," replied Tristan with humility.

Tristan reached down and ran his fingers over the stumpy grass, connecting with a small piece of flinty rock which presumably was once part of much larger piece of the structure. He tossed it vertically into the air and caught it in his jacket pocket, surprising himself in the process. "I think I'll keep that as a souvenir of our trip!"

Benedict flapped his arms, "Pub?"

"Pub" replied a much happier Tristan.

Llandrindod was not a stone's throw from the abbey and both men were glad to get away from the stark wet afternoon and into the Wiley Stag. The town was small enough so that everyone knew each other in that, "Morning David, how's the missus?" kind of way, but large enough that it had supplies for everything it needed and a few luxuries to boot. It had prospered as a trading hub and had grown into a major stopover for travelling salesmen and traders alike, so everyone received a warmer welcome than some of the "You're not from round these parts" villages that were close by. The Stag itself was an old large coaching inn, warm and welcoming with room for a good turnover of guests to stay. It's old tudor whitewashed walls, both inside and out gave off a coolness in the summer, but a great roaring hearth, centred right in the middle of the main lounge heated the place up superbly in the colder months. The bar was glowing with the happy drone of locals laughing over their pints and travelling folk telling stories. As a couple of strangers to the town, Benedict and Tristan walked in anonymously and were immediately at ease with everyone else. The barman pulled a couple of ales for them with a soft creamy head and malty flavour and both took a long gulp on their pints. They found a table near the bar and settled in. Benedict still looked particularly dejected, despite the cheery atmosphere of this hostelry. Tristan looked around, trying to find something to take his friend's mind off things.

"Hey, I tell you what. The landlady here, she's a bit special see?" he conferred in a whisper.

Benedict looked over to the buxom looking woman behind the bar. She didn't seem that special in his eyes. Happy enough, happier than he certainly was as she laughed flirtatiously with her customers. She was a tall woman, in the high fives, auburn hair contrasted by her pale freckly skin. She wore a low cut top, flashing a fairly ample cleavage that was on it's way south. Benedict had no doubt she kept her customers drinking without having to do so much as bend over the pump slightly and give a flirty smile. He turned back and shrugged, "What's so special about her?"

Tristan lent forward as if to impart some great secret, "Well apparently, she once had a love affair with one of the world's greatest pastry chefs." He winked a knowing wink.

"Really?" said Benedict, underwhelmed by this scandal.

"And," Tristan continued, "He imparted on her, the secrets of his oven so to speak and apparently she's one of the finest bakers in, well, at least Powys."

"Lovely," said Benedict, not at all impressed. But with the mood he was in he'd have needed to be told she could fly and regularly stopped the world from spinning just for larks, to be even remotely wowed.

"Yes!" said Tristan excitedly, "I know, let's see if I can procure some of her handiwork."

He got up from his stool and walked across to the bar. Benedict cast a further glance over his shoulder and saw Tristan engaging the landlady in chatter and before long, smiles, money and a plate were exchanged. Tristan came back to the table, beaming with boyish pleasure at the tasty morsels which sat on the crockery in front of him.

"This one's a local honey tartlet, and this one's a wild strawberry whirl, which one d'you want?" he asked. Benedict mused over the sticky goods. To the landlady's credit, both did look exquisite. But with strawberries coming into season, he could have honey any time of the year. "I'll have the whirl please".

Tristan looked a little deflated, not that that was going to stop Benedict who was firmly wearing his, "Obstinate child, in a strop and needs cake to placate him," hat. He slipped a plate from underneath the one that was holding the pastries and took the strawberry whirl. Benedict bit into the cake and at once his mouth was filled with the most extravagant memories of strawberry picking with family, hot summer's days when swallows cried out and the heat baked the pale skin on his neck to a bright red and then a deep brown as the salad days rolled on. And the pastry; he wondered if some of the top restaurants in London could do better and doubted it. Crisp, sweet, light as a feather, but unpretentious, as if his grandmother herself was in the room baking the cakes.

"Good lord, these are impressive. I wonder who she trained with?"

Tristan didn't answer, he was too busy making orgasmic faces just above the brim of his plate. Benedict had devoured his in one, but Tristan was taking the time to savour every morsel as if it was a substantial Sunday dinner. It seemed to take forever for him to eat and Benedict was quite glad when a couple of local farmhands engaged himself in conversation rather than watching the gurning twerp come to climax in front of him. The cakes were tasty, but come on now.

"Here, mate, enjoying Bessie's cakes are you?"

Benedict looked to the bar and saw that the two fellows were clearly both back from a day in the field. Both were of stocky build, wearing blue dungarees over tatty shirts and heavy boots which were muddy from the pastures they'd been working in. The one who addressed him was a slightly older gentleman. His receding hairline and large mutton chop sideburns were once a golden ginger but now heading towards a sickly yellow white colour. His friend was completely bald, red and ruddy, heavy skin on the face making him look rather like a humanoid beagle. His voice, was a deep bass and cavernous and matched his hound-like features.

"Looks, like they have Howell. Look at his mate, look at his little hampster cheeks going," he said with more of a Bristol accent.

Tristan shrugged and threw up his hands mumbling, "I can't help it, these are bloody brilliant."

"So, not familiar with your faces. You come far?"

"London."

"Ooh, a posh boy Howell. Business or pleasure?"

"Pleasure mostly, my friend has some family up here, thought we'd take the air so to speak, do you know the Bradfields?"

The other man next to Howell, tutted, and ran his hands over his greasy brow. "How few Bradfields do you think there's going to be? I can think of at least......three that live here. You might like to be more specific."

Benedict was a little taken aback by the dourness of this other chap, with a face as maudlin as his prospects.

"Oh, sorry." Tristan chipped in with a cakey response, "You know Mfanwy and Gwyffan?"

Howell smiled, "Oh yes, lovely pair. They're a nice couple as well". Both men fell about in guffaws, Benedict knew it was in reference to Mfanwy's ample chest. When they had recovered sufficient resolve, Howell continued, "So, you been seeing a few of the sights today then, hills and valleys and whatnot?"

"Yes, we've been over by the abbey today, Cwmhir is it?"

"Oh the abbey!" said the ruddy looking one, "Lovely spot for a picnic with the missus I find, good bit a history there too." He propped himself up against the bar and his face turned stern and teacher-like. "Apparently, one of the last kings of Wales was buried there, chap called Llewellyn."

Benedict rejoined the conversation, "So we've heard, we walked over there today to see if there was any truth in the matter."

Howell laughed, "Only truth you'll find there my friend is the definition of the word ruin. Nowt but old rock, solemn memories and ghosts round there if you believe the stories. It is rumoured that if at midnight, you stand naked in front of the abbey, with a daff shoved up your arse and sing the hymn 'Love divine, all loves excelling' then the king will appear in front of you, though why you have to be naked is beyond me. Perhaps the king was a bit fruity."

"That is a lovely hymn," said Tristan staring off into the distance. The two goons at the bar heard what he said and called him a silly sod, offending him.

The fancy pastries had brightened Benedict's mood for about half an hour, but the walk back was tentative, slow and Tristan knew that his companion was thinking about the shortcomings of his misadventure. Tomorrow he would be turning for home, with nothing to show for his endeavours except perhaps a warrant for his arrest. Tristan was glad it was over but a part of him felt for his friend. They would entertain him tonight to send him on his way happier than when he arrived, if he was leaving of course, which as it currently stood, was not a definite.

Chapter 17

After a delicious chicken dinner, a high volume of port and sherry imbibed and so much waltzing in the back garden that Mfanwy was sick in a bin, it was time for bed. A clearly trolleyed Mfanwy waved goodnight to the boys, wiped sick from her hair and commanded Gwyffan to take her to bed. "Not often I get requests like that," he jested, rubbing his big choppy sideburns as both of them disappeared inside. As it was now dark, Tristan and Benedict also strolled to the house from the wonderful evening in the back garden, across the green lawn, back through the kitchen and into the comfort of the lounge. Benedict walked over to the drinks cabinet, pulled out a Speyside malt and poured himself and Tristan a decent measure.

"To your health and family's hospitality, cheers."

Benedict raised his glass to meet Tristan's and then enjoyed the sensation of the delicate peaty flavours running down his throat. He stood, poised for a moment, allowing the smoky tones of the liquor to run through him. He slouched into an old red velvet armchair next to the cabinet and let his legs splay in an ungainly fashion. Regardless of his toasting health, he looked as sick as a dog. Tristan sensed that the moment was right to close the chapter, similarly sought out at an equally ill worn chair opposite him. They both sat in the perfect peace of the late spring night. An owl occasionally reminded the world that the darkness was not a soundless vacuum but otherwise the cool rumble of nothingness came from outside one of the ajar bay windows. Tristan took a sip of the single malt and coughed, spluttering immediately. Benedict sniggered. "Not on good terms with the stronger stuff are you?" he said.

"To be honest I've never really drunk spirits apart from the occasional brandy down the pub. I don't really know what I'm doing."

"It's an acquired taste I think, but as you get older, you happen upon the stuff more and more and I think you just grow to accept it and then like it."

"Devil's cough mixture, that's what my mum used to say to me."

"I'd laugh, but she's probably right."

Tristan left a pause, he wanted to move onto more pressing matters, "But, can we speak freely now, as friends do to each other. It won't do, this dwelling on what could be. I sense behind this veil of discovery and adventure, a lonely man who hasn't quite figured out his purpose in life."

"You got all that from a week with me, good grief. Do you know anyone called Freud by any chance?"

"Don't know the fellow, the point is, that I think perhaps, I represented an opportunity to you. We happened upon a quest of sorts, and given my naivety in the circumstance you saw me as someone who would easily join your merry band and enjoy high adventure with you. But as we now know, come tomorrow morning I'll go back to my life and you'll go back to yours and this quest, this daring, criminal, laugh-some, dangerous quest will be over. And for why? Because we now know Boudicca's crown either doesn't exist or is so strewn around, both geographically and historically that Boudicca's crown can now only fail to exist. Either way, this is finished and I'm worried that you'll go back to London and dwell on it and find some other ridiculous avenue where you could get into trouble or start chasing some other fantasy."

His chin resting on his slumped chest, Benedict considered the scathingly accurate summary. A minute later he murmured, "Well, thank you for the pep talk. You are of course right, but I shall go back to my life of high society and you shall go back to sheep shearing."

It was a low blow; Tristan downed the rest of his whiskey, this time stifling the cough that came from the throat burn and made for the living room door to the stairs. He looked back at Benedict and in one last appeal to reason said, "It doesn't do to dwell on the past."

Tristan closed the door, Benedict listened to the clump clump of footsteps heading towards a room with a soft bed.

Benedict continued to listen out for the floorboards creaking above him, waiting for the moment when the house would fall silent again. He was still in a slumped position, staring out to nothing, dwelling on everything. His final comment to Tristan had been made in poor taste and in the morning he would readily apologise for it, except he wasn't dwelling on the past, far from it. He was thinking about the immediate future, or by checking his watch, the future approximately forty five minutes away. It was quarter past eleven by his reckoning and he'd need to be in a certain abbey by midnight.

He needed to prepare, needed to assemble his props for the theatrical night ahead. But inertia gripped him to the seat, like invisible claws had bound his legs hard into the chair. Anticipation and tricks whispered sweet nothings in the quiet rumble of the night, giving the kind of false movement and sound that only a four year old can give physical form and be frightened of. Benedict couldn't move, aware of his task and how pressing it was becoming, but still stalling. He was frozen, stuck in a moral dilemma, a moment only a criminal can know before actively committing the crime. It was that moment which evaluates every reward and every cost associated by that action until gut kicks in and a result of fight or flight occurs.

Another ten minutes passed and still he sat, but pressure began to bear down on his mind and another quick look at his watch made him realise that he would soon be late if he was to undertake this endeavour. Benedict thought that ghosts probably wouldn't take kindly to tardy timekeeping. That pressure made up his mind and Benedict pushed himself up, out of the chair and he started to creep towards the hallway and then the kitchen door. Allowing himself little margin for noise, he gingerly moved on, into the pantry. It was an internal room, so he had no reason to worry about light and so he flicked the switch on. What did the farmhand in the bar say, two leeks? He found the Bradfield's vegetable rack and moved onions aside, withdrew a bag of spuds and there, happened upon three leeks. He quickly quality controlled them, rolling them over between his fingers for inspection. One fell quite short of the mark, all withered and loose. He reasoned that if one was going to get his privates out in public he would do it with a fine medley of vegetables. The other two looked ready for the pot, firm, with that green length dipped in white at the root end. He had two of his props, now he just needed the final adjunct which would be outside.

Benedict crept back through the hallway to the front door and then by some twist of stupidity found himself deciding that it would be absolutely for the best if he went out in some sort of disguise. He reached for the coat rack on the wall and selected what he felt was the right choice for such a momentous occasion. Being removed of any sensible thoughts, Benedict thought the best way to disguise him in late spring was to wear a heavy over coat. At least it was navy and would do a half decent job of shrouding him in the darkness. To finish his ridiculous disguise he spotted a deerstalker and plopped that on his head to complete the look of a mildly vampiric Sherlock Holmes.

Benedict shuffled out the front door, breathing a sigh of relief as the hinges twisted silently, the oil allowing his charade to continue without waking those above. He clicked the front latch shut and crept like a theatrical villain up the gravel driveway to a flower border at the side of the farmhouse. A light attached to one of the barns cast a feint glow over the sleepy flowers. He stared into the various blooms, searching for the yellow which would highlight his choice. Then the truth politely knocked on his addled brain and reminded Benedict that it was nearly summer and all the daffs had stopped shaking their pretty little heads about a month ago. The soily farmhand in the pub had specifically said a daffodil clenched between the bottom cheeks; this could derail everything. Benedict looked at his other non-daff-like but feasible options, a choice between a short stubby marigold and the long stem of a cornflower which was in bud but yet to reveal it's blue loveliness so technically not even a flower yet. Considering the merits of both blooms, it was decided that the stem of the marigold was too short and his backside might swallow the flower whole, irritable leaves and all. No, his weapon of choice would be the cornflower, he could clench the stem and be trouble free from the rest of the plant. Benedict plucked the plant from the base and once again set off on his devious night-time wanderings.

He'd quickly covered the ground between the farm and the end of the small country lane that led from it. The gravel had been tricky to navigate quietly but then the lane had been a quick walk. He met the crossroads and followed the signs back to Cwmhir Abbey. The moon was both blessing and curse. It generated out enough light to guide his footing safely and providing the scant knowledge of shapes ahead but then was bright enough that he too would be highlighted to any late night pedestrians. Fortunately, the geographical location of the farm and the road to Cwmhir was remote enough that only the weirdest of people would be travelling that road at ten to midnight on any ordinary day. Benedict was the only man that fitted that description in the whole of the country on this particular evening.

He made his way to the edge of the wooded copse and walked parallel to the tree line along a worn path to the Abbey. Suddenly a guttural scream rang out to Benedict's right in the wood. Having jumped in surprise into a pot hole and fallen onto his backside, he recognised it for what it was, the call of a roe deer picking it's way gracefully through the bracken. Unnerved and with his heart firmly lodged in his throat, Benedict composed himself, removed his colon from his chest and continued up the small track. He turned the corner of the copse and there, across the poorly rested grass, the old stonework of the abbey lay, broken in front of him.

Now, the chap down the pub hadn't exactly been specific as to where one should drop one's pants and sing hymns in the altogether, so Benedict was presented with a conundrum. There was no real structure to the place anymore, a few walls that formed old windows or arches, but Benedict couldn't tell if he was in the abbey, by a font or in the old vegetable patch. Already there were gaping holes in this plan. Benedict thought about turning back, but after a moment's consideration of the alternative, figured there was nothing else for it. Besides, who cared? No one was about.

Once again, the feeling of the moment was upon him, he froze, listening to the sounds of the country's nocturnal creatures. Benedict looked around the abbey, just to be sure he was totally alone. He paused again for a minute until he was absolutely sure he was the sole occupant, with just the wind for company and then using his feet alternately to hold the other's heel down, slipped out of his brogues. He dropped the two leeks and the stemmy cornflower to the ground and began his urgent strip. Benedict was glad to take off the deerstalker, his head a sweaty mess, through both nerves and the warmth of the late spring night. He gladly threw off the overcoat too and started to set about his trouser belt. His brown coloured cords fell down and he feverishly attacked his shirt buttons, panicking as his hands shook, all fingers and thumbs. At last he got the top button undone and he pulled the shirt off his sweat soaked back. Only his long johns remained but Benedict was hit by a wave of paranoia. He'd left himself unguarded whilst changing. Anyone or anything could have roamed into the area since, a drunkard, a pervert, a bear? *Do they still have bears in this country? Did we ever have bears in this country, or was that wolves. If not wolves then we definitely still have wild boars, all rough and tusky. Oh God!* He crouched down, ready to make a grab for his clothes and to flee the site with haste. It was fight or flight time and Benedict was captain of the high speed chicken team. His heart impolitely knocked on his rib cage, desperately wanting to be let out as it felt it had a fairer chance to escape if a proper set-to occurred. Fortunately, that moment of bending down low also provided a moment for rational thought, as he listened and could only hear the gentle sigh of the wind in the trees. He stood up again, anxiously glancing around and then announced to himself that it was time for the show to start.

Benedict thumbed the top of his long johns and then slid them down in one fluid motion and stepped out of them, totally in the buff. He cupped his modesty and

cleared his throat, ready to belt out a couple of verses of
the required hymn, what was it? Love divine all loves
excelling? He looked down and realised he was not yet
appropriately attired, forgetting of course the leeks and the
would-be daff substitute, the cornflower. He gulped,
uneasy in standing there totally full frontal, but picked up
the leeks and then reached around and clenched the stem
of the cornflower twixt cheeks. It may have been a
summer's night, but Benedict's manhood was showing all
the signs of it being minus thirty, shrivelling to something of
an angry little chimp's willy. Now, dressed like a naturist
traffic conductor. Benedict cleared his throat again and
then tentatively, with his voice breaking, began to sing a
few bars of the chosen hymn.
"Love divine, all loves excelling;
Joy of heaven to earth come down;
Fix in us thy humble dwelling;
All thy faithful mercies crown!"
He grew in confidence, throwing caution to the wind,
puffing out his chest and adding a deuce more substantial
bass to his voice.
"Jesus, thou art all compassion;
Pure unbounded love thou art..."
Someone coughed behind him and Benedict jumped so
high it was a shame there was not an Olympic selection
committee member nearby.
"Aaaah!" he shrieked twisting on the spot and replaced the
sight of his flapping winky with the long green stem of a
leek. He ducked down, back to his clothes and hugged his
trousers to his chest, mortified he'd been caught in the act.
He looked at the cougher, an old man wearing similar
brown cords to his own, with a chequered shirt on, a dark
drown gilet and on top of the weathered tortoise like face, a
brown flat cap. The stranger was resting his weary body on

a large shovel, half dug into the ground. How Benedict had not heard that penetrating the soil was anyone's guess.

"Lovely night for it I spose......." said the stranger.

"Oh please don't kill me, I have money. I mean..... not on me right now but I can get money, oh please don't touch me too much," Benedict whimpered.

The old man coughed hard and hacked up brown spit onto the ground, the effects of forty years of smoking unfiltered tobacco.

"Reckons I'll let you go I will, but first you'll be telling me what you're doing on parish property," he reasoned.

"I could ask you the same question," Benedict replied in a more defensive tone.

"Well, you see the funny thing is, I'm both Groundsman and Gamekeeper for this abbey and the copse nearby. So you could say I have every right to be standing here right now, whereas your claim, I think is still very much up for debate, wouldn't you say?" He gave a wrinkled smile.

Drat! Benedict's poor addled brain box went into overdrive trying to think of a plausible excuse for his sudden nudity on holy ground. An idea popped into his head and his voiced raised seven octaves too high to make it anywhere near genuine.

"My good man, do you not know what day it is?"

"Sunday," was his factually accurate response.

"Yes well, beyond Sunday it is also....Saint......yes.....Saint Bartholomew's tide."

"Righty ho, and what will that be meaning then?"

Benedict charged headlong into his excuse, "I'm surprised you don't know from living round these parts. For it is on this day that Bartholomew the Armourless, lost his armour prior to fighting the foul scourge of the countryside which had been killing livestock for weeks. It was a beast only known as.......the budgie of hell's dyke?" That was weak.

"Big animal was it, bird of prey perhaps?" asked the man resting his forearms on the shovel handle.

"Bigger, perhaps an old relic from before humans walked the earth. Besides, I'm digressing from my story."

"And that's definitely all it is," grumbled the old codger.

"Well, Bartholomew had been tasked by the country folk to slay the beast and he would be rewarded for his valour with the hand of the most beautiful women in all the nearby villages. However, another suitor, jealous of Bartholomew made off with his armour the night before the encounter. Realising he had no choice but to save face, Bartholomew went out completely as God intended with only his faithful sword, erm, Budgiebane to protect him."

"Happy ending then, he killed the big old Budgie of hell's dyke as you called it?"

For whatever reason, Benedict rationalised his story as he just couldn't see it as a likely victory. "Oh heavens no, he was eaten and subsequently martyred. But, but, since then, a small group of templars, yes that's what we are, have taken to celebrating this day."

"By parading nude in what is technically my back garden."

"........yes."

The old man mulled Benedict's reasoning over for about five seconds.

"Well now, that is an explanation of sorts. But you've told me a story, I'll tell you another. An idiot, and by no means was he the first, walked into any of the pubs in the small town of Llandrindod, a foolish looking chap, probably not from the area but with 'mug' written on his forehead in invisible ink."

Benedict could see where this was going and flushed red. "In the pub, he is spotted by some villagers, who to keep the passerby entertained tell the story of the last King of Wales, coming from the area and dying here up at the abbey. They then also recollect a version of events whereby if said stranger stands in front of said abbey in the emperor's finest clothes and a selection of veg shoved up his ass or thereabouts, then the king will be revealed. Now I have only one question for you young man, prior to me fully well expecting you to sling your hook before I reach you with my shovel. And I may be seventy but I still got a first step like an angry ram who's had his favourite ewe troubled by a ne'er do well upstart sheep. Would the aforementioned idiot have talked to Howell, bloody nuisance that he is, and also, how many previous idiots do you figure there has been?"

Benedict meekly replied, "Yes, and to the other question, one?" He felt guilty and as if he was the only person stupid enough to entertain the notion that by singing a song naked, some spectre from the past would be dead chuffed about this, pop out for an ogle and to impart some advice as to where someone might thieve his crown.

"Don't flatter yourself. You're the fourth stupid idiot that I've found out here and accounting for the nights when I stagger home in a beery fug and topple straight into bed, I would say there's been a few more. Now, unaccustomed as I am to rudeness, I suggest you flee the area before your forehead becomes extremely closely acquainted to the flat, spade shaped object beneath my foot. If you want to warm up, I'd imagine Bessie is just finishing her lock-in, she'll see you right. Now, clear off!"

Benedict did not need to be asked twice and in a surprisingly graceful motion managed to scoop up his clothes, shoes, the long coat and managed to cover his groin as he scarpered from the scene. In his panicked state he felt like he'd run a mile and was out of breath quickly. He looked back and realised he'd only jogged about a hundred meters and the old groundsman was still staring at him. He lumbered on and ducked behind an old stone wall. As he struggled on with his long-johns, the sweat and nerves making it nearly impossible to get a leg through, the old voice echoed behind him from a fair distance away, "Oy, you forgot your leeks!"

Chapter 18

Benedict ran away so fast from the scene of his one-man public outing as a nudist that the world seemed to be rotating on his every footfall. When a sufficiently challenging asthma attack brought him to an abrupt halt, Benedict realised he was once more just outside Llandrindod. Cowering behind the small garden wall of a cottage, the lack of interior lights turned on meant that he could probably change back into his clothes with relative anonymity, save for any more random groundsmen that might be lurking in the bushes. That was not the case and once more ensconced in his clothes and with the long coat folded over one arm and the deer stalker in hand, a drink sounded like a mighty fine idea. Benedict was shaken from his ordeal but the one thing he did agree on from what the old groundsman had said was that a nice pick-me-up might be the order of the night.

As he approached the Wiley Stag, it seemed like he may have even missed the lock in. The pub's windows did not have that happy welcoming glow, but the sombre dim half-light of most of the equipment having been switched off. Benedict was about to head for home when the side door of the pub opened and Bessie the landlady came out, a small empty barrel firmly gripped to her chest, ready to be put with the rest of the empties round the back. She stopped and looked at Benedict.

"Hello lovely, you were in here earlier weren't you?"

"That's right, my friend and I came in for a short while."

"Well, I'm just shutting up for the night; lock in's done and I'm a bit tipsy if I'm honest." She tottered forward, "Oh hello, I'm about to spill this barrel. Quick quick!"

Bessie lurched toward him, the barrel slipping from her grasp. Benedict ran forward and slid his hands underneath, stopping the inevitable village waking clang of the drum hitting the ground. He took it off her and walked the short distance to the storage area round the back of the pub. "Thank you for your assistance; I suppose that as you've been such a kind gentleman and spared my blushes from some annoyed neighbours, you might like to come in for a nightcap?"

"Oh that would very sufficient, thank you," beamed a very happy Benedict. "And would a strawberry tartlet go amiss?"

"You might be in luck sonny, I'll go and check the larder."

As Benedict walked in to the light of the hallway, Bessie looked him up and down and with a quizzical look asked, "Here, very warm night for a coat and deerstalker, why you got them on your arm?"

Benedict scrambled around in his brain for an answer, looking under cognitive books and piles of imagination. Finally he had his excuse, "Well, you never can be sure at this time of year. Best to be safe or you could catch your death."

Bessie laughed and replied, "Aren't you a mummy's boy?"

"Who needs friends when you've got mammy's bosoms?" Benedict chuckled.

The pub's dim light had a kind of romance to it, it was sultry and old smoke hung in the air. Were it not for the dart board and pub skittles, Benedict could almost kid his senses into thinking he was back in a gentleman's club in Kensington. It did not matter though, here he was with this woman of incredible warmth, knocking back rusty nails and giggling like children. They both took to each other and any emptiness that had filled their lives was temporarily quieted.

The bottle of Drambuie was empty and neither Bessie nor Benedict could stomach the quarter bottle of Jameson's that remained, not that it particularly mattered.

The night was growing old, but the flames of their flirty lust were young and kindled and before you could say, "Shall we go again?" Benedict was nodding off, post coitus, as a slightly disappointed and deflated Bessie lay next to him.

"The least you could do is stay awake," she said.

"Eh? Oh sorry."

Benedict stretched out, his undefined, hairy chest raising from the sheets, his nipples daring to peek out like nervous eyes. He reached back with his hands, placing them under his head, resting on the pillow and slowly Benedict's eyelids descended once more. A jab to the ribs with a splinter like elbow propelled him back into reality and he jolted upright. Bessie lit a fag and took a long draw, causing a premature ashy end which she deftly flicked into the ashtray on her bedside table.

"You lack stamina my boy," she mocked.

Benedict flamed red with embarrassment, "Well it is four in the morning!"

"The night is young, old man."

Benedict's stomach rumbled. He tried his luck, "Well, of course, I might perk up with a small slither of tart au citron?"

Bessie sighed, resigned to the fact that he was as much if not more in love with her cooking than he was besotted with her charms, "If you must."

He found resurgent energy and leapt out of bed, his agenda annoying his partner in bed.

"Back in a jiffy, can I get you anything?"

She tutted, "No, I spend the day making the stuff and eating it. I'm more than fine thanks."

He didn't need any further clarification and was down in the pantry quicker than you could say, "I really think you oughtn't, have you seen your sizeable posterior?"

He flicked the switch to Bessie's interior larder and was immediately transported to a utopian land where everything was sweet and sticky. He stuck to his guns though and gently slipped his fingers under the old creamy ceramic of the plate which held the lemon tart and he whisked it through to the kitchen. Flicking the light switch on the wall by the door-less entrance to the steps which led to the upstairs quarters, Benedict then marvelled at the yellowy sheen on the tart. But also, Bessie was clearly a true artisan, as the outside crust had a series of undulating dips imprinted onto it. Benedict yelled up, "Bessie dear, the outside design of this tart is incredible, how do you do it and why on God's earth aren't you baking for a living?" There was a pause and then Bessie confidently shouted from above, "It's because I cheat."

"I'm sorry?" said Benedict, slightly let down by the revelation.

"I cheat!" replied Bessie almost sounding like boasting. "Go to the cupboard to the right of the range, you'll find a handily shaped tin in there."

Benedict was curious as to her deception and did as he was told, walking across the kitchen past the range where so many sugary treats had been born, to the low cupboard at the side. Squatting down he opened the door and looked into the short gloom at a number of metallic baking utensils. There were a couple of sieves, baking trays, large, crusty cake tins and then his eye caught it. There, on top of a neat stack of shallow pie tins, he saw one on top where he could just make out on the far inner circumference, the pattern which Bessie had alluded to by saying that she cheated. Benedict reached in and with a clatter, pulled the tin out from the back of the cupboard.

Baking tins, generally are a perfunctory sort of object to have in the kitchen. If one was to cast one's mind to a baking tin or pie dish, one might immediately think of some dark metallic looking circular object, with a curled edge at the top and either a built in bottom, a bottom that lifts out, or if professional, a springform side which releases the bottom of the tin. It would serve it's exact purpose and nothing more, it is by definition a cake tin. The item that Benedict now held in his hands though could not be described in any way as perfunctory as even he could see it was modified, but modified from what? He flipped the container over in his hands several times. It was well used; the crumbs and grease of yesteryear baked to a hard brown colour in the many crevices of the base and inner ridges around the circumference. It did, however differ in overall colour from the other tins. The others had the grey coldness of a steel, tin or iron. This object however, it was almost, yellow? Brass? Seemed a bit much for a cake tin. He turned it over, so the loose base plate tipped out onto his other outstretched palm. The base plate was clearly not the original for this tin, as it was, like the others, that ordinary, "dull day at the seaside" grey. Then Benedict confirmed his modification theory. The inner metallic lip which the base should have rested on had been welded in place and welded badly, gaps showing between this ring and the side of the alleged tin. This was an adjustment, a make do. And the front of the tin as well had what looked like four socket points, four clasp areas, but the clasps had been long-bent into the metal. They were all symmetrical and surrounded a larger, more oval one in what he presumed to be the middle. Benedict ran his hands over the internal pattern which had turned ordinary pie crusts into something exquisite to look at. Whilst old crumbs and grease came away on his fingers, he also noticed a really soft resistance in the quality of the metal pattern inside.

It hit him, like Bessie had snuck down the stairs and thrown a well aimed brick at him with a message wrapped round it and the word, "Idea," printed upon the sheet of paper. Each of the indentations were made of the same metal as the tin and had been bent into the circumference. Each was a fleur de lis. With greater ease than expected, he slid a fingernail underneath the first of the eight indentations and prised it upwards, off the flat of the tin interior and back into it's rightful place, prone in the air. Underneath where it had covered, Benedict saw the difference in colour, from the burnished bronze colour of the exposed metal, to what was plainly gold. A cold nervousness, a feeling of incredible guilt and yet jubilation crept over him all at once. This was a crown, a great crown! He feverishly prised up another of the fleur de lis and held it away from him to see if the change in perspective mattered. No. And he cast his mind a couple of miles away, back to the farmhouse and the car, and the sword haft that lay secretly in a hold-all in the boot of his Phantom. He was absolutely certain of the size of the precious gems for which the sword was stolen and equally certain that those same gems would fit the outer sockets of this king-maker. Benedict almost wept, realising that his tart au citron had just turned into the crown of Llewellyn.

"Is everything alright down there luv?" a female voice above him said.

Benedict let out a squeaky, "Yes," before having to steady himself against one of the kitchen units.

"So what do you think to my artistry now that you've found out my sneaky ways?" Bessie asked unseen from the bedroom.

Benedict was flustered, he was unprepared for idle chitchat or pillow talk and seemed to panic with the delicate crown in his hand.

"Fine, lovely, well played?"

He cursed himself for sounding like a completely disinterested fool. He could not believe that the crown they had been searching for was now in his possession and what's more, that it was being used for baking! Bessie was either an evil genius or stupid to the point where she had no understanding what her cake tin would be worth if melted down.

"Well played? Well, are you coming back up any time soon?"

"Um, yes, be right there." Benedict so badly wanted to run out of the back door and show his new prize off to the sleeping Tristan and it wouldn't be the first time that night that he'd been streaking in public. But fortunately his common sense strolled across the document littered office of his brain and gave his carelessness a good slap across the chops. Now was not the moment and much as it would pain him, Benedict would have to wait.

Benedict forced the two fleur de lis prongs he had prised up back down again, though they were bent more amateurishly this time and sat away from the internal wall of the tin. If Bessie used the tin any time soon it might take a chunk out of the side of whatever she was using the crown-tin combo for. Benedict slipped the mismatched bottom back into the crown and lobbed the makeshift baking ensemble back into the cupboard with a clatter. He rubbed his hand from the grime of the tin, grabbed a plate and knife off the sideboard, cut a generous slice of tart and put the remainder back in the larder.

Bessie saw Benedict enter her boudoir holding the plate with the slice of tart.

"Couldn't get enough whilst you were down there then? You want to watch yourself, a man of your age. Before you can say strong constitution, you'll be breathing your last with a coronary."

Benedict was a little put out. Yes he didn't have the deltoids of a Greek hero and could be described in a lonely hearts advert as, "cuddly," but he considered himself a half decent catch.

"This is my first piece actually, I was marvelling at your tin."

"Clever isn't it," Bessie replied, breaking off the tip of the slice of lemon tart and sexily slipping it between her lips. "I may not be that rich in talent, but I'm rich in culinary cunning!" Benedict tucked into his early morning dessert with his bare hands and couldn't believe how rich Bessie really was. The question now was how he was going to deprive her of that wealth. Benedict had a few ideas.

Chapter 19

Tristan hadn't heard a peep last night. Mr Sandman had brought him a series of lovely dreams including one where he was a talking unicorn which he happily mused upon through his morning ablutions all the way to the breakfast table. But he felt refreshed from his long sleep and he was now happily drowning bready soldiers in a thick sea of boiled egg. As another able yet wholemeal seaman was lost to Egg-Neptune's aquatic legions, the front door of the farm house clicked open and clacked closed again. From where he was seated, Tristan leant to his left and looked into the hallway at whoever had just entered. To his surprise it was Benedict.

After hanging up the long coat and deerstalker, Benedict confidently walked through to the kitchen. Pleased that it was only Tristan about, a big grin spread on his face.

"Been out taking the morning air have you?" said Tristan, his chops full of egg toast.

Benedict stifled a laugh, "Of sorts."

"Thought I had trouble rousing you. I knocked several times like a woodpecker after a tasty grub. Thought you were either out for the count or had died."

Clear that Tristan had then come downstairs for breakfast after assuming his friend was dead, the smile faded from Benedict lips and he said, "Well thanks for checking if I was no longer of this world."

Tristan shrugged and took another bite of a third, un-soldiered bit of toast, "You stand before me sir."

Benedict returned his grin to pre-fatal thoughts and said, "I've got it!" He looked around to make sure that Mfanwy and Gwyffan had not appeared.

Tristan looked puzzled, "What, got what exactly?"

"The crown man, the bloody crown."

"What? Really, just this morning?"

Benedict sat down and dropped his voice so only Tristan would hear.

"No! Look, last night after we spoke and you went to bed, I er..." Benedict really didn't want to cover the ground where he had stood naked in a field with a flower up his arse which then became an act of indecent exposure to an old man with a large spade, so he cut to the good bit.

"I went out to clear my head and ended up having a lock-in at the pub. Well, it ended up just being me and the landlady."

"Crown my backside," said Tristan, "Someone got lucky last night and hasn't been home yet I'll wager. You gave her your crown more like, hehe," he nudged Benedict in the ribs.

"Um.....no, I really did find the crown. Regardless, we did end up in the sack and afterwards I went back downstairs for something to eat."

Tristan perked up, "Oooh, more lovely tart."

"Right. So anyway, whilst looking for the tart, I noticed a wonderful pattern in the pastry and Bessie alluded to cheating by using a special tin. I rootled about for it and before I could say "Unusual baking discovery," it turns out that the pattern was the fleur de lis of the crown bent inwards and even the stones from the sword would fit on the outside. It's been turned into a cake tin by welding a circle of brass to the bottom so that a separate and entirely different spare cake tin base would fit in. So it exists! It bloody well exists. I knew it, this proves everything, Boudicca's crown exists. Through hunches and a bit of luck, we're really on to something here!"

Benedict flinched, like someone had driven a fist at him and he'd seen it in the periphery of his vision, automatically recoiling from the expected rebuff and dressing down that Tristan would give him. It did not come.

After what felt like an age, where Tristan weighed up everything that Benedict had said, Tristan simply shrugged his shoulders and said, "Lovely."

"Lovely? Letting me off a little lightly there aren't we? I expected to be thrown from the house with clothes in tow." Tristan raised his hand to Benedict's face. "Now, never let it be said I'm not a reasonable man. I've listened to your explanation and it seems perfectly reasonable. Plus the fact that you do not have it in your possession makes me want you to prove it but I'm not going to dismiss it out of hand."

"Oh, right, I almost wish I'd tried harder with my story now, just to make it less plausible."

Another piece of toast met the inside of Tristan's mouth, quickly chased down with hot milky tea. "The bigger question is how you're going to get the crown, reckon you're going to need it if it exists."

Benedict scratched his chin. He hadn't thought that far ahead. "I hadn't thought that far ahead. Er, we could steal it?"

"Always with the theft," replied Tristan.

"Well, have you any ideas?"

"You could always ask her? Has it occurred to you that she might just give it up?"

Benedict scratched the sandpapery stubble under his chin for a moment and said, "I prefer my way. Look, I'll do what I do best and charm the pantaloons off her. There is a back door, you sneak through there whilst I'm making enough noise to wake the dead and we're away."

"I won't even know what it looks like!" said Tristan.

"It's the bloody cake tin which is gold and looks like a folded over crown. It's not as if you'll be searching for it in a stack of other folded over crowns."

Tristan flicked up his hands dismissively, "I give up, I really do. Fine, I'll do it just to get you to shut up and leave me in peace."

"Lovely," replied a happy Benedict. "Now if you'll excuse me I need a bath."

"I bet you do."

After tea time, everyone was sitting quietly, awkwardly in the living room. It was terribly uncomfortable for everyone as the two houseguests had as much veiled secrecy and tact as an elephant in tap shoes on a metal surface. The old grandfather clock drew attention to itself by clacking auspiciously. Eventually Mfwanwy grew impatient.

"Right, what is it with you two rapscallions today? You've been skulking round, looking guilty since early this morning. Something is going on."

Tristan cleared his throat and replied, "Leave it Mfanwy, just a small disagreement. We'll be out of your hair soon." Gwyffan didn't know what to do with himself and avoiding confrontation, stuck the wireless on. They listened intently to a selection of news about the phony war, how Hitler looked ready to accept his gains and not press for further conquest. After all that gloomy analysis, the beeb tried to cheer hearts with a production of 'A Midsummer Night's Dream.' Thankfully after lots of difficult smiles around the room, Benedict stood up and exclaimed, "Golly, is that the time? I think I fancy a nightcap!"

"Yes, mmm, I think a single malt at the local yeomanry would send me in the right direction to Sandy Bedfordshire," replied Tristan, also standing up conspicuously.

What they didn't expect to happen was for Gwyffan to also stand and say, "Lads, I think I'll join you." He couldn't stand the random tension anymore and just needed to get out of the house, much to the raised-eyebrowed annoyance of his wife.

"Oh no, noo noo no, oh we'll be gone a matter of minutes," replied a worried Benedict.

"It's a good half hour walk to the pub!" retorted Gwyffan.

"Oh yes, but we'll just be talking about the route home tomorrow, nothing more." added Tristan.

"Oh, leaving are we?" added Mfanwy, "That's courteous of you to tell us in passing, the day before you go!" She stood up and balled her fists; apparently she was quite offended. Tristan was taken aback by her reaction, "Oh, no no, I didn't mean to be discourteous."

"But you were willing to enjoy our hospitality for nearly a week and then bugger off without so much as a thank you!" she shouted.

"Ah, wa....." Tristan was floundering, Benedict was keeping out of it. As the stranger he felt he could be properly rounded upon if he interjected anything.

"This is what today has been about isn't it? Trying to shuffle off because you thought we'd be offended by you leaving. My goodness what kind of people do you think we are!?"

"Well now you come to mention it," Tristan was going to add, "very lovely people."

"Treat this place like a hotel would you? Come on Gwyffan we're going to bed! Let's leave these two 'guests' to a drink elsewhere."

She snatched at Gwyffan's hand and dragged him out of the room. He gave a forgiving raise of the eyebrows to Tristan and Benedict as he left as if to say, "Sorry lads."

"Oh, she's like a tornado when she gets started. I mean, I couldn't defend myself, what was I to say to make things right?"

"I thought you were quite brilliant," laughed Benedict. "Indeed without your suggestion that we were leaving tomorrow we might have had an unwanted party with us. Now we can toddle down to Bessie's, do what we need to do and be out of hers nice and early tomorrow. And thank you for facilitating our quick exit, I can't say enough about your work tonight, I'd almost applaud."

Tristan shot Benedict a filthy look in retaliation for his condescending smile as he walked out the room to the front door.

As they walked to the pub, they rehearsed Benedict's plan. It was quite straightforward. Benedict would go for the lock-in, Tristan would lurk round the back. As soon as the last few customers had left, Benedict would turn on the charm. When the lights downstairs had gone out Tristan was to approach the back door of the pub, which Benedict would have already unlocked before heading up the stairs. He would then sneak in after six minutes, (Benedict was not proud of his stamina, but it would make the theft process a lot shorter) and once it had gotten noisy in the bedroom, have the crown away. The first thing Bessie would know about it would be the first time she came to make another tart or cake. Hopefully by then they'd be back in London and Benedict's whereabouts masked by the fact that he hadn't told anyone of his address. Tristan was another matter altogether, but as he wasn't going to be seen, it wasn't going to be a problem.

Except there was a problem: They had not parted ways soon enough and as they reached the grounds of the pub, a call went out.

"Whooo, Benny!"

Bessie was already outside, of course that was where he met her the night before. She must have been doing the empties again.

"Bugger it, there goes that plan," said Benedict under his breath before raising a fake smile and saying, "Bessie my darling, how are you this fine evening?"

"Oh I'm right as rain, just about to call it a night actually..........I see you've brought company." There was a hesitance in her voice.

"Yes, umm," Benedict was once more forced to think of a plausible excuse, but all his poor addled brain was giving him were ridiculous motives. *He's here to make a fondue and will use your toes as dippers. He thinks he's found a way to propel you into space. He's here because of the family that live in your optics.* Seconds passed, it was becoming uncomfortable.

"I'm here my lovely, because of the delicious tarts you make," Tristan said, saving Benedict's bacon. "Yes, I'm from the Welsh Federation of Bakers and we're doing an article for our quarterly digest. It's on quality local producers of baked goods who are off the beaten track a little bit so they don't perhaps get the attention they deserve. Anyhow, I was in your lovely pub yesterday and I couldn't help notice your fine home baking and wished to ask whether you'd like to feature?"

Benedict looked at his associate, totally cool and calm, *Genius! Though I'm not sure where he's going to go with this* he thought.

"Of course, I'd be delighted. It's a complete surprise that you would want to focus on me, but that sounds wonderful, I'm Elizabeth Wenchly, welcome to the Stag."

She held out her hand. Tristan took it and replied, "I'm Michel Papillon."

"Oh you sound terribly Welsh for a Frenchman?" she queried.

Quick as a flash Tristan replied, "Oh, I moved here when I was six from Bordeaux, the accent's gone, but you never really lose your love of culture and good gastronomy."

"Of course not!"

She escorted Benedict and 'Michel' into the pub. Again the lights were dim like the night before. She took down a couple of upturned chairs on a table for them to sit on and asked if Michel would like a bottle of wine.

"Oh how thoughtful, well I suppose it's not too late, is it a fine vintage?"

Bessie looked shamed and said, "I don't really know about wine, I'll go fetch it and you can decide." She scuttled off to an unseen cupboard.

Benedict rounded on Tristan and whispered, "What on earth are you doing?! Michel sodding Papillon?"

"I'm trying to improvise, now she knows who you are, but she doesn't really know me. Oh here she comes back."

She plonked the bottle on the table with a couple of wine glasses. Tristan had another idea, "This looks quite palatable, but do you have anything stronger? Perhaps some pastis?"

Bessie had no idea. "I have some vodka?"

"Lovely," replied Tristan.

Bessie nipped across to the bar and detached the optic with Vodka attached. She sat down with the two men and then asked, "Are you not going to use a pad and a pen?" The plan was beginning to unwind, or was it?

"Oh no, photographic memory me. Shall we?"

He poured them both a glass of wine, whilst Benedict sat there like a spectator. He really had no other part to play, but to Tristan this was the perfect opportunity. He could get Bessie as drunk as necessary to hand over the cake tin. If it was just a cake tin, he could hand it back, and the only harm done would be to Bessie's head in the morning when then inevitable hangover occurred, but he assumed she was quite a stout girl from working in a pub. If it was the crown, then in the drunken haze, she'd probably not realise he'd taken it.

Tristan sat back in his chair, took a sip of his wine and then with a serious look on his face asked, "So Bessie, tell me about your childhood memories of cooking."

"Well it was all so long ago......"

Three hours later and Benedict had nodded off an hour ago. They had worked their way through the wine and the vodka. Bessie was plastered, cackling and wouldn't shut up. Tristan was sober as a judge, having poisoned the pot plant next to him with the booze, all well placed when Bessie wasn't looking.

"Blime guffner, you don't sneem dunk at all," said Bessie, beginning to feel the world rotate. She held the edge of the table.

"Oh I tell you, I'm literally about to fall off my stool," replied a deadpan Tristan. "Now, earlier yesterday, I came in here and had a delicious piece of tart with a rather exciting pattern embedded into the crust. Just how did you achieve that?"

Bessie suddenly seemed quite sad. She looked at the snoozing Benedict, feeling guilty that he knew her secret and she sobbed a little.

"Alright guff, s'fair cop, I use a special tin with the pattern printed into it. There, I'fff told you now. Take me away to the pastry police, lock me up and eat the key made out of choux pastry."

"Au contraire my lovely," said Tristan, "If anything it shows a little ingenuity on your part. Er, may I see the tin so I can describe it in the article?"

Bessie huffed at having to move from her seat, but the currency of some fame excited her, so she tottered upright and clinging to the bar, like the world was at a diagonal, went in search of her baking implement. Tristan calmly waited, Benedict began to snore on his left. At least he could make his evaluation in peace.

After a substantial amount of clattering and swearing on Bessies's part, she came back through the hatchway of the bar, clearly holding a circular bronze looking object in her hand. Having plonked herself down again and exclaiming that she needed some air, she handed the tin to Tristan. She then fell off the side of her chair and slid to the floor, at first giggling and then snoring. Tristan briefly cast an eye on her and then realising she was happily out for the count, turned back to the item that had caused all the fuss of Benedict coming up to mid Wales in the first place.

The light in the pub lounge was dimmed and as he turned the grubby metal over, it just looked like brass. He could feel that the inner material did have a raised edge to it which provided the imprint. He couldn't really see it properly though so Tristan got up and walked across to the light switches, putting another two lamps on. And then there it was: The improvement in light immediately showed Tristan that Benedict was right. He saw the fleur de lis bent inward and even felt the raised one which Benedict had been unable to bend back last night. Tristan scratched at the fudge-like crumbs covering the metal and saw the sunshine pure quality of gold underneath. He turned the crown round further in his hands and admired the crafting of the rents where the crown jewels would be placed. He smiled and said to no one in particular, "There goes my plans for a quiet life then!"

Tristan walked back over to the table where the snoozing Benedict and the snoring Bessie were. He bent over Bessie and took the pub door keys that were on a loop on her belt. He then kicked Benedict sharply in the leg and made him jump.

"Ow!"

"Don't ow me mate, I've just gone and got your crown for you. As much as I hate to say it, you were right."

Benedict yawned, "So you believe me now?"

"Oh yes. Previously I thought you mad as a box of frogs, but now? No, there's something definitely going on here, the bigger question is what we do with it now."

"Surely, we hang on to it and see what else we can do, are you suggesting we go to the authorities?"

"I don't know yet," answered Tristan, "That's not for now, let's get home and sleep on it, but the facts do seem to be pointing towards something."

Benedict smiled at this positive reaction.

Tristan helped Benedict to his feet and slowly they pulled the sleeping Bessie upright, leaning against the back of the bar. She happily snored away as they flicked all the lights out, with Tristan last to leave the pub, he locked the door and posted the keys back through the letterbox behind him.

Chapter 20

Benedict lay on his back in bed, bathed in the early morning dimness coming through the curtains of the guestroom. He had awoken early and made a bedfellow of his trophy. He turned sideways to see the crown, as a cake tin, still covered in greasy crumbs sitting next to him like some filthy lover. Benedict rolled the other way to look at his wrist watch, perched upright, leaning against the leather strap so he could see the time without having to pick it up. It was half five in the morning and time to be going. Whilst Tristan's brilliant performance last night had pre-emptively set their departure date, the capture of the crown also meant that they would truly be leaving and the atmosphere between them and Mfanwy was likely to be frosty. Gwyffan was fine, he was a simple man and just wanted people to get on, but Mfanwy, there'd be no living with her now. Benedict imagined her to be the kind of woman to hold grudges. He got up, washed and dressed and was packed before seven. The smell and sound of sausages giggling in a pan downstairs drew his attention.

Hungry and tired, Benedict edged his way down the stairs. He felt like he could murder a plate of Lincolnshire or Cumberlands. However, he did not want to outstay his welcome and take anymore away from the Bradfields then he already had. At ceiling level he bent over the banister and peered into the open kitchen. His stomach gave a sigh of relief as he spotted Tristan, wearing comfortable slacks, a grey cat-sick jumper and a navy pinny whilst tending to the pan. Benedict clumped the rest of the way down the stairs, Tristan turned and saw him coming through the open doorway.

"Thought the smell would bring some down some early birds."

"Well, the early bird catches the particularly fat sausage," chirped a happy Benedict.

Tristan returned to the pan and within five minutes had slid a plate of sausages and fried egg Benedict's way. He quickly helped himself to a portion and then both men tucked into to the savoury breakfast at the table.

As they enjoyed their delicious start to the day, they talked plans.

"So, no sound from Mfanwy and Gwyffan then?" asked Benedict.

"No," replied Tristan, sounding quite low about it. "But if I know Mfanwy, she'll know we're up and will be using the opportunity to have a lie-in and to make us feel bad about last night."

Benedict was confused, "So if we leave, is it a problem? Isn't it a problem? What I'm alluding to is have I wrecked a family relationship here? I don't want you falling on dark days on my account."

"Oh it's nonsense, trust me. She'll be over it by tonight and be right as rain when I see her next, probably won't even remember it. She's just had her pride hurt by us not telling her we we're leaving, she probably feels like a lousy host. Trust me, the last time Gwyffan bought her a dress two sizes too small for Christmas, now that was shunning someone, her own husband in this case. I believe he didn't leave the spare room for two months whilst she slimmed down."

Benedict chuckled at Tristan's last remark and added, "Oh well, at least we can make a quick getaway then. I do hate long goodbyes. I'm all packed and ready to head off back to London."

"Well, that's that then I guess," said Tristan, a hint of resignation in his voice.

Benedict knew what his friend wanted. Tristan had been incredibly useful to him over the past few days, a place to live albeit uninvited, the voice of reason, the pub and therefore by association the crown and his heroic verbal actions last night. He didn't look up from his coffee, and merely said, "Unless you'd like to come back to London of course?"

"I thought you'd never ruddy well ask!" beamed Tristan.

After tidying away the plates and cooking utensils, Benedict and Tristan lugged their cases down the stairs to Benedict's Phantom. Benedict felt guilty for using and abusing their host's hospitality, snuck back into the house, took out his wallet and left them a small fortune on the kitchen table. There was still no sound from the house owners as he started the engine and swung out the driveway.

The journey back to London felt like it had pace to Benedict this time around. There was a sense of purpose and urgency to their activities. As such, the friendly "getting to know you" banter was gone and was replaced with discussions of politics of which Tristan could only describe his locally to Wales but Benedict focused more to war and the machinations of Hitler and where his conquests would end. Both men felt that with the size of the chunk that Germany had bitten off, there would be no further conquest. Still, if Hitler did decide to advance across France, which was highly unlikely, then he'd meet the steely might of the British Expeditionary Force who would give him a damn good hiding and send him home red cheeked. There was nothing to worry about.

Eventually, they rolled back into the busy streets of London, both men with a degree of hesitance and unease due to the fact that the last time they were here they suffered multiple burglaries which caused this mystery and then starred in a caper not too far away, of which the loot was in the boot of the Phantom. But it was here they needed to be. Benedict put his beloved car to bed, back under it's dust blanket and both men strolled away from the lockup, bags in hand, loot in Benedict's. Both cast suspicious glances at members of the public as they walked back into the heart of Kensington, never knowing fully whether someone might make a random snatch at Benedict's belongings to capture the crown and the jewels for a purpose yet unknown. A stranger quite accidentally knocked into Tristan, his unassuming small height being overlooked by some city banker. Benedict immediately came at the man and told him to clear off, with the poor victim left cowering with only his umbrella to shield him.

The stroll back to the house felt long but at last they returned to Benedict's front door. He inserted the long key and gingerly turned it, pushing the door slowly open once unlocked. Half expecting the police to be sitting in the living room with an "Ah, Mr Lukely sir, we've been expecting you, Smith, we've got him bang to rights," agenda, Benedict called out, "I say hello?"

The silence that followed was deafening to all intents and purposes. Not even the sound of a harrumphing Scottish housekeeper. That was unusual.

"Apparently nobody home," said Benedict as he frowned at Tristan.

Both carried their suitcases through to the hallway and set them down. Tristan span around to look at the place, still as ornate and grand as ever and he was pleased to see his mirror still up in the hallway. Benedict tutted when he saw it.

"Shall I put the kettle on?" asked Tristan.

"Well I half expected that my only current member of staff would be here to greet me and offer us a spot of tea what with it being so late in the day, but I suppose we will have to make it ourselves."

"Hang on a second, there's a few bits left here on the coffee table," Tristan said.

He'd stepped into the lounge to establish if the house was safe and had seen the post there. Benedict walked through and picked up the pile. Only the top two contents got opened. He read the note on the top and could not suppress a "Bugger!"

"Something bad happened?"

"I've lost Mrs McDoughty. Her note says that after all the shenanigans of the past fortnight, and the fact that I scuttled off on holiday and was not here to protect her, it would seem she has decided she can no longer serve in my house. Oh that's soured things, good housekeepers are harder than butlers to find."

"I'm sorry for your loss."

"God really? I'm not, stroppy old do-gooder, now what's this? Ah a telegram, don't get them that often."

Again he read through it in silence with Tristan left in a, "Shall I make tea or not?" limbo.

"Good grief!"

"Found another housekeeper already?"

"Not quite, better in fact. This is a letter from Trilby Effingham-Wright, the old codger that we sought advice from initially. In a complete stroke of luck and coincidence, he telegrammed me two days ago requesting our presence urgently as he has acquired new information on the riddle. He doesn't go into detail, but says he expects a visit soon. Oh this is wonderful news!"

"Er, well what do we do? Go now?"

"Goodness no, it's getting on for six. No," Benedict rubbed his stomach. "Mysteries can wait, I'm famished. We'll leave early tomorrow. I feel a fish supper coming on."

"Crikey, not even unpacked and we're underway again," mumbled Tristan as they walked back out the door.

The next morning and the house had that whiff about it which suggested fish and chips from the night before, greasy papers, the tang of old vinegar and a slight Piscean odour to the entire downstairs of the house. The night had left them refreshed and ready for the drive back towards Essex. Benedict brought their cases once more down from upstairs whilst Tristan tidied away whiskey glasses, chip paper and plates. The trip to the Phantom this time was more brazen and careless as if with the knowledge that Trilby could impart, they were protected. Benedict even stopped on the way to buy a quarter of aniseed balls. As for the journey, the car seemed to skim across the roads in double quick time as both their sense of anticipation built in that the mystery of the statue and the riddle might be solved. Soon enough they were rattling down the side road to Trilby's gingerbread cottage and as they reached the courtyard, Benedict threw the Phantom into a hand break stop, showering gravel into the flowerbeds nearby. He tooted the horn twice to announce their arrival and once Tristan had prized his own nervous hands from the dashboard, they stepped out.

"Less haste next time please."

"Come now, you're such an old woman, what's the point of having a car like that if you can't go fast?" replied Benedict.

"Yes, well, I'd just prefer to get somewhere in one piece!"

The front door opened behind them, "What's this? Quarrelling like an old married couple are we, heh heh!" Benedict turned from the boot of the car and saw Trilby making his way towards them across the gravel. Today he was attired in some navy blue slacks and a white shirt covered by a maroon cardigan. His strangely fluffy hair was looking evermore the cloud.

"Ah Professor, good to see you again!" boomed Benedict, "We came as soon as we could, which would have been earlier but for the fact that we were in Wales."

Trilby shook Benedict's hand, "Wales eh? Holiday I suppose. You've given up on the riddle already then?"

"On the contrary, my colleague and I followed your advice and may have happened upon a particular item in Colchester. After a minor tiff, we then ended up in Wales." Benedict reached into the boot for his suitcase. He placed it on the floor and opened it. "We have now completed our end of the riddle, look!"

Effingham-Wright was taken aback by the bright sheen of the gold crown. No longer was it the stained, fudge covered cake tin. The one thing Benedict had managed to do before going to bed last night was painstakingly clean the crown with an old toothbrush, a bucket of water and some polish. He'd also cleaned out the fixtures for the stones and bent the fleur de lis back into position. Now it gleamed, proud and regal in it's natural condition as a symbol of authority. It caught the sun's light and painted the back of the phantom with a gold shimmer.

"Good grief! I'm lost for words.....It's extraordinary."

Tristan chimed in, "Oh, look at that. Up until this moment I'd only ever seen it as a would-be grotty container, but now I feel I've committed a heinous crime calling it a cake tin."

This brought Trilby back to reality, "Excuse me?"

Tristan couldn't take his eyes off the gold, "Long story, might tell you later."

"And we also have this," Benedict reached under a shirt in his case and slowly retrieved the sword haft and passed it to Trilby. While he examined it Benedict reclosed his case.

"I say, this is rather special also," he said whilst turning it over in his hands. He inspected the rubies, admiring their generous size and quality.

"Yes, I had rather wondered whether this would turn up in your possession. There has been a number of interesting pieces in the local news about a daring raid on Colchester barracks and the mugging of two squaddies, but the military police can't work out whether it was thieves that struck lucky or a well planned scare by the Germans or even our secret service checking security. Turns out it was you though eh?" Trilby laughed and tossed the haft into the air, catching it after a complete three-sixty turn.

Tristan however, couldn't see the funny side and panicked. In his eyes, there was already a police hunt going on and now a man who owed them no loyalty knew the culprits.

"Oh please, don't turn us in! I'll do almost anything. I didn't want to get dragged into this. I just wanted to go home to Wales and look after my farm."

"Turn you in?" Trilby looked puzzled, "Nonsense, no, honour amongst thieves old boy. How do you think I 'acquired' some of the items in my home? And besides once I've told you what I need to tell you, I'll be just as implicated as you." He gave a knowing wink that made Tristan feel so much better about things.

Tristan brushed himself down, as if brushing the accusations off of him and picked up his bag which Benedict had sat down next to him.

"Come on in, I've got a pot of coffee on the go."

Once more the two gentlemen walked towards Trilby's front door.

"You big turncoat," Benedict said to Tristan.

Once inside, Trilby waved them through to his study, a room with wall to wall bookcases, a large old oak desk in the middle and three chairs, one nestled into the desk itself and two on the outside. On the wall was a Swiss cuckoo clock which had just sounded the hour and a further door which Benedict presumed led to a utility room and then the orchard like garden which they could also see out of the study window. Effingham-Wright laid the sword haft on the desk amongst his work papers and scuttled off to the get coffee. He seemed incredibly enthusiastic, there was almost a nervous energy about the man since the last time they visited. Benedict liked it, he was clearly pulling in for the big win. Benedict unclasped his case once more and took out the crown. Then with Tristan sitting to his left he pushed the chair back, placed the crown on his lap and then rested his feet on Trilby's desk. Fat and happy with himself, he looked at Tristan. Tristan knocked his feet off the desk. A cough seemed to come from the direction of the other door, presumably that was where the kitchen was too. However, within five minutes Trilby had returned with a pot of coffee and three mugs and served them from the desk. He then plonked himself in his own chair and laced his hands across his chest, taking an air of the old schoolmaster addressing two kids once more.

"Now, where were we? Ah, yes, the crown and rubies, right! Yes, Gentlemen, since we last spoke a remarkable revelation has occurred. I must admit, that when I first caught sight of that little bit of parchment, er do you still have it?"

Benedict tapped the top pocket of his jacket.

"Good, good, well when I first saw it and sent you on your way to Colchester, well I thought it a fool's errand. However, that didn't mean that you hadn't raised my curiosity and my historical instinct. Surprisingly, your story, the story of the riddle, there is a lot more to it which I have only just discovered."

Benedict noticed that Trilby was breathing fast, his sentence pace was erratic and there were a couple of beads of perspiration coming from the cloudy forehead. He hoped he wasn't about to have a fit or something. Nevertheless, Effingham-Wright continued.

"Do you recall, when we last met, that after I told you the story of Boudicca, I said that no document supersedes the Magna Carta in laying out who the ruler of this country is?"

"I do," replied Benedict, stroking his chin inquisitively.

"Well, I must apologise, for it seems I was wrong."

Benedict shifted uncomfortably in his seat.

"You'd heard of the Magna Carta, but if I said to you, have you heard of the Charter of Liberties, could you honestly answer?"

Tristan looked at Benedict and both men said, "No."

"Exactly, well the Charter of Liberties supersedes everything. It does exactly the same thing as the Magna Carta but does it earlier, making it precedent."

"I don't follow, so what's the difference?" said Tristan

"What is the difference? There shouldn't be any difference," said Trilby, "But there is. You see, the Charter of Liberties was written by the scribes of Henry the First in eleven hundred and it was witnessed by several archbishops and other nobility. Henry was a Norman and at his side was another Norman knight, a Robert Malet. Whilst Malet was a good man, unknown to him, his squire was a traitor and an original Briton, seeing the Normans as unjust conquerors. The riddle of the crown and the whereabouts of the components must have been folklore to him and his family. They had passed it down from generation to generation until it was only written in document form once, before disappearing without a trace from history. Gentlemen you hold that document."

"So I hold a very unique antique written by a true Briton, what does this have to do with the Charter of Liberties?" Benedict asked impatiently.

"The document, which your riddle was written on, was the bottom of the Charter of Liberties. In coming together to write the Charter, the squire to the opportunity to add something of his own, if you will. Now, here's where you fall off your chairs Gentlemen. They hadn't signed it when it was written. All the signatories there that day became complacent and celebrated, toasting Henry's success early and in the process all found themselves paralytic. The squire added the riddle to the bottom, and every......single.....one.......of them.......signed it."

Tristan let out a sound like he'd just been hit in the stomach by a medicine ball, and kind of "Cuhhhhhhhhhhhhhhhhhh."

Benedict was equally stunned. An eerie silence hung over the room.

"So you mean to say.."

Trilby interrupted, "I mean to say the document is legal. It's law. It beats everything. It's a command, it's the equivalent of a papal bull. And knowing that he couldn't do anything with it at that moment because the Normans had conquered the land and he did not want them to be the true rulers, the squire tore the riddle from the document and then also tore the riddle in two, one half which contains the main body of the riddle, which you have, the other which contains the other half of the riddle and all the signatures. He then clearly had a blacksmith sympathiser fire the statue which you held until oh so recently and the dockets were inserted."

"So to recap and clarify, whomever holds the reconstructed version of Boudicca's crown is by law ruler of this country?" Tristan asked.

"They'd need the other half of the riddle to prove it, but yes, they would be monarch."

"Good grief, it's no wonder I was burgled with that kind of knowledge out there, scant though it is, These, Frenchies, their motivation could be anything. They could be in it for the Germans, or their own government as a bargaining tool to keep Hitler off their back or just in it for themselves!"

"Well thank goodness we found our pieces first!" added Tristan. "Professor, would you happen to know what the rest of the riddle says?"

"Indeed I do. The final lines of the riddle or should we now call it statement, are, 'The High Cross to show her journey homewards, the sapphire for the lands which she vowed to defend.'"

"Incredible. I haven't a clue what that means." Benedict just stared off into space for a moment, considering all the possibilities of what he had in his possession and the last part of the riddle yet to come. He snapped out of it, he owed Trilby a debt of gratitude.

"Professor my good man, thank you so much for looking into this for us."

Benedict reached across the table and vigorously shook the old man's hand, but as he did so there was a shyness about Effingham-Wright. He wouldn't make eye contact with Benedict, he just looked down at the floor. He also noticed he was still sweating, though the room was quite cool.

"Everything alright Professor?"

Trilby looked back up, "Oh, I'm fine, I'm fine. More coffee?"

Tristan said, "Ooh, not for me, I'll be going all the time on the way home otherwise, or wherever we end up next. It's crazy and quite exciting if I do say so," he chuckled. "Just one question though, how did you come across such rare information and also find out the last few lines of the riddle. Have you seen it?"

Trilby looked down again, he looked ashamed, "No."

The handle on the additional and unassuming door to their left suddenly turned. They had presumed they were alone, apparently not. The door opened but before the imposter entered a voice rang out, with a French accent, "But I have Monsieurs."

Chapter 21

Benedict had immediately recognised the voice that had acknowledged the existence of the second piece of the riddle. It was the Frenchman who had so calmly issued the order for him to be killed back when this all started back at his Kensington apartment. But he had not seen the man that night. Now he was able to face his assailant.

Both Tristan and Benedict sprang from their chairs as the voice entered the room with such easy aloofness. He was wearing a white loose shirt and tanned riding jodhpurs with brown boots. His wispy moustache only highlighted the cruel smile underneath. Together, Benedict and Tristan would have been a match for the sinewy, handsome Frenchman, were it not for the two goons behind him. One was an extremely large fellow, the other a wild looking man with a fearful blaze to his eyes.

As simply as he was pulling out a tissue, the Frenchman retrieved two elegant looking pistols from his belt and casually held them up to his captives.

Benedict glared at Trilby, "You tricked us, this was all a ruse!"

The Frenchman answered for the ashamed professor sitting in front on him.

"Oh now, that is perhaps a little harsh no? In fact, by coming here gentlemen, you have discovered the true value of what you held until very recently, so don't be too harsh on the professor. He was only doing what he was told."

"And who is the man who addresses me?" asked Benedict, angry at the betrayal, his sense of nerves gone, replaced by the annoyance that he could be tricked into his impending death.

"A mon dieu, how rude of me, twice we have now met and twice I have had the indecency not to introduce myself, ooh lalala. Mr Lukely I presume. I sir, am Philippe De Castagnet and these are my two accomplices, Poubelle is the rather large homme and Chevalier is the intense looking fellow over there."

Both Poubelle and Chevalier gave a cheery, "Hello."

Benedict and Tristan awkwardly waved back.

"Now back to your original question, how did we know the contents of the second section of parchment? Well as I'm sure you've worked out by now, that was in the first statue we stole from you, Queen Boudicca's chariot. Now, admittedly when you're aware of a myth, a legend, and are only presented with 'The High Cross to show her journey homewards, the sapphire for the lands which she vowed to defend' it does tend to baffle one. However, Monsieurs, I can only pass on my gratitude to you."

He mockingly bowed to both men in turn.

Tristan looked peeved at his sarcasm, "Why thank us?"

Benedict sighed, "Because, our captor here has clearly been keeping an eye on our movements, and now we've fallen straight into his hands with the crown and rubies."

Philippe clapped, "Excellent deduction Monsieur Lukely! Yes, with just the second part we would not have had a clue where to begin, but you have travailed on our behalf. And now if you don't mind...."

He nodded to Chevalier who snatched the gold crown and then the sword haft away off the top of the desk. Philippe got cocky and slid one pistol back into his belt, freeing up his left hand to swing the crown round and round on one finger, watching the yellow reflection move round the room.

"Ironic, isn't it Monsieurs, that the very crown that you have been searching for is now in the hands of a Norman, the very people the riddle and the crown was designed to prevent from ruling Britain."

"Normans are the French!? Oh now it all makes sense!" Said Tristan, quite surprised as he hadn't understood all events for some time.

"Indeed," Philippe winked at him.

"So that's it, take the crown for yourself or for France and rule this country as your own?" yelled Benedict.

"I wish it were so, trust me, it would be a happier outcome. But no, you couldn't be more wrong," replied Philippe, wagging his pistol at his captives. "What has mother France ever done for me? Left me in the dirt with no father to speak of, no education and no prospects. No, I've had to find my own way in life. But it might surprise you to know that I'm just a pawn in this game of chess. Frankly I'm nothing more than a common crook."

He looked to his left back through the door where they had entered and further, heavier footsteps began to come into the room.

This time an absolute brute of a man entered the study. He made Benedict feel nervous just from looking at him. He was at least six foot seven, yet built like the proverbial best of British outhouses. Benedict was reminded of the ogre in the children's fairy tale, 'The Three Billy-goats Gruff'. His hands looked like they could punch through walls and crush mortar. His face was long, smooth, not unhandsome, but with a square jaw. He dressed in large blue pants held up with braces which looked like they should be holding cargo down on a ship's deck.

Underneath he was wearing a strong red shirt. Benedict may not have known the man but he was almost certain of where he was from.

Tristan whispered, "Good grief, how did he fit in there as well?!"

Philippe overheard, "Trust me, it was a job. If anyone had released a 'faux pas' let's say, there would have been asphyxiations".

The giant man spoke for the first time and immediately asserted his authority on the situation with a firm and deep, "Gentlemen!" He continued, "Allow me to introduce myself." Benedict's suspicion was confirmed, he was German. His English was very good but not that good.

"I am Eric Von Schuler, commander in the Abwehr to a very special unit. We are a small band of men, drawn from the SS, but with intellect and advanced knowledge of the ancient histories of this world. In fact, it may interest you to know that prior to the war, I was an archaeology professor at the university of Vienna. Now, we honour the Fuhrer by using our knowledge to locate lost history, law, people and artefacts which may ultimately give the Motherland the upper hand in such matters as lebensraum."

Benedict was worried, "So you want the crown for Hitler?"

"Yes, but there is more to the matter than conquest."

Benedict found it unusual that this man wanted to justify himself, especially under the circumstances where he completely had the upper hand.

Von Schuler continued, "You and your government must understand, that even as we speak, a force far larger and better equipped than your expeditionary force is massing in areas, unprepared by the French for an invasion by force. Hitler has no genuine reason to hate Britain but if needs be, we will in the next few days following today, invade France and undoubtedly crush the opposition who stand in our way. However, if we were to establish the crown and gain rightful, legal entitlement for the Furhrer to reign as your monarch, don't you see the lives that could be saved by averting a great and bloody war, much drawn along the same lines as the last Great War. How many men would have to die for you to see that?"

"I'm sure our expeditionary forces can handle themselves in the field of conflict." replied Benedict.

Von Schuler smiled, "You have spirit, but also blind faith. The technology and overwhelming strength of the German army is fact, not bravado on my part. Gentlemen, by securing this crown we secure the future of both our countries." He nodded to Philippe and added, "And now it is time for us to leave. I bid you Auf Wiedersehn." Von Schuler stepped out of the room.

Philippe smiled a vile, wicked grin. "Alas, parting is such sweet sorrow Monsieurs. But first, the top half of the riddle?"

Neither Benedict or Tristan said anything. Philippe nodded to Chevalier who walked up to Tristan and slapped him hard across the face.

"Ow! What the hell was that well for?"

Philippe looked at Chevalier, confused and said, "Yes, what was that for? I was merely nodding to ask you to search them and find the parchment. I thought we were on the same page?"

Chevalier stared back for a second and then threw his hands up and shrugged. He moved across to Tristan and stuck his hands into his trouser pockets.

Tristan shot him a look and said, "Do you mind!"

He ignored the Welshman and moved to Benedict, finding the parchment with the top half of the riddle and the car keys to the Phantom in Benedict's jacket pocket. Chevalier gave them to Philippe. He slipped the parchment into his back pocket and tossed the key in the air, catching it on it's downturn with a snatch.

"I saw your mode of transport as you arrive, a beautiful car. Phantom right?" he asked inquisitively.

"Yes," replied Benedict, really hoping the Frenchman wouldn't take his prized possession. Philippe seemed unsure, though he continued smiling. He finally put the key down on the desk and said, "The Renault Viva Grand Sport is also a beautiful car for a summer's day, pity you'll never get to experience it. Chevalier, Poubelle, tie them up and then burn the place down. Gentlemen, do not think me an evil man, just someone with an agenda to complete and cash to gain." He bowed to them, "Adieu," and walked out of the room. Trilby also stood up to leave, Tristan was livid. "WHAT!? But you said honour amongst thieves."
"Actually, if you recall, I said, 'no honour amongst thieves', come on, play the game a bit better or this is no sport at all!" laughed Trilby, shooting Tristan a patronising look. Benedict tried to appeal to his sense of style and history, "But what about your house, your paintings and artefacts. Good grief man, they're priceless."
Effingham-Wright stopped for a second, Benedict's words seem to have struck a chord in his mind. He scratched his scalp and then replied, "Yes, it's a shame to lose such valuable items, but I have been promised a great reward in the new kingdom and as I have said many times before, all of life's a gamble." Trilby too stepped out into the world outside this small office.

Poubelle pulled out a revolver from his own belt whilst Chevalier got to work, briefly heading back into the small room from which they sprang but returning with a length of cord and two canisters of gasoline. Helpless as they were, Benedict and Tristan were secured fast with their hands behind the chair backs and their feet tied together as well. Neither could be sure if they struggled, whether the heavyset fellow would shoot them so they simply did nothing and hoped this would not seal their doom. Tristan stared his assailant in the face and said,

"You'll not get away with this and if you do, then God help us all including you Frenchies!"

Chevalier just laughed and then spat in Tristan's face. The two assailants then grabbed their fuel canisters and liberally splashed petroleum by the doors near where Trilby had been sitting and then around the sitting room, stairs and kitchen. Poubelle went to join the others outside whilst Chevalier walked back into the study to revel in the moment. The fumy stench of petrol was everywhere and Tristan was already feeling a little heady. Chevalier pulled a small box of matches from his pocket. He plucked a single match and wickedly said, "Eeeenglish, this is the match that kills you."

He walked over to the wet gasoline patch by the wall and struck the phosphorus head against the course paper. Benedict winced, expecting a sudden ripple of flames and a short, quite painful death. But there was a dull phut as the match misfired. Chevalier threw it away and drew another. Again he struck the head, but much the same as the last, it sputtered and then died. And another match, and another and another. Tristan looked almost disappointed.

Chevalier, turning red with embarrassment gave a nervous laugh and said, "Un moment, damp matches." He opened the box, there was only three left. This was going to be awkward if he ran outside and the house was not ablaze. Luck was on his side though, but perhaps not Benedict's or Tristan's as the second before last match lit perfectly. He threw it to the ground and quickly the vaporous fuel caught alight, flames licking up from the floor. Chevalier nodded to the two helpless arson victims and scarpered.

In the moment between the last French assailant fleeing the premises and the flames beginning to travel ever so quickly, it became apparent to Benedict that the house was literally kindling for a human barbeque. Orange flames leapt from place to place as ancient dry timbers were appetizers to the thirsty fire. The house squeaked in pain as more and more of the fiery imps spread.

Benedict yelled at Tristan, "Right what do we do? I figure we've got about three minutes tops before we're Sunday roast, any ideas?"

Tristan coughed and said, "None at all. HEEEEEEEEEEEEELP!" He ended up spluttering again as more and more substances were absorbed by the fire and began to churn out black smoke.

Benedict was also panicking and starting to hyperventilate. Tristan struggled in his chair and tried to rock back and forth to break the legs. All this did though was cause him to topple over and bang his forehead on the legs of Benedict's chair. Benedict looked down at his friend who now seemed to be spinning on the floor as he struggled and babbled.

The room was taking on an abnormal temperature now as the heat from the ever-building flames caused beads of perspiration to form on Benedict's brow. Somewhere else in the house he heard the first of the ceiling timbers come crashing down. They were doomed and Benedict could see no way out this time. Whilst Tristan did his weird little jerking jig on the floor, probably coughing to death, Benedict simply closed his eyes and said a little prayer to himself, asking that if there was a God he would be accepted into his almighty and celestial flock. The temperature was starting to become intolerable, unbearable, singeing and so he kept his eyes shut and just tried to think happy thoughts whilst he waited for the end. And he waited..............and waited, the rumbling sound of a fire, boring into his ears.

And suddenly his hands were free? Was he dead, Benedict was not sure, he still felt hot as hell. Oh bugger, what if he'd been sent to hell? He opened one eye. If this was hell, and it still could be, it looked awfully cottage shaped and the devil it turned out, was Tristan.

"Right, hands free, now I suggest we flee," said a familiar Welsh voice. Benedict opened both his eyes and then raised his hands to touch his face. He was very much alive and sweating as a backdrop of flames danced behind his liberator, who had once again saved his life.

"How?" said Benedict in puzzlement, he was sure they were done for.

Tristan flipped a piece of flint into the air and caught it, giving a happy grin at his friend. "It's the piece I took from Cwmhir Abbey and tossed into my top pocket. I'd completely forgotten about it to tell the truth. When I fell off my chair it just leapt out my pocket as if to remind me. Had to wheel round to get it mind, but then I just clamped it between my hands and worked the edge on the rope!"

"I could kiss you right now, but I won't. This place is going to topple like a house of cards if we don't get out now, lead the way!"

Both men legged it across the room to the side door which the perpetrators had come through, guessing that it led to a back door. Fortunately they were right. Benedict was delighted to find an old black key in the lock and he wiggled the door open as a beam toppled behind them. The house was falling apart now and would soon be nothing but a bonfire. He threw the door open and then just as he was about to escape to freedom, he turned to Tristan.

"The key, the bally key to the Phantom. We'll never catch them if we don't have transport." Benedict went to run back into the blaze.

Tristan grabbed Benedict's left lapel to keep him there and shouted at him with fury, "Leave it you fool, you're no use dead!"

It didn't matter. Benedict yanked himself free and ran back into the yellow and amber colours. Not looking back, Benedict entered the office which was now like a furnace and saw that the keys had fallen to the floor. He leapt gallantly over flaming debris and reached down for his beloved Phantom's keys. Just then, he heard a telling squeak above his head and realised his fate. The arm he raised to try and protect himself was too slow as a heavy, smouldering beam came down and struck him on the forehead, knocking him out cold.

Chapter 22

Everything was dark, a dark that only the mind's eye can hold. And it was so peaceful, peaceful and cool. Yes, let's not forget cool. From where Benedict had come from, this was especially cool. And did he mention peaceful? What was this place, this wonderful place of darkness, coolness and what felt like elevation? Was he floating? If so, was he floating in water or in the air? That's important he thought, as if he was floating in water, that was plausible as anyone could float in water, except for those that couldn't swim of course. But he was a strong swimmer, he'd got medals, certificates and who knows how many purposefully tossed bricks out of swimming pools.

But if he was floating in air, that was different. That had an ethereal quality to it and he couldn't naturally do that. And if he was floating in air, in the cool, calm, dark place, then it could only mean one thing. He was sure of it now, he was floating on air. He straightened a tie he didn't have on. *You want to look your best if you're going to meet your maker.* He presented himself as best he could and then he felt the cold refreshing chill of two parts hydrogen and one part oxygen on his forehead.

Nope, definitely in water. And then as air rushed round his ears, as ice cold water splashed his face, Benedict was rushed out of the darkness back into reality and was greeted by the most beautiful face he'd ever seen.

"Hey stranger, thought we'd lost you there for a while," said Lillian Warner, the curator at Colchester Museum. Benedict blinked his eyes and saw before him that he was in one of the great halls of the museum. He lay on a cold polished floor surrounded by suits of armour and other interesting ancient paraphernalia. Everything seemed warm and fuzzy and if he was being honest with himself, there was a distinct ringing in his head. The back of his skull seemed to be rhythmically pulsating and there was a general warmth coming from the beat of every pulse. It then occurred to Benedict that there was no way he should be in the museum unless he had invented a time machine and travelled back to the moment when he and his Welsh friend met Lillian, that most wonderful, beautiful and challenging of women, who had then clearly smacked him round the back of the head with an antique. The last thing he could remember, oh what was it?

The heat, the intense heat. He and his companion Tristan were trying to escape, but from what? Then the events of the recent past hit him and his head really throbbed. He reached to the back of his scalp. Benedict's hair felt matted and sticky. A wave of nausea flowed over him, as he remembered now, the trip back to Trilby's, the deception and capture, the relinquishing of all they'd tried so hard for, the fire and then the beam crashing down on top of him. How he got here was the next question.

Lillian batted his hand away and said, "Leave it Benedict, you'll only give yourself an infection."

Then another marble dropped, Benedict? She definitely called him Benedict. She didn't know, shouldn't know that he was called Benedict, but what was he supposed to be called?

"Er, Benedict my dear? I think you'll find I'm Captain Trousershot or Jeremy Five-Iron and this is my glamorous assistant Rhonda!" he said pointing at a baffled looking Tristan.

Lillian placed another sponge of cold water on Benedict's head and pressed it so that the cold liquid ran over his face and down his neck. She gently said to him, "I thought your names were actually Rhodry Jones and Gerald Updike, Benedict."

Benedict panicked, "Oh, she knows! Tristan sh'knows," his head pounded again. He struggled and Lillian steadied him by placing a warm soft hand on his arm and applied a gentle pressure. Her touch set off a wonderful choir singing in Benedict's head. He flopped again to the floor and then sat up, scratching the uninjured side of his head.

"So to recap, in full, I have no idea how we got here, will somebody please tell me?"

Tristan coughed, "Well, you um, ran back into Effingham-Wright's house to get your car keys and a large beam crashed down on top of you, hence your bleeding head."

"It doesn't look too bad by the way, I've applied some antiseptic to it," Lillian added.

Tristan continued, "So, you'd been knocked out cold in the middle of a house which was about to collapse and well, I, I dragged you out. I didn't know where to go or who to turn to. And the only person I could think of whom I knew locally was Miss Warner here."

"Right, right," said Benedict, "But, I mean, how did I get here, I was out cold, did an ambulance take us or something? Surely I'd be in hospital."

Tristan grinned sheepishly, "Well, you know you said I'd never driven anything like your Phantom before?" he coughed nervously, "Well, I have now". He opened his hands wide as if to say "Tadaah! Hence we're here!"

"You mean to say you drove my car all the way here, without even asking me?!"

"Well, it was a little bit difficult to get your permission, you were unconscious and bleeding profusely after all," replied Tristan, quite put out.

"You drove my.... No hang on, you stole my car and drove it here!? My baby? My beloved Phantom? You could have ruined it!"

"Oh thanks for pulling me out of the fire Tristan, thank you for saving my life by getting help Tristan! Tip of the cap for the ruddy vote of gratitude Benedict, I just saved your life, wish I hadn't of bothered now, you ungrateful shit!" Tristan said.

"Kinda has a point," added Lillian.

"Yes well, I've just had a little juice squeezed out of my lemon, that's all."

Benedict gathered himself together. He sat, slumped forward like a drunkard and looked up. "Tristan, I owe you an apology. I suppose it was necessary to drive my car with me so incapacitated and in danger of losing my life, so, thank you."

"Gracious to the last," mocked Tristan.

"Take it man, it's all you're getting. Now can someone tell me why Lillian knows our true names?" He eagerly eyed Tristan again, ready to retract his apology. "We are, after all back in a place where, SOMETHING, happened earlier, SOMETHING bad. Something to do with some rubies?"

"I had to tell her".

"And what did you tell her?"

"Everything, and stop referring to me as her, I'm in the room," said Lillian who had stopped helping this pompous ingrate.

"Why, did she give you a Chinese burn or something?" said Benedict, still aiming the barbs at Tristan.

"No, because he had no choice. I was just locking up for the night and suddenly two fellas who claimed to be fancy polishers turn up, one bleeding half to death. He had to tell me or I'd have gotten the police involved and by the sounds of it, you wouldn't want that to happen. And trust me, Chinese burn? I could snap your wrist like it was a stick of Coney Island rock candy."

Benedict felt his wrist as if she had unconsciously wreaked damage to his arm with her words. Fortunately she hadn't, but he believed her strength.

"So here we are. I'm awake, what now? Will you hand us over to the authorities?" Benedict asked.

"Well, to paraphrase what I've been told by your little friend over there, through a burglary at your own premises, you have discovered a document older than the Magna Carta, where if the component parts of the crown of Queen Boudicca are found, then the owner with the document will have the legal right to call themselves monarch of Britain. You found the rubies on a sword hilt; nice robbery by the way, you've got the whole of Colchester up in arms on that one."

Benedict blushed.

"You then travelled to Wales where, purely by chance you actually found the crown, but on returning to London you were tricked by an old schoolmaster who had been infiltrated by those who committed the burglary in the first place. It turns out that a Frenchman called Philippe De Castagnet was working for a Nazi who sought the crown and therefore the legal right to the throne for Hitler. On stealing your items, the thieves made off and set the cottage you were tied up in ablaze. You both narrowly escaped but on re-entering to get your car keys you were bludgeoned on the head by a falling beam and your friend here, Tristan, very bravely pulled you out whilst the house collapsed around you and then quite sensibly drove you here to me."

Benedict felt ashamed for the way he'd behaved earlier and with his head hung low, said to Tristan, "Sorry for being a total blaggard."

Tristan shot him a smile back, "Apology accepted."

Lillian continued, "To answer your other question, involving the police. Well, you've infiltrated a barracks during wartime and committed theft twice. I'd say the chances of you not being locked up and having the key thrown away are as much as Hitler having a sense of humour, saying, ' April fool,' and giving all the countries he's invaded back to their rightful owners. But then, if I do hand you in as common crooks and what you've said is really happening, I mean, why would anyone in their right mind make up anything as convoluted as this? It just makes no sense, which in some ways means it makes perfect sense. So as far as I see it, there is only one choice...."

Benedict and Tristan looked at each other, both slightly confused and not sure what the very obvious answer was.

"You have to take me with you."

"I'm sorry?" said Benedict, slightly shocked that this distinguished, learned woman would want any part of their caper.

"You have to take me with you. Think about it, they have this Effingham-Wright guy, who is a solid historian. And can bet your bottom dollar that with him on board they know the location of the last piece, this, 'Sapphire to show the journey home'. Well I'm pretty handy with the history too fellas."

"Ah but it's not as simple as that, surely. We need some sort of high cross to find it and where you stick that high cross is well beyond me," replied Benedict dismissively.

"You readily shoot down my abilities Mr Lukely," Lillian wagged a finger at him, "I can tell you now that as a senior at college, my thesis was based on ancient Roman Britain". She walked away to a cabinet and unlocked it. Before Benedict could see what she was doing, he added rudely, "And?"

"And," said Lillian now unfolding what looked like a very delicate map, "And, I can tell you all about High Cross..." Benedict paused and then replied, "Well, what is it?"

"Not what is it?" replied Lillian placing the map on the floor in front of him and rolling it out, "Where is it?"

Tristan moved across to where they were standing and peered down at the geographical representation. The map was centuries old and showed a very rough looking outline of what they knew as Britain and various cities' and towns' names. It was yellowing, torn in places and the edges were curling away.

"High Cross is believed to be the location of the final battle of Boudicca's reign, the battle of Watling Street. There is supposed to be an old Roman fort there called Venonis. It's near a small village called Claybrook Magna. There isn't much there now of course, just a load of old moss covered ruins and hillocks. But in terms of Roman war strategy the plains near Venonis and the forests which surrounded it would have been perfect for a Roman attack. If I'm wrong, change my name to Nancy and spank me with a paddle, but it should be easy as pie to find."

Benedict became excited, "Well what are we waiting for then?"

"So that's a yes in terms of me coming?"

"Seems like we can't do it without you," said Tristan.

"That's settled then," Lillian smiled that wonderful broad red lipstick smile and Benedict immediately thought about changing her name to Nancy and finding a spanking implement. He shivered at the thought.

"First things first though, you need to get some sugary tea inside of you and rest up. This sapphire won't find itself in a heartbeat, it was meant to be difficult to find. I'll make you both a tea and then grab some downtime. How d'you take it?"

Benedict thought he'd try a cheeky line, "I like my tea like I like my women," he shouted as she walked away to the kitchen.

"I know, slightly wet, bitter and in need of some sugar", she yelled back without turning around. "Gosh you're just full of charm. I bet you're the kind of guy who also has a name for his manhood..."

Benedict couldn't help volunteering this information, he was under her spell and it just tumbled out of his mouth, "Spike?"

Tristan shook his head as Lillian laughed and yelled back sarcastically, "How romantic!"

When Lillian returned with the tea, they sat and talked, Tristan and Benedict told her all about themselves and their chance encounter on a street in London which began this adventure. Eventually the talk turned to Lillian. Tristan asked, "So, how about you, what brings you to our fair shores then?"

"Well", she twirled a lock of hair with her fingers, "Don't laugh, but ever since I was a little girl I wanted to be a chorus line dancer. But when I was eight years old, I was on a pony trek during a family holiday up around Lake Michigan. I couldn't get my pony move and everyone else headed off, so I geed up my steed for the day, but the horse wouldn't stop eating the grass in front of it. So I jumped off and started to push it as hard as I could. Two things happened. Firstly the pony kicked me hard on the shin bone, meaning that I've never been able to put a lot of pressure on that leg in terms of doing ballet, and secondly as I was knocked over, it er, it pooped on me."

"It pooped on you?"

"Yes, it pooped on me, so I don't like horses that much."

Benedict sniggered. "Well as funny as that is, that only explains a lifelong aversion to equestrian pursuits but doesn't explain why you ended up as a temporary curator of a museum."

"No it doesn't, well, knowing that a career as a dancer wasn't in the making, I looked at what else I loved. And when I was at school, history and archaeology were my passions. I was always a bit of a tomboy, always out on my Schwinn, that's a bike, up trees, digging up old fossils on beaches. I just loved what the past could tell us about the future. So, I majored in it at university hoping one day to pass on that knowledge. After graduating, I worked in some of the Chicago museums for a time, but missed drinking, or maybe I didn't thanks to Al Capone, and I came to Blighty. Only kidding, an opportunity came up for a group of historians to exchange ideas in a kind of job swap arrangement. I did a good job for the Natural History Museum as a Researcher, next thing I know a colleague says, 'Hey a temporary curator job at an out of town museum is open, fancy going for it?' Curator sure looks good on your CV so I tossed my hat into the ring. I just didn't understand how small that ring was. And here I am, surrounded by dusty armour and very very old discoveries." There was a touch of disdain now in her voice.

Tristan thought this was ideal though, "But I thought this would be the place that would make you happiest?"

"Well I'm not quite a fossil yet myself at twenty six. For me, the thrill is in the chase. I don't want to be surrounded by other peoples' success, lovely as it is. I want dirt under my nails, I want the hem of my skirt ripped by a bramble bush as I search for a lost artefact. Now that's finding history."

"Sounds like it was lucky that we found you then," winked Benedict

She nodded, "I think I might be your greatest find yet..."

"And modest too!"

The trio of unexpected adventurers fell about laughing.

After more tea and checking that Benedict was not concussed, Lillian disappeared briefly to square away her office and then they stepped out into the gloom of the growing evening. To the man on the street it would have looked like one hot broad and a couple of charcoal smudged down and outs. Tristan approached the driver's side as he still had the key.

"Er, what do you think you're doing?" asked Benedict.

"Well you might have a concussion!"

Benedict thought about it and shook his head, "Fair point I suppose."

"What will we do when we get there?" Lillian asked, looking for a plan of action.

Tristan replied, "Same thing we always do, improvise." He slid into the car and banged his door shut. With some trepidation, Lillian did the same.

Chapter 23

Neither Tristan nor Benedict had had any sleep for over twelve hours and both were exhausted from the day's events. For Benedict, this not a problem, he sat in the back of the Phantom and drooled down the clammy passenger window, gently snoring, dreaming of Lillian being chased by a flock of paddles, each with the word 'Nancy' written on them. For Tristan though, he was in the final spasms of consciousness. His eye lids were starting to drop and the street lamps were beginning to draw pretty dancing patterns on his retinas as he blinked. Then there were the other signs of fatigue, road signs changed before his very eyes. 'Wheathampstead' became, 'We'll hang Ted,' 'Kettering' became 'Lettering,' literally and 'Corby' became 'Can't be,' which was possibly accurate. He'd successfully traversed Hertfordshire, Buckinghamshire and Bedfordshire and was well into Northamptonshire by the time the Tristan nodded off with his fellow passengers. The car drifted aimlessly across the road and somehow kept going without running into oncoming traffic. Thank goodness the automobile was still a relatively recent personal addition to most, as the Phantom evaded collisions whilst they trundled along, passengers asleep, as well as the driver.

Thankfully or not, depending on your view on animal rights, the car hit a badger with a sizeable bump and everyone involved apart from the recently departed wildlife woke up to find the car veering up the driveway of a house. Tristan slammed on the breaks which responded with a highly agitated squeal and a near calamity was averted. "It's no good!" he proclaimed as an old couple with matching his and hers nightgowns appeared with a lantern at the front door of the house fifty metres away. "I can't continue, I need something soft to lay on for a nap."

"How about your head?" suggested the mildly agitated Benedict, more than a little nonplussed about his Phantom nearly ending up as an oversize ornament embedded in a stranger's lounge wall.

Lillian piped up, "I know how to drive, remember, tom boyish adolescence?"

"Well now, I don't know if I'm happy with that," was the sexist reply from Benedict.

"Trust me, this cat needs the woman's touch to make her purr, besides the natives are getting restless."

The tartan coloured home owners had retrieved a garden fork and the husband was advancing down the driveway. Lillian and Tristan jumped out to switch seats before Benedict could say anything. Regardless, he was rendered incapable of speech for the next forty five minutes while the thought of purring and a woman's slight of hand played through his mind over and over again.

A good two hours later and the horizon, which had been a perfect night sky, was beginning to lighten and the countryside took on that dim, misty uneasiness which appeared before the new day. Sparse blackbirds called out their morning song and the undulating Leicestershire countryside rolled as the Phantom and it's three passengers passed through silent villages and foreboding woodland. Finally, after passing through Lutterworth, they exited a small country track and were travelling a short way on the road to Hinckley and Nuneaton.

"This is Watling Street, as it's traditionally known," said Lillian, "I think we should be close."

The hairs on the back of Benedict's neck stood up, partly a mixture of fear and partly exhilaration at the potential showdown to come.

The car travelled for a further ten minutes, then a sign showed another old road named, 'Fosse Way'. It intersected the road they were on and disappeared in another direction.

"This is it, we're here!" said Lillian peering out to look at the fields and hedges surrounding them. She slowed the car down to a crawl and then brought the Phantom to a complete stop, just past the crossroads, in the worn down muck of an entrance to a field where sheep were grazing. She turned off the magnificent engine and they all sat there, Benedict, Tristan and Lillian, taking in the soft play of the wind on the bushes and the harsh morning calls of the crows. After a minute, Benedict was completely underwhelmed.

"Really? Is this it?"

"Yup, this is High Cross, Sugar", replied Lillian.

Benedict who had been expecting an imposing and mildly phallic citadel or fortress could see nothing but condensation on the inside of his window and the hedges surrounding the convergence of the two roads. It was rather a wash-out.

"I don't see anything," added Tristan, apparently agreeing with Benedict's sentiment that High Cross was significant only by it's severe lack of a high cross or anything remarkable at all.

"Well then, shall we stretch our legs and engage our investigative minds?" replied Lillian as she opened her door and confidently stepped out. The two men were less confident however, fearing for an unseen foe, a sniper perhaps, ready to ambush any who would challenge Philippe De Castagnet and Eric Von Schuler. Slowly both men climbed out, stood up to full height and scanned the horizon. The morning air was still but bracing, especially with the gentle mist. Tristan rubbed his own arms and jogged on the spot to warm up a bit. Benedict was looking for the fabled placed called Venonis, he quickly found it.

The four quarter fields that filled the intersection of High Cross were unspectacular if not rather stereotypical of the English countryside. Three of them were occupied by agriculture, one with happily grazing sheep, nervously eyeing up the passers by and the other two by crops that were showing signs of developing into a healthy wheat harvest. However, in the fourth field there shone the beautiful fortress of Venonis. Or at least it would have done, had the Roman empire not collapsed two thousand years ago.

All three of them trudged the short distance across the road to a gated field where a series of green mounds were situated over the space of approximately seventy metres squared. They were moss covered and grassy, in varying sizes although none of them extended outwards to a great degree or had a height above twelve feet. All three of the adventurers stood and stared, leaning on the cold gate, letting the dew that formed on the wood seep into their sleeves. It was Tristan that broke the silence.
"It's not as awe inspiring as I had hoped."
"Well, what did you expect? It's around two thousand years old." replied Lillian.
"I know, I just thought something would have been made of it, all things considered, at least a sign for something so monumental," Tristan added.
"Well we could be missing an absolute sitter. It could be conspicuous in its modesty. We should at least inspect the grounds around for any clues," said Benedict.

It didn't take many strolls round the small remains of the once great Roman fortress to realise that if there were any clues here, they were expertly hidden but more likely non-existent. The old remains revealed nothing but grassy, tufty hillocks and smooth earth beneath. It seemed highly unlikely that anything was buried there. Benedict stood in the middle of the lumps of hardcore, hands on hips mulling over their next move. Only a single prop plane flying low overhead broke his train of thought. He rolled his tongue around his mouth whilst he considered an appropriate avenue and then sucked air through his teeth.

"I can't see it being here, not in an accessible way anyway."

"I'm inclined to agree," added Lillian. "Hey we should try one of the villages over from here. I saw the sign for Claybrook Magna at the cross roads. We could at least snoop around and maybe ask some of the locals regarding the history of the area. It might give us some insight."

"Fine, but we'll need to be cautious though. We don't want to go careening into the other team in this race."

They all left the field, Tristan closing the gate behind them and then jumped back into the Phantom. The day had brightened up now as Benedict put the car into reverse and swung the car round into the cross roads and then forwards toward the village of Claybrook Magna. After a short journey down the small country lane, the car was rolling into the picturesque streets. Suddenly Tristan shouted, "Look!" and pointed at a large public health risk moving slowly, two hundred meters down the road. Benedict immediately recognised the object as the all consuming, fat, lumpen shape of the assailant De Castagnet called 'Poubelle. He glided the car behind a local store's van that had been parked up for the night.

"Do you think he saw us?" asked Tristan.

From where they had stopped, the car was well hidden but Benedict could still see up the road and to the right. He stared into this space, hoping that Poubelle would appear in his field of vision.

Lillian said, "What is it, who was it, was it one of the guys who we're after?"

Benedict just nodded, never taking his eyes off the remaining visible part of the street. The tension in the car was heavy and was punctuated by Tristan's noisy heart racing in his chest. Benedict gave a sigh of relief as he saw Poubelle, still in the distance, cross the road and oil out of view down what looked like an alley.

"Panic over," he said.

"Who was it and what the hell is that smell?" said Lillian.

"Apologies," said Tristan, "It was quite a powerful gust I admit."

Benedict pinched his nose and said with a nasal whine, "That was a chap we believe to be called Poubelle. He's one of De Castagnet's henchmen and as a gambling man I'd be prepared to put a sizeable chunk of sterling on a bet that says wherever Poubelle is, De Castagnet can't be far away."

Lillian was practical as ever, "Well then, shouldn't we be following him?"

This flustered Benedict, "Yes I suppose so. But we'll need someone to keep an eye on our rear end. We don't know just how big this organisation is. We should be casual but cautious and try to blend in. And for god sake, let's get out of this excreance!"

"Again, I'm rather eggbound at the moment, I do apologise."

"Under the circumstances, you are forgiven, now let us away and get some fresh air."

Benedict clicked open his door and stepped out onto the quiet street. He gently pushed his door shut, followed by Tristan and Lillian. Benedict looked around at his surroundings. The village was surrounded by old large trees, whose sapling shoots sparkled in the early morning dew. It was a small village with houses dotted amongst large, wooded gardens and a Saxon church with what looked to be either a rectory or manor house on the other side. There was an old village shop, just close to where they were parked and the shop's delivery van sat out in front, but there were no other cars to be seen. Had the crooks they were chasing arrived by car, which inevitably they would have due to the size of party and speed which they themselves had arrived, it was nowhere to be seen. The two men and Lillian started to walk down the street, Tristan lagging behind slightly, keeping a good eye on what was coming from behind. So far, no net curtains had noticeably twitched at their arrival and only one person had seen them, a farmhand cycling by on the way to work. They nodded their head in greeting and he gave them a nod and "Nin," back.

After a short walk they had reached the point where Poubelle had disappeared from view. To their left was a pub, a local tavern called The World's End, Benedict hoped it wasn't a sign of things to come. To their right, in between two red bricked houses there was a farm track and then a gate which led out into a green pasture beyond. Just in the distance, they could see the slow, lumbering frame of their target unsteadily climbing over a sty into a field not visible to the eye due to the hedge row running along it. Poubelle bested the sty as when cocking his leg over, he lost balance and took the two fencing rungs that were causing his balancing predicament with him as he fell backwards. Lillian stifled a snigger as the poor Frenchman got up and waddled over into the field and away out of view. Benedict said, "Perfect, we can see where he's going without him seeing us. We should move to the hedge line."

They set off, down the alley way and through the farm gate, Tristan, ever vigilant, kept an eye on where they'd come from.

The green pasture was a grazing field for horses kept at a paddock along the right boundary line of the field. Two brown mares happily ignored the new visitors as they chewed the early morning cud. Benedict and Lillian skirted across the field as Tristan kept up the rear-guard action. The morning dew had slowly, unassumingly crept through the leather of Benedict's shoes and he squirmed as the cold, wet feeling entered his socks. They had finally reached the hedge line and ducking down, they took the final few steps at a stoop so as not to be seen.

"Right, what's happening?" said a nervy, slightly out of breath Tristan.

"We've not taken a peep yet. In fact, I'm not sure either I or you should." Benedict whispered to Tristan. He continued, "You and I, we're a known quantity, whereas Lillian is a complete stranger to them. She could be one of the locals for all they know. Lillian, would you be willing?"

"Sure," was her easy reply. She raised her profile from the squatting position into more of a stoop, hand on her knees until her vision was just crowning the top of the bramble bush. The field ahead and its contents were brought into view.

The field opposite to them was not a field as such, but a very large patch of scrub or common land. It seemed to stretch into the horizon, but was flanked either side by the dark tree lines of a forest almost as if this fat strip of land acted as a fire break. The turf was unkempt, with tufty grasses. It did however have one defining feature, a reasonably sized duck pond. Young reeds gently bobbed in the breeze and some cautious mallards had made their way to the far side of the pond due to the stragers that were now in the field. It was these conspicuous people that drew Lillian's attention.

"I see about eight men, standing round a large pond," she said.

Benedict was surprised, "Really?"

He looked at Tristan who was also worried. So far they had only countered Philippe and what they assumed were his only two henchmen. Curiosity got the better of both Benedict and Tristan and slowly they also raised themselves to take a look over the hedge.

Lillian was right and they recognised the bulky shape of Poubelle who was standing at the edge with other men they didn't recognise. He was staring at the ducks and didn't seem that interested in proceedings. Another two familiar faces were deep in discussion a good ten feet away from the others. It was Philippe talking to Von Schuler. Frantic gesturing toward the pond and solemn nods were the order of the day, as if they were planning an approach.

Philippe whistled across to one of the unknown men who walked towards the pond carrying a spade. This man then lent on the handle as he took off his shoes and socks, rolled up his trouser legs to beyond his knees and then waded a few feet into the murky depths. A chuckle went up from the group, as the accomplice stepped on something sharp and danced about holding his foot. He continued; the water had reached his kneecaps and was now soaking his trousers and the lower portion of his thighs. He stopped and looked to Philippe who then gave a subtle nod. The subordinate drove the spade down into the pond and then levered the pond muck up from below. It was an easy movement as years worth of silt gave way to the spade-head. A dark brown cloud spread out onto the surface. He struck the same patch again, resulting in the same outcome. There was a brazenness to proceedings, the cloak and dagger approach of the robberies was long past. The field they were in and also the field that Benedict, Tristan and Lillian were viewing this scene from were both visible to the back bedroom windows of the houses on the street that they had originally walked down. Philippe and his gang didn't seem to care.

"What is it that they're doing in that pond?" asked Tristan in a hushed tone.

"Presumably digging for the sapphire, but how they found the exact place is anyone's guess. Remember that twenty minutes ago we we're strolling around a series of ancient lumps."

"Probably Trilby," replied Tristan, "Can't see him now though."

The old professor was conspicuous by his absence it had to be said. The worst of thoughts crossed Benedict's mind but sadly, on the basis that he had narrowly escaped death twice in the clutches of a particularly charming but tenacious Frenchman, Benedict could only presume that the worst had probably happened.

Lillian surveyed the field, "Perfect spot for it. This was just how the Romans liked to fight, flanked by a tree line so that with their organised tactics, they could hit hard and there was no room for manoeuvre by the opposition. If the sapphire is anywhere, here is as good a place to bury it."

"You said the same about the tufty monuments," replied Benedict.

Lillian held her gaze on the field, "Archaeology is one part education and two parts guesswork dear, do you know which famous person said that?"

Benedict racked his brain, he was sure he knew it, "I give up, who?"

"Me, ten seconds ago, now shut up and keep watching."

The subordinate in the duck pond raised his spade to show nothing but mud. He received unheard instructions from Von Schuler and moved to his right, trying his luck again and again only with a muddy return. He waded further in but the water line rested just above his crotch as apparently he had reached the ponds maximum depth. He struck with the spade a third time, a fourth time and then on the fifth occurrence just when Philippe and Von Schuler had started to mutter and become distracted, there was a noisy CLOINK as the spade hit something other than mud. This sound was hard and metallic and refocused everyone around the lake. A satisfied look sprang on the face of man in the water and he wiped his brow with his free hand and then tossed the spade to the edge of the pond. He gathered his balance and then rolled up his sleeves. Plunging both hands into the muddy pond, Benedict could see that the accomplice was rifling around in the silt underneath for whatever had made the alerting noise. Finally his arms had stopped moving as if they had found the corner of the unseen object. Colour flushed the subordinate's cheeks as he pulled hard and the object began to come unstuck from hundreds of years of being buried. He strained and yelled something at Von Schuler in a language none of them understood, presumably German. And just when they thought he was likely to suffer an aneurism, there was a satisfying gurgle from under the water as the hidden treasure shifted, causing the poor henchman to topple backward and fall fully into the murky depths.

Falling into the mucky, brown and black murk of thepond would have been sufficient to ruin anyone's morning, but the man reappeared, his head first and then shoulders. After he'd blown the water from his fringe he stood up and smiled whilst raising what initially looked to

Tristan to be a large brown log. The man now slowly stood up, his clothes pouring with strings of water at the extremities as he waded back to the shore and his masters. A pleased grin spread across his face as small applause broke out around him from the assembled group. He handed the soggy brown object to Philippe whose mouth was hanging open. Fortunately, from where he was standing, they could see exactly what Philippe was about to do.

On closer inspection, Tristan realised it was not a log. It was a large object, approximately the width of Philippe's chest, with a shallow depth of about a hand. The wooden colouring was actually an old rag. It looked like a large piece of chamois, used to protect its contents. Drawing it away, Philippe next revealed the bulk of the item. It was a dirty looking metal box. The container was yellowing in colour so was either made of tin or perhaps bronze. It was of practical design, not ornate in any way and completely smooth. Philippe trailed his elegant fingers along the ice cold metal lid, fantasizing about the contents which were about to reveal themselves like some burlesque dancer switching feathers and flashing just a glimpse of something taboo.

Philippe could wait no longer, he felt which side of the box was hinged and flung the lid open, causing the weight of the container to shift and for him to nearly drop it. Philippe moved his hands in time and gave himself a self assured raise of the eyebrow as if the spillage was never in doubt. But then the eyebrow fell and a frown descended upon his now confused looking expression.

They all knew why they were standing here in this field, or peeking over the hedge, it was to establish the existence of a long since mythical stone. Philippe had potentially beaten Benedict to the final resting place of the sapphire, but the look on Philippe's face sent waves of elation over Benedict's body. Philippe was staring at nothing but a box full of old rags.

"He hasn't got it! He hasn't got it!" Benedict whispered. Tristan and Benedict shook hands in congratulations. Their moment of triumph was short lived though.

"Stand up," said Lillian, "Looks like there's more."

The hessian cloth was rammed tightly into the tin and it took a good tug from Philippe to free it. For the most part the material was just the end of one extremely large roll, plugging up the container, but it was the potential of what was on the end of the roll which held everyone's gaze. As Philippe pulled the cloth upwards, the ball slowly unravelled until it was the size of a child's fist. One final pull and a clatter occurred in the tin.

Benedict gulped.

Philippe's satanic grin reappeared and he snatched greedily into the tin at the fallen object. The most large and beautiful sapphire that either group had ever seen sat in the palm of his hand. Philippe held it up to his right eye and the morning light. It gave off an almost ethereal blue sheen. This time all the men, including Von Schuler rushed round to congratulate him and despite not having put in the labour to dig for it, it was he who hungrily ate up all the praise.

Tristan's mouth was dry from it being open too long in amazement. He swallowed and said, "I think that's the most beautiful thing I've ever seen."

Lillian too was in agreement, "You could be as dumb as a post and as mad as a blue bottle near a dung heap and I'd still marry you with that surrounded by a gold ring."

Benedict was less emphatic in his praise, he knew what this meant, "Well the game is up then folks." He gave a darkened frown.

To make their day a hair's breadth worse, there was then the obvious click of a pistol being cocked into firing position behind them. Benedict closed his eyes. Of course, they had completely forgotten to continue checking behind them to cover their rears and now had been caught in the act. He hoped it was a local bobby, having been informed by a net curtain tweaker from the houses behind. Or perhaps the army were running drills nearby and had been alerted to the strange happenings. They had seen two planes flying low over the area so maybe British airmen were nearby and had been roused by suspicion. But he knew; Benedict knew it could only be one person.

In unison they all turned around and began to raise their hands. It was as Benedict feared: Chevalier, the slightly deranged henchman. How long he had stood there behind them they could only guess, but it was obviously long enough to draw to pistols and clench a hunting knife between his snarling teeth.

"Bugger it," said Benedict, with a healthy dollop of defeatism thrown in for good measure.

Through the art of looking menacing and making circular motions with the pistol in his left hand, Chevalier got the small party in front of him to turn around with their hands on their heads and step over the collapsed steeple which Poubelle had ruined earlier on. Philippe was square on to them and initially didn't notice their entrance to the field, but now out of the corner of his eye, he caught the weary procession coming towards him and turned to look with Von Schuler. Philippe still held the heavy and exquisite sapphire in his left hand. His right hand which held the metal box now dropped it to the grass below, in shock. *How had they survived the fire? And what are they doing here now?* He then realised that their party had expanded by one, a confident and exquisite woman. Von

Schuler looked on with the calculating blandness of expression that Benedict and Tristan had witnessed back at Trilby's cottage. The rest of the henchmen had now also seen the group being shepherded along by Chevalier and similarly a couple of them drew pistols and cautiously edged towards Benedict, Tristan and Lillian.

Philippe didn't really know what to make of the situation, he felt angry at himself. He should have just shot them when he had the chance. To have them here now just made a mockery of him in front of one of the most important men in the Abwehr. No matter, he had his sapphire and therefore the deck of cards was heavily stacked in his favour. But he would need to act quickly, the sleepy village behind them would soon wake up and the lace net curtains that looked out on this grassy strip of land might be alarmed to see strange men, armed men. They were so close to their goal yet perhaps their open brazenness in this moment was foolish. The crown was not yet ready and all it would take was a call to the police and the game could be up. Benedict was nearly in spitting distance, so Philippe wiped the look of shock and disappointment off his face and affected a smile, but which could not hold a candle to his usual Cheshire-cat like grin. He opened his hands out in a welcoming gesture.

"Ah Monsieurs, just when I thought we would no longer cross paths, serendipity it seems has once more brought a fortuitous moment where you too can witness our eventual triumph."

Von Schuler issued a command in German and all the henchmen apart from Chevalier put away their weapons. Philippe focussed on Lillian, "And what precious flower of the meadows do we have here?" he said, changing his disposition to his normal wormy, flirty self.

"Christina Beauregard", replied Lillian. Benedict managed to hide a smirk, but found it funny that she should give a fake name at this stage of proceedings. Having said that he probably knew as much about her as he did about Effingham-Wright. *Are they all in on this?* He started to doubt himself.

Philippe bent forward and kissed her hand, "Enchanted Madame, and may I say what a happy coincidence that your name loosely translated means looking good, when you yourself are Cupid's bow, which fires the arrow to entangle men's hearts."

"I'm more of a Smith and Wesson girl myself. Bows all sound a little effete for my liking."

Von Schuler nudged Philippe in the back and coughed; this was all getting a tad unprofessional and messy for his liking.

Philippe gave an annoyed glance over his shoulder and returned to his duties as the villainous host. "Well, it does not matter how the three of you met and what part you play in this. Madame, it would give me great pleasure to invite you to witness the birth of a new era, plus we will have some other special guests!"

Tristan's mind immediately turned to who was missing, "Where's Trilby Effingham-Wright?"

His suspicion that he might be the guest was wrong, "Ah Mr Wynd, why the good professor has played his part in this sordid little tale. But alas, on imparting the likely whereabouts of High Cross and the sapphire, his time with us had expired indefinitely." That didn't sound good.

Philippe assured them, "Do not worry though my friends, you will have the opportunity to see this moment drawn to completion, but beyond that, I'm afraid it's too late for you," he turned to Lillian, still willing to extend his sexual olive branch, "But perhaps for you Madame we can choose a happier road?"

"Oh that sounds like a fate worse than death, I'll take death please."

Philippe gave an exaggerated frown, "C'est la vie, you make me sad by your choice."

"You won't get away with this!" said Benedict, raising his voice and hoping it might carry and wake some of the houses nearby.

Realising his game, Philippe tutted and replied, "Oh but I will and when I do, there won't be anything to get away with."

Von Schuler had recognised that Philippe seemed very committed to the ideology of the Fuhrer becoming the new ruler of Britain, perhaps worryingly committed. Why should he care? He was a common French thief in a country that stood shortly to be occupied by Germany, regardless of outcomes here. Was he hoping his loyalty would provide him with the opportunity of power in the new regime? Von Schuler wasn't certain, but something was amiss.

Compelled, he stood by Philippe's side and said, "Yes, a new era of German occupation and British collaboration." This flustered Philippe and he added, "Of course, of course."

Now it was time to return briefly to discretion "Poubelle, could you administer a little nap for our three friends here s'il vous plait."

Poubelle looked confused, "C'est le matin," he replied.

Philippe impatiently sighed and repeated, "Poubelle, Le bon nuit pour trios, s'il vous plait."

Poubelle finally understood this and lumped towards one of the other collaborators who was carrying a satchel. A moment later he came back with a handkerchief and a green bottle, one Benedict was all too aware of the contents of. Philippe had had enough and didn't even acknowledge his captives' faces as he walked away. "Adieu my friends, until this evening."

Desperate to raise the alarm, Benedict shouted, "You're a bungling fool De Castagnet, you've not managed to finish us off yet, what makes you think........"

He was unable to complete his rant as the steel butt of a pistol painfully whipped into his jaw. It seemed to rattle his gums and run from his chin to his nose. Chevalier had struck him heavily and now drew a finger to his lips silently. Meanwhile Poubelle had unscrewed the cap of the bottle in his hands, briefly upturned it onto the handkerchief and made his way over to where Lillian stood. She showed no sign of nervousness and even seemed composed and elegant as the handkerchief was placed over her face and she started to crumple gracefully, caught in the pudgy arms of her assailant. Chloroform, the sandman in a bottle; Benedict looked at the beautiful woman now laid out on the grass and wondered whether it was fair that he and Tristan should have dragged her into this. He laughed at himself thinking it would kill him if she died, the irony not failing him that he was likely to be dead as well regardless. The large hankie finally arrived in front of his field of vision and almost willingly he breathed in the intoxicating mist. Within moments he was falling down the dark rabbit hole to the place where he slept and he too laid spread-eagled on the floor.

Chapter 24

Tristan woke up with a rolling jolt; rolling in as much as he was laid out on a flat surface and a sudden movement had caused him to briefly roll backward from acceleration into something hard. His eyes tried to adjust, but adjust to what? He was clearly in a dark space, but slowly, as the effects of the chloroform wore off he could see and hear where he was. He now heard the unmistakeable rumble of an engine and further jerks and bumps from below drew him to the conclusion that he was in the back of a van which was moving towards an unknown destination. He lay with his face staring up at the ceiling and tried to move his extremities. Tristan realised that both his arms and legs were tied. However, he managed to wriggle toward the metal side of the van and then with a lot of puffing and panting, righted himself to lean against it. Hell felt as groggy as he would after drowning in a vat of rum, but ironically was in desperate need of a drink. He peered around in the dim, grainy light of the empty van. Three other human sized lumps accompanied him. One of them had similarly woken up and was leaning on the wall of the van opposite him.

Lillian looked scared, almost flustered. So far as she had been the coolest hand of them all, but this worried Tristan. He ventured, "Lillian, how are you feeling, are you okay?" She briefly focussed her attention on him and then back to one of the lumpy objects that lay by her side, this one seemed to be in a long, grain sack. But then Tristan saw the detail which caused him to feel physically nauseous and sympathise with Lillian's anxiety. What his female companion was looking at was a dark uneven patch on the side of the coarse threads which made up the vessel and then the gentle white curly hair sticking out of

the top of the sack. Tristan knew who the occupant was and closed his eyes. So far, despite all the actual threats and attempts on their lives no one had died. It seemed that they were living charmed lives; perhaps that luck was about to run out. It certainly had for Trilby who had obviously been promised the world but ended up gambling his life away. Tristan tried to put it from his mind and refocus on the moment. He managed to twist his tied feet toward Benedict who was still out cold, drool running from his lips onto the dirty flat bed of the van. The farmer wriggled onto his side, bent his legs back and then levelled a well placed two footed kick into Benedict's groin.
Benedict, let out a breathy, "Oooooooooooooooooooooooh!"
"Oh goodness, sorry, sorry, sorry," said Tristan, now realising that a shot in the pills must have been as nicer way to wake up as, well, a shot in the pills.
It was a rude alarm call for Benedict who now cupped and nursed his groin with both hands, saliva still plastered to his cheek and his hair standing upright on one side. Benedict sucked air through his teeth, took another deep breath and then, like the others, righted himself to a sitting position in the moving vehicle.
He rested his head momentarily against the cool side and then used his sleeve to wipe off the spittle from his face.
"I say Tristan, next time I'd much prefer you waking me up with a cup of coffee and the papers."
Lillian laughed, her spirits raised slightly. She added, "Well, at least we now know how you look first thing in the morning,"
Tristan chuckled whilst Lillian blushed, realising how this must have sounded. She darted a quick look at Benedict who similarly had flushed red. An awkward pause came over them all until Tristan, ever the pragmatist asked, "Right, how do we get out of this mess?"

The high drone of the engine began to decrease as the vehicle decelerated.

"I haven't a clue", replied Benedict. He looked at the long bag with the white hair poking out of it and realised the grisly end that had met Trilby. "We're going to need to do something though or we'll all end up in a grain sack. I think we're about to find out where we are."

It was a good coincidental guess, as the van drew to a shuddering stop and the engine was turned off. The journey had evidently been brief or the dosage of chloroform light as Tristan could still see some daylight through a gap in the doors. He reasoned that they must still be close to High Cross.

They all heard the dull trudge of footsteps outside the van.

"Whatever happens, we should try and stick together. We'll be most effective if we work as a team." said Benedict.

Lillian tried her binding around her wrists. "Hey guess what, I reckon I could slip my cords now if I had more time."

It was one of many resources they needed and didn't have. A locking mechanism at the back doors of the vehicle started to be turned.

Benedict replied, "No, keep them as they are. Having the element of surprise as our one card might play in our favour."

Lillian nodded her head in agreement.

The back doors of the van were flung open, letting in the dusky sky; at least they now knew what time it was. Two plain clothed men held open the back entrance to the van and motioned with lugers with their other hands.

"Out!" one of them said.

All three captives wriggled toward the exit and as each of them reached the edge and dangled their legs over the side, a guard untied the rope around their ankles so they could walk to wherever their final destination might be. The last out, Benedict took a moment to look around. Coniferous trees lined the road where they'd parked and Benedict surmised that this must still be close to Claybrook Magna, although he could not identify any distinguishing characteristics to be sure. He glanced to his right and noticed another large van parked next to their own. They were definitely going to be in company, but not the jolly good, glass of champers as a welcome kind. Firm hands were placed on shoulders and all three captives were silently willed into the woodland on their left.

After travelling down a fresh path where spring bracken had been crushed and old branches shoved aside by heavy hands, a few dim lights began to glow in the distance. As they travelled further into the woods down this uncertain trail, the sun was preparing to depart this hemisphere and arrive in the next and the lack of light from above exacerbated the falling darkness around them. There was no sound except the noise of their footfalls on years of leaf litter and old twigs. Tristan stumbled and was manhandled and shoved by a petulant guard for slowing down their progress.

The lights in front grew closer and Benedict could see a flicker from them. As the bracken and trees thinned, they could see the dancing lights were actually torches planted in the ground around a large clearing. The light played on the patchy grass in this place and caused long sprites of the twenty or so men that stood in small groups around the clearing. At last they broke through the tree line and Benedict could see the area fully. It was a clearing, strange in it's foundation as it appeared to be rectangular, but not manmade. If it was a fire break or cleared through recent logging, it should extend as far as the eye could see or show the stumps and the debris of deforestation. But there were no signs of manmade intervention, just the unkempt grasses and the odd molehill.

The villainous associates watched Benedict, Tristan and Lillian enter the clearing and then turned back to their conversations. It was obvious that their number had swelled even further from this morning as the twenty or so men were chattering in German. How they had entered the country or how long they had been in hiding was clearly beyond the work of the secret service. Three people were kneeling down a good fifty yards from their position, hands tied behind their backs and with black bags over their heads. Short of sacrificing his own men, Tristan couldn't work out who they had encountered who those three sorry individuals might be, were these the special guests Philippe had mentioned? Benedict knew these three captives and themselves would not be found by the authorities until it was too late. He hoped upon hope that they would catch a break with Lillian's loose knots.

At the head of the clearing stood Philippe, his two chief goons, Chevalier and Poubelle and Von Schuler. There was a long metal foldaway table in front of them with a black holdall sitting on top and the handle of the sword haft poking out. Von Schuler seemed visibly agitated and as he had his back to the arriving party continued a row which had clearly started whilst they were in the woods and was not meant for strangers' ears.

"............Herr Castagnet, you have been paid have you not? I cannot see any further need for the pomp and circumstance you are now placing on events. My men and I can simply construct the crown, piece together the original documentation and then have our witnesses sign it as authentic. I see no point in further drawing out proceedings!"

Chevalier gave him a testy look, but Von Schuler realised that Philippe was ignoring him completely, instead looking over his shoulder at the incoming captives. Von Schuler turned and saw Benedict. He shook his head and said, "I think this is unnecessary."

Philippe replied, not taking his eyes off Benedict, "On the contrary monsieur, I would not have it any other way. This brings a sense of occasion to the matter before it draws to a close and your great leader has his crown."

He emphasised, 'great' with too much sarcasm and Benedict picked up on it.

"Ah Madame, Monsieurs, welcome to our night of celebration and one might say coronation?"

He winked at Lillian who looked disgusted.

"If you please, on your knees." He giggled to himself, "Oh I made a rhyme, how witty!"

The men behind Benedict, Tristan and Lillian pushed them to the floor.

Philippe tantalised them with details again, "Tonight, for your delectation, you will see a new monarch crowned, an old order fall and a new piece of history begin. Before your untimely expiration you will pay witness to all these events."

Benedict snarled back, "Don't be a fool, nobody would ratify the Fuhrer's authority over this country. You may as well drive to Somerset and claim you're the king of cheddar for all the good it will do." Benedict tried a haughty and false laugh.

Philippe gave a patronising smile and shook his head, "Oh Mr Lukely, how you underestimate my ambition, I will have my coronation as I do have that authority, not just in the precedent set by the riddle but by witnesses who will observe the proceedings. Gentlemen if you please!"

He called out to a group of men keeping watch over the hooded captives. Those hoods were quickly whipped away and after their hair had spilled from underneath, Benedict realised to his horror that Castagnet was right. Two of the captives were men, both pushing beyond middle aged, grey hair, dark suits and panic on their faces. The other was a woman, a plump lady in a navy blue dress, her hair unkempt from the static of the hood and dark streaks of wet mascara running down her cheeks.

"Oh dear, he's captured three complete strangers," said Tristan, not having a clue who they actually were.

"Not quite," replied Philippe, "But I am sure Mr Lukely, as a man of society, can tell you who they are. Would you indulge me Mr Lukely?"

From his connections, Benedict immediately recognised the two men and one woman. He sighed and then muttered, "The older of the two gentlemen is the current clerk of the parliaments, the other gentleman is a lord's commissioner and a privy counsellor to the King and I believe the marginally terrified woman is his wife, Maude." Maude nodded.

"So you see my friends, I have all the credibility I need. We will simply proceed with matters, have them witnessed by these willing victims and then they will take the news back to London of this new truth and precedent and I will be all powerful!"

Von Schuler certainly overheard this last comment and vehemently disagreed.

"I'm sorry, De Castagnet, I thought for a moment there I heard you say, you will be all powerful? I cannot allow that to happen." He pulled a luger from his waistband and pointed it towards Philippe. "I thought this might occur. This is not how it is supposed to be, the crown and the charter of liberties is for the Fuhrer and not us. All of this, this is irrelevant and not how Hitler would want it handled. He will want a smooth, amiable transition not some crude, arrogant Frenchman running the show. Do not forget, you are under my command! And I can ask my men to put you down at any moment."

Philippe laughed, "You stupid fool."

In the blink of an eye Chevalier had thrown a flick knife at Von Schuler's hand. The blade completed a full rotation and struck the lower palm, just under the pistol grip, slitting his hand open. Instinctively he recoiled in agony and dropped the pistol.

For an obese block of lard, Poubelle could move with little friction when he needed to and he sprang like a surprisingly agile hippo, knocking Von Schuler to the ground with a clatter and then rolling him to one side to restrain his arms. He heaved the shocked and bloodied German back to his feet, claret streaming down his upturned forearm. The other German troops drew pistols and advanced but it was too late. Philippe had reached down for the Luger and now had it's barrel trained on Von Schuler.

"Another sausage eater takes a step forward and you will lose your esteemed leader for ever, do I make myself clear? Lower your weapons or we all die."

The Germans took their pistols down to their sides, all hesitant to re-sheath them as they looked on as helplessly as the captives.

Von Schuler croaked, "Why De Castagnet? Why betray me when we would pay you in as much bullion as you could ever desire. This crown means nothing to you."

Philippe looked incredulous, "Nothing to me? Nothing to me you say? Well let me tell you about me and then we'll reassess your last statement!"

He started to pace as he spoke. "The moment I was born, I was cast down with the soddomites. The son of a common street whore, with no food, no water and only the public housing system to 'protect me' and when I say protect I mean beat me senseless and use my body like a floor mop. I was stabbed, burnt with cigarette ends and molested by priests, and yet, I learnt. I educated myself, became streetwise and managed to pull myself out of the gutter. I joined a gang in Avignon, thieving from the barges on the Rhone and through sheer determination and cruelness worked my way up to a respectable position, accruing some wealth. When the time came I formed my own band with loyal followers and I started to research my family tree. I found my mother, the useless whore, in a brothel, a moment away from the eternal night of death, high on opium and I left her to rot. As she breathed her last, she whispered to me the family secret, a clue into my lineage and I read further. I found documents pertaining to my ancestry in libraries and public records. My mother was a scarlet lady and my grand mother too before that. However, she was conceived in an incredible tryst of passion which brought infamy to my family name. Gentlemen, my great great grandmother served as a maid to the great French leader, Napoleon Bonaparte. Despite her status, he fell madly in love with this kind, sweet woman and that loved blossomed into a deep passion, until she fell pregnant with his illegitimate child. Rumours abounded round the courtiers and so to defend his honour, Napoleon did the only thing he could do, remove her from ever having any connection to his life. She was transported from Paris to Avignon and thrown to the floor with only her clothes as her sole possessions. She sold herself to pleasure men and lived a life filled only with misery, while Napoleon grew as a hero of France. So you see gentlemen, I have a history as rich as this crown and with all the strength in my body I will avenge my mother and grandmother and great grandmother to be a ruler as great as that small bastard, Napoleon.

"I think it's you who is the bastard sir," said Benedict.

Philippe walked with purpose over to Benedict and with menace and intention in his eyes struck Benedict's cheek with the back of his hand.

"Silence, you roast beef eating toff. Soon you will see my true power and at last Napoleon's Original Brotherhood will rise to the prominence it deserves!"

"You do realise the acronym for that, don't you?" Tristan said with real concern.

"Yes, Yes, I know, I do know that it's an acronym for something else, oh why do people keep telling me! I mean it's not as if this job could be any harder as it is! Mon Dieu!"

Lillian whispered, "I think he might be about to have a nervous breakdown."

"Let's hope eh," replied Tristan.

"I heard that, do you want to feel my hand too?!" yelled Philippe, his voice straining ever higher. "Well, I am about to show you!"

"About," turned out to be an hour later.

Whilst Chevalier continued to look intense and make threatening grunts toward the hostage Von Schuler, he kept his guns trained on the hand-tied Benedict, Tristan, Lillian, lord administrator to the parliaments, lord privy counsellor, his wife and the fifteen or so soldiers of Von Schuler. Poubelle and Philippe had emptied the contents of the bag onto the canvas table and with a series of tools were constructing the crown like it was a very expensive Airfix kit. If everyone else was all on the same side it would have been easy to overpower the three lunatics currently at the top of the clearing. The Germans were starting to get fidgety, Von Schuler was looking increasingly pale and if he snuffed it, well there was no need for them to wait around, they may as well shoot everyone and go home. This was only tense now because it was also boring. Lillian had twice dozed off and forgotten about her loose hand ties, not that there had been a moment to spring into action yet. At the table, came mutterings from Philippe as both he and Poubelle poured over the crown trying to get the various rubies and the sapphire to slot into place.

At last they stepped away from the table and there it was, the most brilliant, golden, bejewelled crown that they had all been chasing after for the past few days. Replete, resplendent with it's luminous jewellery, the torches' flames danced upon the dazzling mirror of the yellow metal. Philippe stepped up to the table. He closed his eyes, drew in an overly dramatic deep breath, held it in for a few seconds and then let it spill from his mouth in a relieving "Hhhhhhhhhhhhhuuuuuhhh."

"My moment has arrived," he announced.

Tristan rolled his eyeballs and tutted.

Gradually, gracefully, Philippe picked up the wonderful crown of Queen Boudicca and placed it gently on his head. It sat perfectly, as if it was made for him and him only. The elegant metalwork only served to make his face seem slightly effeminate. He closed his eyes again, taking in the moment. Only an owl congratulated him in the darkness, otherwise there was nothing but the wind in the trees and the raggedy dance of the flames from the torches. A minute passed.

"Now what?" asked Tristan.

Philippe let his eyes open slowly and focus on the little Welshman.

"Now Monsieur Wynd, I will take my rightful place as your King, and you will bow to me alone! Poubelle bring our parliamentarians to the bench for authentication purposes. A few simple signatures and I will be all powe....." He broke off, his voice fading to nothing. The briefest of shadows in the woodland had caught his eye. It couldn't be could it? Surely not.

A very British voice rang out across the clearing.

"Halt in the name of the law!"

Suddenly, the navy blue uniforms of Leicestershire's finest constabulary were appearing everywhere. Approximately fifty bobbies had now surrounded the area and a further ten plain suited gentlemen also mixed with them. The plain clothed officers all had pistols drawn.

"Oh, no, no no no no no!" exclaimed Philippe.

Two German soldiers to advantage of this break and whipped their pistols up, firing a snap shot at Philippe, who on ducking dropped the crown from on top of his head onto the floor. The other Germans now sprang alive and moved to more defensive positions, opening fire at the police presence coming through the bracken and at Philippe's own party. Lillian took the initiative and quickly slipped off her bonds. Whilst gunshot sounded all around them she untied Benedict and Tristan. They briefly huddled together to assess the situation. Deep within him, Benedict's leadership qualities awoke from under its duvet, stretched its legs and decided to rally the troops.

"Lillian, you lead the administrator, privy counsellor and Maude out to the bushes. Whoever these bobbies and chaps in suits and trench coats are, they are obviously enemies of the Germans and therefore hopefully friends of ours."

Lillian nodded in agreement.

"Tristan, looks like our froggy assailants have got themselves well dug in along with the krauts, we should flank them through the bracken and take them from behind."

"Take them with what?"

"We'll take what we need from the forest floor."

"Oh goody. I've always wanted to attack someone with a piece of bracken before." replied Tristan.

"Don't be sarcastic, it's my job to be sarcastic. You're job is to be plucky and optimistic. We need to ensure that Philippe doesn't make off with the crown and gemstones or he may still have some claim on the country"

"Message understood," said Tristan raising an eyebrow.

As they broke to perform their respective tasks, things certainly had become entrenched. Philippe and Poubelle had run for the tree line behind them and were using the firs for cover whilst Chevalier had ducked next to the upturned table and was rapidly firing salvos at anyone who was close. He'd already downed two of the Germans and put the wind up a couple of the bobbies. Meanwhile the remaining Abwehr agents had also entered the trees and were in a series of pitched battles with the police and unknown plain clothed agents. Benedict and Tristan made for the bracken to the side of the clearing and were soon into the tree cover as well. Benedict glanced back and saw Lillian leading the three hostages to safety. He had little or no concern for them, just that Lillian was safe and sound. A quick confirmation and he was off into the woods.

As they ran through undergrowth, Benedict and Tristan could hear hollering in different languages, gunfire and bullets ricocheting of the trees. In the darkness they only had their instincts to rely on as they ploughed on, headlong into a confrontation with the enemy. Benedict stopped suddenly behind a large fir and slammed his arm into Tristan to stop him going past. As luck would have it a bullet danced around the spot where Tristan would have run.

"You saved..."

Benedict put his hand to his lips to shush Tristan into a whisper. They stood directly behind the line of sight for the last few trees before edge of the clearing. Tristan glared at Benedict and shrugged, questioning why he had paused. Benedict peeped round the side of the tree and there, cracking shots off whilst yelling at each other were Philippe and Poubelle. Philippe had the crown dangling from his arm like an ornate and glittery woman's handbag. Benedict assessed the situation: between them and the villains was only ten feet of ground, yet there was an assortment of very old dry and crackly twigs. If they were to time it incorrectly, they may as well have had a toastmaster announce their surprise attack first. Benedict considered waiting for their next volley of fire, but even then, the crack of the luger was instant and dissipated quickly; their sounds would only be disguised for the briefest of seconds. A tenseness showed across Benedict's face, they would have to enter no man's land and hope for the best. However, fortune favoured the anxious and just at the moment Benedict was going to impart the plan to Tristan, Chevalier, still out in the open by the upturned table, ran out of ammunition.

Rather than doing a quick heel and toe to where Philippe was hiding not twenty metres away, this particular Frenchman had had enough of stalemate, drew two large hunting knifes from the pockets of his trousers and ran at full tilt towards the allied forces screaming, "ROS BEEEEEEEF!"He made an anti-heroic ten yard dash before it became apparent that the bullet was mightier than the blade and he was smited with about fifty of the things out in the open. Chevalier was no more.

"Chevalier!" cried Philippe as his pet psychopath was mown down by a fulsome volley of lead.

This gave Benedict and Tristan the window they needed and they leapt into the gap between their own fir and the two that Philippe and Poubelle were using for cover. As they trampled the bracken and old leaf cover underfoot they had nearly made it to their quarry but at the most unfortunately of seconds, Tristan tripped on a root and hurtled face long into Poubelle's reasonably comfortable derriere. Philippe span round to catch Benedict's blow in time, grabbing his fist whilst trying to angle his pistol with the other hand. Benedict was having none of it though and took hold of Philippe's gun as both of them wrestled in and out of a clear shot between them.

Meanwhile, having recovered from being mildly nudged into the fir he was hiding behind, Poubelle began to round on a very scared looking Tristan, now occupying his favourite spot, cowering on the floor. However, the maddening face of Poubelle and the rest of his planetary size took an orbital amount of time to turn and face his attacker. If an orchestra had been emphasising his revolving menace, it would have packed up and gone for tea by the time he was ready to pounce on Tristan. He crept forward, hands raised in front like an old vaudeville monster, one step at a time with nothing but the promise of lingering death for the man on the ground.

Still Benedict struggled with the hands and firearm of Philippe. Briefly the French villain had the barrel pointed at Benedict's head but he pulled the trigger too late and a shot whistled past Benedict ear and into the darkness. Philippe had relaxed his grip though to crack off the shot and this gave Benedict a small window in which to act. He slammed Philippe's gun toting hand into the rough bark of the fir they fought next to. Again, he struck the hand into the tree, causing Philippe a considerable amount of pain. About to drop the luger, Philippe tried a desperate measure and swung his weight to the right, moving them away from the fir and the barrel back into line with his victim. He squeezed off a final shot, but Benedict had the measure of it and as a keen Waltz enthusiast yanked Philippe into a reverse spin. The shot missed by inches, yet struck the fir behind them beginning a ricochet that would hit seven trees and eventually pass it's way perfectly through the ears of Poubelle.

Tristan saw the bullet briefly whistle through the head of the mountainous giant standing at his feet. There was a moment of uncertainty as Tristan was sure he himself was about to meet his maker through a considerable mauling. Now the tables had turned and even Benedict and Philippe had stopped their death dance to watch what happened next. Poubelle smiled an oafish, fat toothy smile as he departed this life and then Tristan understood the nature of his doom. The twenty two stone blob of destruction began a curved rolling belly flop and until at last he slapped on top of Tristan. Both Benedict and Philippe chuckled as Tristan was enveloped in flaps of skin and fat. With no time to give concern for his friend and with gun battles still happening all around them, Benedict's eyes met Philippe's once more and then were drawn down to the crown, still dangling round his left arm. Short of allies and using the distraction caused by the king maker, Philippe socked Benedict smartly in the eye and legged it into the darkness of the forest.

Whilst cross country was always his downfall at Foulsham, Benedict was determined to prove he was not just a load of huff and puff and asthma attacks. There was no doubt that Philippe had achieved a goodish start by delivering the now forming black eye to Benedict, but he ran now at full sprint through the blackened forest, over roots and branches, aware that one misplaced foot could cause a broken ankle and spell the end of everything if Philippe still had the crown. As the chase moved further into the woods, the crackle of gunfire and fighting began to fade which gave Benedict the opportunity to hear the rustle of Philippe's fast movement in front of him. Suddenly Benedict began to recognise that he was nearing the edge of the forest, as the blue of the night was visible through the slowly thinning trees. He felt confidence grow in his chest as he was sure that in a straight fight, he could put years of shadow boxing practice to good use and best his opponent.

And so it came as quite a surprise that as Benedict blew out of the forest into what looked like a long wide firebreak between woodlands that his chance at victory was dashed. Fifty metres in front of him, Benedict saw two camouflaged light aircraft, the front one of which Philippe was hoisting himself up into the cockpit.

Of course, that's how the additional Abwehr men arrived Benedict thought and he recalled back to their arrival at High Cross and the low flying plane they had seen then. Benedict's chances of pulling Philippe up by the collar studs were slipping away as the first aircraft's propeller kicked into life with a splutter. Benedict had one choice and one choice only.

When in amongst the salad days of the year, Benedict had on occasion been partial to being the co-pilot of at least two of his chums who had spent a large sum of their inheritance on single prop planes. However, his expertise only extended to drinking and spilling Bollinger everywhere and occasionally passing the bottle to the reckless pilot who seemingly always unintentionally threatened to plough into somebody's large country pile.

However, as he strapped himself into the pilot's seat of this small passenger craft, he revised in his mind the brief lesson that one of those crackpot johnnies had taught him. He needed to remember fast as Philippe's aerial horse was already cantering down the firebreak.

Throttle plus direction equals lift, or something like that. He flicked the ignition and the engine choked before building into a satisfactory roar. Benedict found a lever market with 'T' and experimentally, pulled it towards him. The plane lurched forwards and after a series of unforgiving jolts began to roll, building acceleration. Soon the aircraft had built up a speed surpassing his Phantom and it rolled along the surprisingly gentle grassy surface. Philippe's plane clearly wasn't using the amount of throttle that Benedict was as he gained quickly, to the point where Benedict began to push in the T-stick to decelerate. Benedict panicked, what if he was going too fast to take off properly, was that why Philippe was slower? But one question which was immediately answerable was becoming apparent, if either of them didn't figure out how to take off soon, the fire break came off its namesake break time in two hundred metres; beyond that there were only more large, unmovable trees.

The problem was, Philippe had climbed into the cockpit of his aircraft knowing this was his only means of escape with the crown. Unfortunately, he didn't know how to fly either. He'd struck lucky with the throttle and now, as he sped along towards the tree line he really needed to give himself a quick lesson in the old up, up and away. Yanking switches, pressing pedals, nothing worked. One hundred metres. He considered bailing out, but at this speed Philippe realised he would probably do himself a significant injury and the game would be up. Seventy five metres. Something had to make this crate fly, anything.

Fifty metres. Philippe considered the joystick in front of him and pulled back on it. Twenty five metres. Suddenly there was lift. There was actual lift! He looked down at the stick in amazement as the plane gently floated off the ground. Sadly as he looked up again, only the trees were there to give him a warm welcome and a prickly, wooden, splintering hug. Seconds later, Benedict's plane got in on the congratulatory act as well, crashing heavily into the back of Philippe's and catapulted the French man who would be king and his crown out into the woodland.

Benedict didn't so much as park up, as ram his plane into the rear of his enemy's and come to an abrupt halt. The other plane fared a lot worse than his and despite slamming his noggin into the cockpit glass he felt his extremities and realised he was happily intact. He stopped for a moment to catch his breath, and then unbuckled himself from his seat, opened the pilot's door and stepped down into the darkness. Philippe's plane was a mess; the front part entirely smashed into the trees it had collided with, no propellers intact and the cabin was badly mangled. Benedict approached the side, sure that he would see Philippe's corpse draped across the dials, as dead as possible. He reached the pilot opening which was hanging off it's hinges and tentatively peered inside. Philippe was not in there! His head swirled with possibilities, had he made his escape? Had he been flung out and lay mortally wounded in amongst the bracken? He quickly received an answer though as the hard, flat wooden side of a broken propeller was swung viciously by Philippe into the wound on the back of Benedict's head.

He'd had no idea where the Frenchman had come from, but now as he rolled off his front and onto his back, through the dizzying waves of nausea, he looked up and saw his conqueror. Torn and tattered, Philippe was breathing heavily and hotly, the beginnings of steam rising from his breath. He was bloodied and badly cut, but like a wounded tiger looked fierce, psychotic and ready to strike.

"So, at last Monsieur, we have reached something of a dénouement and it is time for us to part ways."

Benedict felt groggy and couldn't properly focus on his enemy. "Where is the crown?"

Philippe laughed but with an air of desperation, "Oh, you know, here and there. It rather inconveniently scattered into pieces when it was ejected with me from the cockpit. I have enough to still be interested but not as much as I need thanks to you." He kicked Benedict's left foot angrily.

Benedict managed a smile and wearily replied, "Glad I could be of service."

"Oh, your retorts are pointless monsieur. Yes the battle has almost certainly been lost between my men, the Germans and the British constabulary, but well, once I am done with you, I shall have myself a nice little bonfire here and use your glowing corpse to find the remaining pieces of the crown. Now, how would you like to die? This propeller blade to the back of your head once again, or the splintered end driven through your chest?"

Benedict chuckled, "Nice of you to kill me before turning my body into a torch, at least you have some honour. By the way, you'll be seen for miles away; you don't stand a chance."

Philippe pulled the large sapphire out from his trouser pocket and gazing at it's beauty, said, "Monsieur, it's a risk I'm willing to take."

What seemed like a blur flew past Benedict and Philippe and before he could realise what had happened, the sapphire was gone from Philippe's grasp.

Benedict's eyes focussed as Philippe cried, "Bitch!" and began his pursuit. It was Lillian!

Staggering to his feet, Benedict lolloped in the general direction of where she had run, knowing the grave danger she was in from this megalomaniac looney and his broken prop shaft. He heard a branch up ahead give a dry snap and the cry of a woman in pain. Benedict hurried on but Lillian hadn't got far anyway and now lay sprawled on the ground, crying as Philippe picked up the sapphire which lay amongst the undergrowth. He saw Benedict and stood up triumphantly.

"Such a shame I must now also kill something so beautiful."

Benedict looked at Lillian as she sobbed clasping her left ankle. He shifted his gaze back to Philippe. He pleaded, "Please, there is no need to kill us both, just take me. I'm the cad you've wanted since the beginning."

"Aw, how sincere, you have feelings for the lady no? In which case, she goes first. You have taken something wonderful away from me Monsieur Bryant-Lukely, my honour. Now I will exact the perfect revenge and take something dear away from you!" Philippe turned to Lillian, "I'm sorry my dear, but this is going to hurt, a lot".

Benedict yelled a helpless, "NO!" as Philippe raised the splintered end of the propeller high into the air, ready to drive it home and end Lillian's life.

A single shot rang out, echoing through the woodland. Philippe paused, confused as blood began to depart from the single exit wound in the middle of his skull. He staggered backwards once and then toppled over, dead. Benedict ducked, searching for where the shot came from. Finally he found his marksman. On the very edge of the wood next two the two collided planes, frozen in silhouette stood one man, Eric Von Schuler, still poised with his luger. He finally caught Benedict's gaze, nodded with no emotion and then he was gone into the darkness of the night.

Benedict exhaled, feeling exhausted from a lack of sleep and the events of the evening. More noises were coming through the trees now, shouts of English words and in the distance, the tring of the bells on Police vans. He groggily got to his feet and made his way over to Lillian, slumping down and then deeply embracing her as she cried on his shoulder. He drew back to look at her face and she smiled through the dark stains of her mascara.

"Are you all right?" asked Benedict.

"Oh fine, fine, it's just a sprain," she replied, wiping her face. "You look a little worse for wear."

"I've had worse," boasted Benedict, "Though I'm not sure when. Now come on, help me up and let's leave this place before we're really in a bad hole."

Lillian heaved Benedict up and they hobbled towards the firebreak.

"When was the last time you saw Tristan?" Lillian asked.

"My goodness, Tristan!" Benedict yelled, realising his friend was still probably trapped under several kilograms of flab. Lillian seemed to know the way that Benedict and Philippe had come through the wood and after ten minutes of hobbling, they came across the heavy body of Poubelle and saw Tristan's legs underneath, showing no signs of movement. Benedict ran across and stood over him assessing his condition, hoping upon hope that he hadn't been crushed beyond repair. He bent down and with an effort greater than all his previous strength rolled the tub of lard Frenchman off his friend.

He slapped Tristan in the chops. "Come on Tris, stay with me, don't be dead. Tell me where it hurts and I'll get some help!" He wept salty tears onto Tristan's cheek.

More activity was happening around him now. Policemen streamed through the trees and were shouting to each other, checking the condition of the dead and wounded.

"Stop your crying you big girl. Any chance you've got an aspirin?" said the prostrate Tristan, his eyes still closed. Benedict stopped crying, looked perplexed and then said, "Bastard," whilst Tristan laughed hard and in pain on the floor.

The administrator to the parliaments, the privy counsellor and his poor wife were in shock and babbling nonsense at the poor bobby who was with them. They were helped into a police van which screamed away from all the activity at the edge of the forest. Police and medical staff swarmed everywhere, carrying out the dead and wounded on stretchers, writing reports and speculating on events. Sitting on the flat bed of the van next to the one which had just left, in between the doors, wrapped in grey woollen blankets with their legs dangling over the end, were Benedict, Tristan and Lillian. None of them spoke, they just stared forward down the country road away from the hubbub of the night's events.

They'd embraced each other tightly when they'd all met up again. Then came the job of trying desperately to explain things to the police whose immediate reaction had been, "Come on folks, pork pies are made just up the road from here, but these are porkier than you'd find in Melton Mowbray, so you're coming in for a lot more questioning." So they hugged and then they'd just sat, slumped against one another, dazed, shocked and confused. A question was brewing in Tristan though, the one they were all thinking.

"So, what just happened back there then?"

He looked at Benedict who could only give a comical shrug. Lillian took her time with the question and eventually replied, "I don't know. I thought we were done for, but those policemen came out of nowhere and...." She signalled with her hands to the woodland they'd just come from. It was about as plausible an explanation as anyone could come up with. Benedict was dwelling on Philippe though.

He said to the others, "I have never been so certain of death as I was when Philippe struck me with the propeller. This crown, this ideology had lit a fire deep within him and I could see it in his eyes. He was not going to let up until certain victory or the end of us all".

Tristan replied in a distant tone, "You could argue that it was his Napoleon complex that was his undoing really, which is slightly ironic." He tapped Benedict's knee and added, "Hey, but look at it this way, you alone have saved Britain from two evil dictators! Congratulations!"

Lillian sighed and said, "I need something stiff inside me."

Benedict coughed, "I'm sorry, I've got a headache."

Sniggers abounded all round.

Chapter 25

Considering the mayhem of the night, the official processing of events was surprisingly quick in every way. Benedict, Lillian and Tristan were packed into the van with other policemen and driven to Leicester's main police station. As they were escorted inside, Benedict noticed three men lagging behind. All were smartly dressed, two were wearing a very similar check sports jacket, black pants and trilby hats. They were tanned, easy, their ties were loose and there was casualness to their movement. Gun holsters hung by their sides. The chap in the middle though looked positively uncomfortable with his companions. He didn't belong with them, dressed in a stiff navy blue suit, dark tie done up to the neck, briefcase and a strained, unhappy look to him. As soon as they were through the police station's large entrance hall, the three men took Lillian's arm and escorted her off to another room. She put up no struggle and Tristan thought he heard American accents and he saw her wink at one of them.

Tristan looked to Benedict, concerned and worried about what they'd be charged with. He whispered, "What do we say to them, you know about the theft at Colchester and then getting caught up with the Abwehr and a plot to take the throne from the monarchy? Nothing I can think of seems very plausible."

Equally baffled by events, Benedict shrugged again as they were pushed into a lonely, quite chilly cell, with one singular bulb, buzzing away above them. A cold thick stone slab jutted out of the wall opposite and was the only place to sit. Benedict and Tristan both parked their bums as the noisily ominous cell door slammed behind them. They both gave each other a worried look.

Two hours later, the cell door rattled back into life and was swung open. A young police constable stood in front of them, he couldn't have been older than twenty. "Right then lads, you're free to go, but I'm to take you back to London," he signalled to Benedict. "I'm PC Gladtiding by the way and my mate, er colleague PC Shallowit will take you sir back to Wales." They noticed another young man in police uniform behind the one that had entered the cell. "But..."

"No buts, sir, you're being released on the strict condition that both of you return to your homes, so on your feet, I've packed butties."

Benedict and Tristan both slowly stood up, unsure of how to respond. Where were the questions, the arrest and interrogation? They'd just seen more bloodshed than a butcher at an abattoir.

"Now hang on...."

"Sir, I'm going to have to hurry you, or you'll be arrested for wasting police time."

"But the bloodshed!" said Tristan.

"Don't know what you're talking about sir, but we are under strict orders, so I'm going to have to hurry you."

"What about Miss Warner?" Tristan asked.

"Left already sir, lovely looking woman. PC Jones got the pleasure of escorting her back to Colchester, lucky sod." Both Benedict and Tristan looked at each other confused. Eventually Benedict shrugged and said "Fair enough." Perhaps after what they had witnessed, this was the best solution, just sweep it under the carpet and forget about it. Or maybe someone else had already done the sweeping.

They trudged back outside into the Leicester night. Two cars were parked outside, one being Benedict's Phantom which he was relieved to see. As they walked towards each car, Benedict realised that this might be the last time he spoke to his friend and colleague in this adventure. He had never thanked him for running into the lounge that night in Kensington and diverting De Castagnet's shot.

"Tristan, I just wanted to say, thank for saving my..." he wanted to say more, but the firm hand of PC Runnymede steered his shoulder to the passenger seat of the Phantom. Just before he ducked down to get into his own vehicle, Tristan yelled, "I know!"

Pushed down into the passenger seat by the young copper he was with, Benedict realised that would be the last he would see of Mr Tristan Wynd.

Approximately six hours later and Benedict woke with a start as the Phantom drew to a halt outside his Kensington apartment. He had not said a word to the police officer next to him for the whole journey. Benedict scratched his head. "How long was I out?"

"Ooh, I think you nodded off just outside Hinckley, so pretty much the entire journey. You must have been knackered."

"Yes, well, long day and all that. Sorry for not being better company."

The policeman was annoyingly chirpy, "Oh not to worry, we made arrangements with one of the local nicks. I've got a cuppa and a comfy cell waiting for me in a jiffy and I'm ready for it tell the truth. It's five in the morning after all!"

Five in the morning, had time really passed that quickly? Was it literally only two days since he and Tristan got back from Wales? He shook his head and the constable look confused. Benedict used this moment as his cue to leave.

"Well, thank you officer, wishing you a speedy and safe journey back in the morning."

"Night sir," said the bobby as both stepped out of the car. The bobby walked away up the road.

It was dark and peaceful in the street, only the sound of scant traffic in the roads nearby. He climbed the small steps to the black, glossy entrance, found the key in his trouser pocket, unlocked the door and stepped in. Closing the door behind him, he shut out the world and any residual nose. He took a moment, in his hallway, to feel the comfort of the four walls in front of him and the promising pong of cigar smoke which stained the very fabric of the building. And then he felt sad, immensely sad, for Benedict was alone. No Mrs McDoughty, her gruff bristling greeting whenever she saw him, no Tristan, this random Welshman who had entered his life through the skilful use of a suitcase and strangely enough no Caruthers, whom he thought he would hate the most after the trouble he had caused. But Benedict somehow missed trying to impress that debonair character. Then there was Lillian, how would he get over her?

He walked through to his sitting room and scanned the familiar surroundings, hands on hips. He licked his lips and let his mind unravel. So many questions lay unanswered, like why Von Schuler had saved his and Lillian's life? Also considering Benedict had just averted the single greatest catastrophe of the war so far, he'd not had so much as a thank you or good show or medal ceremony in the morning off anyone. Considering he had dodged his own death three times, at least someone should have said, "good job." There weren't even any questions asked, which was suspicious enough. He didn't get to say a proper goodbye and thank you to his partner in crime and now good friend, Tristan, or Lillian for that matter. He was still probably wanted by the police for theft and impersonating a soldier of His Majesty's armed forces. Frankly, it was all a bit of an anticlimax.

Glum, Benedict spotted half of the broken Boudicca statue, resting on the window sill on the far side of the room. Benedict marched over to it, grasped the leaden lady and then tossed it onto the waste paper basket nearby. He didn't want any more unnecessary memories of the last week and he was determined not to dwell on events as he walked upstairs with the intention of getting some sleep.

Chapter 26

Two days later and Germany invaded France. On the day in question, a particularly nondescript 10th May 1940, after spending the day at home, Benedict entered his sitting room and flicked on the wireless by the door to catch up on current affairs. As a particularly flighty tea-dance song finished, he poured himself a whiskey and settled into his favourite armchair. The announcer read in his standard English voice that this was the news. Benedict was just taking a sip of liquor when he heard the gut wrenching announcement.

"Our main story this afternoon, the phony war is over as Germany invades France. German gains have so far been rapid..."

Benedict downed the whiskey in one and said to no one in particular, "Well that's a rotten sensation."

So Hitler had done it then. Benedict could only presume that Von Schuler was still on the run and had managed to get a message through to the German high command. Could Benedict have prevented the invasion? Somehow he felt guilty when he had absolutely no reason to, but that didn't stop him from drinking his body weight in booze for the next two days.

Fortunately on the third day, he rose again. Benedict tried to return to normality and had gotten up at a reasonable hour, read the news, even made his own lunch and dinner. Of course, he'd also taken the liberty of advertising for a new butler and housekeeper and couldn't wait to have some company again. Try as he might, the house just seemed too big for him on his own. So he left the house often and tried to catch up with some old chums who had the same toffy nosed opinions on people, cracked the same jokes and had the same social life as before and he found himself despising them. He tried to distract himself with pleasures of the flesh, but on his first appointment, Benedict reached the door of the brothel, paused and turned around. It just didn't seem right and in his mind, there was still Lillian. He walked away, disgusted with himself.

It was early July when Benedict decided to confirm Mrs Peasgood as his permanent housekeeper. Responses to both adverts had been poor and the dilemma of the next butler was still yet to be resolved. However, Mrs Peasgood, a widower from the west country, in her fifties, all chest, cuddly rolls and tanned wrinkles, was profusely good at her job from the get go. Friendly and easygoing, she fitted her work in around Benedict rather than demanding he get out of the way of the carpet beater like Mrs McDoughty use to make him do. She was also an astonishingly good cook. Benedict had given her a fortnight's trial, but was beyond satisfied by the middle of week two. He relished telling her the good news as she was an excitable old sort and when he congratulated her on filling the vacancy, a tear came to her eyes and she wrapped him up in a flappy bat-winged, over exuberant embrace. After straightening himself out after his mauling, Benedict looked at his attire in the mirror in the hallway. He'd recently taken up walking to fill his time and was today decked out in long shorts and a white, short sleeve shirt. His tan was coming on a treat in between air raid warnings and was nearly the same leathery colour as Mrs Peasgood. Furthermore, the three mile strolls were giving him a chance to iron out the kinks in his brain about what had happened as since the events of early May but he'd had no discourse from anyone, Tristan, Lillian, the police or more lunatic assassins. Life was getting better and a mildly dodgy friend of his had shown him the lucrative opportunities that were forming for black market goods. Benedict fancied a piece of that action and almost managed to sound excited about things. Studying himself, he found his eyes drawn to the frame of the mirror, the wholesome, chunky and utterly un-styled oak wooden frame, given to him by Tristan. Very much like the man himself, practical, no frills, but very useful. Benedict laughed to himself.

Just as he was about to reach for his favourite thinking pipe and tobacco, the doorbell rang. It caused Benedict to jump as his mind had wandered onto how Mrs Peasgood had found smoked salmon with the food rationing which was now occurring. Although nothing had come of the adventure and the quite sizeable infractions of the law, Benedict was still wary of unannounced house calls. He walked tentatively toward the door, slid over the bolt and pulled on the handle. He looked down at the woman standing at the foot of the steps. She was red cheeked, sweaty and mildly unattractive in such a condition, but Benedict immediately recognised her. And for the life of him he could not fathom how she had managed to find out his home address.

"What have you done with my cake tin!" yelled Bessie, livid and rosy cheeked with anger.

Benedict paused for one moment, reflecting and then replied, "Ah, perhaps I can explain."

The End

Printed in Great Britain
by Amazon.co.uk, Ltd.,
Marston Gate.